Every Five Years

The Fix It or Get Out Series

Christine Ardigo

Published by the author as a member of the
Alexandria Publishing Group

Every Five Years

First Edition, August 2014

Cover Design by Kellie Dennis at Book Cover by Design
Interior Book Design by RikHall.com
Author's photo by Limpuiu Photography

ISBN-13: 978-1500823658
ISBN-10: 1500823651

Acknowledgements

I would like to thank two very special people in my life.

The first is Danielle Rose-West, the author of five amazingly entertaining books. Danielle kept me smiling throughout the publishing process and taught me to love writing and creating my books first, and then everything else will fall into place.

The second is Sheila Kell, author of the upcoming H.I.S. Series. She has provided daily support during my novel writing journey. I could not have made it through without her encouragement, advice and sense of humor. As both my critique partner and friend, her kind words and daily chats kept me on track. I can't thank her enough for her time and positive vibes.

Dedicated to my crazy daughters, Ashley and Autumn.
Always face your fears. It makes you stronger

Chapter 1

Heather

Heather Di Pietro sat across from Brooke Kempler in Zeke's Pizza and watched her rip the entire slab of cheese off her slice and dump it onto her plate. Too bad you couldn't do that with the crap in your life. One quick tear and into the garbage.

Spring air floated into Sterling Ridge, Long Island and reminded Heather that only a few months remained before she graduated from high school. The past four years, jammed with adventures and escapades, pushed the limit on her teenage restrictions, and made her the zany non-conformist.

The pizza parlor, located across the street from their high school, proved far cooler than the cafeteria. Each day, after a slice and a small Coke, Heather attempted to beat her score in Centipede, the only video game in their hangout. She was currently in second place, trumped by someone with the initials GMW.

Three freshmen boys appeared through the rear door, chuckling. They kicked and shoved each other until one boy careened into a garbage pail and knocked the lid onto the floor. Its *thud* onto the glazed tile turned heads. Their rowdiness caused the cashier with the blue-spiked hair to slam her drawer shut and throw a rag across the counter. Heather giggled and Bobby, the shortest of the three boys, waved at her.

A fresh pepperoni pie emerged from the oven and filled the room with its spicy scent. Heather closed her eyes, inhaled and leaned back in her booth. She would miss this place. She reopened her eyes and found Brooke adjusting her gold hoop earring.

Something stirred to her left. She glanced out the window and watched two boys in black Converse high tops and leather jackets make their way up the snaky path to the high school. It was Matt.

She redirected her attention to Brooke, who was scrunching up her hair like a giant haystack. The bigger the better. "Matt likes me," Heather said.

"Matt who?"

"Matt Balderas."

"Ugh, gag me."

"What do you mean? He's nice."

"You're dating Lance Milanesi. Please."

Heather fiddled with the neon-pink shoelace on her purple Converse. She had doodled all over them with a Tri-color pen. "We pass notes between classes. He leaves them in my locker vent."

"Are you serious? How old is he? Isn't he like, a sophomore?"

Heather didn't answer.

"Fuckin-A, Heather. Lance is eighteen, how can you be interested in a sophomore?" Brooke pushed her half-eaten slice away and took a sip of her Diet Coke. "Does he even have a job?"

"He's getting his working papers next month."

"And working where? McDonalds? You're actually considering dating a sixteen-year-old with no job and no car. Are you totally ill?"

"We talk for hours on the phone. He's interested in what I do."

"Of course he is, remember? No job, no car."

"I don't have a car." Heather gulped the last of her soda.

"That's what Lance is for. Do you know how many people would kill to date him? You got yourself a preppy little boy-toy." Brooke examined her teeth in her pocket mirror.

"Matt's getting tickets to see Depeche Mode this summer at Jones Beach and he made me a few tapes of his Ramones records."

"You're gonna make me ralph, you know that? Put your punk rock days behind you. You're lucky Lance even asked you out. Do you understand? He saved you."

"Saved me?"

"Fer sure. You were buying your clothes in the village at consignment shops. Fluorescent jewelry, purple lipstick, oh, and that ridiculous Boy George hat you used to wear. Still not sure what he saw in you." Brooke shook her head. "Stick with your Guess jeans, Heather. You'll be much happier in the end."

Was she happy? Her classmates certainly looked at her differently. They watched with amazement when Lance and she drove out of the school parking lot together. She also caught them whispering when she entered one of the popular kid's parties with her arm around Lance.

Brooke dug into her bag and then pulled out her gold shimmering lip-gloss. "Heather, think about it, what could a space cadet like Matt possibly offer you?"

"It's just nice to hear someone ask about my day. And he's funny."

"Funny? Funny doesn't pay the rent. You wanna go back to the days of walking everywhere on foot? Begging your dad for rides? You'd be in deep shit. Besides, the prom's just around the corner."

"The old days were awesome. Remember when we went to—"

Bobby strolled toward his table holding a tray overflowing with two slices of pepperoni pizza and a large cup. One of his friends locked his foot around Bobby's ankle. He stumbled and his tray tipped to the right. The cup of orange Crush soda toppled and splattered over the white tile like a mutilated pumpkin.

Brooke, splashed with three whole droplets, sprang from her chair. "Stupid freshman. These are suede boots, you asshole!"

Heather lurched from her seat and dashed to the counter. She snatched a pile of napkins and hurried back to the mess.

"Oh, thank God." Brooke held out her hand. Heather spread the napkins on the floor instead, covering the spill.

"Thanks," Bobby said. His face flushed.

An employee arrived with a cotton-string mop, dispersing the mess and the scene.

Heather plopped back into the booth, took a huge bite of her slice and gazed out the window.

Brooke scowled. "Look Heather, this is exactly what I mean. Enough of this nonsense. We're graduating and have to look sophisticated next year."

"You're going away, I'm not. Sweatpants, hair in a ponytail, then off to work."

"Well, that's one smart choice you made."

"What?"

"If you went away, you'd lose Lance for sure."

"I'm not staying on Long Island for him. I'm just not into all that sorority, rah-rah garbage. Besides, I have a good job, getting my dad's old car this summer..."

"You won't need to work once Lance gets his degree."

"I like working."

"What are you majoring in again, cooking?"

"Nutrition. We don't cook."

Brooke's head jerked toward the window. A gold metallic 300zx pulled into the pizzeria parking lot. The passengers climbed out and Brooke stuck her finger in her mouth. "Barf me out. Look who's with your Lance."

Lance emerged from the car with Robin Levine and her posse, all from the Crystal Lake section of town. Gold earrings, thick chains and matching bracelets shimmered in the sunlight. Lance donned his aqua Ralph Lauren shirt, collar up, and a pink sweater tied around his neck. His khaki pants cuffed to show off his brown leather loafers and argyle socks. Heather's eyes narrowed.

"Told you he's a wanted man. Robin will steal him right from you."

"As if. She won't put out."

"You barely did."

Heather glared at Brooke.

"Take a chill pill, just stating the obvious. You don't make guys like Lance wait."

"I had to be sure he was the right one."

"Trust me, he's totally rad."

Lance had laughed when she told him she was still a virgin at seventeen. Afraid of losing him and terrified of her classmates finding out, she consented one night when his parents went out to dinner.

Under his covers, her B-52's T-shirt still on, he rammed her repeatedly despite the pain. When he finished, he vaulted off the bed, pranced around as if he just finished a marathon, then stared at himself in the mirror and stretched. She found the condom inside her two days later, the pain lasted three.

Brooke lost her virginity at the end of ninth grade. So desperate to fit in, she begged her brother to take her to one of his senior parties. A senior named Victor supplied her with a steady stream of kamikaze shots and Bacardi and cokes, until she couldn't see, then led her to a vacant bedroom. The next day, Victor walked past her as if he had amnesia.

Brooke never told her. She only graced Heather with good news, leaving all the horror stories tucked under her mattress. News of her casual sex with a senior spread around the school, though, leaving only hormone-crazed boys to ask her out. One by one they used and dumped her.

Lance strode in with Robin and her sidekicks and their phony laughter echoed through the pizzeria. The cashier glanced up from her register and then made a face as if she was forcefully vomiting. The employee with the mop snickered.

Robin spotted Heather at the corner table and her face lost its color. She recovered, adjusted her posture, nose upturned, and then jabbed her fingers into Lance's ribs tickling him. He keeled forward, holding his side and snorted. Robin cackled loud and obvious like a hyena on crack. She motioned to her friends, alerting them to Heather's presence. The three girls circled Lance and took turns poking him.

"You're not going to just sit there, are you?" Brooke asked. "Fight for your man."

Lance wriggled in a fit of hilarity and then made eye contact with Heather. His laughing ceased. Heather smiled, but her throat tightened, corking the glob of pizza in her stomach. She quickly hid her red-leather spiked bracelet under her sleeve. Lance sauntered over and she stood to greet him.

"Why are you here? Shouldn't you be in math?" he asked.

"Mr. Roesler's out, we had the period off." Heather gripped her wrist and covered the spikes that forced their way through the cotton material.

Lance crooked his neck toward Brooke and leered at her. "Hey, Brooke."

"Hey, Lance. Looking good."

He put his arm over Heather's shoulder then noticed her sneakers. He frowned. "I thought you said you wouldn't wear those anymore."

"I had gym today."

"Can't you buy yourself a normal pair of white Reeboks?"

"I don't do aerobics."

Lance huffed. "You know nothing about style. You should hang around girls like Robin more. Then you'll fit in."

The soda she gulped returned in her mouth. She re-swallowed and glanced at Robin, who stared her down. She had the same stupid pair of Guess jeans on as Heather. The ones that cost her two days salary.

Heather grabbed the sweater from Lance's neck, drew him in and kissed him, mouth wide and exploring, fervent, she rubbed her pelvic bone between his legs. Lance didn't pull away. Instead, he welcomed her unusual aggressiveness.

She pulled away and smirked. "Still care about my sneakers?"

"What?" His voice hitched.

"I'm going to play Centipede, get yourself some lunch." She strolled over to the machine and ignored Robin's glare. Heather inserted a quarter, her three middle fingers positioned on the trackball, and began her battle. The centipede made its way back and forth across the screen, spiraling down, further, faster. The spider appeared and sprang at her. She twirled the ball to avoid it. She swooped up and to the left and then back down before ambushed. She rolled back to the right and then they surrounded her.

"You think you're so smart, Heather, don't you?" Robin snarled. She leaned on the arcade game and her two friends shadowed her, blocking the sunlight. Lance ordered his Calzone unaware of their threat. "Listen, you may have Lance now, but not for long. Not sure what he sees in you, but soon he'll realize he should be dating someone of my caliber."

Giggles erupted beside her. She continued to twirl the sphere.

"Mark my words, Heather Di Pietro, I'll be going to the prom with him, and we'll be prom king and queen. Not prom king and quack." Robin thrust her hand over the trackball, then walloped Heather in the shoulder as she departed. Her cohorts followed. Heather's gnome player piece knocked dead.

She grumbled, cracked her knuckles, and then reached into her pocket and found another quarter.

HDP, the new initials to take first place.

Chapter 2

Heather

"Heather, can you and Barry come in my office when you're done?" Neil Caywood, the night crew manager at Northford Insurance Company, popped his head out the door.

Heather and Barry, both assistant managers for the file clerks, marched in and sat in front of their supervisor. Neil leaned forward, fingers clasped, and smiled. This could not be good.

"I just wanted the two of you to be the first to know that...I'm leaving. I'm taking a job upstairs, full time, days. You guys have been great, but the nights are killing me. I need to get into a normal routine."

Neil had been their boss for almost two years. Heather liked his laid-back manner and the easy shifts set before her. Her first year of college was harder than she imagined. Anatomy and physiology, and microbiology drowned her. Next semester was loaded with chemistry, food science management and medical nutrition therapy. Her non-stressful job enabled her to continue with her kick-ass grades.

"I'm telling you this for another reason. With my position up for grabs, are either of you interested?"

"I have a full course load," Heather said. "My current hours work perfectly."

"What about you, Barry?"

Barry Rethman was several years older than Heather. His mullet haircut fell below his shoulders and it looked as if his sideburns, cheesy mustache and ungroomed beard all attached and joined together to form a tattered ski mask. He never attended college, but his assistant manager job provided just enough cash for his weekend beer runs and what little rent he paid to his mother.

"I'd definitely be interested. Full time. Benefits. What do I have to do?"

All the blood drained from Heather's face and crashed into her shoes. Barry could not take his position. Her life would be over.

"I encourage you to fill out the necessary paperwork and apply. It'll have to go up on the company's job post, of course, but since I get to choose my replacement, there should be no problem."

Two weeks later, they promoted Barry and within days, the abuse unleashed. Barry's relentless visits to her floor had purpose and direction. Weekly write-ups for showing up to work one minute late, fraternizing with her staff, and unauthorized visits from previous employees went into her file. He prevented her from speaking to anyone for enjoyment. After four weeks, he called her into his office.

"Heather, it appears you don't know how to follow rules."

She rolled her eyes and looked away.

"Don't disrespect me. You want me to write you up for insubordination?"

Why not? He wrote her up for everything else. She couldn't wait to see what she did wrong now. Smile at her staff? Make eye contact? Leave her office to pee?

"I've given this careful consideration and it appears that instead of being a leader to your workers, you're distracting them. It's also been brought to my attention that you're consorting with your staff outside of work."

Consorting? Six months ago, he was the one hanging out in the parking lot drinking beers with everyone.

"So, because of this, I've decided to remove you from your floor and switch you to my old floor. You'll begin tomorrow."

Heather's pulse screeched to a halt. Anger and shock competed for a route through her veins. Hot rage collided with cold fear and she couldn't speak. Barry sneered at her. He had won.

Heather trudged into work the following evening after her Cultural Aspects of Food exam, obtained her paperwork and retreated to her new floor. She sat in her office, drew the blinds and hid. A half hour later, Jack, Wayne and Dean strolled onto the floor. Panic rose inside her.

Heather spent her first evening listening to catcalls and obscene remarks. Paper clips winged at her office window and several made it past her door along with two dozen rubber bands. A pile of office supplies accumulated on the rug aligned with the door opening.

Barry came down several times a night to guarantee the abuse continued. He encouraged them and laughed along. How the hell was this allowed?

On Friday, after four days of abuse, and an hour before her shift ended for the weekend, Jack knocked on her door.

"Um, Heather, my wand isn't working."

The file clerk's job entailed delivering mail by matching a series of numbers on the mail to the insured's file. Several months ago, they switched to a handheld computerized barcode system. The employees had to wave a pen-sized wand over the barcode to match the mail to the file. Jack's had broken. He had no choice but to fold.

"Let me take a look," she said. Heather strolled over to his bucket of mail and waved the wand over a random barcode. Nothing. She twisted the cord, checked the battery and then unscrewed the tip of the wand.

"That thing comes off?" Jack asked.

"Yes. Usually something comes loose." She placed the tip of the wand on the desk and jiggled the insides. She held it up to her eyes and played with it. After several minutes, she screwed the tip back on and swept the wand over the same barcode. *Beep!* Success.

"Wow," he said. "How'd you know what to do?"

"Figured it out." Heather returned to her office, refusing to show her soft side.

At the end of the night, Jack entered her office with a bag of M&M's. "Want one?"

"One?" she teased.

"I mean, do you want *some*?" His face reddened. He let four or five pour into her hand.

Heather picked up a light brown one. "Did you ever wonder why they have two different color browns? I mean there are hundreds of colors in this world and they choose brown? And two shades of brown. Why not blue, pink, or purple?" She tilted her head back and chucked all of them into her mouth. Jack's nostrils expanded. "What?" she asked.

Before he could think of a response, he let out an explosive laugh. "What are you talking about?"

"M&M's. Colors. They're boring. They look like autumn leaves on top of dirt. Why can't they look like spring flowers?" Heather held out her hand for more. He owed her this at least.

Jack angled his head to the side and scratched the back of it, unable to figure her out. He tried to hide his grin, but Heather caught it just before he exited her office.

She came into work Monday and found a bag of Skittles on her desk with a note. *Enough color for you?*

****

Heather sat on the desk outside her office. Jack, Wayne and Dean surrounded her with their Snapple Iced Teas and assorted junk food from the only vending machine in the building. Doritos and Cheez Doodles made their way around the circle, as did waves of laughter, while Wayne told them about the woman that stayed late last night.

"So, I said I'd just be a minute and she's like I can't work with all this beeping, I'm going to report you."

Jack coughed up cheese dust and curled forward. Heather held her stomach to disperse the pain.

"I said, report me? I'm doing my job. What do you want me to do? So, she stands up and she's wearing this ugly, army green turtle-neck sweater with bright, pink pants and I fall back onto my bucket and the whole thing of mail topples over and scatters across the floor..."

Dean twirled to the left and spit his ice tea all over the rug. Heather's laugh caught in her throat, and only huffs of breath came out. Her cheeks now hurt as much as her stomach.

"...she starts freaking out and screaming and coming at me. I'm crouched down on the floor picking up the mail and she's towering over me waving a file and I'm laughing in her face. All out laughing right at her and it's just making her angrier and then..."

Wayne froze. His story sacked. Heather unaware, continued to laugh as did Jack and Dean. One by one, they noticed.

"What the hell's going on here?" Barry barreled at them.

Heather tried to stop laughing, but the image of the woman yelling at poor Wayne while he crouched on the floor, mixed with Barry's shock at their apparent "conspiracy with the enemy," made her snort and gag in quick chunks.

Heather took off towards her office, but remained near the door to listen.

"What the hell are you all doing?"

"We're on break," Dean said.

"That's not what I mean. Why are you hanging out with her? Don't you remember what I told you?"

Silence.

"Well? Anyone?"

"She's not that bad," Jack answered.

"Yeah, she's nothing like you said. She's kinda cool," Wayne piped in.

Silence. Then his clipboard whacked the top of a desk. Heather raced toward her chair. Barry charged into the office and slammed the door behind him.

"I don't know what to do with you anymore. I remove you from your floor and it's happening again."

"What's happening?" She threw her arms in the air.

"Fraternizing with your employees."

"What exactly am I expected to do? Hide in here?"

"Obviously you don't have enough work to do. Maybe I should give you a bucket of mail to deliver."

"But then I'll be too close to them. I might make eye contact, breathe the same air, or perhaps even…speak to them."

Barry squeezed the pen in his hand, knuckles faded to white. "What about last week when Marc came to visit you?"

"I didn't know he was coming. I can't predict when former employees are going to visit. What was I supposed to say? 'Stop. Don't come in. Run. Run for your life. Save yourself. Don't look back!'"

"This isn't a joke. Writing you up has no effect."

"Writing me up for what? Is my work not on time? Are there any problems with it? Have I not completed everything you've handed me?" Heather pointed to the door. "Are their mail delivery numbers not the highest in the building?"

Barry's face turned purple. Speechless. Maybe he ran out of things to yell about. He shook his head, then, as if an idea had formed, his brow elevated. "There's a new employee starting Monday. I think I'll give him to you." He stepped towards the door and clutched the handle. "And take Wayne off your floor."

****

Heather strolled into work an hour late stating car trouble. Believable since she drove her father's twelve-year-old Monte Carlo and had breakdowns before. This would force Barry to teach the geeky new employee until she arrived. A small revenge for the weeklong ordeal of training another high school kid. Some uninterested punk, probably stoned or brain dead.

Heather signed in and walked downstairs to her floor. She peeked around the corner but saw only Jack and Dean, both on opposite sides of the room. Not like them. Barry and the new rookie were missing. The eerie stillness persisted.

She dumped her winter coat in her office and then walked toward the center of the room. Jack raised his head and Heather held her palms up, searching the floor. He used his wand to direct her to her right. Heather combed the space, but still nothing.

She crept past a row of desks and behind the wide support beam. A guy in a black T-shirt arched over the mail bucket. *Ugh.* Barry probably taught him quickly, then dumped him for Heather to finish training. She inched forward, noticing his hunched appearance. How close did he have to bend over to read the barcodes? Was he some thick-eyeglass wearing nerd?

Leave it to Barry to make her life miserable. Intentionally hiring a sixteen-year-old clueless dork and sending Wayne, with his white, Billy Idol spiked-hair, down to the first floor. She grinned, knowing the girls down there would be all over him within hours. Maybe he wouldn't suffer after all.

The boy leaned forward until his face came intimately close to the stack of mail. Was he blind?

Then she realized: no beeps. Asleep? Dead? She mouthed "what the hell" to Jack from across the room. Jack shook his head.

Heather stood less than six inches away and poked his shoulder. The boy flinched, then sprang to his feet, steadied himself and turned around.

This was no boy.

He stood at least a foot taller than Heather. Black feathered hair, blow-dried and poufed back in waves as if he used an entire bottle of mousse. His chest muscles carved and perfectly emphasized in his tight black T-shirt. He grinned, bright white teeth flashed between his hair and shirt like a black-and-white checkerboard.

He tilted his head down but eyes remained up and fixed on Heather. A tiny smirk crept up his face. At first glance, he appeared strong, powerful and in control, but now, as he sat upon the desk, he looked humble, somewhat shy.

"Sorry," Heather said. "I didn't mean to scare you."

"No, not at all. I've been waiting for you."

"Me?" She lost herself in naughty thoughts.

"Yes, you're Heather, right?"

What an ass. Of course he was looking for her. "Yes, I mean…" Heather straightened her posture. "I believe Barry set you up?"

"I guess. Is this what I'm supposed to be doing?"

"Well, yes. Wanding."

"Hmpf." He twirled the cord, spinning the wand.

"He explained everything?" She stepped to the other side of his mail bucket. "Any questions?"

"No. He just said to stroke this over the white labels. Stroke, stroke, stroke."

"You've done this before?"

"Stroke? Yup. I'm quite good at it too."

Heathers face inflamed. She let her hair fall forward to hide her cheeks. "So...you always wanted to work at an insurance company, delivering mail?"

"It's been my dream. Ever since I turned seven, I told my dad I'd be doing this one day. And now, my dream's fulfilled." He flicked the wand over each barcode, pushing the next file forward. Without looking.

"I see. You're rather good. Most new employees don't get the hang of it. We have to send them to the Saturday remedial class. Eight hours of classroom time, slide presentation. They receive a book with instructions and frequently asked questions."

His face puzzled. "Seriously?"

"Oh, yeah. Some even attend the Sunday, three-hour session, that teaches proper hand-wand coordination, how to hold it between the thumb and pointer finger, quicker ways to fly through each desk, proper flicking techniques."

"Are you shitting me?"

"Not at all. Nine-million seven-hundred and eighty-two thousand files are scanned per night. If one file gets missed, just one, it interrupts the entire system the next day."

"Really? I must be doing it wrong then. I thought this was a joke."

"Joke? No way. This is serious business. Let me watch you again to be sure." Heather leaned over his shoulder. His cologne gripped her. She tried to ignore it and watch as he scanned the barcodes more carefully. "Hmm, not sure. You might need to attend the Sunday class at least."

"Ah, shit. I'm supposed to play ice hockey with my friends, Sunday. Do ya think?"

Heather lost her flat effect, crumpled into a ball and released five minutes worth of volcanic laughter. "Psych!"

"You are shitting me. You suck." He stood, flung the wand as far as the cord would go and walked a few paces away. Jack perked his head up to see what was happening.

"Sorry, just a little wand humor."

"I was ready to quit."

"Already?"

"You got me scared, thinking this was intense."

"You just complained it was boring."

"Yeah, well, my last job was in a glove factory...I stuffed gloves in boxes or hung them on glove trees."

Heather stared, stone faced.

"I'm serious. I don't joke like *some* people." He rolled his eyes. "This isn't much better though. I actually fell asleep before."

"I noticed."

"You're not going to say anything to Barry, are you?"

"Me? You're asking the wrong person. I don't talk to him if I can help it."

"Don't like him, do you? Something wrong with him?"

"Where do I begin?" Heather opened her mouth to talk but a strange feeling overtook her. "Actually, I'm keeping you from your work. Let me get some things done and I'll check on you later."

She dashed to her office and then closed the door. A trick! Barry set her up. No way was that man a senior in high school. He also caught on too fast. Who trains someone for a few minutes and dumps them? Barry probably had the new employee upstairs with him and sent some upper management in here to spy on her, catch her badmouthing him, then fire her. She couldn't lose her job. She had tuition to pay for.

She peeked through her blinds. The man stood and dragged the wheeled bin of mail to the next desk. Way too confident. And fast. He undoubtedly worked upstairs in the claims department as a supervisor. Barry would never place a man that looked like that on her floor. Why trade Wayne to deposit an even hotter guy down here? He would not fool her.

Heather stormed out of her office, hands on her hips, and veered down the aisle toward him. Prepare to be told off.

"Heather!"

She rotated toward the voice and found Barry writing furiously on a clipboard. Had the impostor supplied him with an earful already? He shoved the pen behind his ear. His harsh squint alerted her to the upcoming lecture.

She dragged her feet toward him. Another write up? Fired? She needed to think about finding a new job.

"What are you doing hiding in your office with the door closed when we have a new employee? I can't get you to stay in there on a normal day, but when I give you someone to train, you hide?"

"You left him down here alone, not me."

"No. I was training him, left to find you, noticed you signed in, returned to the floor and there he is sitting alone."

"No, I was..."

"I don't want you leaving his side the entire night, do you understand? I already informed Jack and Dean to stay far apart from one another. They should be on opposite sides of the room at all times."

"Eventually, as they get to their last desks, they'll be beside each other. You realize that, don't you?"

His eyes widened at his own stupidity. "Just...just sit next to him. If even once this week I come down and you're not next to him, or you're anywhere near Jack or Dean, I will..." Barry raised the clipboard high above his head. "Just go!" His voice resounded in the silent room and bounced back in fury. He bolted out of the room faster than Heather could react.

She stomped toward the rookie, then sat on the desk across from him, arms folded on her chest.

He grabbed a spot next to her and knocked into her shoulder. "As I was saying, is there something wrong with him?"

Heather chuckled and looked down at her purple acid-washed jeans. "I just realized, I never got your name."

"Nicolo. Trevisani." He extended his hand for her to shake.

A fireball ignited in her palm and spread throughout her body. His eyebrows dipped slightly, but the grin continued to grow.

****

Nicolo whisked the wand over the files, but kept his eyes on Heather. *He thought he was cute, didn't he?* Well, he was. Something about this guy kept her intrigued. Every word that escaped his mouth, she gobbled up. He looked at life differently than the group she hung out with, and Heather wanted to know everything about the first eighteen years of his life. After almost twenty hours of conversation, he gave her more than she could wish for.

"Did you ever break a bone?" Nicolo flicked the wand onto the cart and leaned in letting her smell his cologne.

"Of course. Broke my arm climbing my cousin's tree when I was eight."

"You little tomboy, you."

"What about you? Break anything?"

"I broke my arm jumping on my cousin's trampoline while eating a bowl of spaghetti and meatballs."

She laughed out loud. Hiding her laughter after a week of this was becoming impossible.

"I jumped off my roof when I was nine and broke my leg," he continued. "That was after watching Mary Poppins. My mom kept saying, 'Umbrellas are not parachutes.'"

"Oh, wow. Was it bad?"

"Leg wasn't too bad, but you should've seen the umbrella! Poor thing."

Heather muffled her giggling once more. "I gashed my right shin while riding my bike once. Look." Heather lifted her jeans.

"Gruesome." He ran his finger along the scar as if to heal it.

Goosebumps coated her skin. She quickly lowered her pant leg. His touch was more intoxicating than his words.

"One time, I went inside an abandoned house and fell through a board and ripped apart my whole calf." He raised his jeans to show the damage.

"Whoa." Heather thought for a second and then arched in closer. "I got caught stealing lip gloss from Super-X when I was thirteen. Then I stole rum from my dad's liquor cabinet. I puked in my neighbors bushes and she turned on her porch light and caught me."

"Rebel," he whispered. "I hotwired a mail truck once and intentionally crashed it into a mailbox."

"Stupid!" She scrunched down until her butt hit the floor. "You're gonna get me fired. If you-know-who walks in, that'll be it."

"We're just having fun."

"I'm not allowed. I'm destined to live a life of pure suffering."

"Seems like you *had* a lot of fun."

"I did. But now, between college and my assistant manager position, I guess it's all downhill. You never stopped having fun, I guess?"

"Why stop? Who says life's supposed to get boring?" Nicolo squatted next to her, and accidentally fell back, hitting his butt into hers. He snapped back, then repositioned his large frame underneath the desk.

"You make me laugh, Nicolo. You make me think. You make me want to cry. In a good way, though. You seem to have a very generous nature, always wanting to give. When you're not being goofy, that is."

"More so when I'm goofy. I like helping out. Maybe that's why I hate all my jobs."

"Gloves are very important. Imagine all those frostbit fingers if it wasn't for you."

"Yeah, right. Not buying it."

"What are you planning to do once you graduate?"

He emerged from the desk and his face turned serious. "No clue." He stood and resumed his mail delivery.

"You must have some idea. You'd be great at so much."

"Me? Yeah, right. Like what?"

"How about a teacher? Working in a hospital? There's plenty of jobs for you out there. A police officer? EMT?"

"You have more faith in me than I do. Nope. Wanding it is." *Beep. Beep. Beep.*

****

For the first time in over two years, Heather's workweek raced to its end. For the first time in two months, she did exactly as Barry asked and never left Nicolo's side.

The hand on the clock smacked the number twelve, giving it a high five. Eleven employees raced outside and started their weekend. Heather lingered behind with Nicolo and the two of them strolled to the parking lot, stopping at the bottom of the stairs.

She looked up at him, into his black eyes. What was it with him? A senior in high school with no plans when he graduated. Jumping from job to job. Brooke would kill her if she knew Heather was entertaining him. But there was something about him.

She thought about the story he told. The one where he came home from school last month to find his fifteen-year-old dog, Rocco, lying in the kitchen, panting. Spots of blood on the floors throughout the house. Heather never owned any pets, but she knew it would have crushed her. To face it alone. How could he handle a situation like that?

Nicolo smiled. A moment of awkward silence arose, their first all week. Something was different now. Something had changed in this brief, private moment.

A February squall prevented them from extending their good-bye. Heather clutched the coat tight around her chest. The giant hood sailed up and flipped over her head. Only her lips remained visible. Nicolo curled the hood up to reveal the contentment in her eyes.

"Thank you, Heather. This week was... interesting." He winked, then drifted to his car, blurred by yet another gust of blowing snow.

Chapter 3

Nicolo

The whirling of the blender came to a halt, as Nicolo's brother, Dino entered the kitchen. Nicolo poured his milk, oatmeal, banana, and whey protein shake into a 1986 Mets collectible glass and Dino made a retching sound.

"How can you eat that shit?" Dino asked.

"Pre-workout shake. Better than your Cap'n Crunch."

"Whadda ya talking about? It's cereal. It's good for you."

"When you look like me, we'll talk."

"No time for that. College boy here." Dino gripped the collar of his shirt and tilted his head back. "Got big plans tonight for Valentine's Day with Carissa."

"Yeah, I'd like to caress her too." Nicolo snickered. He chugged a few mouthfuls of his shake, but Dino's hand hurled into his chest before he could finish.

"Watch your mouth."

Nicolo choked on the liquid and a coughing fit followed. "Kidding. Chill out."

Dino opened the door of the cupboard, pulled out the Cap'n Crunch, hesitated then grabbed a pouch of his mother's maple and brown sugar oatmeal. "How's business down at the glove factory? Still giving rectal exams?"

"It's not that kind of glove, you moron." Nicolo rinsed his empty glass with soapy water and then wiped his mouth on the towel. "I quit."

"Again? How many jobs have you gone through this year?"

"They bore me. Working at Northford Insurance Company now."

"Sounds *much* more exciting." Dino snorted.

"$4.14 an hour, I'll deal with it."

"Sweet." He emptied the oatmeal packet into a bowl and stared at it. "Any chicks at this place?"

Nicolo ignored his brother and refilled the glass with cold water. He brought it to his lips, but a powerful slap walloped him in the back.

"There is, isn't there?"

Water ejected from Nicolo's mouth and sprayed into the sink. "What the hell is wrong with you today? You trying to kill me?" He wiped his mouth on his hand and glared at Dino.

"Who is she?"

"Who's who?"

"Give me a break, I know you."

"No, you don't."

"What does she do there? Secretarial stuff?"

"She's not a secretary, she's my boss."

"You're sleeping with your boss?" Dino's eyebrows soared.

"I'm not sleeping with anyone. Man, it's impossible to talk to you."

Nicolo finished the rest of the water, then walked into the den and tugged his Bakerspath High School sweatshirt over his head. The hood caught over his eyes. He shoved it back and Dino stood before him. "What? What's with you this morning? Can't you leave me alone?"

"It must be serious, eh. This girl?"

"I just met her, she's dating someone anyway. Just forget it." Nicolo plowed through the front door and slammed it behind him. He jumped into his 1979 Jeep CJ-7 and headed to the gym.

****

Nicolo finished his last set of squats, heaved the barbell back on the rack, and collapsed on the bench. He drank the rest of his water, this time without it reaching his lungs.

The door to the aerobics room opened. Red, purple and pink spandex drifted out and the fluorescent lights of the gym reflected off their gear. Matching leg warmers and bright white sneakers tiptoed out of the room like a parade of fairies.

He wiped the sweat off his brow. *Bam!* The exercise-room door slammed and shifted his gaze. The aerobics instructor exited with a boom-box and a pair of tie-dye bike shorts emphasizing her ass.

Thoughts of Heather flooded his mind. Her long brown hair bouncing up and down as she walked, her never-ending smile and that laugh that pierced him. God, she laughed at everything. Was he that funny? He doubted it.

For some reason, she appeared interested in him, though. Actually, who was he kidding? He enjoyed talking to her as well. He had no idea what he wanted to do with his life, but she seemed to think he could conquer the world. Was she that blind? He was a big nobody.

He couldn't get her out of his mind. Had she offered to help him study for his English exam, or was she just being nice? Did he really tell her about all the pranks Dino pulled on him over the years? What a loser.

The aerobics instructor bounced toward the locker room and he watched her ass shift back and forth around the neon-orange, thong leotard. Heather's ass popped into his head.

Nicolo felt himself get hard under his sweatpants. He hurried over to the slant board to work out his Abs. He secured his ankles under the support brace and locked his hands behind his head. Nine, ten, eleven. The jerking movements made him picture pumping Heather from behind. *Shit*. He released his arms and fell back on the board, blood rushed to his head.

Nicolo released his legs and climbed off the board. Workout over.

He turned the knob on the shower in the men's locker room and jumped in before the water had time to heat up. He placed his hands on the tiles above and let the cold water run down his face and body. He needed to pick up that part for his Jeep at the auto parts store. He could work on it this afternoon.

The water warmed, then went hot and pulsed on his face. He leaned back and the jets hit his chest and streamed down his legs. He wanted to get the Jeep in top shape for the summer. Drive it to the beach looking fierce.

He imagined Heather sitting in the front seat, hardtop off, hair blowing wildly behind her. They'd talk all day, like they did at Northford. You'd think after talking four hours a day, for five days straight, they'd run out of things to say. But they hadn't.

Heather probably loved the beach. Swimming, running in the sand, making sand castles. She wouldn't care if her hair got wet or sand got into her stuff like his ex did. He pictured Heather eating a turkey hero with sand in it and she wouldn't care about the crunching sounds her teeth made. She was awesome like that.

The stream from the showerhead sprayed directly on his dick. It hardened from the image of Heather ramming the turkey hero deeper and deeper into her mouth. *Damn*. He turned the shower off and grabbed his towel.

Screw the Jeep. He needed to go home and jerk off.

****

Monday arrived like driving behind an old man on a one-lane highway. Nicolo hurried into work, retrieved his bucket of mail and bolted off the elevator, aiming straight for the second floor. He casually sauntered into the room and peeked to his right. Heather's office was surprisingly empty. He started working in the far back corner of the floor and waited for her.

Jack and Dean entered a few minutes later. "Someone's excited about their job," Jack teased.

Nicolo tossed a cool look at the two of them. "Nah, just want to get done early so I can chill out."

"Be careful. Barry will give you another section to do," Dean added, wheeling his bucket to the opposite side.

Nicolo *was* excited about his job, but not because of the work. He thought about what Heather had said to him on Friday. How compassionate he sounded when he told his stories. It embarrassed him, for sure. He'd never tell anyone. But she made him feel like less of a loser.

And then she appeared. Everything he felt for her over the weekend intensified as the grin on her face lit up the dreary floor. What was it about Heather that made her different from all the rest?

She approached Jack first, then Dean, her long brown hair flowing over her breasts. Was she mad at him for something? Had he said something stupid to her last week? Probably. Fifteen minutes passed. He glanced up occasionally, and watched her smile and throw her hands here and there, sharing one of her funny stories.

Nicolo finished his third desk and she finally wandered over to him. He panicked, turned his back to her and leaned over the desk to reach the files thrown in a bin. After waiting for her all this time, why was he acting like an idiot?

"Hey," she said. "How was your weekend?"

"Good, great, how was yours?"

"Good. I didn't expect all this snow though. Some twelve inches. I think we got twenty-six."

"Yeah, tell me about it. I spent the day shoveling with my brother."

"Me too."

Nicolo wrinkled his brow. "You shovel?"

"Yes, what'd you think?"

"I can't picture it."

"What's that supposed to mean? I helped my parents all day yesterday. I think we were out there for five hours."

Now he pictured it. Heather clutching the shovel's handle with a firm grip, bending over, her ass in his face, moaning with each throw of the shovel over her head. "Sorry, didn't mean any disrespect. You just look so tiny."

"I work out."

"You do?" Purple thong-leotard, no bike shorts underneath. Bare ass. Blood surged through his veins and ended between his legs. He sat back in the chair and pulled the bucket in front of him. "Where?"

"Lucille Roberts."

"Oh, a girl's gym."

"So?"

He was blowing it. "I meant...maybe we can work out sometime."

"You do aerobics?"

Nicolo chortled. "Aerobics? Please, what do I look like, a girl?"

Heather's lips parted, she shook her head.

"Sorry, all that shoveling's fogged my brain." Three insults in under five minutes. What was wrong with him? He had no problem talking to her last week. Now he was acting like a jerk. "I work out at Gold's gym. Maybe we can work out together. You use weights?"

"Isn't that for guys?"

"Not at all. I can teach you a thing or two." Nicolo raised one eyebrow.

Heather glanced down, combed her hand through her hair, and let it fall in front of her face. Did she just blush?

That's it. Be cool. You can fix this mess. "So, what do you say?"

Heather swallowed hard. Then, after heaving out a breath...

"How's it going?" Barry shouted, making his way down their aisle.

"Great," Heather blurted out.

"Great." Nicolo repeated. *Damn.* Why did he have to show up now? "She's a great teacher. Gave me all these tips on how to hold the pen between my thumb and pointer finger, and proper flicking techniques."

Heather's eyes widened. "Yes, he picked up on it instantly. On his fourth desk already."

Barry lifted his watch to his eye and nodded. "Excellent. Glad this is working out. Heather, can I speak to you for a minute?"

They marched into her office and he closed the door behind them.

"Yo, dude, you're making us look bad." Jack took a handful of pushpins and winged them across the room at Nicolo.

He grimaced as several hit his back. Nicolo picked up a stapler and flung it at Jack knocking a pencil cup onto the floor. Pens and pencils sprayed throughout the aisle.

Dean searched the desk in front of him and held up a large package of Post-its still cellophaned together. He whizzed it clear across the room, hitting a beam. It cracked, spilling its contents below.

Nicolo yanked open the drawer closest to him and grinned. He climbed on top of the desk and held up a large rubber band ball. Jack and Dean ran to take cover. He threw his hand back and...

"So, I want to see that by the end of the week. I already told Cliff." Barry exited her office.

Nicolo jumped down from the desk before Barry turned, but Heather spotted him. The three file clerks hopped into their chairs and beeping resumed. Barry left the floor.

"Nicolo, can I see you in my office for a second?"

Nicolo's chest squeezed tight. What else could go wrong tonight? He entered Heather's office and stood by the door like a child with a poor report card.

She scowled at him. "Close the door."

He closed it, but not before Jack tossed him a tense look.

"Are you serious?" Heather shouted. "I just talked you up to Barry and I hear banging and crashing outside. Then I find you standing on an examiner's desk? What's wrong with you tonight?"

Nicolo's body overheated like a steam room. Sweat built under his Ocean Pacific T-shirt. "I'm sorry."

"That's the third time you've said that tonight."

"But, I am. I wasn't trying to get you in trouble."

"Look, I really enjoyed talking to you last week. You did your job well, and we had fun. We learned a lot about each other and I thought, well..." She looked away. "Never mind. Obviously, last week was some act. Now I feel like you're the same as all the other employees that take this job for granted and plan to skate their way through for a few months, then *Bam*, you'll quit, give no notice and screw everyone in your path."

"No, not at all. I swear."

"I don't believe you." Heather threw her hands in the air and walked back to her desk. "Just go."

"No, please, let me explain."

"Just go!" She plopped into her chair and grabbed the stack of papers in front of her.

He looked at his sneakers. With nothing to say, he walked to the door and stepped out. Jack shook his head at him. Had he heard everything?

Nicolo slammed the door behind him. "Look," he said.

Heather's head shot up.

"I acted like a total ass and I'm sorry. I had fun with you last week. I've hated every job I've had. This is the only one I've looked forward to, and…" He closed his eyes, inhaled through his nose. "And that's because of you. You made me feel like I'm not a useless piece of crap like everyone else in my life." He opened the door again and charged out.

Nicolo ran to the bathroom and then threw cold water on his face. He pounded the hand towel machine and kicked the trash can over. He had never expressed his feelings to anyone before, always holding them in. His ex made him feel stupid and his brother insulted him. His teachers told him he'd never amount to anything. Last week he felt good about himself.

Sure, he was attracted to her, but it was more than that. For the first time he believed that he mattered. He had a purpose in life. That was because of Heather. She brought it out of him. His workouts more powerful, he repaired his Jeep, he looked forward to graduating high school and thought about his future. One week with her and his entire view on life changed. What was it with her? No one ever made him feel like this before.

He looked in the mirror and the ache in his chest and the shakiness in his legs made him want to quit again. The one person that tried to help him, he disrespected. What a dick.

Four hours later, Nicolo trudged out of the building behind the night crew. He lagged behind, avoiding Jack and Dean, then turned the corner, slumped down the final eight steps and headed to the right. The last of the cars exited the parking lot leaving him alone.

Pow! Something hard and wet struck the back of his head. The fiery pain replaced with bitter cold. Icy liquid trickled down his neck and seeped into his shirt. He reached back to remove the stinging but prickly fluid disintegrated in his palm.

Heather ran down the aisle, away from him, laughing to herself. "See you tomorrow, sucka," she said.

He reached down, formed a tight ball, watched her run with a flood of giggles and then, let the snowball drop to the ground.

Chapter 4

Heather

The sixty-two degree day allowed Heather to ditch her coat and grab her C.W. Post college sweatshirt instead. She signed into work and proceeded down the stairwell to her floor.

"Heather, can I talk to you for a second?" Barry appeared from behind. "You know the old files in the basement?"

"No." Maybe if she lied, he would find someone else to help him.

"Yes, you do. Old car accident claims? Cases from years ago that we store in the basement?"

"Maybe."

"You were down there with me once, remember?"

How could she forget? He tricked her into looking for a file and then attempted to put his crusty hands on her. "Vaguely."

"Good. Management has decided to attach barcodes to all the files down there and then wand them into the system. This way, if an old claim is reopened, we'll be able to locate it quickly."

She gave her head a slight shake. "And?"

"Well, I nominated you to do the job and they agreed."

"Me? Who agreed? Why me?"

"Because you're the fastest and you're familiar with the area."

"I was down there once, a year ago. Why don't you ask Cliff?"

"He's too slow."

"So, I'm getting punished?"

"No, it's a great honor." He sneered.

"An honor? To sit in a dusty basement and stick barcodes on files? It'll take weeks to do all of them. Why don't you get one of the night crew clerks to do it?"

Barry rolled up his sleeves, his eyes turned cold and his tone deepened. "Okay, sure. How 'bout Wayne? Should I tell Wayne you selected him? Or maybe one of the girls from your old floor. Pam, Kathy, Tina?"

Her shoulders sagged.

"Or how 'bout one of your own staff? Jack, Dean, or maybe, Nicolo? Fine, instead of you, I'll pick Nicolo." Barry hopped back up the stairs.

"Okay, I'll do it."

"I knew you would." He snickered. "I'll meet you in your office in fifteen minutes."

****

Nicolo strolled into Heather's office with that huge grin on his face. His smile was the only thing that kept her sane anymore. When she told him her news, though, his face plummeted.

"What do you mean? How long will you be down there? Who's watching us?"

"Supposedly he has this all figured out. I'm sure he spent days plotting it. I'll be down there for several weeks and he'll be mostly on this floor checking up on you three, having Cliff check on the fourth floor periodically."

"Why would he have Cliff on his floor when their counts are down, and ours are at their highest?"

"I think it has something to do with him catching us by the water fountain last week."

"We can't drink water together?"

"Apparently not. I'm not allowed to do anything but sit in here alone and cry."

"That's bullshit."

"You know what he told me a few weeks ago?" Heather leaned back in her chair and folded her arms. "He said if I didn't refuse him that day, things would be different."

Nicolo sat on the edge of her desk. "What day? Refuse what?"

His warm eyes comforted her. After two months of sharing stories, she felt she could tell him. "A year ago, they were missing a file. They assumed it was in those large storage cabinets upstairs. They sent the file clerks in there every night for a half hour hoping to find it. One evening, Barry approached me in my section, from behind."

Nicolo reached back and closed the door.

"He touched my hair and it startled me. I turned and saw it was him. He came closer until he was only a few inches away. He told me he fantasized about me. He pictured me naked in his bed."

Heather unfolded her arms and laid them in her lap. She stared at her hands, unable to look at Nicolo. "He said he had this one porn video, and the girl looked just like me. She was his favorite. And when he jerked off to the video, he imagined my mouth covering his..." She closed her eyes.

Nicolo put his hand on her shoulder. "Don't. Don't even think about it. He's a fucking pig."

"He asked me to make his fantasy reality. I told him I was dating Lance. He said he heard the two of us arguing on the phone every night and he could make me forget all about him. Make me feel real good. Then he ran his grimy hand down my arm. I backed away. He clenched his fist and I thought he was going to hit me, but he leaned in and whispered in my ear instead. He asked if he could at least have the underwear I was wearing. It would make a good jerk off tool. Then he tried to grab my..." She looked away.

Nicolo snapped his head back, stared at the ceiling, and then ran his hand through his hair and yanked on it. "Heather I...I'd kill him if I was working here at the time. Why didn't you report him?"

"I was too embarrassed. I didn't think they'd believe me and then they'd fire me. I needed the job, it was good money. My parents don't have a lot. Financial aid wasn't enough. The loans would've drowned me."

"What did Lance say? What did he do?"

"I didn't tell him. He wouldn't have handled it well."

"What would he have done? Threatened him? Beat the shit out of him?"

"No, no, no," Heather shouted. "He wouldn't have done anything. He would've blamed me. Asked me what I did to tempt him."

Nicolo's face distorted and filled with disgust.

She looked away. "Nicolo, he'll be back for me any minute. Please go, or he'll do something to you too."

****

After blowing her nose for the fourth time, Heather dumped the wad of toilet paper into the bathroom garbage. Her daily routine after spending two weeks in a dust-filled basement. Every morning she woke with a stuffed nose.

She left the bathroom and trudged back to her hell. She had only completed a third of the files so far, at least another four weeks before she completed the task. She went to the right and towards the third row of the eight-foot high shelves, back to where her Walkman was. Today she brought her Thompson Twins greatest hits tape and had already listened to it once.

A crackling sound came from behind the shelving unit. Heather stopped and listened as the rustling continued. Barry again? He had already commented on her slow progress, as if she wanted to stay down here any longer. Being alone with him in the deserted basement gave her the creeps.

She tiptoed down the second aisle towards the back. She wanted to catch Barry in the act of rummaging through her counts. His micromanagement pissed her off.

She paused at the end of the cabinet, slid her foot forward and peeked around the edge. Then jumped back. So did he. Both screamed. "You scared the hell out of me!" she said.

"So did you."

"What are you doing here?"

"Visiting you." Nicolo inched over and met her behind the four-foot wide cabinet base. The dim lighting and secluded area made him look broader, taller and sexier. The letters on his brother's Farmingdale State College T-shirt warped, as they stretched across his beefy chest. The chest that was eye level. He placed his hand high above her on the shelf, reaching the top.

"I should have you reach the files up there. I use the step stool for them."

"Maybe you should say you need help."

The thought of being alone with Nicolo made her quiver. With Jack and Dean constantly around, Barry checking on them, and that incessant beeping, there were always interruptions. The silence and darkness down here made all that disappear. They were alone now.

He glanced at her shoulder. She had removed her sweatshirt thanks to the lack of any circulating air, and only her black tank top remained. He scanned her arm, then detoured to her boobs.

She peeked down at her cleavage. Her tank top had shifted, exposing the lace of her bra. Instead of running for her sweatshirt, Heather's breathing quickened. She let him continue to roam, his examination aroused her. Visions of him clutching her shoulders, and pinning her against the cabinet with his hot lips, surfaced.

The corner of his lip curled up. God, this was wrong.

"Speaking of step stools..." Heather slunk passed him. "Why don't you grab a seat while I work?" Heather plopped the package of barcodes on her lap wanting desperately to fan herself with them.

Nicolo removed a yellow folder hidden between two claims files and opened it. "What's this?"

"Nothing." She snatched it from him, but he held her hand and took it back. His strong grip made Heather flinch, but her brief second of alarm, quickly switched to curiosity. What were his hands capable of?

"Hmm, let's see, *Diabetes is a significant risk factor for cardiovascular disease.* Doesn't sound like a car accident report to me."

Goosebumps replaced her overheating body. "I have finals in three weeks."

"Guess you're not in that much of a hurry to get out of here. Maybe you're trying to avoid me."

"Silly. I'd rather be up there with the three of you."

"Oh, the three of us, eh? Jack and Dean too?"

"Of course. You're like the brothers I never had." The musty, unventilated air made the sweat creep out of her pores.

"Brothers, hmm." Nicolo closed the folder and slipped it back into its spot. "Not sure how you do it. Working thirty hours a week, going to school full time."

"I don't have a choice. Gotta pay the bills."

He nodded then reached for her Walkman and popped open the cover. "Cool. You like new wave, too?"

"Yeah. Used to listen to this great college radio station last year."

"Used to?"

"Lance listens to rock."

"So?"

"So, since I'm with him all the time, I started listening to rock."

"I thought you liked to dance. You can't dance to that."

"Lance doesn't dance. I haven't gone dancing since eleventh grade."

Nicolo's brow collapsed. "What about your friends?"

"They all went away to college. I met a girl at Post but she waitresses at night."

"What do you do on the weekends then?"

"Hang out with Lance's friends at their homes. Rent movies, play cards."

"Are you kidding? You sound like a bunch of old people." He jumped up, stood on top of the stool and balanced on one leg. "This is the time to party and have fun."

"It is what it is."

"You say that a lot. Why are you settling?"

"Settling?" Heather tossed the wand back into the cart. "You think I'm settling?"

"You just don't seem happy when you talk about him, that's all."

"What's not to like? He's studying criminology at Hofstra University, drives a nice car, lives in a big house."

"You sound like an ad in the classifieds." He hopped off the stool and kicked a file on the bottom shelf.

"He's a good guy."

"Maybe he is...but not for you."

"How would you know?"

"I know more about you than you do."

"What's that supposed to mean?"

He inhaled a deep breath, then his pinched, tension-filled expression released in a heavy sigh. "Heather, you talk about the past all the time. You get all excited, your cheeks hurt from smiling so much, your hands fly around like my grandma telling one of her stories. But when I ask you about your weekend, you look away, change the subject."

"I'm doing what's best for my future. Isn't that what you're supposed to do?"

"You changed your music, your clothes, friends, weekend activities."

"I grew up, moved on. That's what's supposed to happen." Her mouth went dry, but her eyes swelled with moisture.

Nicolo's arms fell to his side. "I'm sorry. Forget it. Let me go before Barry catches us. I'll talk to you later."

He walked to the end of the cabinet, hesitated, and without looking said, "Heather, you know I only want the best for you. I care about you. A lot."

****

Heather and Nicolo reclined in the last row of cabinets and rested the back of their heads on the files, their legs extended in front of them. He had managed to sneak down every night for the past four weeks. With no interruptions their conversations deepened, their questions multiplied, and their actions became more flirtatious.

She had succeeded in getting inside his head, learning things most guys would never reveal. He was someone she could talk to about anything, and she never wanted the conversations to end. He might have thought he was a nobody, but to Heather, he was the gateway to a life filled with possibilities and adventures. His thoughts on how to live life with passion drew her in. Nicolo knew how to live.

On Heather's final night in the dungeon, Nicolo brought in a plastic bag full of red grapes and another filled with pretzels to celebrate the completion of her final exams. He flicked a pretzel stick at her, but it wedged in her hair. Heather's fingers clawed through the strands, attempting to remove it, but the salt particles clung to her hair, refusing to let go.

He arched forward to help her detach it. His cologne floated past her nose. The pretzel clasped onto each strand as he tugged, like quicksand grabbing at a leg. He freed it, held it in front of his mouth and then bit down. The tiny crunch pierced her heart.

Only an inch away from her mouth, Nicolo's perfect teeth nibbled on the tiny stick, then his tongue slid across his upper lip, removing the salt particle. She saw her reflection in his black eyes. Neither of them budged.

His soft voice whispered to her. "When are you coming to my gym?"

The scent of sweet grapes escaped his mouth and she leaned back. "Soon, I promise. When you graduate next month."

"You've been putting it off for four months now. Nervous?"

"Of what?"

"Me, training you." He placed his elbows on his knees and curled in closer.

"Should I be?"

"Yup." He wriggled his eyebrows up and down.

"What are you going to do to me?" She already knew. She dreamed about it every night.

"Show you what you're capable of, how strong you are, how you can transform your body with hard work and dedication."

"And proper nutrition."

"Of course." He winked. "You should see if they have a major in sports nutrition, you'd like that."

"I would?" Heather said, blinking flirtatiously.

He leaned in more and placed his palms on her knees. His persuasive hands warmed her legs. What would she do if he tried to slide them up her thighs further?

"What the hell is going on here?" Barry stood at the far end of the cabinet and hurled his clipboard onto the floor.

Nicolo sprang from his stool. "I'm on my break."

"You are not allowed down here."

"Says who?"

"Excuse me?" Barry gritted his teeth and took a step closer.

"Where does it say where I can or can't take my break?"

"You cannot interfere with Heather doing her job."

"She's on break too. Plus, she's down here six hours a day for the past six weeks. Alone."

"That's her assignment."

"Would anyone know if something happened to her?" He stepped in front of Barry, inches from his face. "What if someone attacked her down here behind a file cabinet? How would we know?"

"I come down and check on her."

"That's what I'm afraid of."

Heather leaped in between the two of them. "Nicolo, please stop. Just go."

"She's entitled to a break too, you know." Nicolo jabbed his finger in Barry's face.

"Your break's over," Barry said. "Both of you."

Chapter 5

Nicolo

Nicolo drifted the wand back and forth over the files, missing every other one. With his motivation gone, he performed slower each day.

Just when Heather finally returned to their floor, Barry removed Nicolo from it and stuck him on the fourth floor in a section directly in front of his office. With nothing to look forward to and no contact with Heather, he could care less about his job. Barry watched him like a hawk, even followed him to the water fountain on four occasions over the past three weeks.

Nicolo concentrated on passing his finals and graduating from high school on Saturday. Maybe the summer would be better.

Heather tried to talk to him when he entered the building, but Barry was quick to drive Nicolo away as soon as he signed in. Most nights Barry kept Heather and Cliff late to discuss stupid things. Before long, Heather stopped trying and Nicolo's hopelessness returned.

****

Nicolo came into work Thursday and found Heather waiting for him at the front door. His heart woke up. "What's going on?"

"I escaped." She pulled the hair on her scalp with both hands and waved her tongue in frustration. "Are you finished? All done?"

"Yup. Took my last final this morning. Officially done."

"So happy for you!" Heather bounced up and down.

He missed their talks; his life was empty without her. A one-minute conversation restored his energy. "I have something for you," he said. "I left it in my car, though. Didn't think I'd see you."

"I'll walk you to your car tonight. I promise. Wait for me by the front entrance."

Nine o'clock slinked onto the plain white clock and Nicolo hurried off the floor as if a siren had blasted at a sporting event. He took the steps, skipping every other one, then waited at the front door.

Ten minutes later, Heather exited the stairwell and skipped over to him. They ran down the walkway, laughing and shoving one another, and then raced each other to his Jeep. Once there, he reached over to the passenger seat and handed Heather a magazine.

"Muscle and Fitness?"

"It's great, you'll love it. Read it from cover to cover. There's some nutrition articles I'd like your opinion on, too."

"Mine?"

"Yes, you're the expert, not me."

She flipped through the pages. "Thank you, I will."

"So, I'm officially done with school. No more stalling, when you coming to my gym?"

Heather stared at the front cover of the magazine. "We'll see. I'll try."

"Try? I thought you wanted to."

"I do, it's just...we'll talk about it next week."

"Next week? How 'bout tomorrow? Maybe we can set something up for Sunday. I'll have to see about getting you a guest pass and—"

"I'm off tomorrow. Lance is taking me to a Broadway show. It's a surprise, not sure which one."

Nicolo's heart shriveled. What was he doing? Where was this going? Could they really have a friendship when she had a boyfriend? The gym, the beach, dancing. Did she agree to do all those things just to shut him up? Only used him for his company while downstairs?

"A Broadway show. That sounds cool."

"I guess. I've never been to one. He's gone to so many." She rolled the magazine up avoiding his eyes. "Yeah, so, I'll be back Monday. We'll talk more then."

He wanted to erase the past month and start over. They'd have to find another way to talk. Maybe he could call her.

She smiled, giving him hope, her green eyes filled with a promise. He wished to be close to her. Wanted to comb his fingers through her hair, push it back to reveal her gorgeous face. He pictured her lying on his bed, naked, her long hair cascading over her breasts. He wondered what her lips tasted like. Plump and wet with...

"So, I guess I should go." Heather said.

"Yeah, sure."

She held her arms out wide, tucked her head into his shoulder and wrapped herself around him. "Congratulations again."

Her gesture shocked him. He hugged back, gently at first, then squeezed hard, feeling the warmth under her thin shirt. He didn't want to let go. Ever. He looked up at the blackening clouds of the night and grinned. She felt just like he had imagined.

She pulled away, but took the tip of her finger and tapped him on the nose. "See you Monday. Have fun at graduation. Don't lose your cap. You have to pay for those things, you know." She winked.

He watched her skip away, her delicious ass moving perfectly below her cropped shirt. Watched her walk to the far end of the aisle, watched until she climbed into her car. His face beamed. Her car reversed and exited the parking lot, taillights disappeared around the corner. This would be a great summer after all. He'd show her what she was missing in life.

He finally turned to leave, but recoiled. Barry perched himself on the final step of the walkway. He glared at Nicolo, motionless, teeth clenched, chest heaving and eyes locked on him.

How long was he there? Did he see them hug and the look on his face as he held her? See the way his eyes escorted her to her car?

Nicolo turned and left, freaked out by Barry's continued threatening expression. He backed out of his parking spot and started down the aisle. Barry appeared in his rearview mirror planted in the parking lot, his legs and arms were rigid but pulsing.

Chapter 6

Heather

Lance and Heather left the Ritz Theater and he clutched her hand, giving it a little squeeze. "How'd you like the show?"

"It was...different," she said.

"You got that right. *Penn and Teller* what a bunch of sickos." Lance tipped forward and grabbed his stomach in a fit of laughter.

"When you said Broadway I was thinking *Les Misérables.*"

"Why would I take you to some mushy girl show?"

Heather released his hand. Her shoes glued themselves to the sidewalk. "Because I'm a girl."

Lance continued to walk, failing to notice her frustration. "I'm taking you to this new restaurant. Large family style portions of food."

Heather jogged in her heels and caught up to him. "But there's only two of us."

"More for us then!"

"You do realize there's a growing number of people in this world that are overweight, some even obese?"

"Nonsense, look around. Do you see any obese people?"

"And there's a real threat of children becoming obese one day."

Lance exploded in hysterics. "You're too much! Are you making this up? Obese children. What are they teaching you in that school? Sure, we had one fat kid in high school, but that was it."

Heather scrunched her face. How ignorant could one man be? Their conversations consisted of long drawn out discussions about oral advocacy or client interviewing. Any reference she made about her work or school ended in dismissal. Petty issues in his eyes.

****

Monday afternoon, after enduring another comatose weekend with Lance and his boring friends, Heather bounded into work. She would accept Nicolo's offer to train at his gym. Why not? She had the summer off and her gym lacked inspiration. His workouts would provide the incentive she needed.

She signed in and stuck the pen back in its holder. "Psst." She looked behind her and found Cliff hiding in the far corner of the large storage cabinets. What job had Barry dumped on him now? Scanning the millions of files in here? She was glad it wasn't her this time. She snuck over to him.

Heather waited for him to speak, but he lowered his gaze to his sneakers refusing to look at her. "Heather, I have to tell you something before you find out yourself."

Oh, no. Please don't say Barry demoted her, took her off her floor, put Cliff on her floor? What more could he do to punish her?

"Friday, when you were off...Barry—"

"Barry what? What did he do?" Heather's face turned ashen, her hands clammy.

"He..."

A noise erupted behind them. Heather dragged Cliff down the next aisle and shook him. "Spit it out," she hissed.

"Barry fired Nicolo Friday. He's gone."

Heather released Cliff, fell back against the cabinet and gasped. All heat drained from her body and left her with biting cold. Her breathing increased, a shriek threatened to spew, but Cliff threw his hand over her mouth to silence her. "We think it was planned. He knew you were off and couldn't interfere." He removed his hand and stepped back. "I'm sorry."

The dull linoleum beneath her provided no explanation.

She shot Cliff a frenzied look, her body began to tremble, and she sprinted towards Barry's office. Cliff tried to latch on to her shirt, but it was pointless.

Heather stormed into Barry's office and slammed the door. He lurched up to grab the phone, but she shoved it back in the cradle. "How could you! What the hell is wrong with you? He was the best employee we had. You had no reason to fire him!"

Barry flopped himself into the chair and grinned. "His counts were down and he wasn't producing."

"He was the fastest employee we ever had and you know that."

"Not recently. Over the past month, he only scanned half the files he normally did. Examiners complained their mail was missing, desks left in disarray, mail delivered late. It's all there in black and white." He threw a stack of counts at her.

"That's your fault. You moved him off my floor."

"He's a big boy. If he can't handle moving to another floor, then that's his fault. There's no guarantee employees will stay on a certain floor."

She pointed her finger at him, baring her teeth. "You did this to punish me."

Barry relaxed in his chair and placed his arms behind his head. "Heather, you did this to yourself. I merely asked you out and you refused me. Repeatedly. And embarrassed me. Think of it as karma."

"Karma? Because I wouldn't go out with you? I have a boyfriend, what don't you understand?"

"But it's okay to date Nicolo while having a boyfriend?"

"Nicolo? I'm not dating him."

"I saw the two of you hugging in the parking lot last week. Just touched the last step when I saw you pull away from him. I questioned what I missed. A long, tongue kiss perhaps? Groping you under your shirt? I wondered what he was still doing out there fifteen minutes after his shift. Waiting for you obviously."

"I congratulated him on graduating high school. Are you serious?"

"Oh, I'm very serious. What else did I miss? What naughty things did the two of you do in the basement? Give him a blowjob in the back aisle? Sex in one of the bathrooms?"

"You're sick!" He leered at Heather but she no longer feared him. "Listen here, asshole. I'm warning you. You better stay away from me, far away. If you so much as look at me the wrong way, give me any projects to do or come within five feet of me, so help me I'll go right down to human resources to report you. Tina was there the day you harassed me. She heard the whole thing. Stay away from me or we'll go in the morning and your ass will be fired. You hear me!"

Heather bolted out of his office and rocketed down the steps missing several on the way. She located Jack and he attempted to calm her.

The two of them strummed through countless phone books looking for Nicolo's phone number, but there were no Trevisani's in Bakerspath. She asked Jack to distract Barry so she could search for Nicolo's file in his office, but he had already purged it. They attempted to sneak into human resources, but the locked office revealed their outcome.

"I'm sorry Heather," Jack said. "We tried everything. Maybe he'll contact you. Maybe he'll be in the parking lot tonight or leave a note on your car."

"No. Cliff told me they escorted him out. Barry warned security that he was a threat."

"A threat to what?"

"Barry told them that Nicolo threatened his life."

"Are you kidding me? What the hell!"

Heather left that night without signing out, but not before she stopped at the job post to look for another job. Her life would change this summer, but in ways she didn't anticipate.

Chapter 7

Nicolo

Dino spotted Nicolo buried in a lounge chair under a tree in the corner of their backyard, avoiding the guests at his parent's Fourth of July party. "You gonna hide there all day? Mom thinks you're being anti-social and dad's getting pissed."

"Does it look like I care?" He rolled onto his side. The lounge chair almost collapsed from his weight.

"So, you're just gonna mope all summer?"

"Yup."

"What happened to spending the summer at the beach? You haven't even gone out dancing with us."

"Little hard to do when you have no money."

"What'd you do with the money you made?"

Nicolo turned over. "I only worked there five months. Every dime went to fixing my Jeep. Now I'm broke."

"Maybe the glove factory will take you back." He snickered.

"Get the hell away from me, will you."

"Just busting your balls, can't take a joke?"

Nicolo looked away.

"It's the girl, isn't it?" Dino squatted in front of him and handed him a beer.

Nicolo peeked over his shoulder, then reached for the bottle. He struggled upward, cracked off the cap, and took a swig. "You don't get it. I'm not sure how it is with you and Carissa, but I went through high school not knowing what the hell my purpose in life was." He took another gulp. "When I talk to her I can see my future. She makes me feel like I've got a lot to offer the world. I can say the simplest thing and she turns it into some giant discovery."

"You're not that interesting, bro. That says a lot."

Nicolo sprang from the chair and ran toward the house. Dino grabbed him by the arm. "Look," Dino said. "I'm sorry. Not used to seeing you like this. Normally everything skims off your back. Didn't realize you were worried about your future. Thought you didn't give a shit."

"I do give a shit. I think about it all the time, but it's impossible to talk to you 'cause everything's a fucking joke. She listened to me though, gave me advice, believed in me." He finished off the last of the beer. "And now she's gone."

"So, call her."

"Never got her number."

"Then go up to the job. Find her."

"What's the point? She's got some rich boyfriend that's going to law school. What do I have to offer? I asked her to hang out a dozen times, but she always blew me off." He looked at the twenty guests parading on his property. Smoke billowed from the barbecue. "I'm kidding myself. She's not interested in me. Who would be? Just some high school loser that got fired from a stupid job."

Chapter 8

Heather

"**I** can't believe Jeff, I hate him!" Brooke jabbered on the phone while Heather washed the dinner dishes.

"What now?"

"I tried beeping him all day and he didn't answer. I was going to call the precinct to see where he was stationed but—"

"You didn't!"

"Well, why not? I'm his girlfriend and it was an emergency."

"What was the emergency?"

"I needed to know what we're doing tomorrow night."

"Brooke!"

"Anyway, I gave up and went to the club to see if he was bouncing, and asked the bartender for him and you know what he said?"

Heather rolled her eyes. "No, what?"

"He said, you're old news, girl. Jeff's been hanging with a new chick for over two weeks now."

"He said that? Why would he say that?"

"Who knows? I'm never dating another cop again."

"I'm sure it has nothing to do with him being a cop."

"Yes, it does. They're all screwed up! Why does this keep happening to me?"

Heather wanted to tell her that nothing had changed since high school. Brooke still threw herself at guys, and guys still used her until they got sick of her whining. She went through more guys then all their friends put together.

"Maybe I should date someone of a higher class, like a doctor, or a lawyer."

Heather peeked over at Lance, fast asleep on the couch. Not even eight-thirty yet. Law school was kicking the crap out of him. Moving in together proved to be a practical decision with both their grueling schedules. Between their full school course-loads, his internships and her job as a diet tech at the hospital, they barely saw each other.

Heather had only two months left before graduating with her master's degree and then she would have the summer free. At least until September, then she'd start her ten-month internship. Lance still had one year left of law school.

Their apartment allowed them to study next to one another, eat an occasional meal together, and, as Lance put it, every night despite their crazy days, he could lie beside her in their bed, holding her.

"I need a drink, Heather. Happy hour tomorrow night?"

"Sure. Meet me here after work. Say five?"

****

Heather drove to Buttles, a club in Levittown and parked her car in the last available spot. They waited on the huge line, then Brooke rushed inside while Heather attempted to put her license away.

Brooke returned a moment later, eyes wide. "This is not happening," she yelled over the thunderous music.

Heather stepped inside and despite the darkness, it was evident what surrounded her. Rows and rows of men in police uniforms. "What the hell?" Heather turned back to the bouncer, "What's going on?"

"Funeral for a police officer earlier today. They got here 'bout an hour ago."

"We're not staying," Brooke wailed.

"Relax. I have work in the morning and I'm not driving all over Long Island. What's the chance of him being here anyway?"

"How would we know? It's so damn dark in here and they all look exactly the same."

The club, eclipsed of any significant lighting, enclosed them inside a cave of thick smoke, irritating their eyes and clouding their vision further. Pounding bass from the DJ echoed off the billows of haze.

They squeezed their way through the crowd to the bar. Elbows stabbed into their sides and spikes dug into their toes. "Two Mooseheads, please," Heather shouted. The bartender crouched below the counter to retrieve the beers. Across the bar, on the opposite end, a police officer stared at Heather. Then grinned.

"Hey, Brooke. That cop's checking me out."

"Which one?" She glanced across the room, but the bartender sprang back up and obstructed her view.

Heather snatched the two beers and handed Brooke hers. "Drink fast, you need it."

They guzzled their beers, then wandered to the dance floor through the smog. The icy beer washed the burning in her throat from the relentless cigarette stench.

"What if Jeff's here?"

"There's too many of them. Plus, it's packed. He'd never find us." Heather looked to her right and saw the hot cop again on the other side of the dance floor. He tilted his head and watched her sway to the hammering music. His smile persistent.

Heather stiffened and redirected her attention back to the dance floor. Only her heart moved now. It twirled and pranced beneath her sheer blouse.

Brooke seized Heather's hand and pulled her away. "I'm ready for a shot."

"Are you serious? Why'd we leave the bar then?"

Brooke dragged Heather by the arm and navigated them to the right. Brooke ordered two shots of tequila but then pretended to look behind her when it came time to pay.

Heather threw down four more dollars and then held her shot in the air. "Cheers. To a better summer filled with—" Brooke slammed her shot back and shoved the lemon in her mouth before Heather could finish. "Okay. Never mind." Heather did her shot, then sucked on the abnormally large piece of lemon. Her face scrunched into a tight ball, eyes closed and lips pursed. *Blech*! When she opened her eyes, hot-cop positioned himself across the bar from her. Again.

"Heather, I'm gonna grub a cigarette off someone. Be right back."

"You're not smoking again, are you?" But she was off through the crowd and out of sight. Heather gritted her teeth, smashed the lemon rind into her glass and then banged her shot glass on the counter. The bartender's head shot up from her hammering.

"Hello."

Heather turned.

"Lemon too sour?" Hot-cop lowered his head and smirked.

"Actually, it was. Really sour."

"I noticed."

Heather's body engulfed with heat. At a loss for words, she twisted back to the bar. "Do you want a shot?"

"Nah, I'm on duty."

"Oh, okay. Wait, what?" Heather scanned his expression and then peered down at the beer in his hand. "Think you're funny, don't you?"

"I've been told I can be pretty funny."

"And with your sense of humor and uniform you figured you got it made tonight?"

"Don't women like uniforms?"

Heather studied the tight material over his shoulders. "I'd have to agree, you do look quite handsome."

"Thank you." He glanced away pretending to drink from his empty beer bottle. "Can I get you a beer?"

"Sure." So much for being sober for work in the morning. Luckily, her job correcting menus in the diet office didn't require many brain cells. Speed, on the other hand, would be a problem.

He held out the beer for Heather but tightened his grasp when she tried to pry it away. "Wise guy, eh?"

He let go, winked then raised his beer. "Here's to an evening of meeting new friends."

"A new friend is always a good thing." Friend indeed. Lance would love her new friend. Speaking of friends, where the hell was Brooke?

They spent the next half hour talking about the police officer's funeral, the events leading up to his death, and the two young children he left behind. Heather listened intently as he choked on his words regarding today's events. His compassionate account made her feel as if she knew the fallen hero herself.

"How long have you been a police officer?"

"Almost three years. My last job made me lose faith in people, so I decided to do something positive and help society."

"Like a superhero of sorts?"

"Yeah, I guess." He hid his grin.

"Where'd you work before?" She took a sip out of her third beer knowing she'd be in trouble in the morning.

"At Northford Insurance Company."

"Northford? I used to work there. Years ago. What department?"

"Night crew. Had to wand these annoying files with this hand held computer. Sucked."

"I...did that...too." The chaos and congestion in the room muted. Heather's heart quickened, pounding rapidly against her chest. She squinted, then edged closer to him. She shoved him back into the light over the entrance and then edged his chin up. His eyes shut from the harsh light, then reopened. She stepped back, shook her head and her mouth flew open. "Nicolo?"

He narrowed his eyes also. Then, as if the club suddenly threw on floodlights, he saw it. "Heather?"

"Oh my God, it *is* you."

"Holy shit..."

"Never in a million years would I think—"

"I watched you at the bar and wow, I didn't realize. I couldn't—"

"Of all the cops in here, you—"

"...and I've never been in here before."

"This is unbelievable."

"You look different, your hair."

"I abandoned the perms and cut eight inches off. Too much to deal with for work and school."

"Still going to school?"

"Almost done. Getting my masters in exercise physiology."

"Really? I'm impressed."

"Learned how to take blood pressures, read EKG's, did underwater body weighing, designed my own gym."

"Wow, cool. You look...great. Really great."

"Except for my sour lemon face, right?"

Nicolo laughed. "Even with the sour face."

"I can't believe I didn't recognize you."

"It's been several years," he said.

"But still..."

"And the lighting in here's pretty shitty." He leaned his shoulder against the wall and bowed his head. He cast his devilish smirk as if no time had passed.

Heather and Nicolo caught up on the past few years, lost in each other's enthusiasm. Their eyes never drifted. He didn't mention being fired from Northford, she didn't mention how she painstakingly tried to find his phone number. He didn't speak of the worst summer of his life, she didn't ask why he never tried to contact her again.

Heather glanced at her watch.

"Leaving already?" He frowned.

"I have to work tomorrow. I shouldn't even be here, but my friend was upset and...where the hell is Brooke?"

They both giggled and then stared into each other's eyes. "You look amazing, Heather. I'm glad we bumped into each other tonight."

Thoughts of him removing the pretzel stick from her hair returned. What would have happened that night if Barry hadn't barged in? She never forgave herself for dodging his invites. What was she so afraid of? As each day passed, she knew he wouldn't contact her. But he was here now, and she wouldn't lose him again.

Nine o'clock neared and the police officers stumbled out of the club. Heather spied Brooke sitting at the bar with a man in a suit and tie. "I should go. I have to be at work at five o'clock."

"In the morning?" Nicolo glanced at his watch.

"Yep, but that's what friends do for each other."

He motioned to Brooke. "Doesn't look like she needed you, though."

"Oh, never when a guy's around. If Mr. Executive fits the bill, I won't hear from her for a few weeks. Unless of course he proposes, then I'll be the first one she rams it down...I mean, calls."

"Sounds like a great friend."

"Best friends since eighth grade."

"Can I have your number?"

"What?" Her muscles locked.

"Your phone number. So I can call you."

"Well, I..." A gush of shame engulfed her. "I live with...Lance. We moved in together, a year and a half ago."

Nicolo's shoulders sagged, a long, low sighed escaped his mouth. "Oh, still with him? I just assumed, well, you didn't mention him all night."

"I'm sorry, there was just so much to talk about." That was a lie. "Listen, give me your number. I'll call *you*."

His chin lowered to his chest, his eyes raised up to meet hers. Vacant eyes, lips flat and still. He played with the wrapper on his beer bottle, then his teeth chewed on his bottom lip.

Would he tell her how much she hurt him? How she rejected him in the past and he refused to be hurt again?

He glanced at the bar, then strode to its edge, leaned in and hunched over the counter. That was it? He wouldn't even say good-bye? How dare him! What a waste of time. What was the point?

Brooke slunk off her bar stool, as did Mr. Executive, and she reached up to kiss him. Instead of anger, Heather's stomach hardened from envy. Would she ever feel that sense of wonder at meeting someone new again? When your heart flutters and pounds, you shake from adrenaline and fear. The promise of someone who stands before you, brush in hand, ready to help you paint your future.

"Here." Nicolo held a pen in his hand and a white napkin. "My number."

Chapter 9

Nicolo

Nicolo hung up the phone and leaned back on his pillow. His weekly talks with Heather made it feel as if no time had passed between them. He looked forward to every Saturday when she called from work. His wake-up call, his motivation to get out of bed and enjoy his weekend.

She made him laugh. How he missed that silly laugh of hers. Her giggles and snorts that had him rolling in bed. His mother stopped knocking on his door to see why he was laughing so early in the morning by himself in his bedroom. Used to it by now, she shook her head when he finally made it downstairs for breakfast.

He flipped over and looked at the sunny, cloudless day. It was supposed to rain on Tuesday for Heather's graduation, but he visualized her smiling and dancing as droplets soaked her face.

He threw on shorts and a tank top and headed down the street for his jog. He ran quicker, knowing Thursday they'd finally hit the gym together. He rounded the corner and leaped over a sprinkler. What would she wear? Would he have to touch her? Would she let him? Adrenaline pushed him faster, his long legs grabbing hold of the concrete, heart beating at a good pace.

****

"I'm so sorry I'm late. Are you mad?"

Nicolo swung around to find black-and-silver striped leggings that clung to Heather's beckoning thighs and a matching sweatshirt that he wanted to unzip to reveal her honeyed flesh. She twirled her keys around her finger multiple times.

"Still don't carry a pocketbook?"

"Nah, they're for grandmas." She stuck her tongue out and punched him in the arm.

Although they spoke weekly, he hadn't seen her since that night in the club. Now, in the intense sunshine that flooded the lobby, her face glowed. Nicolo searched every inch of her beautiful face, eyed the sheen of her hair and the curves of her—

"Come on!" Heather shouted. "I'm pumped and ready to start." She leaped into the air like a cheerleader and then slapped him on the back several times, pushing him forward.

He led her into the weight room and his heart began racing. "Let's start with shoulders." He picked up a five-pound weight and twisted back to her. She unzipped her sweatshirt, whipped it off and tossed it on a bench. *Holy shit.*

Heather's thin-white tank top squeezed her breasts together popping them out of the V-neck. Her nipples grew with each second that passed. He handed her the weight as he breathed through his nose. *Don't get hard.*

She raised the weight in front of her, but her shoulder lifted up to her ear. "No, you need to keep your arm straight, locked elbows, don't move your shoulder."

She looked into the mirror, puzzled.

"Like this." He repositioned himself beside her and rested his arm along the full length of hers. Sweat grew under his shirt. If she weren't still with Lance, he would have grabbed her right then and there. Two months of safe phone conversations left him wanting more.

"Mmm, you're so warm. It's cold in here," she said.

He studied her enlarged nipples and agreed. Nicolo redirected his attention to the mirror before them and jerked back. Heather wasn't assessing her form. She was staring at him. Her eyes, flirtatious and playful, watched his every move.

He quivered, released her arm and turned away. "Okay, that's better." His chest heaved. He grabbed a ten-pound weight and walked back to her. "Lie down."

"What?"

"I mean, I want you to do triceps now."

"Shouldn't I do my other shoulder first? That's what it says in the *Muscle and Fitness* magazines."

He slammed to a halt. "You...still read that?"

"I have a subscription."

The memories resurfaced. The last night in the parking lot, handing her the magazine, watching her walk away with it. He felt dizzy and dropped onto the bench.

"Are you okay?"

Nicolo lowered his head. All those phone conversations and they still hadn't addressed the day Barry fired him from Northford. "I should have tried to contact you after I got fired. I thought about leaving a note on your car, but didn't see the point."

"The point?" Heather's face tightened. "We were friends. At least, I thought we were."

"I was a disappointment."

"To who? I lost it after you left. I bawled out Barry, applied for another job. I tried to find your damn phone number, but you're not listed."

He raised his head, eyes wide.

"My summer sucked." Her voice went flat. "I thought I had more time, thought I could think about it over the summer."

"Think about what?"

"What it would be like to be alone with you."

"I didn't think you wanted to. You kept blowing me off."

"I was scared."

"Of me?"

"No. Of me."

He stared at her, stared for a long time, then grabbed her hand and pulled her down next to him. "I just wanted to show you what you were missing. You were living in someone else's world."

"School and work keep me occupied."

"Is that what you want? To be occupied? What happens when school ends, you get bored of your job?"

Heather looked away. Tears filled her eyes.

"I'm sorry." He held her hand and sandwiched it between his.

"No. You're right, you always were. I realized after you left, but it was too late."

Nicolo had refused to bring up the past, but now it was flying in faster than he intended. He only wanted to move forward, glad that he had a second chance to have Heather in his life. But man, all those wasted years. He wouldn't let anything ruin this again.

Chapter 10

Heather

Heather threw her Tigger shirt over her purple bikini and located her beach bag. She drove to Nicolo's house and parked in front, but before she could compose herself, he rushed out his front door, down the steps and over to her window like a child running into Disneyland. He ripped her door open, clutched Heather's hand and plucked her out of the car.

She stepped onto the silver bar of his new Jeep Wrangler and clutched the roll bar. Black and aqua flames shot over the hood. The top was detached and removed. A pair of thumb cuffs dangled from the rear view mirror. "Nice," she said, touching them.

"Better behave or I'll have to use them on you."

Her heart skipped a beat. Breathe. You can do this.

The sizzling sand crunched under her feet and the ocean breeze twisted her hair, flipping it across her eyes. Heathers pulse pounded in her ears.

They set up near the water, glad the empty Monday beach offered privacy. She straightened the blanket, placed the folded towels on the top half and eased herself around. Nicolo stripped off his shirt revealing his six-pack Abs and then exposed his perfectly carved chest. He wore a muscle shirt at the gym, but now he stood before her in nothing but a small blue bathing suit that encircled his huge quad muscles. She tried to ignore the thing poking out in front.

She fiddled with the towels again and then repositioned her flip-flops on the corners of the blanket. After pretending to look through her beach bag for the second time, she felt his hand on her shoulder.

"Can I help you find something? Suntan lotion, sunglasses, *pride*?"

"What?" Her voice quavered.

"You worked out hard, let's see the results." He crossed his arms in front of him.

Heather examined her purple painted toes. She removed her shorts first, then placed them on top of her towel. She grasped the bottom of her T-shirt, lifted it and watched Nicolo's eyes turn from an arrogant gleam to a wide, incredulous stare. He ogled her. His hands fell to his sides, lip curled in and he shifted on his feet.

She expected him to look away, uncomfortable. Instead, he took a step closer. "Wow, you look amazing." He lifted his hand as if to touch her, but then shuddered, and slipped his fingers through his hair, instead.

"It's all you. You did this," she said.

"No, you did all the work. I just watched, I mean, trained you."

If it wasn't eighty degrees, he would have seen her blush.

"Come on. Let's take a run on the beach before it gets too hot."

They ran a good half mile, then returned. Their cheeks crimson, Nicolo headed into the water and dove headfirst. The icy waves struck Heather and when the water reached her knees, she howled.

"It's not that cold," he said. "You must be hot after that run."

"I'm always hot, baby. Check out these biceps."

Before she could make a muscle, Nicolo pounced and shoved her under the water. She jumped back up and he broke into hysterics.

"Think you're funny, huh?" She shivered.

"No. But that huge chunk of seaweed in your hair's pretty funny."

She removed the seaweed and hurled it at him, hitting him square in the face. He swept it off, then grabbed a larger clump next to him.

"Don't even think about it. I'm warning you."

He edged closer, wad of seaweed in his hand. "Oh, yeah, what're you gonna do to me?"

She stepped back, but before Nicolo could throw it, a wave ripened and clobbered her. Heather's head smacked into the sand. The crunch of her shoulder was the last thing she felt before the wave spun her. She attempted to stand, but before fully erect, another wave smacked hard, buckling her knees, and pushed her toward the sand. The taste of salt water burned her throat. Strands of hair coiled and blocked her vision.

Heather struggled upward, unaware which direction she faced. A mounting wave walloped again. The taste of gritty sand in her mouth and the inability to see sent her into a panic. She coughed, spit, then pushed up on her palms one more time. She needed to escape. Now.

Powerful arms swept her from the water's depths. With her toes flying over the foamy surf, Heather coughed and clawed the hair away from her eyes and mouth.

Nicolo placed her on their blanket and removed the sand from her face. Her breathing adjusted and she opened her eyes. He blocked the sun with his hand. "Are you okay?"

She sputtered. "Yes, thank you."

He brushed the suffocating hair off her neck, pushed it back over her forehead, then gazed at her, silent. His hand continued to stroke her hair, and gently caress her face. Droplets glistened off his skin. Waves of black, slick hair dripped with seawater and landed on her chest.

Feeling his magical fingers on her, seeing his face this close to hers again, made Heather want to taste his lips like she had imagined so many times in the past.

"You scared me." He ran his finger down the side of her face to her chin.

"Don't worry, you won't lose me again."

"Promise?"

"Promise." She smiled.

Nicolo collapsed next to her on the blanket and snuggled in until the warmth from their arms merged. She tilted her head onto his shoulder, wishing he would wrap his arms around her. He rested his chin on top instead, and held her hand, squeezing it tight. Their eyes closed.

School and work no longer occupied her mind.

****

Two hours into Lance's parent's barbecue, Heather begged for a reason to leave. Stomach virus? Sick father? Death in the family?

Lance hooted with his college friends by the outside bar. He had not acknowledged her in over an hour. Their collection of haughty girlfriends took over the only patio table, and drank wine coolers while chatting about the latest episode of Beverly Hills 90210. She considered it a blessing that they didn't save her a seat.

Heather picked at the red grapes on the dessert table, thought of Nicolo, and popped a few in her mouth. The sour flavor, mixed with her bitter beer, was fierce. She squeezed her eyes shut and swallowed, then took another swig of beer to wash out the tang.

"Oh, hello, Heather." Lance's mother, Bianca, stood behind her with another woman. Heather smiled, choking down the beer. "Heather is Lance's...girlfriend." She hesitated as she always did when introducing her.

"Hello, Heather." The woman assessed her from head to toe. "And what do you do?"

What kind of question was that? Was she on trial?

"Heather's going to school for home economics."

"Nutrition," Heather corrected. "And I just finished my masters in exercise physiology."

"Yes, well, not sure where you'll find a job, although I do believe I had a friend whose daughter scrounged for one all the way out in the Hamptons. But then how would you get home in time to cook Lance dinner?"

Heather cringed. Bianca's verbal abuse never stopped. "Lance actually gets home much later than me, remember?"

"That's because he's in school dear, law school." She emphasized. "Have you even looked for a job yet or are you just spending all your time at the beach?" She eyed Heather's tanned skin.

"I can't start a full time job yet. I have to—"

"You mean you can't find one. Just what I thought."

"No, I'm starting my internship in September and it's full time."

"More school? How long does it take to learn to cook?"

Bianca's friend huffed. "I learned to cook from my mother. I never had to take classes."

"That's not what dietitian's do. We don't prepare food."

"According to Lance you don't. Not very well at least."

Heather's mouth fell open.

"Come. Let me introduce you to some of Lance's friends." Bianca ambled away with the woman. A ketchup stain waved to Heather from Bianca's white shorts.

Chapter 11

Nicolo

Nicolo strolled next to Heather along the coastline. The intense, late summer sun beat off her tanned skin. The bronze color intensified the little muscles popping out on her arms. He almost hoped that she would step on a shell, or tumble over an abandoned sand castle, so that he could hold her once again.

Her hair had grown a lot in the past five months. It waved and called to him. He had pictured her long locks rippling in the wind in his old Jeep, encircling the roll bar, tangling in it. He fantasized about taking her to the beach, tying her wrists to the bar. She'd wriggle as his mouth ventured in between her legs and spread—

"Penny for your thoughts."

Nicolo flinched. "What?"

"You've been quiet all day."

"Sorry. Just thinking about you starting your internship next week. Wondering when we'll be able to see each other."

Heather looked at the waves behind him. "Why do summers have to end?"

"Because we live in New York." He chuckled. "But it doesn't mean the fun has to end. Autumn brings pumpkin picking, hay rides, corn mazes, haunted houses, colorful trees, leaves to jump in."

"If I didn't know better, I'd think you were seven."

"In my heart." Nicolo scooped up a handful of foamy water and doused the two of them with its spray. "Every day you have the choice to do something great. You have the power to change your life."

Heather played with the heart-shaped ring Lance had bought her.

"Stick with me, kiddo. You'll feel things you've never felt before."

Damn. Why'd he say that?

"We'll find a way to see each other. I'll still call you from the hospital on weekends. Not sure when I'll have time to go to the gym, though."

His eyes clenched shut with heartache. Seeing her two or three times per week filled his life with purpose. How could he carry on without seeing her so often? And how had he managed to keep his hands off her all this time? Their friendship meant more to him than anything, though. He would never destroy that.

"Can you ever go out at night?" he asked. "Maybe we can go dancing. You know, to burn off calories and stress."

"Definitely, I'd love too."

Did she just say yes? He had asked her so many times at Northford, always with an excuse. Now, he pictured hidden dark corners, music pulsing through their muscles, and sweaty, tight skin. Dancing close and...touching her.

Chapter 12

Heather

Thanksgiving eve, the biggest party night of the year. For the first time in three months, Heather had a day off. Monday through Friday, she trained at different hospitals within the five boroughs of New York. Unfamiliar commutes, numerous dietitians training her, extensive assignments due.

She worked every weekend too, needing the money for their apartment. With her overwhelming schedule, she had yet to venture out with Nicolo. Except for their weekend phone calls and an occasional session at the gym, their time together deteriorated.

She told Lance she was downing a few beers tonight with a girl she met in the internship. She made up a name, but buried in his papers, he didn't seem to care. Heather left in a pair of jeans, an oversized sweater and her white Keds, but once in her car, pulled off the sweater to reveal a tight red shirt. She slipped on a denim mini-skirt with high heels before pulling out of the parking lot.

Once at his house, Nicolo introduced Heather to Dino and Carissa, and then the four of them made their way into Queens. Carissa spent the ride faced backward talking to Heather, revealing embarrassing tales of Nicolo and Dino in their younger days. Dino laughed and tickled Carissa to get her to stop yacking.

Their collective friendliness warmed her. Thoughts of Lance's inattention, his mother's cruelty, and the overall sense of feeling out of place with his friends, evaporated.

They valet parked the car and Heather stepped out. An empty feeling overtook her. Had Nicolo told them about Lance?

They headed to the bar while thunderous music pulsated

throughout the walls. The DJ shouted to the already crowded dance floor.

A bottle of champagne appeared in Dino's hand and soon they each held a champagne flute high to toast.

"Here's to a fun and interesting night full of magic," Carissa said.

Fizz and sparkling bubbles exploded across their faces. They finished the bottle and ordered a round of Michelob Lights. Carissa swayed back and forth with her hips, beer bottle held high. Dino turned to Carissa and put his hands on her ass. She tilted in, clasped her arms around his neck and the two kissed feverishly.

Thrashing music, half-naked bodies and watching Dino's tongue explore Carissa's mouth, aroused Heather. Lance never kissed her like that. What was she missing? A snapshot of Nicolo lying naked in his bed with his hot body, shot across her mind.

She gulped the last of her beer to distract her thoughts, deposited the bottle on the counter, but turned to find Nicolo staring at her. He inched closer and wiped the droplet of beer from her lower lip. What would he do to her if he could?

Nicolo held out his hand and steered Heather to the dance floor.

His hips began to roll, slow at first, then rotated in and out towards her. He raised his arms above, closed his eyes for a beat, then released them, displaying his hypnotic smirk. He moved in a little, but she noticed. He inched in further still. Succumbing to his spell, she mirrored his movements.

He took one final step toward her and surrounded her leg with his thighs. Only inches apart, his jeans rubbed between her legs and her skirt lifted as she squatted closer to the floor. He placed his hand on her lower back and guided her. Heather's hand touched his shoulder, his deltoid firm, solid. Her other hand found its way onto his chest. The chest she inspected so many times on the beach, was now in her palm.

Heather glided her fingers back and forth, feeling the firm muscles underneath. Her grip tightened, his head fell back and Nicolo exhaled. She moved her hand to his shoulder and buried her head in his chest.

He lifted her chin, then shook his head, not allowing her to hide her feelings any longer. He placed his other hand on her ass and gave it a tight squeeze. She flinched, excited yet petrified. Nicolo clenched his teeth and moaned. She had pictured this side of him so many times in her dreams. Why had he hidden it?

After months and years of holding back, Heather positioned her finger into Nicolo's jean belt-loop and tugged him closer. Her other hand ventured under and up the front of his shirt, feeling the sweat roll off the hard contours of his Abs. Her eyes met his ardent gaze. She took deep, savoring breaths unsure if from dancing or his yearning expression. The ache she'd come to accept, softened and dissipated. She couldn't escape her feelings any longer.

The music amplified, or possibly lowered. The masses around them swelled, or might have diminished. Everything blurred and she saw only his magnetic lips. Heather tightened her arms around his neck. She pulled him down and her mouth covered his, tasting the juiciness, ripe and ready. His hunger equal to hers.

The crowd thrashed and hammered on the dance floor, but the two of them slowed until only their lips moved.

Nicolo carried Heather up the stairs. Her legs wrapped around his waist, mouth sucking and biting, extinguishing all her regrets.

His own appetite now insatiable, Nicolo clawed at her shirt unable to wait a second longer. He released her onto the stairs leading to his bedroom. He leaned back, unable to catch his breath and braced himself with the railing.

Heather pushed her hair away, her shirt now discarded on one of the steps below. He smiled, satisfied, like a kid that just stole third base. Nicolo nuzzled her neck, and she heaved out a loud gasp. He chuckled, placed a finger over his lips and then guided her past his parents' bedroom.

Chapter 13

Nicolo

Nicolo stood at the foot of his bed and examined her. Heather edged back towards his pillow, her body sprawled across the mattress. She had arranged herself on his comforter and her purple-lace bra and underwear tortured him.

Her chest heaved up and down duplicating his, their breaths ragged. Curls of hair corkscrewed and settled between her breasts. He pictured this moment countless times, and now, Heather lay spread-eagle on his bed.

Crawling to her, his fingers grazed her calves. She smiled, fearless and determined like the centerfolds in his magazines, unfolded and with the staples removed. Nicolo arched over, slipped his fingers around the lace underwear and slowly trailed it down her legs. *Fuck.*

He unhooked her bra. His finger nudged the thin purple strap clinging to her shoulder until it slumped, then plunged, dragging the cup with it. Her eyes closed, head tilted back.

Nicolo examined her naked body unsure where to begin. Where do you start when all your fantasies become real? Was this really happening? Why was she letting it? He didn't care. His thoughts would not spoil this moment.

He zigzagged his tongue over her flat Abs, wanting to touch and caress every fragment of her, please her for all the times she brought a smile to his face. He couldn't do enough for Heather. His hands reached up from her stomach to her breasts and then down between her legs. He didn't know what to touch first.

Nicolo kissed her lips once more, greedily sucked on her breast, and then slid his mouth between her legs. All previous plans of what he would do to her if he ever had the chance, vanished, and Nicolo became a crazed animal.

Heather clutched his pillow and pressed her mouth into it, stifling her grunts. He wanted to hear how loud he could make her scream. Why were his parents home?

His bulge, now more than apparent, almost embarrassing huge, begged to be released. He whipped his black briefs down, and shoved them aside with his foot.

When he thought he couldn't hold back any longer, he flipped her onto her forearms. Missionary position was not an option tonight. He needed to see that sweet ass of hers. She eased herself into position and her ass elevated toward his face. *Shit*. Heather, the love of his life, kneeled before him with her hot ass waggling back and forth. He ran his fingers between her cheeks and grinned, knowing his wicked imagination, all his desires and wild fantasies, he could now experience with her. The only girl he'd ever loved.

Nicolo slid himself inside and the immediate warmth caused him to convulse. He closed his eyes and the reality of what was happening struck him. Months, years, of fantasizing, and he still had to hold back. How was that fair? He concentrated. She was here in his bed, naked, and he held her silky ass in his hands. Patience. He had all the time in the world.

Chapter 14

Heather

Heather tried not to feel bad as she left her apartment. Again.

She arrived at Nicolo's home and greeted his parents, something she had grown more comfortable with over the past two months. His mother called out to him, but then shooed Heather up the stairs before he had a chance to answer.

Her heart raced with each step. After that first night in his bed, they'd only squeezed in a few times when his parents were out to dinner. Tonight was special though, and she would not be denied.

Nicolo met her at the top landing and spotted the hunger in her eyes. He cast a cautious eye to the lower level, and then led Heather to his room. He closed the door behind them and his lips fused to hers. His fingers massaged the back of her head while his mouth continued to devour her.

Heather moaned but he broke away, holding a finger to his lips. She stepped back, refusing to behave, and untied her coat's belt. The heavy fabric slipped off her shoulders and fell to the floor. A fluttery white bra with ruffles across the top greeted him. The sheer material draped beneath was transparent enough to see her white see-through panties.

Nicolo shook his head. "I don't even know what to do with this."

Heather giggled. "I'm your present."

"For what?" he whispered.

"Valentine's Day, silly."

"Oh, shit. I didn't think we were exchanging. I mean I thought, well, you know." He angled his torso away, arms fell to the side.

"That's okay. We weren't supposed to exchange. I mean we

shouldn't. I just saw this and well, actually, I didn't just see it. I went to the store purposely to buy it and I'm the one that's embarrassed."

Nicolo spun around with a small, rectangular box. "Surprise! Just kidding."

She gasped, and then dove onto her stomach atop his bed to remove the cute wrapping paper.

He sat on the edge of his bed, lifted the mesh cloth that separated his mouth from her ass and ran his fingers over the parts not covered by the thong. Then bit her bare ass.

"Ouch." She chuckled.

"You never complained before."

He ran his tongue between her thighs, but before penetrating, Heather flipped over holding the necklace in her hands. The tiny sterling-silver heart dangled from her fingers. "It's beautiful. I don't know what to say."

"Say you love it and you'll wear it tonight while I spoil you."

Nicolo clasped the necklace around her neck and it fell gracefully between her breasts. She touched it with her finger, then pressed her lips onto his.

Sex took on a new meaning as the silver necklace rose and fell on her chest, perfectly synchronized with each of her muffled cries.

****

"Are you planning a huge party for Lance this summer?" Bianca asked.

Heather drew in a deep breath before she answered. "What?" was all she could muster.

"He'll be graduating from law school. Surely you have something big planned."

"I still have a month left of my internship, then I have to study for the RD exam. I'm a little busy myself."

"You're comparing your silly little internship of cooking all day to Lances' law degree? Are we a bit jealous?"

"I don't cook, how many times do I have to tell you? We assess patient's nutritional status, make recommendations to physicians, and counsel them on special diets."

"There you go, talking about yourself again. The fact is, you failed to plan for Lance's celebration. I guess I'll just have to do it myself as usual."

"I'm swamped. I have to finish my syllabus packet, I have an oral presentation on AIDS to prepare and also the—"

"You certainly find time to go out at night, though. Time to party, but no time to plan a party for Lance?" Bianca deliberately angled her head to study Heather's expression.

Heather clenched her fists by her side to hide the trembling. Had Bianca followed her one night? She wouldn't be surprised. "I'm entitled to go out with my friends once in a while. Lance goes out to lunch every day with his."

"Lance needs to eat. And they study while eating. He also doesn't come home at one in the morning."

How did she know? Had Lance told her? There was no winning with this woman. "If you feel you have the time to throw him a big, fat party, do it. I'm graduating also and I don't see anyone throwing me a party."

"It's not my fault your parents don't have the means."

Heather's nostrils flared. "My parents raised an independent child. They don't baby me and treat me like I'm twelve. They worked hard their entire lives and gave me things more important than money. Love, support and the drive to do things on my own. They showed me not only how to survive in this world, but to enjoy life and not constantly find fault with everyone around me. Now, if you'll excuse me, I have to take a shower. In the future, please call before showing up. This is my apartment too. The one *I'm* paying for, with *my* money."

****

They rode along the Robert Moses Causeway and turned onto Ocean Parkway surrounded by sailboats that bobbed in the beautiful evening sky. The wind blew through Heather's long hair, warm and tantalizing. Blues and pinks circled the floating clouds like Cotton Candy Swirl popsicles. Seagulls soared high and low, searching the ground for throwaway food.

She sank into the passenger seat of his Jeep and with her hair flowing wildly, raised her arms to the sky. The salty air tickled her nose and enhanced the scenery.

Nicolo drove into a small parking lot and then the two of them jumped out. He clutched her shoulders, drawing her into a deep kiss, then released Heather's lips, secured her hand, and pulled her along like two kids skipping in the warm summer night. "Come on, before it's too late."

They strolled along the narrow boardwalk lined with tall grasses and marsh plants. Halfway down the wooden footpath, he stopped, gently wrapped his arms around her and directed her gaze to the beauty that surrounded them. They stared as magnificent swirls of aquas and greens sat on top of yellow and orange ripples. The low clouds soon burst with reds and deep oranges, which demanded the oceans attention, turning the water to dapples of blueberries and cinnamon.

Nicolo placed his arm behind her waist, pulled her in, and she leaned her head against his chest. They watched the giant orange ball cut in half, a semicircle encased in purple and red hues. He took out his mom's Disc camera and twisted them around, positioning the camera in front. A picture to remember the best year in her life.

Only a narrow line of burnt orange remained, melting into the splattered dark ink. The sunset left them alone in the night. Nicolo hoisted her up on the boardwalk railing, squeezed her thighs and his eyes held her view. She kissed him gently, while small waves crashed against the marsh plants providing a rhythm that pulsed through her body.

He let his lips slowly separate from hers, biting down on her bottom lip, then grasped her by the waist and helped her down. They coasted to the end of the pier where the enormous black ocean engulfed them. He pointed out stars that he knew; his wisdom of the natural world fascinated her. Heather broke her gaze from the empowering sky and caught him studying her. He scanned her face as if he had never seen it before. His brow low, his expression lost.

Nicolo took her hand and led her over to one of the wooden benches perched around the end of the small pier. He unzipped her jacket, releasing each of the metal teeth from their captivity and tossed it on the floor. Her T-shirt next, until only her soft pale-blue lingerie remained.

She removed his dark blue jeans while his thumbs slipped under her bra, circling. She turned her head to look up the walkway where they had come from. Would someone see them? Nicolo touched her chin and directed her attention back at him. With the last of their clothes heaped into a pile on the sea-mist covered floor, he attempted to lay her down, but instead, Heather eased him back and had him sit on the wood bench. She straddled him, and he entered in one smooth motion.

Heather glided in and out effortlessly, unleashing strong, powerful thrusts. A seagull squawked above, the low rumble of a boat-horn echoed in the distance, small waves continued to lap against the wood frame of the pier. The dock creaked beneath them as Nicolo watched her sail up and down. A foghorn warning, faint yet mysterious, called out to them.

Her rocking slowed, tapering the back and forth rhythm. Barely moving, she studied his dark eyes instead, unhindered for the first time. His brows squinted, narrowing the openings, and he stopped moving as well.

Heather paused, rested her weight on his thighs, her mouth opened slightly. Nicolo stared at her in wonder, his eyes probing hers, looking for something deep in her soul. They both froze. Stared. Unable to find the correct words for what they were feeling. A slight breeze whipped her hair up, but she did not move.

Although they sat motionless, their breathing quickened. Without speaking, they knew at that moment.

Chapter 15

Nicolo

Nicolo waited for Heather to call. The phone rang at ten o'clock Saturday morning and he jumped for it. Hearing her voice after several days always elevated his mood, but the awkward silence that followed, sent Nicolo's heart racing. Never before were they at a loss for words. He was afraid of this. "Heather, about the other night..."

Silence.

He'd imagined it. He knew it. She'd probably laugh at him if he brought it up. He should be thankful for what he had with her, it was more than he'd ever imagined. Now, was it gone?

"By the pier?" she asked. "Yes, I know."

Know what? *Damn it.* He wished he could read her mind.

"I felt it too, Nicolo. It was different."

He fell back onto his bed and sighed. "Then why didn't you say anything?"

"I was afraid. I don't want to hurt you."

"But if you felt it, it means something." He paused. "Doesn't it? It's not just sex, is it?"

"No. I don't think it ever was. We both knew that. It was always more than that. Since we worked together at Northford. I think we just finally broke down our walls."

Chapter 16

Heather

The sun began its descent in the sky when she found her flip-flop under Lance's T-shirt. She shoved it on her foot, grabbed her sweatshirt and bolted out of her bedroom.

She opened the door to the apartment and then frowned. "I asked you to call first."

"I'll only be here a second," Bianca said. "I came by to drop some papers off for Lance. Besides, I did call."

Heather glared at Lance, sitting on the couch.

He winced. "Sorry. I thought you'd be gone by now. You said you were going out."

"Out, again?" Bianca asked "And on a Monday night? Maybe you should be spending your free time looking for a job?"

"For your information, I had three interviews and was offered two positions. I'm just waiting on the last one before I make a decision." Heather turned back to Lance. "Goodnight."

Heather entered her car, but then took a minute to calm down. She refused to let Bianca ruin her evening. Tonight would be the night. Whitney Houston's *I Will Always Love You* played its final note, restoring her mood. She drove out of the parking lot and toward her future.

****

They headed down Robert Moses Causeway again, toward the beaches. "You're not going to tell me what we're doing?" Heather asked.

"Nope." Nicolo reached for her hand and held it.

They pulled into the deserted beach parking lot. Nicolo exited his Jeep, grabbed two blankets, then secured Heather's hand and ran with her down the sandy path. They giggled and tugged at each other, skipping as they went.

He plopped the blankets on the sand and kissed Heather. "Ready?" he asked.

"For what?"

"Ever run into the ocean naked?"

"No! Never."

"Trust me?"

She looked at him hard. He was serious. She tried to suppress her fear. "Yes."

"Then, let's go." They tore off their clothes and ran into the waves. She shrieked from the icy rush on her feet, but he continued to tug on her before she changed her mind. Artic blasts of needles stung every pore. She screamed while he laughed and then he embraced her and placed his frozen lips onto hers. Warm tongues, joined and converged, combatting the cold, while waves crested over their shoulders.

When they could stand it no longer, they sprinted back through the clingy sand for their blankets. Nicolo picked one up and wrapped it around Heather first, his own body shivering. She snuggled into it and watched while he reached for his.

They fell to the ground and he flipped the corner of his blanket onto her as well. "I love you," she said.

"I love you too. All the way to the moon."

Her lips warmed from his mouth. "Mmm, you're crazy," she said.

"Life's short, you have to enjoy it."

She looked down. "I got two job offers today."

"You did? Terrific."

"One only offered twenty-eight thousand. I told them no. The other thirty-two, but I really wanted the one at St. Elizabeth's Hospital."

"You'll get it."

"You believe in me more than I believe in myself."

He stroked her face. "You were different back at Northford. More confident, a fighter."

"Surrounded by people that never compliment you, it gets to your self-esteem."

"But you've achieved so much."

She ran her hand over his scruffy cheek. "You're so good to me. Good *for* me."

He smiled and kissed her hand.

"I've done a lot of thinking, Nicolo. With all the changes in my life, finishing school, starting my career..." She looked up at him. "I want to make a complete transformation."

"Okay." Nicolo waited for her next words.

"I'm leaving Lance. I decided yesterday. I love you and I don't want anyone else."

He sprang back. "Are...are you sure? I mean, I don't know what to say."

"Just tell me you love me and you'll never stop."

He grinned. "Stop? Never. Are you kidding?" He kissed her again, more powerful this time. "Heather, I've never loved anyone else, I've never found anyone like you and I never will. I should have called you after I left Northford. I should have fought for you every single day. All those years we wasted living apart. Five additional years I could have spent with you in my lifetime. I won't let another day pass."

"You've made me so happy, Nicolo. One amazing year with you has brought me more joy than the previous twenty-three. I couldn't wait to tell you tonight. I finally have something to look forward to in my life, instead of just keeping myself occupied."

Nicolo ran his finger across her lower lip. "I promise to make all our days memorable, for the rest of our lives. I look forward to the day we're sitting on our rocking chairs while our great-grandchildren splash in the ocean in front of us."

"We'll marry on the beach and live there too. Sunrises and sunsets will surround us every day."

Nicolo eased her back onto the sand and kissed her long and hard. A kiss that seemed to last forever, but one that she never wanted to end. If she could spend the rest of her life just kissing him, it would be enough.

"I'm going to tell Lance this weekend. Sunday night."

"Let me know if you need anything." He brushed the wet hair away from her neck and she shivered. "Cold? Come on, let's go. Our night's just beginning."

They hiked back to the parking lot wrapped in their blankets. Before she could scramble onto her seat and get dressed, he grabbed her waist. "Come in the back. There's something I've wanted to do for a long time."

They hitched up their blankets and climbed into the back.

"No fear, remember?"

She nodded. Nicolo revealed two red bandanas from the back

floor and grinned. He removed one of her arms from the blanket and raised it high above her. She inhaled.

He tied one wrist to the left side of the roll bar and when he lifted her other arm, the blanket unfastened and slumped to the floor. She hung in the middle of the parking lot, facing outward, completely naked. The lamppost they parked under lit the area, allowing Nicolo to examine every inch of her. Light wisps of ocean breeze touched her frozen skin and caused her nipples to enlarge and harden. He ran his fingers over them, his tongue joined in, twirling and teasing.

She squirmed.

"Open your eyes," he said. "I want you to watch me." He moved his hand between her legs. Her body trembled, but with fear. Although alone, the vast open parking lot made her feel like a stripper performing on stage, exposed and vulnerable.

"Tonight's all about you, Heather. A little piece of what our future will be like."

She tried to relax and enjoy this. Her body wriggled, savoring what he was doing for her. Nicolo intensified the thrusting of his fingers, gyrating until all the deep crevices inside her vibrated. He arched in and let just the tip of his tongue barely touch her firm nipple. It tortured her, then sent shivers up her arms.

Heather remained silent, worried that even a seagull might hear her, but allowed herself to watch Nicolo's expression as his excitement grew. She rotated for him and his fingers stroked her into madness. "Yes," she managed to murmur.

"That's it? I want to hear you. No parents in the room next door tonight. We're all alone."

This was true. For the first time she could scream and not worry if anyone would hear her. Heather let herself drift away. Her panting increased, loud squeals set free. There were no restrictions tonight, no reason to suppress. Her body convulsed as she finally let herself go and released a blistering howl.

"Yeah, Heather, that's it. That's—"

Lights flashed on them from across the parking lot. Her breasts magnified in the beam. Heather looked down at her exposed breasts, then froze. Were the passengers in the car watching her all this time? Aroused by her show?

The car engine hummed and then the vehicle pulled out of the parking lot.

"Don't worry," Nicolo said. "They were probably doing the same thing we were. A lot of people come here to have sex."

"I'm scared, please get me down."

"Of what?"

Heather twisted in the bandana ties, her muscles tensed and she gasped for air.

Nicolo giggled.

"Please, take me down. Nicolo, please!"

He frowned, then removed the bandana on the left side. "I'll build that confidence back up. Your problem is you confuse fear with excitement. This is excitement, like a roller coaster ride."

"I hate roller coasters."

"What? Are you kidding?" He untied her right hand and she reached for the blanket, covered herself and then ducked her face into it.

"Dino and Carissa usually hit Great Adventure at the end of the summer. Let's plan a date with them, we'll have fun." He wrapped his arm around her.

She faked a smile, but the humiliation still consumed her.

"God, Heather, there's so much I want to do with you. Our life together is going to be one giant roller coaster."

Chapter 17

Nicolo

Nicolo strutted up his walkway and through the front door still fueled by the evening Heather and he had last night. He tossed his keys on the foyer table, but their jangling was offset by the sound of chatter in the kitchen. The usual scent of dinner simmering on the stove, non-existent. He peered into the room. His parents sat at the table, Dino and Carissa stood behind them. Four sets of eyes stared at him.

Carissa flew at Nicolo and shoved her hand in his face. A small, square, diamond sparkled in the kitchen light. "We're getting married," she squealed.

"I can see that. Congratulations." He tossed his arms around her while Dino looked at him for approval. "It's about time. Seven years. What the hell?" He winked at Dino.

Of course he was thrilled for them and he kept his mouth shut, not revealing that there would be another wedding in the near future. Tonight was their night and he'd wait until tomorrow to tell them his news.

Chapter 18

Heather

Heather paced the living room, her heart unable to relax since she arrived home. She inhaled slowly, exhaling slower. She glanced around the apartment at the furniture and items they collected over the years. Memories of get-togethers, late night studying, dinners and stress. Lots of stress. Were there any good memories?

Lance sauntered out of their bedroom with his suit jacket over his shoulder.

"Hey," she sputtered. "They offered me the job at St. Elizabeth's Hospital, the one I really wanted. I accepted."

He looked for his car keys and ignored her news.

"They want me to start immediately. It seems one dietitian retired and another went on maternity leave a month early, leaving them short."

"Is that what you're going to wear?" he asked.

She scanned her pink pantsuit. "What's wrong with this?"

"Why don't you put on a dress instead?"

She shook her head, then marched into their bedroom and slammed the door behind her. Always criticizing her clothes. Since high school, nothing she wore was ever good enough.

She ripped a black satin dress off the hanger. Way too fancy for dinner. She had worn it to his cousin's wedding but she'd show him. She slipped on her four-inch heels and then finished it off with Nicolo's heart necklace.

They drove to the restaurant in silence. He had laughed at her outfit, telling her she was being ridiculous. She didn't care. She'd go out with a bang.

The pulled into the parking lot and fear returned. Why was she doing this at a restaurant? And when would be a good time? After dessert? When they received their drinks? Would he make a scene?

The maître d' escorted them to their table in the back, hopefully next to the busy kitchen. Lance walked ahead as usual. Nicolo had always held her hand.

The faster Lance walked ahead of her, the quicker her strength restored. She'd start an argument with him as soon as they received their drinks and then tell him she'd had enough.

They reached the back of the restaurant, but there were no available tables. Where had he brought them? Lance and the maître d' drew back the accordion room-divider and stepped aside.

"Surprise!" Thunderous applause filled the catering room. Over fifty guests packed the area, loud banter reverberated. She briefly spotted her mother, Brooke, a neighbor. And Bianca.

Confused, Heather glanced around the room for an answer. They had already thrown Lance a graduation party two weeks ago. Could this be her graduation party? But who paid for it? Not her parents, not a catered event this size. Lance? Did he ask his mother for more money? Would he ever celebrate any of her achievements, though, and would Bianca really give him the money? Had Bianca's heart warmed? Did she feel bad seeing Lance worshipped at his party, lavished with envelopes full of cash while Heather received nothing? Unlikely, but then who?

She rotated back around to hunt for an answer, but Lance kneeled before her, captured her hand and removed a tiny box from his jacket pocket.

Her stomach twisted and buckled as if she had completed three thousand crunches holding a fifty-pound dumbbell in her hands. A sour taste filled her mouth, her body overheated.

Lance pushed the ring onto her finger and she shuddered. The ring scraped and jammed over her knuckle. She panned the room and saw her mother crying.

Tears raced down Heather's face too, but not the same kind as her mother cried. This was not happening. Some kind of cruel joke.

Lance lurched up. "Well?"

Her soft tears transformed into gasps. Unable to speak, her body collapsed and she arched forward, her head landed on his chest.

"I'll take that as a 'yes.'" He held Heather's hand up displaying the ring as if brandishing a prize.

The crowd cheered. Were they all that stupid?

One by one, they tackled Heather to give her their blessings.

"Congratulations," Uncle Pete said.

"I'm totally excited for you," Brooke squealed. "I'll be the best maid of honor ever."

Maid of honor? She didn't want Brooke.

"Honey, I'm so happy for you." Her mother beamed. "You'll make the most beautiful bride."

"Am I gonna be the flower girl?" her cousin's four-year-old daughter asked. "Mommy said so."

Flower girl? Whose wedding was this?

The next several hours, a blur. She barely spoke, never ate a morsel. She sat by herself at a corner table and sipped water to restore her dry mouth. Lance tottered drunkenly in front of her and then held on to a chair.

Eight years they had dated. She never thought he would ask and thankfully, he never did. Brooke wondered why also and blamed it on Heather, who was obviously not attending to his needs. Brooke bragged that she kept Mr. Executive pleading for more, and soon they would marry.

Heather guided Lance to her table. "Are you okay?"

He wobbled, then placed his hand on her shoulder. "Yes, fine, fine. Wonderful party."

"Lance, you're drunk."

"Just a little nervous, I guess."

"Maybe you should sit for a while, drink some water. Did you eat?"

Lance dropped like the dead into the chair, then clutched a glass of water. It cleared the way for Heather to see Bianca's reflection in the wall-to-wall mirror, her arms knotted together.

Heather passed Lance another glass of water and he sucked it down. Bianca materialized above him.

"Lance, darling, why don't you make a toast to your lovely fiancée now?"

"Toast?"

"All these guests attended your party, you must say something." She helped him up.

"Maybe now's not a good time." Heather pushed him back down.

"Nonsense. Now is the perfect time." Bianca led him to the front of the room.

Lance leaned onto the shaky partition, steadied himself and then clinked his water glass with a spoon. The room silenced. "The last eight years with Heather have been demanding."

Oh, no. What would he say? Heather caught Bianca's eye and her smug expression. She knew he would embarrass Heather in his intoxicated state. God, she hated her.

"But, although these have been some of the most challenging years of our lives, we've supported each other through every step. Moving in together proved to be a sound decision as we struggled through school, long hours in the library, and summers working and interning." He took another gulp of his water.

"But it's over, and with that, time to do the right thing and get married. Make Heather my wife. She stood by me during my darkest moments and always found a way to make me laugh, keep me strong." He swayed, but caught himself "In fact, her enthusiasm and sense of humor brought us together in the first place. Did I ever tell you how we met?"

Heather cringed. The toast veered into a stroll down memory lane.

"The summer before our senior year, my parents dragged me to one of their boring weddings of some friend of a friend. I hid in the back, avoiding the mind-numbing conversations and then in the middle of the dance floor, this cute, little thing in a tight, black dress started sashaying all over the dance floor. Slam dancing, doing the Cabbage Patch."

He was nuts, a regular loon. What was he babbling about? Slam dancing? The Cabbage Patch?

"Dancing to some Duran Duran song." Lance swayed and threw his hands in the air. "At first I thought 'what the hell?' But then, I was intrigued. I approached her, of course, and she spent the evening sharing her view on everything from how she despised top-forty music, to how she was on a mission to prove that ketchup was not a vegetable.

"Initially, I thought she was insane." The guests broke out in unison laughter. Heather wanted to hide under the table. "But her not caring about what others thought fascinated me. She had her own set of rules.

"When it was time to leave, she refused to give me her number. Me. Can you believe it?" The crowd howled again. "I tracked her down, but she still refused to meet me. Finally, by August, she agreed to go to the beach. By the time the sun set on that hot day, I knew I was in love."

The audience released a collective "*aw.*" Heather slumped back in the chair and her mouth fell open. She clutched her heart and her chin trembled.

"Her humor kept me from losing my mind. How she keeps such a positive attitude, adding in sarcasm at just the right moment, is beyond me, but I'm honored to have her in my life. Now that school is behind us, I look forward to spending the rest of my life with her." He held up his water glass to her. "Heather, I love you and plan on making you as happy as you have made me."

Glasses raised in the air, clinked and then applause rang out. Lance never expressed himself to her, never conveyed why he held on to her. His words dissolved her animosity toward him.

Guilt engulfed her. What had she planned to do tonight? He organized a surprise engagement party and her only thoughts were to crush his heart over dinner? She should have communicated with him, discussed their issues, worked together as a couple. Instead, she embarked on an affair. What kind of person was she? She stared at her feet and clutched her stomach. What was she going to do now?

"Darling, why so sad?" Bianca towered over her. "He did better than I thought he would."

Unable to make eye contact, Heather glanced around hoping someone would rescue her.

"You have big shoes to fill, young lady. I will ensure that you keep him accustomed to the life he's used to living. Still not sure what he sees in you. There were girls far more suitable in our neighborhood, but he seems to be charmed by you. Lucky for you, I'm only interested in my son's happiness, so I will no longer persuade him to find someone else. He has requested this from me, and I will abide."

She tried to leave but Bianca grabbed her arm. "By the way, Lance asked me to help him with this party, but I refused. Not only don't I approve of his choice, but I suspect some infidelity on your part."

Heather's body stiffened. She kept her expression as blank as she could. Would Bianca start tracking her every move?

Bianca held her chin high and flipped her hair away from her face. "This will be quite the busy year for you. It looks like all your free time will be spent planning your wedding with me."

"With you? But my mother will of course—"

Bianca took a step forward. Her intense eye contact shut Heather up. "Since Lance deserves a grand affair, we'll obviously be paying the bill. Therefore, I'll be accompanying you on all your outings, not your mother."

"Listen I really don't think that—"

"No, you won't think. I'm in control and I'll be keeping a close eye on you." Bianca leaned in within an inch of Heather, the smell of gin on her breath apparent. "With every ounce of your free time filled planning this wedding, there will be no time for any more outings."

****

"Five minutes and the processional begins," the lady in the nauseating, fluorescent-yellow dress called out.

"Okay." Brooke smoothed her dress in the mirror.

Heather glanced around the room at her maid-of-honor and bridesmaids. Their robins-egg blue dresses twirled and fluttered around the bride's room. Brooke lowered herself to the seated make-up table and applied her lipstick.

Heather stood in the center of the room as if in the middle of a chaotic Manhattan street during a morning commute to work.

This was just one of her recurring nightmares, right? Soon she would wake up screaming, sweating. But this part she never visualized before. Five of her supposed dearest friends fussed with their stockings, straightened their jewelry, and clogged the room with suffocating hairspray.

Heather wanted a small wedding, a maid of honor only, but Lance had so many close buddies, and then Bianca accused her of not having any friends. At least not any female ones.

She asked a cousin, a new co-worker that she forced a friendship with, her best friend from college, and then there was Kelly. Their long-lost friend from high school that suddenly reappeared when she heard the news.

Not real friends. If they were, they would know about Nicolo and recognize Heather's spiral towards depression. All a façade, a big show, and they were all part of the illusion.

How could they not tell? Did they even notice her now, standing in the center of the room, petrified?

A week after the engagement she broke down and confided in Brooke. Told her she wasn't in love with Lance. That she was deeply in love with Nicolo.

Brooke exploded. Was Heather insane? Out of her freaking mind? She'd consider throwing away a lifetime of luxury and comfort for some cop she met in a bar? This was marriage, not a silly crush. She refused to discuss it ever again, only increasing Heather's guilt.

The wedding neared and with no one to confide in, the panic grew. Heather's mother cried with joy each time she purchased something new, expressing how thrilled she was that Heather found someone to provide for her. Her parents would no longer have to worry.

Her bridesmaids chatted amongst themselves about their dresses, the bridal shower, and bachelorette party as if Heather was merely a lifeless doll they were planning a celebration for.

Bianca made all the final decisions. A band instead of the DJ Heather wanted, a rose bouquet even though Heather hated roses, and the invitation of over two hundred guests, only fifty of them from Heather's side of the family.

The entire affair resembled a flight with the pilot locked in the bathroom while the passengers took charge. All of them headed for the bottom of the Atlantic Ocean.

"All right, let's go," the glowing canary beckoned them. The four bridesmaids scampered out, snatching their bouquets as they went.

Brooke turned so that her back faced the mirror, caressed the silky material covering her butt and grinned. She had ignored Heather all afternoon. Whose wedding was this? Some maid-of-honor.

"I can't," Heather finally spoke.

"What the hell is wrong with you?" Brooke grabbed her bouquet.

"I can't do this. Please, Brooke. Help me. I can't marry him."

"Not this again. Don't tell me it's about that cop?"

"Brooke, you're not listening." Her red eyes brimmed.

"Ladies come on!" The banana lady stomped her foot.

Brooke scowled. "How could you be so selfish? For some reason you were given the gift of Lance and you don't even appreciate him. I wonder why we're even friends sometimes." She stormed out of the room.

Heather rushed to the bathroom and dry heaved. Then giggled like she had gone mad. What could she possibly throw up? She had barely eaten in months. Her gown hung on her. Any muscle she had built, disintegrated.

She rinsed her mouth and then struggled toward the window. Uncle Pete bounded up the steps and raced into the church. She laid her hand on the pane. Heather examined the wood frame, the latch, and the height of the window from the grass.

Her hand drifted to the latch and unfastened it. She hoisted the frame with both hands. Balmy air mingled with the chilly room. The gust warmed her nose and trembling arms. Birds sang, dark green grass surrounded her, leaves shimmered in the trees, a woman jogged by.

Run. She needed to run away and find Nicolo.

"Close that window, the air conditioning's on." Big Bird slammed the window shut. She clutched Heather's arm and the bouquet and then dragged her into the alcove.

Heather caught sight of Brooke's train entering the church and the door closing behind her. Why couldn't Brooke hear her?

"You look so beautiful," the woman said.

How many other girls had she said that too? How many others ran away, out the door and down those stairs to freedom?

The double doors flew open and her knees buckled. Nausea returned. Her mother cried, Bianca frowned, Lance wore a huge grin. The wedding march began and she took her first step. Her vision blurred and the music sounded like her grandfather's old phonograph player.

Couldn't anyone hear her screaming? Her father lifted the veil over Heather's head. Was he beside her the entire time? Didn't he hear her cry out?

Coward. She never called Nicolo.

Chapter 19

Nicolo

Nicolo stood in front of his bedroom mirror combing his wet hair, wearing nothing but a towel. Dino sprinted by in his tuxedo, then took a step backward into Nicolo's room.

"Yo, hope you fit into your tux. You're huge. Whatta ya taking steroids or something?"

Nicolo turned his head, slow and robotic, and stared Dino down. His new tribal tattoo covered his upper arm.

"Sorry, just want everything to be perfect for Carissa and me."

Nicolo glared, then unhooked his towel and let it fall to the rug.

"Okay, then. Guess you're in a bad mood."

Dino left and Nicolo looked at himself in the mirror. It was Dino's day. The best man should be supportive, not a total dick. He yanked his underwear on and strolled into Dino's room. "Sorry, bro. Being a dick of a best man."

Dino fixed his bow tie, turned, and upon seeing him half-naked jumped back. "Whoa! You gonna rape me now or something?"

"Yeah, that's my plan. A second bachelor party." Nicolo raised his eyebrows and winked.

"Get the fuck away from me." Dino laughed.

"Kidding." Nicolo extended his arms behind his back and stretched.

"Thinking of Heather, aren't you?"

"Yeah, sorry. It's cool. I'm okay." Nicolo left and began the task of putting on his tux. He wouldn't dare tell Dino what he just found. Not on his day. He took a deep breath and smiled. He was happy for them, and Carissa became a sister to him.

Initially, he was worried when Heather didn't call that weekend. He only wanted to give her a pep talk, lessen any fears for her talk with Lance. But she never called, Saturday or Sunday. She had never missed one weekend in almost fifteen months.

Maybe she wanted to keep her head clear, calm her nerves. Understandable, but when he didn't hear from her the following weekend, he panicked.

What happened that Sunday night? Had Lance murdered her? No, he would have heard it on the news. Nicolo searched the police records for any domestic violence reports. None. But would she have reported it? Too embarrassed?

Why no phone call? By the third weekend, he called the hospital. They connected him with the diet office and a girl stuttered her greeting into the phone.

"Can I speak with Heather?" he asked.

"Heather?" She paused. "Oh, Heather. She doesn't work here anymore. Got a new job or something."

"Do you know where she went, what hospital?"

"No, sorry. I'm new here. Didn't know her."

What hospitals did she say she heard from? Which ones offered her the job? He raked through the phone books and wrote down hospital names and numbers. He went as far as holding the phone to his ear, but what would he say? Does a Heather Di Pietro work here? Can I talk to her?

Besides, if she wanted to speak to him, she would have called. Something had changed her mind.

He had scanned his memory of their last night together at the beach. It was perfect, romantic, and they said they loved each other. She said she would leave Lance.

Wait. That night he made her run into the water naked. Tied her to his Jeep. Forced her to look at him while he pleasured her. Then the car, it frightened her. She begged him before he finally released her.

What an ass. She was scared and he frightened her more. And his plan to drag her on a roller coaster, too? How much did he throw at her in one night? She probably pictured a lifetime of fear and pressure if she stayed with him.

He wallowed in self-pity for weeks until Carissa came running into the house one Sunday. Dino's and her engagement photo had made *Newsday*. She read it to them, sputtering, so that he barely caught every other word.

She finished and handed the paper around the kitchen table.

Nicolo glanced at the photo, having seen it before, framed in his living room. Then he saw it. On the right hand side, a photograph of Heather with Lance. He read their engagement announcement and broke into a sweat. He read each word carefully. Their wedding would be in June.

Their picture made him sick. Lance in a double-breasted suit with a pink tie and Heather in a tight, black dress. Their hands clasped together, a diamond ring dead center. A huge grin flooded Heather's face.

Nicolo's chest heaved. So that's what it was? A big fat diamond? That's what she wanted? A huge wedding, publicity and all the hype? Women were all the same.

With nothing else to do on his days off, he spent his time at the gym, lifting. Heavy, heavier. He spent hours there, every day, sometimes with injuries, in pain. New pain to drown out the old pain, but it didn't work. Even getting the tattoo didn't drive the pain away.

A year passed, he needed to know. Needed proof that she went through with it and married a guy she couldn't stand.

And then it came.

Like he did every Sunday, Nicolo retrieved the paper and flipped to the Wedding Announcement section. Today, on his brother's wedding day, *Newsday* displayed Heather's wedding announcement. *June 11, 1994, Heather Di Pietro and Lance Milanesi were wed.*

It was official.

He drifted down the stairs in his tuxedo and let his mother attach the white boutonniere to his lapel. She smiled at Nicolo the way Heather always did, then kissed his cheek and patted him on the shoulder.

Chapter 20

Heather

Karen Kastopolis, the Chief Nutrition Manager at St. Elizabeth's Hospital, swept her blonde hair back repeatedly with her left hand. Her agenda for their meeting had ended, but she hesitated and lingered. One o'clock. The only thing on Heather's mind was lunch. "One last thing," she said. "Since spring is just a few weeks away, I decided you're no longer allowed to wear open-toed shoes or sandals of any kind, and pantyhose must be worn at all times. Any questions?"

Cara and Samantha stared Heather down. She pretended not to notice.

"Very well, then this meeting's over." Karen walked out in her pink floral dress, leaving Heather alone with the two new dietitians.

"This is ridiculous!" Samantha said.

"What is this, a prison?" Cara added. "And why didn't you say anything, Heather? You never speak up."

Heather closed her folder. Cara and Samantha, both new graduates, had limited experience as dietitians and with life in general. Whine, whine, whine. She had enough.

"Yeah, first we couldn't wear fake nails, then no nail polish."

"Don't forget we were forced to start wearing lab coats too, and each time you say nothing."

Heather placed her hand on the bottom right of her belly, and felt the baby kick. Only three weeks to go and she'd be away from these dimwits. "Guys, I have a two-and-a-half year old at home, so fake nails are impractical and nail polish a luxury. Second, as much as I hate lab coats, covering these old maternity clothes that I wore during my last pregnancy is a blessing. As for the sandals, my feet are swollen and I wouldn't want anyone to witness them first hand."

"That's not the point. We have to stick together."

"You could say something too, you know," Heather said.

"You've worked here for almost five years. She won't listen to us."

Heather eased herself out of the chair and clutched the edge of the table. "I have a lot going on right now. Sandals are not high on my priority list when I have a toddler and a house to take care of, not to mention a newborn on the way. I'm sorry."

She left the conference room and waddled to the elevators. If they didn't want to eat lunch with her, she didn't care. Thoughts of applying for a job at another hospital returned. She considered it after Laurel was born, but ill prepared for the demands of a new baby, she clung to the familiar atmosphere here. Working alongside these two any longer though, strengthened her decision.

After lunch, Heather returned to Tower-8 and made her daily visit to room 815. The lingering smell of meatloaf filled the hallways. "Hey, Mr. Gentile, how was lunch?"

"Hey, ho, how's my favorite dietitian?"

"Good, but I'm concerned about you. They said you didn't eat much today."

"Well, I didn't have my usual company."

Heather felt a twinge of guilt. "Sorry, I had a meeting at twelve."

"Oh, no, no! No problem, my little lady, just something to look forward to after four weeks."

"Have you been here that long?"

"Twenty-nine days to be exact." He coughed through his last few words, unable to catch his breath as usual. He attempted a few shallow gasps, but then wheezing ensued. "It's like I'm breathing through a straw, Heather. Ever breathe through a straw? Can't get any air no matter how much you suck in."

"Where's your oxygen?"

"Took it off to eat but then never ate."

"Do you want a respiratory treatment?"

"Damn mask hurts my face. Look, I don't want to talk about my damn breathing, how's that baby doing?"

"Almost here. Three weeks from today."

"I still say it's a girl. Don't care what everyone else says. *Boy*. What do they know?"

"You're in the minority, everyone's guessing a boy."

He coughed again, his raspy voice returned after spitting into a napkin. "Sorry. A young lady like yourself shouldn't see things like this."

"Nonsense, you're my favorite patient. Hey, the nurse said you gained another pound."

"What's one pound when you're five-eight and only weigh ninety-eight pounds?"

"I'm trying. I'll get you all beefed up before you leave here."

He laughed, but it twisted into another coughing fit. "You're something special. One lucky husband you have there. Tell him I said he better go out and buy ya a pretty bouquet. What's it you like? Tulips?"

"Yes, my favorite."

"Well spring's here. Shouldn't have any problem finding 'em."

"You rest. I'll come back later and make sure you get some dinner in you. Are you drinking the Ensure at least?"

"As long as it's chocolate. Can't stand that strawberry. What numbskull invented that? Bad enough we're sick but they force you to drink that crap. Sorry, pardon my language."

"Nothing I haven't heard before." She turned to leave. "You get your rest. I'll see you later."

"Oh, Heather, wait. Thank you for that piece of cheesecake on my tray last night. You went to Lucibello's Bakery, didn't you?"

"I don't know what you're talking about. Must have come from the cafeteria." She exited before he could see her blush.

****

Heather hurried through the daycare centers' entryway. Upon seeing her mother, Laurel charged full force at her despite Heather's belly providing a significant roadblock. "Mommy!"

"How are you, my fruit punch girl?"

"How'd you know I had that?" Her red mustache was comical.

"I have special powers and can tell what you drank today. Mommy's know everything."

"Like magic?"

"Something like that." Heather hugged her tight. How could she possibly love the new baby as much as Laurel? She gave her such joy. Heather wanted to squeeze her cute face every second of the day.

They ambled into the house and Laurel ran to the TV. "Barney, Mommy. I want to watch Barney. Pleeeease."

"The tape's still in there from yesterday. Let me just turn the TV on for you."

Barney began his repetitive, aggravating song and Heather slipped away before the tiresome melody worsened her headache. She removed her green dress, one of the few things she still fit into, threw on her dull, gray pajamas and hung the dress back on the hanger. *Uck.* It looked like one of the muumuu dresses her grandmother used to wear. What a dork she had become.

A languid clip-clop echoed in the hallway. She tensed, inhaled, then readied herself.

"Hey," she said. "How was our day?"

Lance entered the bedroom, then dumped himself onto the bed. "Liquid lunch today. The boys and I went out and never came back. Split a six-pack on the train ride home, too." Beer breath competed for air in their bedroom. Lance removed his leather shoes and flung them in the center of the room. She waited for him to ask about her day. The only sound came from Barney.

"I've been thinking a lot and decided that while I'm on maternity leave I'd start searching for a new job."

"Too much to juggle? Told you you couldn't handle it."

Heather cringed. "No, it's the new dietitians. They're not interested in anything I talk about. When I try to tell them how Laurel started potty training or how she knows all her colors, they don't even acknowledge me."

"Maybe you're boring the hell out of them. Did you ever think of that?"

"It's my first child, I'm excited. It's what's important to me. They monopolize our lunchtime discussing how drunk they got over the weekend or what guys they picked up—"

"Sounds like you're jealous, Heather."

"Jealous? They have no idea what the real world's like. They complain that their mothers didn't do their laundry. Do they know what it's like to take care of a child or clean an entire house?"

"Once again...jealous. They're partying and living the single life while you sit at home on the weekends taking care of a child."

Heather frowned, then shook her head. "I am not jealous. I love my life. I just have nothing in common with them. They're materialistic, clueless and—"

Lance stood and hauled his drunk ass out of the bedroom. "Is dinner ready?"

****

Monday morning, Heather gathered her papers and proceeded upstairs before the other two came in. If she could avoid them for another fifteen days, maybe work wouldn't be so miserable.

She unloaded her belongings on Tower-8 and headed straight for room 815. Mr. Gentile's engaging conversations kept her coming back. He understood her better than her own husband did. It was silly to talk to him so much, but she missed strong, one-on-one conversations. As amazing as Laurel was, how many times could she talk about Barney or her farm animals? And Heather was sure that Cara came back from her lunch hour drunk the other day.

Heather wanted to ask Mr. Gentile what she should do about her job. Would he tell her to stick it out for another year? Another child would add more to her already hectic schedule. Two kids under three years old, a house to clean, and with summer approaching, the outside responsibilities as well. Impossible. But another year working beside those two? Not to mention how she hated eating lunch alone.

Laurel would be a big help, even at her age. Lance had yet to change a diaper or feed her. Heather didn't mind, but if he helped with the housework then she could find more time to play with her. With the new baby, would she neglect Laurel? So much to coordinate. Cara and Samantha were in for a big surprise one day. That's if they remained sober long enough.

Heather knocked on 815's door and smiled at the man in bed A. She continued to the next bed and peeked around the curtain. "Mr. Gentile, I brought you something." She found a man in his late twenties sitting in bed watching *Regis and Kathie Lee*.

"Oh, I'm sorry. They must have moved him again."

"No problem," the patient said.

Heather tottered over to the unit secretary who had the phone to her ear. She finished her call and then smiled. "Hey, Heather, that baby still in there? When's he coming out?"

"Not soon enough." She patted her belly. "I hate to bother you. Do you know what room they moved Mr. Gentile to? I'm hoping the change of atmosphere—"

"Heather, Mr. Gentile passed away over the weekend. Saturday, I believe. I'm so sorry."

Heather stepped back. "No, he couldn't have. He was fine on Friday. Even gained weight. I had a whole conversation with him."

"I thought you knew. I'm sorry. You helped him a lot and he always asked for you."

"Did he ask for me on Saturday? What did he say? What happened?"

"I wasn't here. I'm not really sure."

"Excuse me," Heather said, wiping her nose on her lab coat. She ran to the bathroom and hid in the stall, ripping wads of toilet paper from its holder. They warned you not to get too close, but she cared about so many of them. How many of their wakes had she attended? What was the point of nourishing them if they were all going to die anyway?

She felt the baby kick her. Hard. Please, let her water break now. Please.

****

Heather entered the mall at five o'clock in a rush. She needed to buy Brooke's gift quickly so she could make it in time to pick up Laurel before the six o'clock closing. Brooke's baby shower was next Saturday at Martini Bistro. She already had an elaborate shower for her first son Jacob, but had no trouble throwing herself another shower and registering for extravagant gifts like cribs and dressing tables, armoires and dressers. Brooke also hinted that her best friend would surely help with these purchases, even though Heather felt it was her parents place to buy the larger items.

Guilt overtook her, though, and despite the fact that she bought several items on the registry already, she'd decided to dash into The Pampered Peapod and pick up a few blue outfits. Daniel had to be well dressed of course. She wondered what Brooke would say if she bought him clothes from the clearance rack at K-Mart.

Heather cut through Macy's to enter the main section of the mall. Dozens of flowery scents invaded her nose, as she weaved in and out of the perfume-wielding women. Did they think a thirty-seven week pregnant woman wanted to be doused?

She passed a mirror at the Clinique counter and recoiled. She had thrown her hair into a ponytail after lunch and strands of hair had escaped, making it look like someone did a static-electricity experiment on her. She spit on her hand to smooth the hairs back into position. Was there any makeup left on her? *Holy crap.* Mascara dripped under her eyes exaggerating the fact that she hadn't slept. Was the mirror defective or did she really look that puffy? The twenty-five pound weight gain clearly went straight to her face. She used to be so attractive. What happened?

She made it to the other side of the department store unscathed, and pushed open the main doors. She held the door for a cluster of cackling teenage girls who trampled through, snorting their words and stumbling over each other. They didn't notice her mushroomed abdomen or thank her for her gesture. Had she become that much of a loser?

Heather smoothed back the hair on her head again and stepped into the main concourse. The scent of buttery baked goods struck her instantly and she wanted to forgo dinner to eat a few Auntie Anne's pretzels.

Then Heather saw him.

It didn't matter that he was clear across the other side of the mall or that years had passed. She knew his walk, the glide of his fingers through his hair. It was Nicolo.

Excitement turned to panic. He approached with such confidence, like a smoking-hot model strutting down the runway. She remembered her reflection in the mirror. Hideous. Not to mention nine-months pregnant. *Pregnant.* What would she even say to him? She never said goodbye, never explained herself and fled like the coward she was. To see her now, pregnant, and still with...Lance.

She surveyed the area. He headed straight for her. With nowhere to run, she ripped the ponytail holder out, bent her head down, and let her hair fall, hiding her face from his view. Heather raked through her plaid pocketbook/diaper bag, looking for an escape.

She sensed his presence, his body, a *swoosh* of air as he passed. Reachable, touchable. He grazed her and headed for the department store she had just exited. Rocketed past her in a blur.

Then he was gone. Strode into Macy's and never noticed her existence. The only thing that remained was the fading image of his black leather jacket and matching biker boots. The scent of his Ralph Lauren cologne prevailed over the pretzels. She inhaled deeply as if to bring him back.

She lingered for several minutes staring at the empty doorway. Shoppers glanced at Heather and her dazed expression. Guilt of what she had done to him resurfaced. Her deep love for him, something she tried desperately to forget, emerged.

Fate. Gone.

Chapter 21

Nicolo

Nicolo rushed into the mall and glanced at his watch. *Shit*. He'd be late for his date for sure. He raked the hair back on his head. Would she notice if he didn't re-wash his hair? He sniffed under his jacket to see if his armpits smelled, but the scent of the cologne he spilled on his shirt this morning won out. The overwhelming scent of buttery pretzels hit him next. *Yum*. He should have eaten a larger lunch.

Did it matter if he stunk, though? Every girl he dated was a waste. Maybe if he smelled she wouldn't want to date him and then he could avoid that awkward break-up conversation. He hated telling someone it wasn't working. Sometimes he continued to date them just to avoid having the talk.

Then there was Deidre. Calling him in desperation because her house alarm would not shut off, only to find her naked and spread eagle on her kitchen table. *Ugh*. He closed his eyes and massaged his temple with his left hand.

He opened the door leading into Macy's and then ran up the escalator two steps at a time. He reached into his back pocket to find the name of the pots Carissa had asked for, for their new home. *Home*. They purchased their first home, had two children and Nicolo was still single. He reached the top step and once again felt that pain.

Calphalon. He weaved in and out of the display pyramids. Bakeware, knives, utensils. He found the brand and searched for the eight-piece set they asked for. Unsure of the correct one, he hunted for a sales associate.

A young couple held up a wooden bowl and checked the price. A pregnant woman with a toddler in her stroller lugged a food processor under her arm. Another couple, in their late fifties, laughed at the unidentified utensil in their hands. The housewares department contained a future he had yet to experience.

Nicolo turned, and his elbow slammed into a dozen rectangular boxes. The display of outdoor, summer dinnerware went flying across the room, sending plaid salt-and-pepper shakers all over the floor. He panicked and kneeled behind the elaborate presentation, sweeping the boxes into a mound.

Heather would hate these. Plaid, how boring. She'd choose something colorful and fun. Perhaps with giant strawberries on them, and smiley faces.

What the hell was he thinking about? He gathered the last of them into a pile and a hand reached out to him. "Need any help?"

Long brown hair fluttered and dangled before his eyes. It hung just below her breasts. He grabbed five shakers under his right arm and sprang up. She scooped up the other three and smiled.

"They pack these aisles so damn tight." He tried to act cool.

"I put this picnic display together," the cute saleswoman said.

"Sorry, didn't mean to insult you. I'm just a clumsy guy." He thought of the complicated Tae-Bo workout he completed last night.

"You don't look clumsy." She glanced at his chest and then her eyes travelled to his jeans.

"Yup, clumsy Nic, they call me. Always knocking over condiment containers." He rolled his eyes.

She giggled, then arranged the remainder of the salt-and-pepper shakers back on the table.

"Great picnic items," he said.

Her face lit up like a tail light. "Do you like…picnics?"

"I do," he grinned.

"Miss, can you help me?" an elderly woman called to her.

She sighed. "Excuse me for a minute."

She rushed toward the back of the store, her muscular calves pounded their way across the linoleum, and left Nicolo to find the eight-piece Calphalon set himself.

He threw several bills on the counter as the elderly woman continued to question her on every coffee maker they sold. Five thirty. His watch reminded him of his date.

He glanced back one last time, but she had one of the boxes open and the contents of the coffee maker scattered across the shelf.

****

Nicolo drove to Ornello's and then helped Jada, his date of the month, out of the car. She spent the car ride explaining her role as an assistant buyer for Bloomingdales. He tried to appear interested but every time a good song came on the radio, he had to stop his hand from turning up the volume.

The hostess seated them near the front entrance at the last table-for-two. Nicolo decided on the roasted salmon with white wine sauce, but pretended to read the menu to avoid Jada's incessant chatting. The roasted asparagus sounded delicious, too. A waiter passed their table with a plate of bruschetta, the sweet basil and onions roused his appetite further.

"So, it's really a fast-paced job. It's as much about crunching numbers as it is about having taste. Luckily, I'm good at multi-tasking, very analytical and outgoing." Jada sounded like an ad in the employment section of a newspaper. "It's very demanding though, and you have to be able to adapt to a stressful environment."

"Do you know what you want to order yet?" Nicolo interrupted.

"No, actually I haven't even looked."

Nicolo had enough of her babbling. Bla, bla, bla, bla, bla. How exciting could it be to buy and sell handbags? He put the menu down and stared at Jada's platinum-blonde hair. Could he ever date someone and not compare them to Heather? Probably not. That woman at Macy's did seem nice though. He never got her name.

"I think I'll get the Caesar salad, without the chicken."

Great, another salad eater. Don't eat any protein, but drown the poor lettuce in salad dressing and croutons. Heather would have ordered a fish entrée. Then finished it off with a giant brownie a la mode.

Nicolo shook his head. He had to stop these constant comparisons. "So, Jada, what do you do on the weekends?"

"Sometimes I work on weekends, if there's a special sale, conferences..."

"No, I mean what do you do for fun?"

"I usually hit the mall and shop. Mostly to check out other stores, what they're selling and—"

"Do you have any interests, hobbies?"

"What do you mean?"

The waiter arrived and took their orders. Nicolo skipped the appetizers so he could leave the restaurant as soon as possible.

Their food arrived and he pretended to cut his salmon, but glanced at his watch instead.

"A typical day could involve forecasting sales, going to designers' showrooms, choosing what's going to be in stores—"

"Jada, do you like the beach? Do you like amusement parks, the zoo, sports? Do you work out at the gym?"

Her face stiffened. "The gym? I don't need to work out at a gym. Are you saying I'm fat?"

"What? No, that's a myth. People that work out at the gym are fit. The ones that don't..." He paused, knowing where that would end up. "I'm just trying to find out what your interests are, so I can plan something for us to do next time." Did he really want there to be a next time? Why was he so nice to all of them?

"I haven't been to the beach in years, and I don't participate in any sports because I have to uphold an image and, well, with the clothing I have and the manicures..." She glanced at her nails. "The zoo? I can't say I've been to a zoo since I was little. Amusement parks? Nicolo, do you have children? Nancy didn't say anything about children. Now if you do, I'm not sure if I'm ready for that and—"

"No, no. I don't have children. I just thought it would be fun once the weather gets warmer."

After dinner, Jada excused herself to the ladies' room. Nicolo paid the bill and decided to use the bathroom also. He asked the waiter where the restrooms were and headed toward the back. He neared the alcove and heard the unmistakable voice.

"He's all right Nancy, but he wanted to know if we could hang out at an amusement park. Who does that? Could you see me on a roller coaster?...I know. My nails would break off and then I'd have to find time in my busy schedule to get them fixed." Another pause and then, "and another thing, he drives a Jeep. Do you know how embarrassing it was to pull up to the valet in a Jeep? Please, I almost died...No, I didn't say anything... No, I'm not sure. You said he was a cop, but he hasn't mentioned his job all night. They make good money, don't they?"

Nicolo hid behind the wall and firestorms surged through his veins. A girl around five-years-old glared, questioning why he hid behind the large plant. He took a few steps back, then strolled into the alcove with his head turned. He collided with Jada.

"Oh, sorry, Jada. I didn't see you."

The kindergartener stuck her tongue out at him.

Jada excused herself and hung up the pay phone. "No problem, I was just...checking in with my co-worker. Big day on Monday. Meeting with a new vendor."

"I'm just running in here, then I'll meet you back at the table."

****

Nicolo waited outside for his Jeep while Jada stood in the lobby to keep warm. Despite the sixty-degree days, the nights still dipped into the forties. He remembered how Heather snuggled up to him when they waited for his Jeep that one night he took her out to dinner in Queens. Any extra time spent together meant the world to them. Or so he thought.

The Jeep, barely nine-years-old, still had a lot of kick left in it. Never had any problems with it either. Was it immature though? Not appropriate for a twenty-nine-year-old? He eyed the aqua flames shooting over the hood.

He wanted to buy a house if he were still single by the time he turned thirty. Dino purchased a sizeable ranch for a hundred and seventy-nine thousand, but the prices had jumped in the past year. A new car would mean another loan and less money saved towards the house. Could he afford a car loan and a mortgage?

"Did you hear what I said?"

Nicolo flinched. Jada stood eerily close to him. Suddenly the word 'stalker' entered his head. "No, I'm sorry what did you say?"

"I inquired as to where you were taking me now."

How about home? If he was going to grow up, buy a new car, invest in a home, he needed to stop the charades. No more pretending he enjoyed the date or had a good time. He needed to be honest with them.

"Actually Jada, you're a great girl but I don't think we have very much in common. I don't see this going anywhere and I'd hate to waste your time. I mean, with your busy schedule and all."

Her mouth fell open and hung there like a broken construction crane. Jada wrenched her head towards the valet for support.

This was the beginning of his future. Time to grow up, sell the Jeep, buy a house and most importantly forget about Heather. Move on and find a different path. The current one led to constant dead ends. And dead ends never led to anything.

Chapter 22

Heather

Heather left Brooke's baby shower, fuming. The ridiculous amount of money she spent and Brooke never said "thank you," as if she expected it. Her neighbors loaded her up with cheap items like stuffed animals, blankies, a basket of bibs, and a few freakin' onesies. Only large groups of family members purchased the expensive gifts. Her abdomen tightened and squeezed.

Luckily, her parents offered to keep Laurel overnight. Heather's current mood would ruin everyone's evening anyway. She entered the house and tossed her party favor on the kitchen table. It landed with a *clunk*. A lavish metal bookmark with a giant stork on the top and *Daniel* inscribed across its wing. Like she would ever use that.

She tore her jacket off and chucked it over the chair. When it refused to stay put and slid onto the floor, Heather kicked it. Tingling and irritation on her thighs increased until splatters of liquid coated the floor. Oh God, not now.

She dialed Brian's number and asked for Lance. "Now?" he asked. "The basketball game's almost over, can't you wait?"

She ripped off her ugly beige dress and threw it in the hamper knowing she would never have to wear another piece of maternity clothing again. She yanked the shower curtain back and stepped into the shower. The warm water poured onto her aggravated skin. At least she wouldn't have to see Cara and Samantha ever again. No fake good-byes. She'd update her resume as soon as possible.

The hot jets kneaded her aching back. Heather closed her eyes and let it relax her. When would she take a peaceful, uninterrupted shower again?

Nicolo. She remembered the day they returned from the beach covered in sand from the horrible gusts of wind that day. Their ocean-drenched bodies coated themselves in gritty, coarse sand from the windstorm that forced their early departure. She wanted to jump in her car and shower at her apartment, but with his parents at work, he convinced her to stay and bathe with him in the master bathroom.

Their lips blended and water trickled into their mouths. Rolling and mingling, their sugary flesh greedily consumed each other. He bit down on her bottom lip while his hands surrounded her face and embraced her cheekbones. Hands that made her tremble. Strong calculating moves, gentle at times, but then powerful when the mood demanded. Nicolo bathed her with the silky bar of soap and let it wander all over her body. Once the sand and grit sank to the bottom of the tub, he lathered his incredible hands and allowed them to finish the job.

Nicolo's palms surrounded both her breasts and he eased her against the wall. Arms like steel beams pressed her into the cold tile and he extended them until his hot ass touched the shower curtain. His hands massaged and kneaded until the rest of her body numbed. His thumbs magically circled her nipples without missing the rhythm.

Nicolo growled. His wolf eyes devoured her, but they would have frightened anyone else. His lustful inspection aroused Heather and she knew what was about to be unleashed. She welcomed his aggressiveness as his mouth pressed her against the tiles, lips rolling over her teeth.

He pulled away just long enough to flash her a wicked grin, then his right hand skimmed down her Abs and came to rest between her legs, stroking the smooth, eager flesh.

His mouth found the sweet, responsive spot on the back of her neck. Nicolo nuzzled and sucked on it, knowing it would drive her mad, and that he would leave yet another mark on her skin. On her soul. Caught between his hard muscles and the hard tile, Heather nevertheless felt soothed, and she melted into his velvety skin.

Contractions spread, blurring the image. Tears trickled down her face, mixing with the water sprays. Her life sucked. A life that grew from trying to please everyone. Shallow co-workers, pretentious best friend, egotistical spouse, vindictive mother-in-law.

She wanted Nicolo back. She had made a terrible mistake. God, how she missed him.

****

Heather rested on the crisp, sterile sheets in the hospital bed with Gia in her arms. Mr. Gentile was right. A girl, another beautiful daughter. Would she love her as much as Laurel? How could she? Laurel was so affectionate and loving. Laurel played with Heather's hair during their long talks, and gave her life a purpose. The soon to be three-year-old, the one that never went through the terrible two's, helped Heather through tough moments not knowing she was doing it. Laurel provided the only enjoyment in her life.

But holding Gia on her chest, faces only inches apart, her itsy-bitsy nose like a doll's, her pink grapefruit lips pursed into a smile, she would provide a wealth of happiness as well.

Lance strolled in with Laurel and she immediately jumped on the bed asking to hold her little sister. Heather positioned Gia in Laurel's arms and then she leaned back. The three of them laid there holding one another, warm and full of love.

Her family grew. Two daughters cuddled delicately in her arms, her family was now complete. Their body heat thawed her bitterness. They would comfort her and provide the joy needed to endure her dreadful life. She vowed to make their years happy and unforgettable, make them as wonderful as Nicolo had made her life that one spectacular year.

Heather's lunch arrived and she placed Gia in the plastic bassinet beside her. Laurel shifted on the bed and then dug into the yellow rice on the plate. Heather laughed, letting her eat as much as she wanted. Laurel ensured that not a grain of rice fell from her plastic spoon.

After twenty minutes, Lance stood. "Okay," he started. "Your mom's coming in a half hour, right?"

"Yes, why?"

"I need to do a few things before you return tomorrow."

"You just got here and my mom's been helping out."

"Look, you know I hate hospitals. I can't sit here, I can't stand the smell."

"What smell? It's a maternity floor, it smells like baby powder."

"Daddy, I don't want to go yet. Please."

"You can stay. Grandma will drive you home."

"You can't leave Laurel here. I can't watch both of them."

"She'll be here in a half hour, what's the big deal? Wheel the baby back into the nursery if it's too much for you to handle." Lance strolled out, leaving Laurel on Heather's lap.

****

Gia settled into her cherry-blossom painted bedroom, swaddled in her flamingo-pink blanket, on top of her fuchsia plush carpeting. She wriggled and squeaked in her cocoon, eyes still shut tight.

"She'll love her new room." Laurel patted Gia's forehead.

"You don't think there's too much pink in here?" Heather scrunched her nose.

"No, Mommy, it's beautiful. I want a pink room now, too."

"I made your room yellow because we didn't know if you were going to be a boy or girl."

"Silly. I was a girl Mommy, can't you see?"

"Now, but when you were in my tummy, I didn't know."

"You painted Gia's room after she came home. Why didn't you change mine?" Laurel flipped onto her stomach next to Gia and rubbed her blanket-wrapped belly. "We going to be best friends."

"I hope so." Heather pushed a strand of Laurel's hair behind her ear. "The three of us will polish each other's nails, have make-overs with silly mud masks, and wear pink tutus and eat lots of chocolate and have girls' nights and watch kissy-face movies..."

Laurel giggled and rolled over onto her back. "Ew! No kissy movies, mommy."

"Why not? I love kissy movies." Heather tickled Laurel's belly and watched her squirm. "Kissy like this?" She leaned over and kissed Laurel on her cheeks and forehead, then down her neck. "I'm the kissing monster." *Smooch smooch.*

"Leaving an infant on a dirty floor, how barbaric."

Laurel and Heather gazed up at the beast, Grandma Bianca. She insisted they call her Bibi, her nickname. Heather grimaced. "It's a brand new carpet. Just installed yesterday."

"Disgusting." She rolled her eyes. "Where's my son? I can't find him anywhere."

"He went for a drive with Brian."

"I came all this way for nothing?"

Heather's eyes widened. "I thought you came to see Gia?"

"Who?" Bianca ran her fingers across the top of the crib checking for dust.

"Your new granddaughter."

"Oh, yes."

"Why didn't you visit at the hospital? Everyone came but you."

"Heather, this wasn't your first child. Must I come every single time?"

"She's your granddaughter. I would think you'd want to see her."

"I was able to bear a son, a fine son. One who will carry our family name on. You give Lance only girls."

"I give him? You do realize the man's the one that decides the sex."

"Please, Heather, I did my job, the least you could do was yours. Now our name will not continue on."

"What's wrong, Mommy? Why's your mouth not closing?"

"Tell Lance I was here. Have him call me when he has returned." Bianca tossed her head up, her gaudy gold earrings jingled as she disappeared out the door.

Laurel took a step toward Heather and pushed her jaw closed. "Does your mouth hurt, mommy?"

"No, it's just at a loss for words, as usual."

"Do you want my ABC book?"

Heather smiled at Laurel and then stood up. A mere six-pound baby and her thighs were weak. How did she ever do ninety-pound squats with Nicolo? She placed Gia in her crib and Laurel skipped towards the den.

Heather had to get Nicolo out of her head. Since seeing him in the mall, the aching for him only intensified with each passing day.

Heather had succeeded in doing it again. Finding things to occupy her mind. Things to distract her. Avoiding the problem.

But now, she craved his hugs that pressed away her fears. If she could look into his black eyes once more, hear him whisper to her under the covers, hold his hand. What she wouldn't give to go back in time.

Laurel attempted a somersault on the den carpeting, but tumbled to the side instead, never completing the roll. "I did it, Mommy!"

"I saw. How cool." Then again, she wouldn't have Laurel, or Gia. Meant to be. An angel sent them to rescue her. Rescue her from whom? The very people that she chose to spend the rest of her life with? If she stayed with Nicolo, she would not have Laurel or Gia but perhaps she would have a lifetime of happiness and other wonderful children. Children that they could both enjoy and have fun with.

"Look, I can stand on one foot." Laurel balanced for one second, then repeatedly lifted and lowered her left foot. "See?" She lifted her foot again, holding it much longer, then fell backward.

"Ooh, are you okay, honey?"

Laurel's chin quivered. "I fell on my butt."

Heather rushed over and picked her up. "I'm going to call you Boom-butt from now on." Laurel rubbed her butt and pouted her lips. Heather combed Laurel's hair back to reveal the glow of her cherry-tinted cheeks. She pulled her in and hugged her.

Selfish. What was she thinking? Giving up her children for some crazy sexual encounter? That's all it was. A weak moment in her life. She was stronger now, mature, head clear and focused. Her family depended on her.

Nicolo's black leather jacket and boots flashed in her mind. She hugged Laurel tighter, fighting back tears. Why was he in the mall? Did he live nearby? Was he married? Did he have beautiful children of his own? Jealousy flashed over her at the thought of him having sex with someone else. Was she serious? This was her choice. She had no right to be jealous.

"Mommy, you're hurting me."

"Sorry." Heather released her. "Do you want to read a book before I feed Gia again?

"Yes, I'll go get it." Laurel hurried off and Heather crashed to the ground in tears.

Was it really just a fling? Brooke had grabbed her at the wedding reception and shaken her. Drunk, Heather collapsed in her bridal suite thankful for waterproof mascara. Brooke reminded her how she was the luckiest woman alive and to grow up. Lying on the floor now, recollections of her outburst that night returned.

Why did she have to see him? She had moved on, his face almost vanished from her memory. The last two and a half years she immersed herself in Laurel's world, erased the past and saw the direction she needed to travel.

What was the point? Was it some cruel joke, or a second chance?

✳✳✳✳

Heather struggled back up the eight flights and one hundred and sixty steps to her nursing unit. A task she performed for five years, but after three months of maternity leave, the undertaking seemed agonizing and depressing.

Life at home with two small children made it impossible to rewrite her resume. She found the time to print her old one off the computer, jot down a few rewrites, but then the document became lost among the stacks of papers piled on the desk.

How would she go on interviews anyway? Leave her kids in the waiting room? She asked Lance to mention it to his mother, but he exploded, informing her that she was too busy to watch children. What Bianca did all day was a mystery, even to Lance, but he assured her that his mother's life was indeed hectic. Heather's parents worked, as they probably would until they were in their eighties.

There was no welcome committee in the diet office for her first day back. No baby gifts. She spent her morning and her lunch hour listening to Samantha and Cara talk about the spectacular time they had with the temporary dietitian, Eryn. The three of them quickly grew close, spent every Friday at the bar across the street with other hospital employees, even shopped together and bought new wardrobes. They called themselves *three peas in a pod*.

Cara never asked about Gia. Samantha asked what she named her *son*. They even finished their lunch break by stating that they were surprised when Heather came back. They thought for sure she had planned to find another job. How heartbroken Eryn was to have to leave such a wonderful position.

Chapter 23

Nicolo

The escalator steps hummed beneath Nicolo's feet. He held onto the rotating railing, rehearsing the speech in his head again. It had been over two months and this was his third visit to the housewares department. He decided if she were not there again, he would ask for her.

He rounded the corner and scanned past the rainbow display of glass pitchers. A gentleman in his fifties wearing a brown suit and navy-blue tie, stood behind the counter. Gray hair bounced upon the top of a saleswoman's head as she helped another elderly woman with a toaster oven.

Where was she? Nicolo should have returned the following week. He neared the counter and waited for the man to finish the transaction. His stomach churned and he jammed his hands into his jean pockets.

"Can I help you?"

Nicolo spun towards the voice of the gray-haired woman. Her customer had left without the toaster purchase. She looked pissed.

"Yes, I was looking for a salesperson that worked here. A woman in her late twenties, little shorter than you, long brown hair."

"I'm not sure whom you mean, but I'm confident I can help you. What was it that you wanted to purchase?"

"No, I needed to speak to her, specifically."

"She no longer works here, so please allow me to assist you."

Nicolo shifted on his feet. He had waited too long. Everyone disappeared from his life. "No thank you. Sorry to have bothered you."

"It's not a bother at all. We're here until eight if you change your mind about your purchase."

"Thank you again, but I didn't want to buy anything. I just wanted to find her, the girl." He turned and trekked away, avoiding another family with a stroller.

"Sir. Sir!"

Nicolo glanced back to find the older gentleman waving his hand at him.

"Are you asking about Kim?"

Nicolo hustled back to the knives section. The saleswoman frowned at the man in the gray suit. "Yes. I mean, I think so."

"Cute, little, Italian girl, about five three, tiny waist?" He winked at Nicolo. The saleswoman huffed and stormed away.

"Yes, sounds about right. She quit though?"

"No, no. Just not in this department anymore." He grabbed Nicolo's arm and pulled him a few feet away, looking back over his shoulder. "She's in the children's department now, on the lower level. They moved her when the wicked witch of the west demanded this department. Seniority or something."

"Is she here today?"

"Not sure. Can't hurt to look, right?" He winked again and hurried back to the cash register.

Nicolo took the escalator down two floors and headed to the left unsure where the children's section was located. He weaved past woman's bathing suits, the juniors department and then another left. He found the boy's department, but with no sight of her, made another left into the girls' department. Nothing.

He weaved in and out of the infant's section and held up a green and pink bathing suit with a large flower on the front. Size 3 months. Too small for his niece.

"Need help with a size?"

How embarrassing. They probably thought he was a pedophile. "No, just looking for my niece." He put the bathing suit back on the rack and turned to the voice. The saleswoman walked towards a table of infant toys and began rearranging them. Was it her?

He crept toward the table and stopped. Her back was to him. What would he say? Nicolo quickly grabbed a red, white and blue shorts set and held it up. "Excuse me. Would this fit a two-year-old boy?"

She turned and reached for the hanger. It said 5T. What a moron.

"It could," she said. "If they were...tall and...big."

It was her. She looked hotter then he remembered. The children's department did her well. "Oh, well, he's not that big. Now that I'm looking, it looks too big."

"Do I know you? You look familiar."

Nicolo tilted his head down to avoid her gaze. "No, I don't think so."

She leaned in as if to study his features. "Hmm."

"I shop in here a lot. Maybe you saw me before."

"That must be it. I see many of the same people run through here." She hung the patriotic outfit back on the rack.

Nicolo stepped back to give her room and his ass knocked over the display of stuffed animals she just fixed. He jerked around and stepped on a blue elephant and the thing let out a distressful squeak. "Oh God, I'm so sorry." He squatted, scooped up a pile of animals in his arms, and then placed them back on the table in a disorganized mess.

"Now I know. You're the one that knocked over my picnic display in housewares."

"What? Me?" Nicolo tried to arrange the giraffes and lambs into some kind of pattern and then sighed. "Oh, housewares, yes. I remember now."

"You're right, you are clumsy." She giggled.

He held out his hand to her. "I'm Nicolo."

"Kim."

****

Nicolo let Kim walk in front of him as they made their way to a rear table outside of the Bayville Tiki Bar. The heat from the noontime Memorial Day sun beat off his bare shoulders. They sat across from each other at one of the wooden tables and browsed their menus.

"Do you want to share a dozen clams on the half shell?" he asked.

"Raw clams?"

"They're really good. Some horseradish, tabasco, lemon."

Her face scrunched up. Like Heather's did when she sucked on that oversized lemon-wedge at the bar. "No, thank you."

"Do you know what you want to order?"

"Probably the Caesar salad."

"That's all?"

"What do you mean? It has Romaine lettuce, croutons, cheese."

Nicolo kept quiet. The waitress returned. "I'll have the grilled chicken sandwich with lettuce and tomato, but instead of French fries can I have corn on the cob?" he asked.

The crowd grew as did the laughter and noise. A bunch of college guys clinked bottles and then tossed their heads back downing half their beers. Two girls behind them, in belly shirts and cut off jean-shorts, sipped their strawberry daiquiris. Caribbean music streamed through the speakers atop the bar's grass roof. French fries and grilled beef whizzed past his nose.

"This place is so quaint. What great weather for it too."

"I used to come here all the time. I almost forgot about it. When I saw the weather for today it popped back into my head."

"Great choice." Kim smiled and took a sip from her water.

"You sure you don't want a beer or something?"

"No, I don't drink beer."

Visions of Heather and him finishing off two six-packs of warm Michelob at the park near his house weaved through his mind. Rocketing on the swings, careening down the slide backwards, falling on top of one another. Nicolo hid his grin. "Pina Colada?"

"Oh no, too many calories."

"It's Memorial day, eighty degrees, surrounded by great music and crazy people. Come on, order a fancy drink. You'll get a cute umbrella." He winked.

Kim smiled, but then shook her head. "No, my water's fine. I usually drink wine."

"Sorry, I don't think they have wine here."

"That's okay." She twirled the ice cubes in her glass with her straw.

The waitress brought their food and Nicolo eyed her salad-dressing drowned lettuce. "Do you want some of my chicken sandwich? Half my corn?"

"No, this is plenty. It fills me up."

He shook his head and reached for his beer. The amount of fat in the salad probably equaled the amount in the Pina Colada.

"Did you hear me?" Kim asked.

"I'm sorry, what?"

"I said, how's your chicken sandwich?"

"Really good. They have this honey mustard sauce on it. Gives it a nice kick." He took another large bite. Too big to chew, he attempted to push it to the other side of his mouth. The image of Heather eating that colossal burger at the Old Mill Shack made him smile. He remembered the elderly bartender that always served them. He would lean on his elbow, watch Heather down the entire burger, and then say, "Look at that little girl eat."

Nicolo couldn't stifle the laugh any longer. The large mass of food went down his windpipe, causing him to choke. He coughed it up, chewed quickly, and swallowed half of it. Heather could out-eat him, out-drink him. Only half his size, but...

"Are you okay?" Kim stood and offered him a napkin.

"Yes, fine. I guess I just bit off a little too much." *Damn, Heather.* "What do you like to do for fun, Kim?"

"My sisters and I go to the city a lot. Usually a Saturday dinner followed by a show or dancing. Do you hang out in the city?"

"I worked as a New York City cop for seven years, then transferred to Suffolk County about two years ago. Got tired of it."

"Tired of it? It's magical."

"I guess if you're there for fun. My fun revolved around robberies and shootings."

"What do you like to do then?"

"I love the beach, fishing on my friend's boat, hiking. I used to own a Jeep but then traded it in for the truck, and now I feel the wind on my head through cycling instead. Signed up for a few bike races across Long Island at the end of the summer, and thinking about doing a Duathlon next year."

"You're one of those outdoorsy kind of guys."

"Definitely. Do you like your job?"

Kim paused for a second, then bit down on her lip. "I worked at A & S for years but when they closed, I transferred all over the place. I ended up in that Macy's. I loved housewares, but then they transferred me again. The children's department is giving me this love-hate relationship with kids."

"What do you mean?"

"The cute ones make me want to have a hundred, the bratty ones make we want to run."

Nicolo laughed. "Most kids' bad habits are due to parent's laziness. Not that I'm saying parenting's easy, just that it's simpler to take the easy way out. Give in, give up."

"How do you know? Do you have any I don't know about?" She wiggled her eyebrows.

"My brother has two. A baby girl and a two-year-old boy."

"Do you want kids?"

"Definitely, lots of them. I always wanted a big family."

"I have three sisters."

"Wow, lucky you. Tons of sharing, huh?"

"When we were growing up our house was small. Three bedrooms. I was the oldest, my sister Lily was born a year later. But then my grandfather became ill and moved in with us. My sister and I had to share my room. My mother didn't think my grandfather would make it past that year, but eleven years later, he was still alive and kicking. Two years after my grandfather moved in, my mother had twins. My sisters and I all moved into the master bedroom."

"That must have been hard. Four of you in one room?"

"Sure, there were times when we'd argue, but, well, did you ever have a slumber party?"

"Uh, no, can't say I ever did that. Not really a guy thing."

"It was like we had this giant, fun slumber party every single night. We shared toys in the center of the room, stayed up late, talked about everything. We spent every minute together."

"That's great."

"Three years before my grandfather died, my parents decided it was ridiculous. Four pre-teens in one room? They searched for a bigger house, my grandfather said he would help with the bills and we moved about a year later. Two sisters in one room and two in another."

"That must've been better."

"I was devastated."

"What do you mean?"

"Although they were right next door, it felt like they were miles away. It almost felt like I was being punished." She took a sip of her water. "When my grandfather died two years later, Lily decided she wanted her own room!"

Nicolo tried to look shocked but he was obviously missing the point.

"It got even weirder after that. I received a scholarship and was off to college, and the three of them were in the house without me! I wondered what they were doing, what fun they were having, what I was missing. Then after she graduated college, Lily moved in with some loser guy, and the twins still had two years to go before they graduated. I was living in an empty house."

Nicolo took a bite out of his sandwich not wanting to react the wrong way. Luckily, some honey mustard sauce dripped onto his fingers and he grabbed a napkin to clean it up. *No eye contact.*

"To make a long story short, I rented my own apartment and have been there ever since. Of course, now, the twins are back at home. Lily thankfully dumped that guy, but now she's back home, too."

"Why doesn't she move in with you then?"

"I asked, but she wanted her own place. It was a terrible break up. She never should have dated him."

"Why?"

"He wanted Lily around him every second of the day. It was ridiculous."

They dumped their napkins onto the plates and Nicolo tossed money on the table for the waitress. They walked toward the exit and the cool sea breeze from across the street teased his nose. "Hey, do you want to walk along the beach, Kim?"

"Is there a boardwalk?"

"No, but we can take our shoes off and walk in the sand." She glanced down at her high-heeled silver sandals. "We don't have to. It's just such a nice day out."

"Is there a place to wash my feet afterward?"

"Not sure, but I always carry a towel in my car. I can grab it."

Ten minutes later, they were wandering along the shoreline, Nicolo with his feet grazing the icy cold water, Kim standing away from the splashing waves that rolled in.

"Mmm, the ocean air smells so good," she said.

"Doesn't it?"

"I can see why you love it. Cooped up inside a mall all day you forget how close we are to the water."

"Maybe we can have a beach date next time?"

Her eyes widened. "Um, maybe."

"I mean if you want." Silence. "Or we can wait a few months if you're uncomfortable."

"No, I'm sorry. I'm being silly. Sure, we can go. I should get some color on this pale body of mine."

Nicolo gazed at the curves running up the back of her legs. Her calves muscular, her thighs slim. Her toenails painted white with sparkles that attracted the light. Her hair flowed over her shoulders and covered the bare part of her back that the tank top failed to cover.

She turned and glanced at him. The sunlight reflected off her chest magnifying the cleavage within her red tank top. Brown curls of hair corkscrewed onto her breasts.

She studied him. "What?"

"Nothing." He took a step closer. "It's just so beautiful here. Everything's beautiful."

She grinned and Nicolo pushed her hair behind her shoulders and leaned in. Their warm lips met for an instant, tasting each other for the first time.

"Mmm, that was nice," Kim said.

And it was.

Chapter 24

Heather

Heather pushed the stroller with Gia cuddled up under her crocheted blanket. After two blocks, Gia fell asleep looking cute as all hell with her black-cat costume, now covered under pink fringes. Laurel ran alongside, dancing in her Cinderella gown. Heather, disguised as a pirate, adjusted her eye patch so it sat more smoothly.

Laurel skipped up the walkway to the next home and then opened the princess castle bag that Heather's mother made her. She held up the Mounds bar that the chubby man in black sweats gave her and smiled. "Thank you," she said, and ran back to her mom.

"Coconut," Heather said. "My favorite."

"Mine too. Look it all the candy mommy. The most ever."

"What are you going to do with it all?"

"Eat it."

"All of it?" Heather gasped in jest.

"Except for this." She held up a thing of Whoppers.

"Ew, moth balls."

Laurel leaned in and whispered. "We'll give it to Gia."

Heather giggled. "Already trying to get over on your sister, eh? Be careful, one day she might trick you."

They headed home as the biting wind picked up. Once inside, Heather slipped on Gia's one-piece feety pajamas and then placed her in the crib, grateful she went right back to sleep.

Laurel scampered to the den, then dumped her Halloween bag on the rug, creating good and bad piles. Heather loaded kindling into the fireplace and soon the room lit up and warmed their chilled bones. Laurel sifted through the stash. "Look it mommy, this one has a cute bunny on it."

She took it from her and read the side of the candy bar. *Easter Greetings. Cheapos.* "This one's bad. Leftover from Easter. Sorry, honey."

The front door opened and Lance entered. Laughter from numerous voices emerged. The boisterous men accompanying Lance ambled into the kitchen. The racket drowned out the gentle crackling of the fire.

"Daddy!" Laurel sprang from the carpet and scurried over to her father. Lance extended his arms, but to stop her rather than lift her up. He rested his palms on her shoulders. "Laurel, relax. These are my friends from work. Say hello."

The three men admired her Cinderella costume. Laurel let the tip of her glass slipper peek out from beneath the gown. *Oohs* and *Ahhs* resounded. Lance glared at Heather. She strode over to them, hat and crossbones still on her head.

"Ahoy there mates! Can I get ye scallywags a drink?"

Lances' eyes widened.

Rex Bacon, Lance's college buddy, raised his hand. "Got a bottle o' rum, Captain?"

"Sure thing, matey." Before Heather made it to the liquor cabinet, Lance pushed Laurel away, put his arm around Heather and guided her to the dining room where they kept the liquor.

"Are you insane? What the hell is wrong with you?"

She bent in. "It's Halloween, booooo. Are you scared?"

"Yes, as a matter of fact I am. Are you drunk?"

"Drunk? I haven't had a drink in over four years. One sip and I'd be trashed."

"Why are you wearing a costume?"

"Why aren't *you* wearing a costume?"

"Because I'm a grown man and a professional lawyer."

Here we go again. Heather tuned him out as he jabbered on about the law firm. She located the bottle of rum and strolled back into the kitchen with it.

"Yo-ho-ho and a bottle of rum." Heather thrust the Bacardi into the air.

Rex stepped toward Heather and wrapped his hand around the bottle also. The two danced in a circle, the rum held high in both their fists.

"Thank you, me beauty."

"Welcome aboard, Rex. Let's drink grog before the fog."

Lance snatched the bottle away from them. "Okay, that's it! Enough. We'll be in the den if you need me." Lance ushered the men into the candy filled room, booting Laurel and her away from their cozy fire and Mounds bars. Rex looked back and gave Heather the thumbs up.

****

"I'm just calling to let you know I'm having a handbag party at my house on November 15th," Brooke said. "Darlene is making out the invitations for me so keep the date free."

"You just had a jewelry party two weeks ago and a Tupperware party over the summer." Heather picked up all of Gia's Cheerios that missed her mouth but made the floor.

"I know, and did you see all the free jewelry I made out with?"

"I didn't get any free jewelry. I had to pay for mine, and then I gave it to my mother. I don't even wear jewelry anymore, except for my wedding rings."

"Then have a party of your own. Stop refusing the offer."

"You know I hate these parties, Brooke. Everyone sitting around with wine, bragging about their kids' awards and soccer goals and report cards. How great their marriages are, even though we both know divorces are already brewing."

"It's a time for all us mothers to pull together and support one another."

Heather held the phone away from her face and stuck out her tongue as if to vomit.

"I've introduced you to a collection of inspirational woman to get you out of your rut."

"Rut? What rut?"

"Come on. We've all noticed the change in you. You should quit that job of yours and hire a nanny like the rest of us."

"Why would I need a nanny if I wasn't working?"

Loud cackles arose from the other end of the phone. "You'll have more time to network and socialize and then join the PTA in the future."

Heather rolled her eyes. "With these inspirational women, right? And what exactly have they done? Their kid's science projects? Run fundraisers forcing kids to beg people to buy stuff they don't need? Make designer cupcakes for school birthday parties? Sashay around with name-brand clothes to show their self-worth?"

"Heather, if you hung out with them, you'd fit in more and then they wouldn't look at you funny."

"They look at me funny? When? What are they saying about me?"

"Becky Meyerson saw you playing on the slide the other day at the park."

"So? I was with Laurel."

"And Terri Steward swears she saw you exiting Payless the other day."

"I was. I'm not spending a million dollars on shoes that the kids scuff up and grow out of in six months. Besides, I bought myself this really cool pair of high top sneakers. It was BOGO."

"They wouldn't ruin their shoes if they took care of them. I buy only the best for Daniel."

"He's only five months old, Brooke. He doesn't even walk yet. Laurel runs through dirt and mud and does cartwheels in the grass."

"Jacob is not allowed to touch mud or other things that may ruin his clothes, and neither will Daniel."

Heather tossed the phone down on her bed and let Brooke ramble on. She yanked on her *Hong Kong Phooey* T-shirt but then covered it with her robe so Lance wouldn't see. She eyed her funky new sneakers hidden in the back of her closet, still in the bag. She picked up the phone and took a deep breath.

"Will you be attending the party or not?"

"Brooke, you know I hate handbags."

"How can you not carry a handbag with two kids?"

"I have one bag, a small one. Want to know what's in it?" She reached for the twenty-dollar pocketbook she bought at Target and flipped open the top. "In the side pouch is my license, one credit card, a pen and a ten-dollar bill. In the main compartment I have two diapers, a plastic baggie with wipes, another one filled with Cheerios, and a small book about animal sounds."

Silence. "I really don't understand you Heather, and I never will. You're never going to be happy."

Chapter 25

Nicolo

Nicolo steered Kim to the free weight section of his gym. Her gray yoga pants dragged over the dusty floor and her long baggy T-shirt covered all body parts.

He initially hesitated inviting her to the gym. More memories of Heather would appear. They had fun over the past few months, though, and he wanted her to be a part of his life in every way.

"You never lifted weights before?"

"I've never been in a gym before."

"Really? You've done sports though, in school?"

"Nope."

Nicolo wondered if she was teasing him and narrowed his eyes. "Your legs are so toned, I just thought—"

"I took ballet for many years, until I entered middle school, then dropped out. That's all."

Nicolo swallowed hard. "Okay, then let's start slow." He grabbed a five-pound weight and had her begin with her shoulders.

She grimaced and only raised the weight a few inches. "Are you trying to be funny? This weight's too heavy. Trying to show me up?"

With five pounds? Was she serious? Nicolo grabbed the pink plastic three-pound weight scattered underneath the rack of iron dumbbells and handed it to her with a patient smile. "This one's lighter, try again."

Kim lifted her arm again, performed four reps and then stopped.

"What's wrong?"

"My arm hurts."

"You're in pain? Did you pull something?"

"No, I mean burning. On fire."

Lactic acid burn from four reps with a three-pound pink weight? *Yeesh.* "That's all right, keep going until you can't lift it anymore, no matter how much it burns. Once you physically can't lift it anymore, stop."

She glared at him as if he was joking. "That sounds painful."

"No, not at all. It's good pain. It means you're working those arms."

She tried again, but after the same four reps put the weight down and then sat on the bench behind her. "Tell me why we're doing this again?"

"You don't like it?"

"It's just, boring."

"You haven't even completed one set of one muscle group. We're just getting started. I promise it will get better."

"Is there any water around?"

"The water fountain's right there." He pointed next to the lat-pull down machine.

"Bottled water?" she asked again.

He sucked in his lips, then smiled. "I'll run upstairs and buy one. Practice on the other arm now and try to do five reps."

Nicolo jogged up the stairs missing every other one and paid one dollar for the plastic Evian bottle. He headed back down remembering the time the water fountain broke in his old gym and Heather tiptoed into the men's locker room and slurped water straight from the sink's faucet. An elderly man emerged from the sauna naked, and stared her down.

Nicolo chuckled. *Weirdo.*

He paused at the top of the step and closed his eyes. *Stop it.* Why can't he erase these damn memories? Did he have to move to another country? Heather filled his mind more and more lately and he wondered if he should see a shrink.

Kim was beautiful, had a good job and a kind nature. He would mess this up for sure. He had to stop comparing her to Heather, move on and work on this relationship. Make it work and not smother it with ridiculous thoughts of a girl he hadn't seen in over five years. A girl that dumped him without a word and couldn't care enough to at least explain why, or say good-bye.

Kim would never do that to him. Heather obviously used him to escape her horrible life. What an ass. The gifts he bought her, the dinners, and trips to the beach and dance clubs. He treated her like a princess, but every night she still went home to Lance.

What a chump he was. She never planned to leave Lance. What a great act she put on. It was all clear now. When they worked at Northford she blew him off all the time. Years later, she's suddenly interested?

Was it just for sex? She said it was horrible with Lance, his selfishness in the bedroom, his awkward actions and positions. Had she used him for sex?

Probably not, but the second she finished school and landed a job, she dumped him. Perfect timing. Just some loser that helped her burn off some steam. Was it always her plan to go back to Lance? Had she lied to Nicolo? Yes. She moved on to a stable life, one with security. Not some unpredictable one he would give her.

But what about that last time on the beach? The night she said she loved him and would leave Lance for him? Just another act? She never called Nicolo after that night. Was that her way of delivering the final blow? But why? Was he that pathetic?

She was who he compared all potential wives to? Was he insane? He was done. This had to end. From this day forward, any thoughts of Heather he would squash.

****

Nicolo helped Kim out of the car with the Christmas presents for his family. The arctic blasts threatened to slam the door back into her, but he held it tight as she balanced herself and the gift bags. Her high heels caught in the cracks between the walkway and she wobbled the rest of the way to the door.

"Nervous?" he asked

"A little. Do you think they'll like me?"

"Like you? They'll love you." He leaned in and kissed her on her cold lips. "Come on, it's freezing. Let's go before those toes of yours get frost bit."

Nicolo juggled the gifts in his left hand and then opened the front door of his parent's home with the other. Kim stepped in first and then waited for him to follow. Heat from the oven hit them immediately. Garlic and tomato sauce drifted through the air along with his mother's pine-scented air fresheners that she always hid behind their fake Christmas tree. He swore he'd buy a real Christmas tree when he owned his own home.

The two of them veered into the kitchen and found his mother positioning button mushrooms on the antipasto platter. Prosciutto and salami competed for space with the green and black olives. Nicolo popped an artichoke heart in his mouth, then grabbed a toothpick with a slice of mozzarella and roasted red pepper on it.

"Hey, stop ruining the beautiful platter mom slaved over." Dino slapped him on the back and then they both hugged. "Merry Christmas."

"Merry Christmas," Nicolo said. "And I'd like you all to meet Kim."

Everyone dropped what they were doing and faced her. His father put down his beer and his mother rushed over and secured Kim's hands inside hers. "Welcome Kim. Nice to finally meet you."

Dino and Carissa followed, and their son Dante took a step forward, peered down at his feet, then ran back into the living room. Their daughter Mariana crawled in between Dino's legs. Grandparents, uncles and aunts soon joined in and Kim struggled to remember all their names.

After everyone devoured the antipasto platter, Nicolo's mother led them to the tree to open presents.

Tiny white lights twinkled on the tree. The wooden Christmas manger with its porcelain figurines still looked the same. Dino and he used to pretend one of the three kings was a bad guy who kidnapped Jesus and they had to ride on the animals to save him. Dino always grabbed the donkey, leaving Nicolo to ride on the small sheep.

He glanced over at Dino and mouthed, "Jerk." Dino's face puzzled and he held up his palms. Nicolo snorted and then finished off his beer.

Nicolo's' parents opened the Mikasa vase that Kim bought them. His mother broke into ridiculous tears and his father took the vase away from her, rolling his eyes at how emotional she gets.

Dante tore apart his gift from Nicolo and Kim. The Thomas the Tank engine lit up his eyes, and he flew off the wood floor with it held high. "Thomas! Thomas!" he screamed for the next two minutes. Nicolo couldn't wait until he opened up the huge track set.

Mariana sucked on the edge of the box that her Kick and Play Crib-Piano came in while they inserted the batteries. Her hands flapped and her legs jerked when the sounds and lights finally came on.

Kim had wanted to buy them both clothing from her children's department, but he refused to be that 'boring uncle' that bought them clothes.

An hour later, the piles of torn wrapping paper made their way into the giant, black garbage bag, and the gifts escaped to various corners of the living room. Kim turned toward Nicolo and handed him a rectangular box.

"Wait, I have mine too," he said.

He unwrapped his first. A cool looking black-and-green fabric Swatch watch. "Awesome," he said.

"It's water resistant, has a stop watch, back light and an alarm. I thought it would be perfect for your runs and bike races."

"Definitely." He removed it from the box and slapped it on his wrist. Was it a peace offering since she admitted she hated everything about the gym and could she please, please not go anymore? He wanted it to be something they did together, but decided that as long as she didn't drag him into the city every weekend, she didn't have to go anymore.

He placed a small box in front of her and admired how much he improved with his gift-wrapping. She stuck the bow in his hair and ripped open the red paper. After removing the cover, she drew in a breath of air. "Oh, Nic, it's beautiful."

A teardrop, aquamarine crystal hung from a wrap of sterling-silver wire. He helped her undo the clasp and surrounded her neck with the bright silver chain. "Your birthstone. I looked it up. It matches your eyes too."

"You're incredible." She leaned in and kissed him long and lingering. Happy and content, he consumed her. He let his fingers comb through her long hair and pulled her locks forward covering both their faces. He enjoyed watching her stand in his bedroom naked, her hair cascading over her breasts and down over her belly button like Lady Godiva. Her white skin contrasting with the darkness of her hair.

Their sex life had improved after a slow start. Her shyness with her body persuaded him to take her to the gym in the first place. Kim, like all the others, except for that insane Deidre, wanted the lights off, the curtains drawn, and her shirt to remain on, under the covers.

Soon Kim agreed to let him light a candle or two. After several months of compliments and purchasing outfits from Victoria Secrets, she let him turn on his bathroom light. Although not muscular, she was slim and had perfectly round, huge breasts.

After a romp in his bedroom, one afternoon, when the wind repeatedly blew the blinds back and forth allowing light to stream in, she loosened up. On her next visit, he whipped the blinds open smack in the middle of an intense round on his couch, and she didn't complain as the sunlight spilled across her body and he brought her to orgasm.

She had laid across from him on the opposite side of the couch, naked. Sweat glistened off her breasts as he examined her. She tried to catch her breath, but couldn't, and panted instead, her thighs still open, exposing her hot glory. He extended his legs and spread her thighs wider. "See," he said. "Look how beautiful you are."

Kim didn't budge. She sucked in air and blew it out just as fast. She threw her head back and mumbled, "I hate you," and then laughed.

After dessert, Dino and Nicolo let the ladies talk while they hung out in their old bedrooms, still untouched and perfectly preserved, in case either decided to move back home.

"Remember this?" Nicolo reached into his closet and removed a box labeled *Jaws*.

"Oh, man. You had to fish for all that broken crap inside his mouth."

"The fish bones were the worst."

"Nah, I always thought the anchor sucked."

"Where is that piece?" Nicolo searched inside. "You probably hid it so you could win."

"Fuck, yeah. Couldn't let my little brother win."

They laughed like a bunch of eight-year-olds and then Nicolo chucked the game back in the closet.

"So, Kim, huh? How's it going?"

"Good, real good."

"You guys gonna tie the knot or what? I'm two kids and a house ahead of you."

"Please, it's only been seven months. I dated Deidre longer."

"Deidre was messed up. What the fuck was that? Was she a stripper or something?"

Nicolo smirked and looked away. "Something like that."

"She was, wasn't she? I knew it."

"Why? You saw her perform somewhere?"

"Yeah, like that'd go over well with Carissa. No, she was just always biting your ear and sitting on your lap like your pants were undone and you were doing her."

"What? Don't exaggerate."

"I'm not. She was some kind of nympho. Mom almost had a heart attack. I heard her praying in her room one night."

Nicolo threw his NY Giant's pillow at Dino and landed it square in his face. "Stupid."

"I kid you not. Praying to God that you'd find a good woman to marry."

"All right, enough. Look, Kim's great, but I'm not rushing into anything. She's only twenty-six and it's not like her baby clock's ticking. The first six months are the easiest. After that, you learn a hell of a lot more about the person. Everything comes out, ya know?"

"Yeah, I hear you."

Carissa walked in with Dante in her arms. "You want to get going? He's getting irritable."

"No, I'm not." Dante rubbed his eyes with Thomas still glued to his hand.

"Yeah, sure." Dino stood from the bed.

"Where's Kim?"

"She's talking to your mom. She's really...sweet."

"Yeah, sweet. That's what everyone says."

"She's a real sweetheart, don't lose her." Dino added.

"Kim looks familiar, don't you think?" Carissa eyed Dino.

"What's vamilar, mommy?"

"Familiar. It means when someone looks like someone else."

"Oh," Dante yawned.

Dino grabbed Dante from Carissa's arms. Dino and Carissa stared at one another.

"Oh, yeah?" Nicolo said. "Who?"

Chapter 26

Heather

Heather sprinted into the house and dumped the party favors onto the kitchen table. A Laa-Laa Teletubby fell out of the bag and dragged a pink-and-white, polka dot #1 birthday candle with it. Then she spied the white plastic bag on the chair. *Damn.* She forgot to mail the invitations for Gia's birthday party during her errands. In no mood to drive to the post office, she hoped the mailman had not yet delivered the mail.

Gia's party was in two weeks and she prayed the weather in April would be warm enough for guests to venture into the backyard for a little while. Forsythias, and hopefully her tulips, would greet their guests. The weeping cherry was due to bloom as well. Laurel helped her plant bulbs and perennials around their home last fall, and gardening became Heather's new passion.

Laurel's first birthday had over forty guests, but now with new acquaintances, family and friends bringing children, and neighbors whom they had become close with, the list exceeded sixty. Laurel insisted on the Telletubbies theme since it was Gia's favorite. Heather knew Gia had no clue what danced or sang inside that square box. Gia only flailed her arms while Laurel sang the theme song. At least Laurel had forgotten about Thomas and the Tank.

Heather piled the party favors in the den with the matching tablecloths, napkins, dinnerware and balloons. She heard a familiar truck outside and remembered the invitations. She scooped the bag into her arms and ran to the porch.

The mailman hiked up her walkway and waved hello. Heather exchanged her stack of invites for today's mail. "Thank you, Eddie. You saved me a trip."

"Anytime." He smiled.

Heather reentered the house and then made herself a cup of coffee. She overloaded it with sugar and half-n-half and then sifted through the mail. She threw the circulars into the recycling bin and then whizzed the junk mail in the same box. A large, blue envelope stood out. Her teeth clenched. The return address read: Bianca and Anthony Milanesi.

What now? All this woman did was plan gatherings. It was obvious she had no real friends and invited people to her home as a charade. The more parties, the more guests, and the world would envy how popular she was. What ridiculous celebration would it be this time? The red-vested Robin taking flight and ushering in spring?

Heather ripped open the thick envelope and removed the fancy invitation. A square of blue tissue paper fluttered to her feet. Heather's Tinky Winky invites looked cheap compared to this grand piece. She held up the heavy document with its gold lettering, and read.

Bianca and Anthony Milanesi
are celebrating their son Lance's new job as
Senior Associate at Weiner and Raper Law Firm.
Please join us as we celebrate a new chapter in his life,
at our home, on Saturday, April 10th, 1999,
at twelve o'clock noon, for lunch.

Heather crumpled the envelope in her left hand and dropped the invite in her right. It careened to the floor and lay face up, mocking her. She didn't! Heather clenched her eyes and fist, wanting her body to implode.

She snatched the phone off the wall and dialed Bianca's number. Anger propelled her, but fear took over when the ringing stopped.

"Hello, Bianca speaking."

"How...could you," she hesitated.

"Pardon me? Who is this?"

"You know darn well who this is. How dare you throw Lance a party on the same day as Gia's."

"What are you talking about?"

"Gia's first birthday. The party, it's on the 10th."

"Well, how am I supposed to know that? Did you send an

invitation?"

Heather glanced at the now empty kitchen chair, the mailman long gone. "Her birthday is the 11th. I told you last weekend over dinner that I was having the party on the 10th."

"I never received an invite. It's truly not my fault, Heather. Maybe you should have mailed them sooner."

"You had professional invitations made. You knew it was her birthday and knew I was having the party that day. You did this on purpose."

"How dare you raise your voice to me. Who do you think you're speaking to?"

Heather tried to calm down. "What am I supposed to do now?"

"Have it the following week."

"It's Easter, and I just mailed the invites today."

"Then I guess you'll have to go ahead with your party. Unfortunately, I already received quite a few responses and it appears that everyone will be coming to my house that day."

"How can I have her party if her father won't be here?"

"You can still have your family and friends."

Heather plopped into the kitchen chair. She arched forward and rubbed her forehead.

"Heather, it's not like she's going to remember. She's one."

"That's not the point. It's her first birthday."

"Answer me this. Who do you think will care more? An infant that has no clue what's going on, one who will whine the entire time and then fall asleep half way through the party, or Lance, a man that has achieved great success that will affect all of you?"

"Don't turn this around on me. You did this on purpose and you know it. I told you the date on Sunday, there was a whole discussion during dinner. I told you I was mailing the invites this weekend. When will you stop?"

Snickering made its way through the phone. Pitches of breath hissed into the mouthpiece. "Heather, you have disgraced this family and you are a constant embarrassment. Luckily, I put an end to all the gallivanting you used to do. What *were* you doing and whom were you doing it with? Perhaps, to pay for all your college loans, you went into prostitution?"

Heather's head whipped up, she couldn't speak. Her ribs tightened, squeezing her heart.

"You do not appreciate what you have Heather. You take Lance for granted and try in every way to embarrass him. He has worked hard to get where he is today. You only drag him down and humiliate him. Humiliate me. One day you will surrender, be the wife he deserves, put him on that pedestal. Until then, you are forewarned."

Chapter 27

Nicolo

Nicolo unlocked the door to his apartment and threw his keys on the end table. He rubbed his temples to relieve the stress from his day. His long day. He wasn't sure what was worse, the days that dragged on with no problems, his partner and him just sitting around talking about crap, or the days when the action was nonstop. Fights, arrests, paperwork.

The worst had to be all the negative bullshit in the world. Whether it was a simple fender-bender or a domestic dispute where kids were involved, everyone was so angry. Yelling and blaming. Screaming, even after you asked them multiple times to calm down.

Nicolo wanted peace, in his job, his home life. Quiet.

He kicked off his shoes eyeing the television. Maybe he could watch a National Geographic special on fly bacteria. Something to put him to sleep.

He flipped on the TV, collapsed on the couch, and adjusted the pillow behind his head.

Click.

Nicolo spun his head toward the other side of the apartment. What was that?

Snap. Then, the *clip clop* of...shoes? What the—

Nicolo jumped up from the couch. Whoever they were, they were in the kitchen now. He crept toward the noise. Was it maintenance? He didn't get a notice they were repairing anything.

Two steps before he reached the kitchen entrance, a figure came barreling at him. *Smack*, right into the intruder. Pain shot across his chest. Nicolo stumbled back, then his eyes widened and he lunged forward.

Kim tumbled back and fell to the ground, hitting her head on the counter.

"I'm so sorry. I didn't know it was you." He rushed over to her.

"I thought I was alone, then I heard the TV and I was scared."

"I thought someone broke in. Are you okay?" He held out his hand for Kim, then hugged her.

"I'm fine, just shaken up."

Nicolo rubbed the back of her head, the smell of hairspray apparent, then pulled back. "How'd you get in?"

"You...you gave me your key on Saturday."

"Oh, yeah. I did but, I...well are you okay? I mean, I gave it to you in case you ever got here before me, but I wasn't expecting you today."

"Is it a problem? You said you were working late and I thought I'd bring some dinner for us and—"

"No, it's fine. I guess I was just surprised. I had a bad day and..."

"You were hoping to be alone. I'm sorry. I messed up. I should have called. I thought it would be a nice surprise after a long day."

Nicolo huffed. He was being an ass. A dog-tired one, but still an ass. "It's great. Really. Picking up take-out is great. I probably wouldn't have eaten otherwise."

"Actually, I made dinner. I had off so I prepared a pot roast with mashed potatoes and green beans and then I made a Bundt cake at home and brought it all over and—"

"Oh. Cool." *So much for sleep.*

"And look, I brought over this new brand of potato chips." Kim grabbed a large bag from the counter and held it up.

"I don't eat chips."

"But this one you can. It's WOW! Potato chips. They're fat-free made from something called Olestra. It inhibits you from absorbing any fat, so you can eat the entire bag. I thought we could try them together."

"But they're still chips."

"I also brought over some wine and was about to put the food in the oven to heat it up. You can help me set the table." Kim marched back into the kitchen before he could answer.

He stood frozen in the hallway, and stared into the kitchen. Pots and pans clanged against the oven rack. Nicolo glanced back at the TV. The news was on. The reporter spoke while police and ambulance lights flashed in the background.

The couch looked more comfortable now than before.

Nicolo finished setting the table and then sat back on the couch. Kim joined him when the food began simmering. She seized the remote, changed the channel, and put on *The Nanny*.

"I hate this show. That voice."

"It's hysterical, are you kidding?" Kim plopped herself on the couch and edged closer to Nicolo until their hips touched. Her elbow dug into his stomach. She bent over for the bag of chips and ripped the top open. "Wanna try one?"

"No, I'm waiting for dinner."

Kim took a handful of chips and crammed them into her mouth. "Mmm, delicious. You should try them." She inched closer, her shoulder now resting on his. She kicked off her shoes and bent her legs up so that her feet rested on the couch. She tossed a few more chips into her mouth and sipped at her wine. "Ooh! I also got a manicure and pedicure today. Want to see?"

"Um, sure."

Kim fluttered her fingers in front of Nicolo and then held up her ten toes and wiggled them.

"Very...nice. Pretty." Is that what he was supposed to say?

"Hey, your neighbor Ethan, did you see his new girlfriend?"

"Yes, he introduced me the other day."

"I saw them when I was carrying all that *heavy* food into your apartment. On my *second* trip up the stairs, I saw them walking out of his apartment."

"Did he introduce you?"

"Yes, her name is Diane." Kim twisted around to face Nicolo. "What did you think of her?"

Nicolo flinched. It was one of those trick questions. "She seemed nice."

"Just nice?"

"It was only a quick introduction. I didn't have a conversation with them."

"What about the way she looked? Did you think she was hot?"

Nicolo sat up straight. Fran Drescher let out a loud honk and waved her hand. He tried to focus on the TV and not Kim. "I don't remember."

"You don't remember if she was hot?"

"It was a long day at work. I wasn't focused on his girlfriend."

"It's not a focus question, just yes or no? Hot is something quite noticeable."

He searched for the pillow again and hugged it against his ribs as a shield. "No then."

"Why'd you pause? You're not lying are you?"

She might be more open in the bedroom, but her insecurity still loomed. "Kim, I did not think she was hot. I didn't even notice her, so obviously she wasn't hot."

Kim reached for another handful of chips. "I thought she was hot."

Nicolo shifted on the couch, the scent of onions filled the room. "The pot roast smells great. It's filling the whole apartment. Smells like a Christmas feast."

"Which reminds me, did you think of what you'd like to do this weekend? It's your turn to choose and it's supposed to be really warm."

"Carissa asked if we could watch Dante and Mariana on Saturday. They have a surprise 40th birthday to go to. I said, yes."

Kim made a face as if he had asked her to go mud wrestling with a pack of flamingoes.

"What's wrong? That's okay, isn't it?"

"Didn't we just watch them?"

"Two months ago. They don't really get out much. And hey, one day they return the favor and watch ours."

She raised her eyebrows but her view remained on the TV. Was she annoyed with him? She chucked another handful of chips in her mouth and then drowned them with the rest of her wine. Kim got up and then stomped into the kitchen. "The food should be just about ready now."

Did she have a problem with their kids? They were so well behaved. Nicolo flung his pillow across the couch. It laid there happy and content, unlike him.

He helped Kim serve the food on the plates and then poured a glass of water for himself. The food was delicious. The pot roast melted in his mouth, hot gravy slid the meat down even easier. Mashed potatoes were similar to his moms. Green beans, crisp and not boiled to a pile of mush. The flavors mixed in his mouth and quieted his stomach.

After Nicolo washed the dishes, Kim cut pieces of the plain, vanilla Bundt cake for the two of them.

"We should top it with strawberries and blueberries." He opened the fridge. "I picked some up from the supermarket last night."

"Berries?" Kim scrunched her nose. "On a Bundt cake?"

"Sure, it makes it even better." Nicolo poured some over his piece and dug in with the fork, shoving a large bite into his mouth.

"Are you saying it's bad?"

"No! I'm just always looking for ways to make things healthier."

"Bundt cake doesn't get berries. I did bring some whipped topping though." Kim reached into the refrigerator and brought the tub to him.

Nicolo lifted it to his eyes and read the food label. This time, his nose scrunched.

"What now?" Kim jammed her hands on her hips.

"Nothing, I just like to read these, that's all." Nicolo examined the ingredients. Hydrogenated vegetable oil, high fructose corn syrup, xanthan and guar gums, polysorbate? "No thanks. I think I'll stick with my berries."

Kim slapped a dollop of the whipped topping on her slice and then plopped two more on that one. He wondered how she stayed so thin with all the crap she ate. And no exercise.

She finished her piece faster than he did, then stood to wash the plate. He downed his last bite and followed her back to the sink. When he dried the last dish, Kim's eyes widened. She shifted on her feet and then placed her hand on her stomach.

"You okay?" he asked.

"Yes, of course." She turned away and took a few steps back toward the kitchen table. Then clutched the chair. She squeezed the top rail, her fingers clenching as if she was crushing a wad of paper in her fist. "I'm just going to use the bathroom." Kim raced away without looking.

Nicolo took off, back to his couch. His pillow was in the spot he wanted to be in. He laughed at his jealousy of the inanimate object, then took a flying leap and landed next to it. He snatched it back up, laid down and hugged it. He searched for the blanket his mother crocheted but it was on the recliner across the room.

He was lucky to have found Kim. They never had one fight over the past year. That says something, doesn't it? They say it's supposed to be easy in the beginning, and it was. They ignored each other's differences and found a happy middle ground every time. That's compromising, right?

Love must be when you find someone you're comfortable with. No drama, no headaches. Nice, calm and laid-back moments in your life. It balanced out the chaos from work. Peaceful evenings, diplomatic discussions, relaxing afternoons. There were no fiascos in this relationship.

He reached for the TV's remote control, but before he could turn it on, he heard a moan. Then another. Then...what was that? A deck of cards being shuffled? Some kind of trumpet?

Nicolo jumped up from the couch again and stepped toward his front door. What now? The walls in this apartment were way too thin. Was someone releasing the air from balloons? He opened the door, but no one was in the hallway. He closed it and stood in the center of the room.

Then it came again. From the bathroom. What the..? He stepped closer to the door and once near, he knew. The gurgling echoed. He snuck back to the couch and flicked the TV on. Then raised the volume. A lot.

Nicolo eyed the empty bag of potato chips on the cocktail table. He read the back of it. *This Product Contains Olestra. Olestra may cause abdominal cramping and loose stools.*

Shit. This evening was turning into a disaster. Nicolo took the pillow and dug his face into it.

Chapter 28

Heather

Heather sat in the cafeteria across from Rebecca, a social worker from her floor who she quickly became chummy with when she returned from maternity leave, over three and a half years ago. Sitting with Samantha or Cara one more day, one more hour, made coming into work impossible.

Rebecca was six years older and had three children. Normally, Rebecca ate lunch at her desk, but Heather convinced her to have lunch one day and for over three years now, they spent their days bashing their husbands, venting about their kids, and sharing parenting tips. Their friendship grew and Rebecca became another blessing in her life.

They also compared mother-in-law stories. Rebecca hated hers as well. Heather's favorite story was the year Rebecca decided to trick Louise, her mother-in-law, who criticized her cooking no matter what she prepared.

One year, after several references to the tasteless food, how she starved her husband with her poison, the lack of fresh ingredients, and then went as far as to compare her meals to Delancey's Crown Restaurant, and how she should take lessons from them since they were by far the greatest Irish restaurant on Long Island, Rebecca decided it was time to take action.

After Louise condemned the entire Sunday meal, from the rotten appetizers straight through to the horrible dessert, Rebecca stood with the empty plate from the devoured Irish Whisky cake and beamed. In front of Louise's entire family, Rebecca informed her that Delancey's Crown Restaurant had catered the entire meal.

Rebecca's father-in-law broke into hysterics. "She got you," he said, pounding his fist on the table.

Rebecca inspired Heather. She wished she could be more assertive, and armed with the same quick comebacks.

She stilled feared Bianca, and with that fear, Lance became more powerful. She wondered if Lance's lack of interaction with Laurel and Gia had to do with Bianca's bombardment of snippy attacks against the kids, in addition to her constant reminder to Lance that he had a reputation to uphold if he was to succeed in this world.

"Behavior that goes unchallenged goes unchanged," Rebecca would tell her. Heather just found it easier to take the girls to a children's puppet show or Chuck E Cheeses and avoid them both. Parks and beaches were also great escapes. Rebecca reminded her frequently that escaping didn't solve any problems, it only made it more difficult to conquer them when they arose.

Heather wished she could run off and hide on a deserted island somewhere away from all the people that drained her. For now, Rebecca made work manageable, and her daughters made their home enjoyable. She tried to look at the positive things in her life.

On a balmy Tuesday in June, Rebecca and Heather sat on the opposite side of the cafeteria from Samantha and Cara. The two desperate girls struck up conversations with every new resident that strolled into the room. They leaned in frequently and whispered, glanced around at any eligible bachelors, and pointed at a few, hiding their childish giggles.

"How do you put up with them?" Rebecca asked, cutting into her pecan stuffed chicken breast. The spinach and dried cranberries tumbled onto her plate releasing the aromas.

"I only ate lunch with them the first six months they were here. I've been sitting with you ever since."

"Still, I wouldn't last a day. When you were off yesterday, Cara sat at your desk and talked on the phone all afternoon."

"That's all she does. I don't think she even goes into the patients' rooms. She figured out a way to write vague notes in the charts, making it appear like she did. *Patient on Regular diet. Tolerating well. Will follow.* I could do that too.

Dr. Barnett, one of the new residents, in his finely starched lab coat, rushed through the door towards the hot food counter. Samantha gasped, then whacked Cara in the shoulder.

"Don't you feel like you're back in high school?" Rebecca asked.

"I don't think they ever left."

Samantha removed her lab coat and unbuttoned one of the top buttons on her shirt. She borrowed Cara's pocket mirror and picked food out of her front tooth. For a full minute. What was stuck in there, a leg of lamb? She fixed her hair so that each highlighted piece laid in perfection succession.

"Do you believe this shit?" Rebecca said. "Watch this." Rebecca released her spicy ginger-red curls from the plastic hair-claw and stood. She thrust her chest out and strutted over to Dr. Barnett. What was she doing?

Rebecca tapped him on the shoulder and an exaggerated grin exploded across her face. He mirrored her by flashing his teeth, like a row of French nail tips. Her arms flung wildly as if she was warning him about a hurricane that was about to touch land. He let out a roar and Rebecca clutched onto his shoulder.

Heather's face stretched back like a bad facelift and she shook her head in disbelief. Rebecca was at it again. What the hell was she doing? Asking him out?

Samantha's face tightened and squeezed, she could have made a mean batch of lemonade. Cara, with her gritted teeth, egged her on.

Rebecca finished her stage performance by whipping out her business card. She scribbled on the back, then slapped his arm and projected her fake laugh clear across the cafeteria. What could she possibly be doing? She returned to the table, oblivious to the venom hurled at her from snarling teeth.

"What on earth did you say to him?" Heather asked.

Rebecca continued her dramatic presentation by tossing out another hoot and waving her hand at Heather as if she couldn't stop laughing.

"Tell me! Did you tell him you thought he was cute? Give him your number? Told him to call you if he was free? What did you say?"

Rebecca glared back at Samantha and Cara, then leaned in to whisper at Heather. "I just told him that Mrs. Vincent, the 102-year-old on our floor, thought he was the sweetest thing since her mother's marmalade. She just adored his bedside manner."

Heather shook her head in admiration. Rebecca held her hand in the air for a high five. "You're too much," Heather said.

****

Heather returned to her nurses' station and checked the two lists she had posted on the corkboard. One titled, *Let me know if any patients may benefit from a nutritional supplement* and the other labeled, *Have any of our patients lost weight?*

Heather called out to Otis, one of the nurses' aides on the floor. "Mr. Samuelson's not really eating?"

"Nah, he only ate farina at breakfast and a piece of stew for lunch. Maybe a little apple juice."

"Okay, I'll make sure he gets a Health Shake for dinner."

Otis gave her a thumbs-up. "Oh, and 818b was askin' for some info on gout."

"Gout? I haven't given out literature on that in years. Let me see if I can find it. They have medication for everything nowadays."

Heather searched her desk, looking through folders with yellowing paperwork, long forgotten diet copies, and outdated research articles. She thought she had an old copy of the diet somewhere. Granted, it was probably from 1987, but possibly, it still held some helpful advice.

She yanked out a red folder on the bottom of the dust-filled shelf and rummaged through it until she came to the back. A crumbled sheet lay there, forgotten. Her resume. Something she planned to update during her free time, but she could never think of leaving Rebecca now.

Heather found the diet, photocopied the discolored sheet to make it appear new and entered 818b's room.

"Hello, Mrs. Davis? I'm Heather the dietitian." Her usual cheery grin emerged. "You asked for a copy of a gout diet?"

The woman sat with her bare feet propped up on two pillows. Peeling cracked feet, adorned with corns and bunions, met her gaze a few seconds before the stench hit her nose. "It's about time," she hollered. "I asked for this over an hour ago."

"I'm sorry. I was just informed. Can I go over it with you now?" Heather wondered if they expected doctors to run into their rooms that fast.

The woman glared at her. "Well, don't just stand there looking stupid. Read."

When did Heather become the magnet for abuse?

****

Heather carried the veggie platter out of the kitchen and stopped in the den to shut off the TV that Laurel and Gia had left on. Brooke sat outside at the patio table, her arms and legs crossed, her eyes squinted and her lips pursed. She looked like someone tied her in a strait jacket and fed her some Sour Patch Kids candies.

Heather slid the screen door to the right and spied Jacob and

Daniel sitting on the stoop, hands in their laps and frozen as if a professional photographer waited to snap their picture. They both wore matching white shorts and pink Ralph Lauren polo shirts. Their white boat shoes and pink socks completed the look of a commercial advertising 'Come vacation on Long Island where you can sail our beautiful waters.'

Jacob was five-and-a-half and Daniel turned three this month. Heather was happy their children were close in age, both only a few months apart from each other. They were able to share in each other's pregnancies, and raising their children together meant a lot to her.

Heather placed the veggie platter in front of Brooke. "Come on boys, I have some snacks."

"They don't eat vegetables." Brooke waved her hand at her.

"None? These are raw. Perfect crunching foods."

"They won't touch them and I have no time to fight with them."

"But that's your job, as a mother. To feed them healthy foods and teach them what's right." Heather flung a baby carrot into her mouth and then ripped the cover off the dip. "You can have them help you cook and then they'll think it's fun. They'll want to taste it."

"I don't cook anymore. I have Inez do it."

Inez was Brooke's nanny. She failed to see why she needed one since Brooke didn't work. "Maybe Inez can have the boys help cook and she can teach them."

"She has no time for games. She has to cook and clean the house and watch the boys as well."

Isn't that what all mothers did? Even ones that worked? "Well maybe if you asked—"

"Carrots!" Laurel shrieked. She dug in, grabbing four baby carrots. She snatched a cherry tomato and then tossed it three feet in the air and caught it in her mouth.

"She never misses," Heather said. "I don't know how she does it."

"You must be so proud." Brooke looked away and pretended to adjust her dress.

Gia skipped over to them and looked into the platter. She grabbed a broccoli spear and held it in the air like she was the Statue of Liberty. Gia had on a yellow-and-black polka dot shirt, red leggings, a pink tutu and no shoes. Her feet were black.

Laurel grabbed another tomato and flung it in her mouth.

"Girls, why don't you take Jacob and Daniel to play on your swing set?"

Brooke's head whipped up. "Is it clean?"

"The swing set?" Heather's face knotted.

"I mean, is it dusty and full of dirt?"

"Well, I haven't gotten around to...furniture polishing it lately. It did rain the other day, though, so I think that—"

"Has the rain been wiped off? You know how slides are. The tops always have pools of water on them."

"Mommy made a cool water slide last week," Gia said.

"Yeah, she took the hose and hung it over the top of the metal bar thing and then faced it to the slide and then turned the hose on and it shot all over and when you went down it wet you and it was cold, but then it was warm and then the bottom got all muddy and we were sliding in mud and it was fun and—"

"Um, I don't think so boys. Better stay here with mommy."

Heather frowned. "And do what, watch us? Listen to us talk?"

"I don't want their new clothes to get dirty, that's all."

"Then why did you dress them like that? You should have thrown on their play clothes."

"Those are them." Brooke fingered a celery stick and bit off a tiny fragment.

"What do they usually do for fun?"

"Educational toys, of course. We just bought them both LeapPads."

"I mean, what do they do outside?"

"I think once in a while Inez pulls them in the wagon that Clifford's parents bought them."

Heather leaned back in the patio chair, put her leg up on the other chair and stared. Her mouth threatened to open, but she forced herself to clench her teeth instead.

"Can't we open up this umbrella? The sun is so..."

"It's gorgeous out. They're saying seventy-three degrees for today, and with all the rain we had this month..."

Brooke ignored Heather and studied the top of the umbrella.

Heather huffed. She bent forward and cranked the handle on the umbrella as fast as she could, rotating the lever in furious bursts. The umbrella opened and smacked into Brooke's face.

"Oh!" Brooke shot up, causing her chair to fly back and crash to the floor. Her boys giggled.

Gia rocketed past them with a sword in her hand. "Ninja!" Her hair had fallen out of her ponytail and hung loose, draped across her face. She had a diamond-and-ruby tiara on her head instead.

"I wanna play ninja." Jacob ran over to his mom.

"I don't think it's a very safe game."

"It's just a foam sword," Heather scoffed.

Laurel ran towards the table, grabbed another tomato, threw it up high and caught it in her mouth, again. Her Barbie Rapunzel shirt was now on backwards.

"I want a tomato," Jacob said.

"Me too," Daniel followed.

Jacob grabbed a tomato, threw it over six feet into the air, and on its way down, it struck Brooke on her head.

"Jacob!" She toppled backward and swatted her hair as if the tomato had exploded and spewed its contents all over her. "Go! Go play, just go."

"That's all it takes to get you riled up?" Heather kicked the red ball into the bushes.

"A tomato just hit me in the head! Did you not just see it?"

Heather chuckled. "Do you remember Bobby Robinson's party in ninth grade? He got so high he started chucking gummy bears at everyone and they stuck in Lonnie Fischer's birds nest hair?" Heather curled over holding her stomach. "And then...Lonnie tried to remove it, but she didn't see...what was his name...the big guy with the red hair...anyway, she trips over him and lands on the couch where Kelly and Brian were making out and spilled his beer down her shirt..and—" Heather laughed until tears fell down her face. "You were sitting on the floor and you picked up one of the gummy bears and started eating it—"

"I did not!"

"You totally did. You were so stoned. You refused to eat before the party so you could fit into those jeans and..." Heather couldn't speak anymore. She gasped for air and tears dropped out of her eyes faster than she could wipe them.

"I don't remember any of this."

"I'm sure you don't." Heather snorted.

Gia came running from the driveway, stopped, and looked at her mom. "Mommy, why you crying?"

"I'm not sweetie, I'm laughing. Haven't laughed this hard since high school."

"What's high school?" Gia asked.

"A place where big, dumb teenagers go." Laurel whacked Heather in the head with her sword.

"Be careful," Heather said. "I never lose a sword fight." She flinched and the two girls dashed off, their shrieks filled the air.

"I need a drink," Brooke said.

"Really?"

"There's too much commotion and disorganization."

"It's lunch, in my backyard. Should I have a schedule of events?"

"I'm just not used to this. Can I have the drink?"

Heather shook her head. "Do you want a beer?"

"Beer? I haven't had a beer since college. Have any wine?"

"You want me to open a bottle of wine? At twelve noon?"

"Is that a problem?"

"No, it's just that I don't drink wine, but if you want it, I'll search for a bottle opener."

"No, no, it's fine. Do you have any rum or vodka?"

Jeez, Brooke was a real boozer, eh? "Yes, but I don't think we have anything to mix it with."

"Soda, juice, anything."

"We don't drink soda or juice. The girls have never had it."

Brooke tossed a baffled look at Heather. "How could they've never had soda or juice?"

"Empty calories, all sugar."

"And people say I'm a strict mother." Brooke looked away, nose in the air.

"I'll look for something." Heather stepped into the den closing the screen behind her, then went into the dining room, opened their liquor cabinet and searched through the bottles. In the back was a plastic jug of cranberry juice. She checked the expiration date.

She placed the juice on top of the table and searched for a bottle of vodka. After pushing aside the rum, she saw the bottle of Cuervo. Nicolo shot into her mind.

Heather peeked out the window. Brooke was admiring her French manicure. Heather didn't even wear nail polish anymore. One less thing to do. Brooke reached into her duffle-bag-of-a-pocketbook, pulled out a mirror and inspected her teeth. How much celery could have wedged between her teeth with one nibble?

With the tequila lid cracked open, Heather took a quick swig. The liquid burned her mouth, killing any bacteria that threatened to linger there. She winced, swallowed, then shook her head, gasping for fresh air. *Wow! Good times.*

Heather moseyed outside with Brooke's cocktail and a bottle of Coors Light. "Vodka and cranberry. You used to drink these the summer before college, remember?"

"That was a long time ago."

"Feels like yesterday to me."

Brooke tipped the drink to her nose and sniffed it. Then took a nice long, lingering mouthful. Heather took a sip of her beer and caught Gia running behind the swing set. She was now naked, except for wearing one of the boy's pink polo shirts.

Heather rolled forward, choking. Some of the beer drooled down the side of her lip.

"Are you okay?" Brooke handed her a napkin.

"Yup, no problem." She wiped her mouth.

"So did you hear? Kelly and Alex are getting divorced."

"Really?" Heather raised her eyebrows. "I'm not surprised."

"Are you serious? They were the happiest couple we know."

"Yeah, right. Her, with her snooty, petite, party hors d'oeuvres and all that fake tittering, while Alex was off at strip clubs."

"Strip clubs? Heather don't exaggerate."

"I wasn't."

"You have a vivid imagination."

"Think what you want. It's a fact."

"Heather, the poor couple's getting a divorce and you're making jokes."

"It's not a joke. Why are you blowing it off?"

"If I was getting divorced, I'd be devastated and I wouldn't want people making up stories about me."

Heather grabbed another carrot and bit down on it in an exaggerated manner while staring at Brooke. "So. Moving on. How are you? What's new?"

"I've been elected as president of the PTA at Jacobs's school."

"Already?"

"It's extremely demanding. I have to elect members to serve on school leadership teams and community education councils. Hold meetings, elect future officers. The most arduous part is getting other parents involved in school activities like parent-teacher conferences, open houses and curriculum nights."

"It's not just licking envelopes?"

Brooke frowned. "No. Last year eleven of us spent almost three hours discussing which catalogue's we should use for prizes for the end of the year school carnival. It's very time consuming. I missed my yoga class that afternoon."

"Yoga, huh?"

"It relaxes me and keeps me in shape. It's a stressful world, but between yoga and Inez, I have peace and also time for myself and then of course, it only improves my sex life."

Daniel chased after Gia and darted behind the shed. It appeared they were playing hide-and-go-seek. Neither of them had shoes on now.

"You're still having great sex?"

"My sex life's incredible. We go at it for hours."

"You do?" Heather took a slug of her beer. She couldn't picture Clifford being good at anything except crunching numbers. It was amazing he knew what to do at all. You never know with those nerd types.

Heather only had sex with Lance once since Gia was born. Once was enough. It was awkward and made her want to vomit. She had just stepped out of the shower and Lance ambled over to her like he was Hugh Hefner, ripping the towel from her.

She had no idea where Laurel or Gia were since Lance was supposed to be watching them, but he wrapped his thick thighs around hers and steadily moved back, forcing her in the direction of the bed. Heather collided with the mattress, half on, half off, as he attempted to lie on top of her. She slid off the bed, her naked butt crashed with a *thud* onto the hardwood floor, and found Lance's crotch in her face. He tried to pull her back up, but his hands slipped from her wet skin and she smashed back onto the floor.

Heather righted herself and then he grabbed her right boob pulling it into him. She stood in the middle of the room, nude, while he slurped away in a disturbing manner. Was he always this bad?

Lance's hands reached under her armpits. He lifted her in the air and threw her onto the bed. She bounced as if on a trampoline and vaulted to the other side of the bed, landing back on the floor with a *thump*. Before she could get up, Lance had already sprinted around the bed with his pants dragging by his ankles. He shoved Heather over the mattress and entered her from behind, despite the dryness.

He pumped her like they were wild dogs, while her dripping hair stuck to her face, veiling her. She tried desperately to remove the strands of hair, but when her sight restored, he was already done.

"How often do you do it?" Heather asked

"What do you mean?" She took another sip from her glass. It was almost empty.

"You said you do it for hours, but how often?"

Brooke seemed bewildered, then refocused. "Oh, you mean Clifford and me. At least three times a week."

"Three times? A week?"

"Honey, I've always known how to please a man. They beg me for more."

Heather wrinkled her brow, then she heard Laurel scream, *charge!* from the front of the house.

"That's great, Brooke. Really."

"You and Lance don't have sex anymore?"

"Of course we do." Heather hated lying, but Brooke always made her feel like the disadvantaged of the two. Even in high school, Brooke had clothes that were more expensive, a bigger house with a pool, and a huge sweet-sixteen party at a dance club, where her parents invited their entire grade.

The time Nicolo and she had sex on the beach in some secluded dunes, entered her mind. She had to change the subject. "How are the boys doing?"

"Excellent. Jacob excelled in school last year."

"He was in kindergarten."

"Yes, but he can already read and write quite well."

"That's wonderful."

"Actually he's behind Daniel. We enrolled Daniel in an advanced preschool. He can already spell and write most colors and gets weekly spelling tests. He can count and write the numbers one to a hundred. For daily homework, he gets—"

"Homework?"

"Well, yes, Heather, how else do you expect him to remember what he learned in class?"

"Gia is just fooling around with blocks and puzzles, and playing dress up. She does know how to use a scissor pretty well, though."

"You must be very proud. No, we made the mistake of not putting Jacob in this program. We need to find something else to put him in so that Daniel doesn't exceed him."

"When do they have fun?"

"Who?"

"Your children."

"Fun? This is when they learn to grow into fine human beings. It's our duty to make sure of this. We are responsible for them, we have to teach them well and give them the proper tools they need to succeed."

"Kinda like not giving them soda and juice, right?"

Brooke rolled her eyes. "What does that have to do with anything? You are failing your daughters, Heather.

Was she? They weren't as advanced as Brooke's boys were. Maybe she should practice with them more. Buy some educational activity books. Sit down with them every night and study. Her sex life sucked too. Was that her fault as well? Maybe she needed to please Lance more in the bedroom. More? Hadn't it always been about him?

Brooke was succeeding in all aspects. Her well-pressed, lemon sundress, the designer sunglasses that Heather had no idea who manufactured, her golden sandals. President of the PTA. A nanny and a long list of prestigious friends, as well. What was Heather good at? She was apparently a failure as a wife and a mother.

Laurel flew by in her Rapunzel dress with a cowboy hat on her head. She carried a pail full of dirt and a purple shovel. Gia raced by them in nothing but her Thomas the Tank underwear. She held a jump rope in one hand, and her stuffed lizard tied to the end of a rope, in her other.

"Gia's potty trained already?" Brooke asked. "Isn't she two?"

Heather's pout turned around and she shook her head. "She turned three last month. You were at her party. And yes, she's been potty trained for over six months now. Isn't Daniel?"

"Well of course, Heather. Don't be ridiculous. I just forgot how old Gia was."

"Gia and Daniel are only six weeks apart, Brooke."

From around the corner came Jacob and Daniel. Jacob was shoeless, but wore Laurel's pink ballet costume from last year. On his head was a hat with a giant shark, which made it look as if it was eating his skull. He had a broken water gun in one hand and the foam sword in the other.

Daniel came last. He had a green, leprechaun top hat on and its matching orange beard around his chin. The only other thing he wore was a sopping wet, droopy diaper.

"Mommy, this is fun. Best playdate ever! Can we come back tomorrow?"

Brooke sprang from her chair in horror. Her hands flew over her mouth and her eyes broadened.

"Another vodka cranberry?" Heather asked.

Chapter 28

Nicolo

Nicolo opened his eye enough to see Kim slip on her pink sweater. He raised his head a few inches and grinned. "Time to go?"

"Yes. You slept right through my shower."

"So tired, I didn't even hear it." Nicolo glanced at the clock. Eight-thirty. Her strawberry shampoo drifted into his bedroom. "Late night for us. Too bad you don't have off. We could lie in bed all afternoon."

"Actually, I was thinking, Nic." She took a few steps closer and sat on the edge of the bed. He moved his legs to make room. "Since I'm at your apartment a lot and, well, I sleep here at least three times a week, shouldn't we, I mean, haven't you thought about me moving in?"

Nicolo sat up and rubbed his eyes. He dreaded this conversation. She had hinted for over six months now, but he ignored her remarks. Kim had her own apartment, loved her five-minute commute to work and she was good friends with her landlord, but after three years of dating, Nicolo knew he needed to make a decision. The fact that her three younger sisters were still single helped, but there was no getting around it any longer.

It wasn't that he didn't want her moving in. They spent all their free time together anyway. She grew to love the beach and he tolerated the vineyards. Her sisters, although loud, were as sweet as she was. The nights that he hung out with his niece and nephew, Kim went to the city with her sisters. They had their romantic nights alone, but she kept a few nights for herself.

But moving in meant the next step was inevitable. Only a matter of time.

"Do you want to?" Nicolo removed the covers from his body. "I mean, your commute to work will be longer."

"Only by ten minutes. I don't mind. Unless...you do?"

"No, it's a good thing, right?" Was he agreeing or waiting for a sign? He listened for a boom of thunder. Nothing.

"I think it'll be great." She leaped forward, landed on his blanket and hugged him. "I'm so excited. I'll tell my landlord right away."

****

Nicolo called Dino and asked to meet him for lunch. They parked themselves on a few bar stools in Shooters, a local pub near Dino's job. The intense sun streamed through the window that overlooked the main street. They ordered their meals, shared a few jokes and then waited for their food.

"So, what's up? You usually spend your days off at the gym. For a good twelve hours."

"Ha ha, still a comedian." He took a sip from his water. "Kim's moving in with me."

Dino narrowed his eyes and waited for a reaction, but Nicolo dodged his view. "This is great. Congratulations."

"Yeah, I guess."

"Her idea?"

"She asked me this morning. Moving in October first it looks like."

"It's time, right?"

Nicolo didn't answer. What *is* the right amount of time? Some people marry in less than a year. Why? Did they know immediately? Why did others take years before they made the commitment?

"How'd you know that Carissa was the one?"

Dino exhaled. "You're asking me to go back fifteen years?" He gazed up at the ceiling, mulled it over but the waitress arrived with their food. They helped her distribute the plates, and then Dino grabbed the largest of the steak fries as soon as she left.

"No, just in general," Nicolo stirred the New England clam chowder in his bowl.

"We're good for each other. We complement one another, you know, support is there all the time. Good friends, with fringe benefits." He nudged him with his elbow.

"Yeah, I see it. Always have. Lucky guy."

"And soon you'll be. I guess the ring's next, huh?"

Nicolo tossed his fork on the counter and leaned back. "One step at a time, this is too much already." Sweat emerged through every pore of his body like the dam had split. He clutched his glass of water and chugged it until the ice cubes struck his nose.

Dino put down his burger. "Nic, if it's dead-on, you'd be the one asking her to move in. And you'd be flying to the jewelry store after lunch today."

****

Sunday football games with the guys at Nicolo's apartment, went out the door with the beers and wings. Kim felt they could come occasionally, but every Sunday was getting on her nerves. 'What if she wanted to watch her own shows or lie around in her pajamas? What if she was sick?'

Then the plants marched in, arranged on top of his two-hundred dollar speakers. His "Lunch atop a Skyscraper" picture came down and a painting of a couple eating in Paris went up. The two decent-sized bedroom closets, she jammed with her clothes, leaving him half of one. The bathroom went from smelling like Irish Spring soap to cinnamon and apples.

Evenings that Kim had off, she prepared delicious meals and relieved him from the task of cooking or the expense of eating out. Not that he was able to eat, though.

Several weeks after she moved in, his appetite moved out. After drinking a protein shake one morning and puking it up, he could no longer stomach it. He only picked at his dinners. Although they looked delicious, the smells invaded his nose and left a rancid taste in his mouth.

Even Jim, his partner at work noticed the change. Apples and carrots left untouched until Nicolo stopped bringing them altogether. One or two bites of his sandwich and he was nauseous. His partner snatched it up each time, finishing the sandwich off with pleasure. Whatever weight Nicolo lost, Jim put on. Hearty grilled chicken sandwiches beat out Jim's boring ham and mayonnaise on a roll.

Nicolo continued at the gym. At least he had a place to hide, a place to release stress. But soon, his lack of nutrition wrecked his workouts. Weights he had lifted with ease fell to the ground after only six reps. An hour session at the gym, fell to a half hour, if that.

By the end of the summer, Kim's continued hints at their engagement, stacked with her nagging trio of sisters, forced him to buy the ring. And, for the first time in almost four years, Nicolo thought of Heather.

He remembered the ring on Heather's finger in that engagement photo in *Newsday*. She looked happy. Where was she now? Big mansion, four kids, driving a Mercedes, housekeepers and nannies. Then again, what if she was miserable? Had no kids or drove a brown Ford Tempo. What if they divorced?

Suddenly his anger melted. He had buried his feelings for so long that he couldn't remember why he was mad at her. Carissa once told him that something had to have happened to change her mind. A real good reason.

He thought of the night by the dock, the night they fell in love. Well, the night she did at least. He had always loved her, since their days at Northford. That night everything changed, though. The look in her eyes, the expression on her face. Heather freed herself at that moment. After years of holding back, she let go. He sensed it and so did she. He wanted to grab her face and say, "I love you, Heather."

He used to think of that evening often. Never forgot the way her mouth dropped open with realization. That gave him faith on the lonely nights he laid in his bed staring at the ceiling. Someone out there loved him. She made him believe that he was special.

But the one main question remained. Why didn't she call? He would have understood. Moved on quicker with his life. Sure, it was easy to say now, but as the pain and resentment disappeared, what remained clear was that Heather was a good person. She wouldn't have intentionally hurt him. He needed to believe this and move on with his life.

They fell in love and it wasn't either of their faults. Two decent people in a messed up situation.

****

Nicolo drove into his apartment's parking lot and turned off the ignition. He watched the red leaves fall from the tree beside him and slump to the ground. A pumpkin rolled off a stoop from the wind, and lay sideways on the leaf-covered grass. Brown leaves curled and withered, untouched by the groundsmen.

He glanced to the left and spied two boys, one dressed as Spiderman and the other as Harry Potter, hop into the back of their mother's minivan. Halloween, two days away, and Nicolo had yet to enjoy the autumn season. Kim was too busy planning their wedding, and had refused invites from Carissa and Dino to check out the White Post Farms Fall Festival with their kids. The haunted house in Bayville, which they had checked out last year, way too scary. No time to carve pumpkins, run through corn mazes, or buy candy apples.

A teenage girl from the apartment across the way, skipped down the steps and headed toward her car wearing purple alien antennas. His gut wrenched from the memory of this afternoon.

His seven-to-three shift, had twisted into a seven-to-seven shift. A peaceful Sunday ended with a fatal car crash. Two cars welded together. Acrid and syrupy fumes of oil and coolant burned. The flashing lights of the ambulance intensified. A firefighter had used the Jaws of Life on one of the vehicles, a Toyota Corolla.

Although positive that Heather must have bought a new car by now, he still wondered if it was her lying in that Corolla. Blood scarred the face of the driver, but as he peered over the firefighter, he saw it was a much older woman. He wondered what Heather looked like now, had it been almost ten years?

Nicolo had arrived at the home of the deceased and paused before ringing the doorbell as always. He hated doorbells. A girl around seventeen, reminding him of Heather when they first met, answered the door. Nicolo held his hat in his hand, the naïve girl smiled. Heather would have known in an instant, known this wasn't a pleasant visit.

The girl was alone, no one to comfort her. Nicolo stayed, called her father and waited for him to drive home, praying he wouldn't crash on the way, leaving the girl an orphan.

Nicolo stepped out of his truck. He trudged up the walkway and then inserted the key into his apartment, four hours later than planned. Distraught, sick to his stomach, and glad he had off tomorrow.

The door opened to the cackles of four women sitting on his couch, around his coffee table, listening to his stereo and eating his dinner.

"We're looking over various bridesmaid gowns, want to see?"

Sure, that's exactly what he wanted to do after today. That teenage girl would marry one day, but without the help of her mother. He suddenly wanted to call his mom.

Kim's three sisters looked up from the magazines and joined in the fun.

"Wow, look at you."

"Men in uniform, it's true."

"Never saw you in your uniform. Now I know what Kim sees in you, Nicky."

He attempted a fake, cheerful smile. He hated the name Nicky. His Aunt Bea always called him that. He removed his coat and the stabbing pain returned from the hole in his stomach. Bile climbed up his throat and burned his mouth. Another evening without food.

Chapter 29

Heather

Heather and Rebecca rushed into the cafeteria on Ice Cream Sundae Day, a yearly treat hosted by the hospital to thank the employees for all their hard work throughout the year.

They turned the corner, zigzagging through the congestion of employees, and witnessed the madness. Sprinkles flew onto the floor, whipped cream exploded from the cans, cherries rolled all over the table. You would think dietitians would have more self-control. Samantha and Cara strolled by them with their mile-high sundaes.

Rebecca and Heather made their sundaes and took a seat in the back. Rebecca licked the whipped cream off her spoon and shivered. "You'd think they'd have this in the summer instead of the first week of January."

"Maybe the ice cream tubs are cheaper the week after New Year's."

Rebecca laughed, licking the chocolate syrup from her bottom lip. "Reddi-whip is the most amazing discovery ever. Mmm."

Heather sucked the maraschino cherry into her mouth. "You know, I used to spray it in my breakfast cereal when I was little."

"Ew, you did not. The cereal had enough sugar as it was."

"Then I'd hold up the bowl and slurp the red and blue milk into my mouth."

"Are you sure you're a dietitian?" Rebecca giggled. "Actually, I caught my kids squirting it in their mouths one time."

"Totally. Who hasn't?"

Silence. "Me," Rebecca murmured.

"Get out."

"I don't know. I just never did. My mom would have killed me."

"Mine too, but I didn't tell her. I'm bringing in a bottle of whipped cream on Monday and we're downing it in the bathroom on Tower-8."

"You're crazy. I could just see the two of us walking out of the bathroom together with a bottle of whipped cream. We hang out too much as it is."

"Good, give them something to talk about. My life's so boring." Heather finished her sundae and plopped the bowl in front of her.

"I'm supposed to take my kids to the Children's Museum in Garden City on Sunday." Rebecca wiped her mouth on a napkin.

"It's supposed to snow."

"I heard rain."

"Which will turn to ice."

"Great." Rebecca dumped her bowl next to Heather's.

"We have to get the kids together again. They had a blast last time."

"How about February break? I took the week off."

"Me too!" Heather practically sprang from her chair. "Let's plan out the whole week."

"It'll be great. It's so hard trying to keep them occupied in the middle of February."

"I know. My parents took turns watching Laurel this past week and they're losing it, even with all her new Christmas toys. Luckily, Gia's in day care."

"Can't Lance take off and watch Laurel?"

"Oh, please, he wouldn't know what to do."

"So? You're enabling him. Tell him your mother can't do it. Force him. He'll learn. You do too much and he takes advantage of you. Brad and I split the chores down the middle. He vacuums, does laundry, cooks."

"Get out!"

Rebecca shook her head. "Why are you allowing it? Why are you letting him win?"

****

Heather scooped the last of her scrambled eggs and ketchup onto the fork and shoveled them into her mouth. Cryptic babble, intertwined with whispers, came from Samantha and Cara, who sat shoulder-to-shoulder on the other side of the room. Their attempt at preventing her from hearing their story made Heather choke down her food as if the place was on fire. She only made out a few sentences, a random word here and there.

"Can't believe it." "So hot." "Drunk." "No condom." "Works on Tower-6." "Vodka." "Hasn't called."

The pair still hung out with Eryn after four years. Their weekly drunken carousing always made for interesting conversation on Mondays. She could swear Cara was high half the day and the diet office reeked of alcohol after lunch on occasions. Rumors flew of Cara sleeping with a handful of residents and now it appeared Samantha was in on the merry-go-round as well.

The phone rang and the diet clerk informed Heather it was for her. Who on her floor would call so early, Otis? He was outstanding at updating her on patient's meal intakes. Rebecca? With another morsel of interesting gossip? Heather was always up for that. At least the call would rescue her from Tweedledee and Tweedledum.

Heather reached for the phone, knocking over the container of Reddi-whip she brought in for Rebecca. "Hello?"

"Heather, it's Brooke."

No. Her day could only get worse. "Are you okay?"

"Of course. What could possibly be wrong in my life?"

God forbid she shared any of her miseries with her. Heather was sure there were plenty, but Brooke never let on. Same old Brooke from high school. "Well, you're calling me at work at nine a.m."

"Sorry. Am I disturbing you from serving your patients their peas?"

Heather crushed the Styrofoam plate in half and crammed it into the garbage pail. "I don't cook or serve food. How many times do I have to tell you that?"

"I'm kidding, I know. You...monitor the cooking...or something."

"I don't work in the kitchen, Brooke."

"It's early, my brain's not awake. The menus, you pass out menus?"

"No. I don't pass out menus, or cook, or serve the food or decide on the cafeteria meals. I have nothing to do with the kitchen or food service."

Samantha and Cara both snickered, then Cara made a face motioning toward Heather and rolled her eyes.

"Do you want to know why I called or not?"

Not really. Heather glanced at the ceiling, mouth gaping. She squeezed her eyes shut and took a deep breath. "What is it Brooke?"

"I was selected as head of the winter fundraiser dance."

"Weren't you the head of the Christmas wrapping paper

fundraiser?"

"And the Halloween Hoedown. Don't forget about that one."

Heather's body tensed. "And what about the 'Easter Beagle crowning the new team mascot on Columbus Day' fundraiser?" Her sarcasm flowed like the bullshit in this office.

"There's no such thing."

Heather snatched the beeper from her waist, jammed it into the phone's mouthpiece and clicked the red button three times, releasing a stream of earsplitting beeps that caused Cara and Samantha to swivel in their chairs.

"Sorry, Brooke. My patient just coded and they intubated him. They need a STAT consult to start parenteral nutrition since his GI tract is non-functioning due to the perforated viscous and peritonitis that caused his sepsis and multi-system organ failure. His abdominal wound from the hemi-colectomy, dehisced and they fear his intestines, which are friable, have resulted in a fistula."

"Friable? What?"

"Gotta run." She slammed the phone down with great satisfaction. The twosome gawked at her. Heather stuck her tongue out and crossed her eyes. Her patience had run out.

She grabbed her binder and the Reddi-whip, then attempted to exit the office, leaving the two of them to continue their asinine conversation.

"You forgot your lab coat." Cara placed her thumbs in her ears and wiggled her fingers up and down.

"Thank you," Heather snarled.

A knock thumped on the door and Coleta, a food service aide, entered and retrieved the callbacks for late patient trays. The diet clerk handed them to her as Heather shoved her arm through the lab coat's sleeve.

"More for Tower-8?" Coleta asked. "That floor's a mess today."

"It's Heather's floor," Samantha snorted.

"No. Because of what happened. Everyone's crying."

"What happened?" Cara asked.

"One of the staff was killed in a car accident on the way to work. Slid on ice, car overturned."

"Who?" Heather asked.

"Not sure, Renee or something. I think she was a social worker."

"Rebecca?" Heather shouted.

"Yes, that's it. You know her?"

Cara and Samantha turned their backs on Heather and pretended to do their sheets. Violent shuddering burst through Heather's arms causing her to drop her books. They fell and spilled their contents across the floor. She dashed towards the elevator and repeatedly smashed the *up* button. Unable to wait, she hooked to the left and then clutched the door handle for the stairs.

Darting up the stairs two at a time, she only made it up three flights before her legs and lungs gave out, thighs burned and her gasps for air quickened. She crawled up the additional five flights, infuriated with herself for blowing off the gym for the past ten years. Flab had replaced muscle after her two pregnancies.

She ran past Rebecca's unlit desk, then to the nurses' lounge. She thrust open the door and it slammed against the wall. Waves of sniffling surrounded her. Heather stepped in and silence cut through the room. They stared, not knowing what to say. Some looked away, pretended to grab tissues, one aide walked out.

Otis stepped forward and placed his hands on her shoulders. Heather froze like a stone wall, tense under his grasp, but the warmth of his hands and heart triggered the tears.

"She was on her way to work, slid on all that goddamned black ice out there. Musta lost control. Car overturned. She was already gone by the time they got to her. They brought her to our ER, but there was nothing they could do."

Heather opened her mouth. No words formed.

"Seatbelt coulda saved her life. All those kids. Don't know if they even know yet."

Her knees shook and threatened to give way. She reached for the back of a chair and collapsed into it. Her head wilted into her folded arms and she cried for the first time in almost five years. Weak and vulnerable, in front of all her co-workers, she cried until she purged the last of her strength. Without Rebecca, there was no way she could continue. Her drive and spirit, trampled for the last time.

Chapter 30

Nicolo

The lock on their front door clicked shut. Kim hurried to work and the compression around Nicolo's muscles gradually released. His heartbeat slowed, his shoulders relaxed, the pain in his gut flushed away.

He shoved back the pink curtains on his living room window and let the January sun flash on his face. He stared directly at it, then closed his eyes. The bright glow continued beneath his eyelids, cracking the chill in his spine.

Despite the forty-degree temps, Nicolo tugged on his sweats, then jogged out the door and down his walkway. It had been weeks since he ran, but something nagged him out of the apartment today.

If naked trees didn't line his street, he'd think it was a summer day. Cloudless blue sky, no winds—

Crushing pain slammed into his shoulder. Nicolo careened to his left, knocked off the sidewalk and into a parked car.

"Oh, no! I'm so sorry!" A girl no more than twenty, blonde hair in a high ponytail, wearing nothing more than yoga pants and a T-shirt that said *I hate everyone,* stood above him. "I didn't see you. Are you okay?"

Nicolo braced himself against the car and then hoisted himself up. "No. I think I fractured my hubris."

"Hubris? What's that?"

"My pride." Nicolo smirked and stopped rubbing his hip.

Her alarmed expression twisted into a tightened knot. "If I didn't just slam you into that piece of shit car, I might—"

"Might what?" He took a step closer. At only five feet, she barely reached his chest, but her collapsed eyebrows showed no fear. "Hit me up with some karate?"

"Don't temp me." She thrust her hands onto her hips.

"Such an angry girl at nine-thirty in the morning. What's got you so pissed off?"

She considered his question, glanced back at her apartment and then yanked the tie in her hair. "Look, you wanna run or not?"

"I was trying to, 'til you got in my way." He winked, then took off down the street leaving her trailing behind. She caught up quickly.

"Are you some kind of a jokester?" she asked.

"Jokester? Who says that anymore?"

She huffed, then sprinted ahead of him.

Nicolo's long legs propelled him to her before she reached the end of the block. "Aren't you cold?"

"It's forty-six degrees. It's gorgeous."

It *was* a beautiful day. The little pixie's attitude shook off the last of his gloom. He ran beside her for another block and then she turned toward the right. "That's a dead end," he said.

"Not the way I go. If you like following rules then get lost."

He chuckled and headed in her direction. She attempted to hide her smirk. They touched the end of the court and leaped atop the sidewalk. Overgrown bushes tangled into masses of cold wire, but she ducked under a low-lying tree branch and disappeared.

Nicolo struggled to find the opening. His height was bad enough, but he didn't possess his running partner's double-jointed body parts. He emerged a minute later to find a vast open field. Was this the back end of Morley's Park?

He paused. She had disappeared. He took a few steps forward and scanned the edges of the field. Although fast, there's no way she'd make it to the other side. He spun around and there she sat, on an abandoned milk crate.

"Man, are you slow. Is this what happens when you hit your thirties?" She snapped a lifeless tree branch in her hands.

"Actually I'm fifty-one."

She squinted, examining his face. His rapid weight loss helped his bold lie. Damn, did he really look that old?

"You are not. Forty maybe, but I'm not buying fifty."

Did he look forty? Her frankness cut through him. Several months of neglecting his body couldn't have done that much damage. His face did cave in from the—

"Geez, I was just kidding. You're not going to cry, are ya?" She threw the stick at him.

He broke out of his trance. He was like a pathetic, emotional woman. "Well, I..." Nicolo shook his head and folded his arms into his chest. "I got nothing, my little sprout."

"Didn't think so." She stood. "Come on, it's nice out, but not that warm to just sit around." She jogged ahead.

He followed, intrigued by her dominant behavior. They headed west toward the entrance. "So, what got you so riled up this morning?"

She ignored him for a second, coughed and then let out a growl. "I'm running to forget, not talk about it."

"Maybe it'll be good to talk it out. These will be our venting runs."

"Oh, like this is ever going to happen again. Once I talk, you'll never see me again."

"Kinda like, now that you know my secret you must be terminated?"

"Again, don't tempt me." They reached the far end of the field and turned left. Morley Park's baseball field stood before them. "Besides, you won't see me after this week anyway."

"Why?"

"Moving out February first."

"Don't like the apartment?"

"Don't like the roommate."

"Some girl that doesn't appreciate your charm and kind-heartedness?"

She made a quick dart around the baseball bleachers and headed toward the campgrounds. "Look who's talking. What's with Ms. Prim and Proper?"

"Who?" Nicolo asked.

"Ms. Fancy Pants, your wife. I see her in her expensive fresh-pressed clothes. If it wasn't for your cop uniform, I'd think you were one of them, also."

"One of them?"

"Yeah, those snooty rich types."

"What are ya, stalking me?"

"Nah, I just stare out my window a lot. But soon, I'll have a new view."

"Where you going?"

"None of your business."

Nicolo dragged his hand across his face and rubbed his eye. Her passive-aggressiveness only sucked him in further. "What are you running from?"

She ended her sprint in one jarring halt. Nicolo rocketed forward another five or six steps. He huffed and gasped, sucking in the air from around them. He bent forward and rested his hands on his knees.

"Getting divorced, okay?" She dared him to stare back. "Need some oxygen, old man?"

"I'm sorry," he wheezed.

"For what? Not being able to keep up with me?"

Nicolo leaned back attempting to look composed. "No, the divorce." How old was she when she married? Twelve?

"You didn't force me to marry some numbskull right out of high school."

"Who did?"

"No one. Just thought I knew it all. You grow up and learn some things about yourself, ya know?"

He kept quiet.

"Thought I was cool, getting engaged and all. Didn't think about money or being broke all the time. You gotta plan ahead, though. I'm gonna finish college and get a good job. I don't need an unemployed drunk that gets fired all the time. I need stability. That's what we women need. Not good looks and a Mustang."

Nicolo plopped onto the dirt in the campground. A lonely charcoal grill, overflowing with blackened debris, stood before him. Is that why Heather dumped him? For stability? Not a stupid Jeep? He threw a rock over the grill and hit a tree. "Smart girl. What are you majoring in?"

"I got accepted to FIT. A fashion design school."

"I know what it is."

She stuck her tongue out at him. "But the expense of the train into the city, well, it was either pay rent or go to college and..." She choked down her last word. Her body shuddered.

"Cold? Come on. I think my old lungs recovered by now."

They jogged through the parking lot. She kept her eyes on the yellow lines that separated the parking spaces to avoid his inspection. They ran in silence until they circled around to the community pool.

"So, what's your deal?" she finally spoke.

"You tell me. You seem to know a lot about me, stalker."

Her eyes squinted and the tips of her mouth climbed upward until a huge grin engulfed her face. What *did* she know? The she-devil restrained herself and kept quiet. Or maybe not.

She cut her steps and Nicolo bolted several yards ahead of her again. "You like watching me make a fool of myself, don't you?"

"Nah, just like watching your ass."

Nicolo's eyes enlarged.

"Relax. I don't date old men."

He rolled his eyes.

"You wanna know what I think of you?"

"Not really." He tried hard to look in shape this time, hiding his pounding heartbeat.

"You became a cop because you feel bad for people and want to help everyone. You look miserable when you come home from work, though. Not sure if it's from a bad day or having to come home to Ms. Foo-Foo."

Nicolo shook his head and bit down on his lip.

"Because when you leave *for* work, you're happy. You don't jog as much as you used to. You lost weight though, which makes no sense. When you and the princess go out to some fancy dinner party, you walk in silence, but her mouth never shuts up. I only see women coming in and out of your apartment, so either you have four wives or no friends, or she doesn't let you have any friends over."

"Are you done?"

"Nope. You sit in your car a lot before entering your apartment. There can't be that many good songs on the radio. Either you're jerking off 'cause she won't put out anymore, or you're avoiding her for as long as you can."

"You don't like her do you?" Nicolo took a few steps back and headed toward the campground. She followed.

"I just know her type."

"Which is?"

"They've got the 'name brand clothes and handbags syndrome'. You know, showing off their stuff to their friends, even though deep down they're miserable inside. They think those things make them feel better, but they don't."

"This coming from someone that plans to design clothes and handbags one day?"

"Hell no! I plan to open a little shop that sells cool clothes. Inexpensive ones that you can be yourself in. I designed this T-shirt myself." She pointed to her chest.

"How'd I know?" They passed the baseball field again and continued their stroll. "What else?"

"You married her 'cause you were either desperate, which I don't really see because you seem...normal."

"Normal? That's all I've got going for me?"

"If you think I'm going to lay it on thick, think again. I already told you I liked your ass."

"Even if it's old?"

Her cheeks deepened in red. Possibly from the cold, probably not. They began their final jog.

"Or you married her because she comes from money and thought you could squeeze her for all she's got. But you don't look like that type either."

"What type do I look like?"

They neared the secret passage and she stopped. She stood directly in front of him, only inches away, and gazed deep into his eyes. "You're a good person, compassionate and helpful. You try to make everyone happy, but end up miserable yourself. Regardless of why you chose her, you tolerate her because you're a good man. You'd rather jump on a trampoline, than sit at some fancy restaurant, but you do it because it's the right thing to do. Sometimes we do what's right, but it's not necessarily what's right for us."

With that, she punched him in the shoulder and ducked beneath the scraggly tree branches. Nicolo watched her gray pants blend in with the dead branches, and then disappear. Her words strangled him like the dense bushes themselves. Was he that transparent? Was it that noticeable? Why had no one else picked up on it?

He bent down near the milk crate and located the opening. Branches grasped at his arms and left scratches on his face. He veered to the right, met a fence and then turned back to the left. He pushed back the lifeless tree branch and the curb appeared.

She was gone. He jogged to the dead end sign and searched the street that led back to their apartments. Nothing. He went into full sprint to their quarter mile long street, but she had vanished. He never got her name.

****

Saturday morning, the screech of truck tires interrupted Nicolo's relaxing cup of coffee and the NBC news.

Kim exited the kitchen and peered out the window. "Thank God," she said.

"What?"

"That little twit is moving."

Nicolo sprang from the couch and ripped back the curtains. And grinned. His little sprout mounted herself beside a U-Haul truck with a large box in her hand. No one else in sight. "What's wrong with her?"

"That's the one I told you about. The idiot that whacked me with her dead Christmas tree, and knocked me over. She broke the heel off my boot. Stupid kids."

"She's the one?" Nicolo turned his head to hide the outburst of laughter.

"I told her to open up her damn eyes, and next time, buy a fake tree like normal people."

Normal.

Nicolo took one last gulp of his coffee and tugged on his sweatshirt. He strolled down his walkway and along the sidewalk. The brisk air woke his listless bones more than the coffee had. He reached the moving van, took his right hip and thumped it into hers as she attempted to lift one of the heavier boxes onto the truck.

He bent over and picked up the largest of the remaining boxes, making sure she got a good look at his tired-old ass. She shook her head, finally releasing a giggle. Nicolo loaded the box onto the base of the truck and then climbed in. She handed him another one and he pushed all three boxes toward the back. Kim spied on them from the window.

Chapter 31

Heather

Heather's eyes sparkled. She hummed, swung her arms and practically skipped up the sidewalk leading into Norlyn Plains Hospital. Less than one month after Rebecca's death, her life took a new direction.

Employees around her scurried into work to avoid the bitter cold of February, but Heather's body charged with warmth.

Heather opened the door to what would be her new home. A new start. With the only positive influence in her life gone, she knew she needed to disconnect from the negative ones. Away from Samantha and Cara, her life would finally change.

In the evening, she hid from Lance, visited her parents more and signed the girls up for various activities. She read them books, cuddled on their beds, and played Hi Ho Cherrio or Pretty Pretty Princess on their bedroom rugs, with the door shut. She waited until Lance fell asleep before she crawled into bed.

Bianca didn't believe Heather when she said she quit her job after almost ten years of employment. She assumed they fired her. She asked what Heather had done: killed a patient with her cooking? Bianca's usual piercing laugh followed.

Heather checked in at the front desk and a security guard in his late fifties, with a sizable paunch, escorted her down the hallway.

She bit the inside of her cheek and scanned the corridor to see if anyone was eyeing her, then studied the red and blue swirls in the carpeting, avoiding their gazes. She adjusted her dress and cleared her throat, then clutched her old-lady pocketbook in front of her like a tiny shield. Good fear, she thought.

The security guard knocked on a door with a pale-blue sign labeled *Dietitian's Office*. A woman in a lab coat, at least ten years older than Heather, greeted them.

"Hi. I'm Heather, the new dietitian."

"Hello. I'm Victoria. Nice to meet you."

Chapter 32

Nicolo

The explosion of women wearing red and pink in the restaurant caught Nicolo's eye. Kim wore a red dress too, with the teardrop necklace he had bought her so many years before. Mind-numbing elevator music streamed through the speakers. The dim lightening emphasized the anxiety and panic felt by the table candles as they flapped wildly. Or was it Nicolo that felt uneasy?

"We found the perfect party favors for everyone."

"We?" He wiped the sweat from his forehead.

"My sisters and I."

God forbid she included him.

"Anyway, they're these seahorse bottle stoppers. They have these cute, silver seahorses that sit on top and I thought it would be great since the reception's on the water."

"Seahorse?" Nicolo took a sip of his water.

"They're so adorable."

"What if people don't drink wine or they don't drink at all?"

"Who doesn't drink wine?" Kim waved her hand at him in jest.

He resumed scanning his menu, but nothing interested him. Had he eaten lunch today? He couldn't remember.

"What are you getting?" Kim placed the menu next to her. Before he could answer, she sputtered her request. "They have the Valentine's special, two lobsters and two petite filet mignons. Do you want to split that?"

"Sure, that sounds great." It didn't matter what he ordered, he wouldn't be able to get it down.

A girl in her early twenties squealed at the table next to him, then shot up from her chair holding a necklace in her hand. The guy at her table stood also, and helped her put it on.

An ache ripped through him. It couldn't be. Nicolo had given the same heart necklace to Heather a decade ago. He excused himself with his usual bogus smile and then hurried to the bathroom. He splashed water on his face, grateful no one occupied the stalls. His stomach heaved, but there was nothing inside to come out. He swooshed a few handfuls of water into his mouth and then wiped his face with a paper towel.

This was insane. What was wrong with him? He was losing his mind. Was this normal? It had to be. He remembered reading something in one of Kim's wedding magazines about grooms freaking out. He felt the small box in his coat pocket and inhaled, but the overwhelming sickly-sweet odor from the urinal cake deodorizer, made him want to gag again.

Nicolo returned to the table and immediately placed the dark blue box in front of Kim. "Happy Valentine's Day," he strained.

"Oh, how cute! I'm so excited." Kim ripped off the ribbon, followed by the paper and cracked the hinges back. "They're beautiful, Nic. I can even wear them with my wedding gown." She removed her pocket mirror and held the earrings against her ears. "They're gorgeous, thank you." She smiled and touched his hand. "I'm so lucky to have you. You make me so happy."

Had the wine gone to her head, because he felt like an ungrateful jerk. His life moved into an incredible new direction: marriage, a home by next year, and then children. Why was he so miserable? Could it be immaturity? No, he saw a lifetime of tragedy during his police career and knew what rotten was.

Their food arrived and atop both their steaks were two shrimps joined together to form a heart. "How romantic," she said.

They clinked glasses and he gazed at her, long after she took a sip and picked up her utensils. She was beautiful. Her eyelashes flashed in an optimistic rhythm. She slid the juicy red piece of meat into her mouth and moaned. "Delicious."

Nicolo giggled. "You love food."

"Good food, yes." Kim glanced at his utensils, still erect beside his plate like soldiers. "Please tell me you're going to eat tonight."

"Of course." He picked up his fork and knife and cut a small piece of steak.

"You've just...lost so much weight. I'm worried about you."

"Nah, just felt like I was getting too big. Need to slim down to fit into that tux, ya know? More important things in life than just lifting weights all the time. "

"As long as that's all it is."

"Sure, what else could it be?"

"You're not nervous are you? Having second thoughts?"

He swallowed hard. "Second thoughts? What makes you think that? We're already living together. It can only get better, right?" He winked at her and forced a piece of lobster in his mouth, hoping the butter would slide it down his throat more easily.

She was right, though. He had lost a ton of muscle. He felt weak, scrawny, pathetic. His T-shirts hung off him, his police uniform loose.

Every day he lied and said he went to the gym, but stayed late at work or walked around the mall instead. His few attempts at the gym were useless. His head wasn't into it. He did a few sets, then left.

A couple of times he just sat in the parking lot and watched people walk in and out. Inspecting their clothes, guessing their body fat, timing how long they stayed, noticing how none of them made any real changes in their bodies after months. He felt like a detective on a stakeout.

A neighbor from his childhood bumped into him in the supermarket last week and thought he was Dino. A total insult. How long could he go without eating? How long would this aversion to the gym continue?

"Did you reconsider what I asked about Dante and Mariana being in the ceremony?"

Kim inhaled and clenched her knife in her fist. "Nic, we talked about this. I don't want any kids at the wedding."

"They'd make such a cute flower girl and ring bearer, though."

"Look, you're the one always saying that Dino and Carissa don't get any nights out alone. This would be a night out alone."

A night he wouldn't have to hear her complain about babysitting them.

What was it with Kim and his niece and nephew? They were good kids, well behaved and quite funny. At five and seven years old, they were much more independent now.

"This place is wonderful. I'm so happy to be here with you tonight, Nic." She changed the subject abruptly, as if he wouldn't notice. "This is going to be a great year." She held her wine glass high. "Here's to an amazing future!"

He clinked her glass with his, then leaned in and kissed her. He perfected the fake smile routine and then pretended to cut another piece of steak. His head throbbed, his stomach contorted and a repulsive taste appeared in his mouth from the stench of the mushroom sauce at the table behind him.

Something had to change. He couldn't live this way anymore. He couldn't spend the rest of his life in this sickened state. He needed help.

Chapter 33

Heather

Heather packed her car's trunk with a beach chair, pink and purple shovels with matching pails, a beach ball, a sand strainer and a green polka-dotted watering can. She filled the rainbow striped beach bag with turkey sandwiches cut into fours, apple slices and chocolate teddy grahams. She plopped water bottles in a separate cooler and then found another bag to stuff their Tinker Bell towels and an oversized blanket in.

Laurel waited patiently for Gia to finish using the bathroom, and once finished, the three scooted into the car on the first day of spring. A seventy-five degree, Saturday afternoon.

Lance left yesterday morning for a weekend golf getaway in Florida with his co-workers. Instead of annoyed, she eased out of her constant tense state and spent her Friday planning the next few days without him. Why couldn't he do this more often?

The girls giggled in the back seat. They played with their favorite Barbie dolls and Laurel helped Gia put a yellow bathing suit on her doll. They neared Sunken Meadow Beach and the smell and flavors of the crisp air lured her back to her favorite place.

Christina Aguilera's *Beautiful* played on the radio and Laurel sang along, lowering the window and singing to a strip of pale, green grass. Gia attempted to copy her, but only belted out an occasional lyric, mumbling the rest.

Heather pretended to laugh, but the lyrics triggered a spasm in her chest and overpowered her emotions. She knew what she had to do, thought about it all week. She sniffled, then thought of Rebecca, as she often did. She still couldn't believe she was gone. Heather's tears though, were not for Rebecca, they were for the fight that lay ahead. She had to do it. Do what she should have done years ago.

Gia tilted to her side and reached for the Ken doll beside her. She wiggled the doll in front of her Barbie. "Sorry, can't go to the beach, have to work." The Barbie slumped over. "Please go, please." "Sorry, work is very impotent."

Heather laughed at Gia's pronunciation of the word, but then she slumped over the steering wheel and let the tears fall. Their joke of a relationship had spilled over onto the girls now. Only seven and five years old and they already thought this was normal. It didn't matter what she taught them, they would learn more from what they saw in their own home.

What kind of role model was she to her girls? They'd grow up marrying a man like Lance and spend their lives trying desperately to get him to notice them. They'd do whatever it took to be what he wanted in his perfect world. He'd surely love her then.

"Leave him in the car," Laurel said. "He's too busy. Dump him on the floor with the umbrella."

Gia studied Ken for a minute, scowled then chucked him across the back seat and watched him land by Laurel's feet.

She'd search for a lawyer next week. She couldn't stand to live with Lance's verbal abuse another month. Trying to please him all these years took a toll on her. Never good enough, and his mother the cause of it all.

They drove into the parking lot of Sunken Meadow Beach and thoughts of Nicolo materialized. Where was he now? Did he think of her every time he went to the beach, like she did?

Heather unloaded the trunk. She handed Laurel the bag full of plastic toys and let Gia carry the Barbie dolls and accessories. She threw the bags full of food and towels over one shoulder, and the bag of water bottles over the other. In one free hand, she clasped her beach chair and in the other, the umbrella. Then closed the trunk with the hand that was holding the umbrella, and slammed the back doors closed with her foot.

The girls sprinted ahead as Heather struggled with the heavy weight. Gia paused to look at the geese poop sprawled across the grass divider and her hand reached down to touch it. "Stop! Don't touch that, it's poop!" Gia stared at her as if she was lying, but then ran off to catch up with her sister.

Heather tried not to think of the repercussions, how much worse her life could get. She needed to get the girls away from Lance before they witnessed any more crap. Before their impressions of men set.

She thought about how Gia treated the Ken doll though, and she was only five. Did Laurel notice too? Gia displayed a lot more spunk than loveable Laurel did. Maybe Laurel sensed it, but kept her feelings to herself. That was worse.

Heather had to do it. Maybe Lance wouldn't even want to see the girls anymore, and Bianca would disappear as well.

They climbed the pebbly path to the boardwalk and once Heather reached the wooden walkway, the aquamarine water embraced her. A cloudless sky, a single seagull overhead and a near-empty beach, aside from two volleyball nets set up with their jovial players, welcomed her.

The girls stepped onto the cool sand and sprinted, dumping their bags of toys and dolls. "Wait for me, stop! Hold her hand, Laurel."

Heather plopped her heavy beach gear down near the silver railing that overlooked the sand and bay. The chair crashed to the ground, her shoulders ached. She huffed, out of breath, and rested, already winded from the less than a quarter mile walk. The breeze from the water whisked her hair up in tangles. The pale, blue sky cut the deep blue water in half. The rocky beach added another layer of color underneath, like three rectangles of color sewn together. New beginnings, new year, new life.

Heather rolled her shoulders and stretched her neck. She raised her arms over her head, then bent side to side, exhaling like a chain smoker out of breath. *Pitiful.* She hoped no one saw her crazy antics. She glanced to the left and only saw a lone couple approaching from far away.

Just an exhausted, out-of-shape, mother here. No need to look at how pathetic she is.

Heather bent forward to touch her toes, but only reached her shins. The girls neared the water and she panicked. "Get back here," she screamed. "Girls, Gia, Laurel! Don't go near the water." Heather grabbed the bags, flipping one over her shoulder, but knocked the napkins out and sprayed them across the boardwalk. "Damn it!"

"Get back here!" The girls ignored her demands, unable to hear her over the waves and thirsty sea breeze. She snatched the parade of napkins and continued to scream like a lunatic. She hauled the two beach bags over her shoulder, but as she reached for the chair, the bag with the towels slid off and banged into it.

Gia and Laurel walked toward the left, and away from her. *Shit.* She flailed her arms, coming across like an unbalanced, drug addict. The couple neared, only a few yards away as she continued to scream and wave both her arms. "Stop right there! Come back! Wait for your mother!"

The girls removed their sandals and let their toes touch the tiny waves. She wanted to scream again, but the couple neared within only two or three feet. She tossed them a smile, and remained calm. How slow could two people walk? Gia stepped a few feet into the icy March water, waves crashing into her shins, and Heather freaked.

"Gia! Gia! Damn you."

The couple finally strolled behind her. They must have thought she was a psychopath. Her face and neck ignited. She waited for them to pass and then scooped up all her bags, turned, and started to run after her kids.

"Heather?" The man dropped the woman's hand and stepped toward her. Heather gawked at the unfamiliar face. She glanced back to the girls, both in the water now.

"Heather Di Pietro?"

Someone from her past obviously. "I'm sorry, do I know you?"

"It's me, Nicolo."

Heather's eyes narrowed. This man looked nothing like him. Her heart began racing. Breathless, adrenaline pulsed through her body and nausea consumed her. Was it him? Thin, scrawny, gaunt face. She tipped her head to the right.

"Trevisani?" he added.

Blinding light hit Heather. She clenched her eyes and looked away, then stepped to the right to avoid it. It came from the diamond ring on the woman's left hand. It twisted back and forth, reflecting the sunlight and firing it into Heather's eyes.

Was he ill? Dying? She tried to shield the light from the ring. Was this his first marriage? Second? Was she marrying him as his dying wish?

"Oh, hello," Heather managed to sputter. "Sorry, um, the kids and all." She looked to her right and saw them playing with long pieces of reeds.

"How are you?" he asked.

"Great." What could she say? Her daughters were about to drown, his fiancée smothered him like a clingy child while blinding her with her evil ray gun, and Heather had dumped him ten years ago without so much as a word. "How are you?"

"Great." The woman gave Nicolo a slight nudge but Heather noticed. "Oh, sorry, this is Kim. My...fiancée."

Heather's stomach knotted. She couldn't think of anything to say.

"Nice day for a stroll on the beach," he stammered.

She heard Laurel scream and looked toward the water again. "Sorry. My daughters ran off without me."

"Two girls?"

Why was he being so nice to her? "Yes, and you?" What a stupid question, he was engaged. Even if he had other kids, did it matter? Holy shit, he was engaged. Engaged!

"No. No kids." Nicolo steered his attention to the woman. "Heather and I worked together back when I was in high school."

Heather heard screams and glanced back at the girls who were hitting each other with the reeds. Her shoulders ached from the beach bags. Her heart crushed from embarrassment and the awkward situation.

"You recognize her from over fifteen years ago?" Kim probed.

Heather adjusted the bag on her shoulder and shifted the chair to the other hand. The gleam from the diamond ring sliced through her eyes once more. The Gods were torturing her again. It would never end. Mocking her and letting her know she made a huge mistake.

She already knew! Everywhere she turned, there were reminders of the love she gave up. Why did his fiancée have to be here with him? Heather needed to tell him she still loved him. She had never stopped. But she needed to stop their marriage before it was too late. What she wouldn't give to throw her arms around him right now and tell him. *I love you, Nicolo. I'll always love you. To the moon. Don't marry her. Don't die.*

Gia let out a shriek that carried itself straight across to Connecticut. Heather felt her knees buckling. She would faint in front of them, for sure. "I'm sorry. My girls are killing each other. It was so nice seeing you after all this time."

"Yes, you too." Nicolo grinned but it looked awful with his sunken temples. He hesitated for a minute. They both did. Until his fiancée yanked him away.

Heather hurried to the area where they dropped their toys, then dumped her load a few yards away and jogged to them. Despite being out of shape, the shock of the reunion propelled her forward and away from the ordeal. It slammed into her like a punch in the back.

Heather scolded the two innocent girls and her face contorted. They recoiled and ran from her.

Heather continued to scream, unsure what rattled her the most. Nicolo marrying someone else? Heather stupidly abandoning him without a word? Her rude callous behavior to him and his fiancée just now? Nicolo dying? Lawyers, divorce, Rebecca's death, a new job?

With so much change in the past two months, her life fell into a downward spiral. Confused, she took it out on Gia and Laurel. Shocked by their mother's new behavior, they broke into tears and collapsed onto the sand, clutching each other in fear.

Chapter 34

Nicolo

Nicolo leaped out of his apartment after eating more than he had eaten in months, and took to the streets. Six o'clock, dusk, clouds rushed in painting a black and orange sky.

He passed a teenager dribbling his basketball down the deserted street. His neighbor walked her German Shepherd before the night fell. A man close to his age pulled his garbage can out into the street for tomorrows pick up. He was free.

He wasn't angry with Heather after all. His new energy came from knowing she was safe. Heather, still gorgeous, and with two beautiful little girls.

Her daughters could have been their kids.

She had a wedding ring on. That he noticed. Still with Lance? Guess he turned out to be a great guy. She must be happy.

The clouds increased, creating instant darkness. Kim must be blind. Why did she want him? He had been so distant with her this year. The year they planned their wedding.

He continued to jog. He needed to move on, stop thinking about the past. He had a beautiful fiancée who was devoted, loving, a great cook, and had a nice family.

Selfish. The wedding, only six months away and he was somewhere else.

A droplet fell on his nose. He whisked it away, but more fell and then crashed around him. He ran faster through the obstacle and turned the corner sprinting in the opposite direction of his apartment.

The downpour continued, but his energy restored. The gym called him back and he was suddenly hungry. No. Ravenous, for life to begin.

His life, the one meant to live. A wife, a house, and children of his own.

Nicolo headed into the darkness. The downpour so substantial, the sheets of rain obstructed his vision, but he could see clearly for the first time. See through the torrential rain, past the gloom. The road clouded before him, like fog settling in the neighborhood. Even the large pine trees grayed and blurred under the deluge.

He turned a corner and headed downhill, following a fast moving current of water barreling down the hill. The rain pelted the street like thousands of crickets leaping away to freedom. The howl and gusts of wind drove the rain into him hard. Gutters overflowed, roads flooded and a steady stream of rain followed him downhill on both sides.

The cold March air froze the soaked clothes onto him. They hung heavily, but he sprinted harder, letting the drenching rain cleanse him from months of haze. It fell sideways, smacking him in the back of his head. Water gushed from his hair like a wrung out towel, much too fast for him to bother wiping his face clear anymore. But his path was clear. He needed closure and today he found it.

Between 6:21 and 6:27pm, a quarter of an inch of rain pelted down on Nicolo, washing away his depression. He slept well that night.

Chapter 35

Heather

Heather wriggled until flat on her back and then pulled the blanket over the two of them to mask their sexual encounter. Fingers meandered up her shirt, searching, until they glided across her breasts. They continued to roam and explore her bare skin, smooth and tingling. Her body relaxed and she exhaled, releasing any footprints of her unhappiness.

The fingers wandered and slipped under her satin underwear, interlaced with the loose mound of threads, discovering the soft flesh that was already wet.

How long had it been since his hands touched her? She ran her hands through his thick, black wavy hair, glanced into his equally dark eyes. His smile reassured her as it always did, and she let him continue the churning between her legs.

The brilliant sunbeams glistened off the sand, creating a shoreline of diamonds around them. Vivid and clear, each moment brought her back as if time rewound.

When the willowy fingers no longer satisfied her, Heather reached to her left and brushed over his bathing suit. She stretched further, navigating underneath to grab hold of the dormant bundle within.

He rolled toward her. She turned to her right, delighted when he finally entered her in their spoon position. Her face beamed with strong color and sheen. After reveling in the immediate gratification, she joined in wanting more. Heather drove her ass into him harder and harder. Why was he being so docile? She wanted him to pound her as he used to do, relentless and wild. The harder she thrust into him, the more lax he became. Lifeless, almost apathetic.

The sunlight on the beach dimmed, the waves darkened, then blurred. A hushed tone overtook the seashore. Complete silence followed. Cold, unresponsive, subdued. He pulled out after only two minutes.

She opened her eyes. Thick crust held her lashes closed. She rubbed them clean. Crimson light met her gaze. 3:27a.m.

Heather turned over. Her bedroom dresser, lined with photographs of Laurel and Gia stared at her. The bed creaked beside her. Lance crawled out of bed and yanked his boxers over his flat ass.

No!

****

Heather only met Victoria two months ago, but an instant bond took hold between them. Maybe because Victoria was close in age to Rebecca. Maybe because she had two children the same age as Rebecca's oldest. Or maybe it was the compassionate nature she emanated. It didn't matter. Heather had to tell someone.

Heather asked Victoria to meet her in the nurses' lounge on her floor. Victoria entered, a puzzled look surfaced on her face, but she remained composed.

"I'm so sorry to unload this on you Victoria, I just...I have to tell someone." She sat on the old green couch.

"Something happen on Easter?" Victoria sat across from her.

"Easter? No, nothing like that." Heather unlocked her arms and crumpled into the back cushion. She sucked her lips deep inside her mouth and stared at her. "I'm pregnant."

Victoria studied her for a reaction, but Heather displayed no emotion. Heather pushed her hair back, and then the tears began to fall.

"I guess this wasn't planned." Victoria leaned over and touched her shoulder.

"Planned? I was planning on telling Lance I was leaving him."

"I'm so sorry. I didn't realize."

"I made up my mind that day. Then I saw him. I don't know what happened. I was dreaming, but it was so real. I couldn't tell him after I just slept with him. I planned to wait a few weeks, but then I was late. Two weeks late. I took the pregnancy test yesterday while the girls played with their Easter toys and now, what the hell am I going to do Victoria?"

"Woah, woah, woah, slow down. What are you talking about? I don't understand. Who's him? What dream?"

It all came out, everything. Heather's friends pressuring her to date Lance due his popularity. Meeting Nicolo at Northford, and how the only time she ever felt alive was in his presence. Meeting him five years later and their affair. She spoke about her engagement to Lance and subsequent deterioration. How the only thing that saved her was the birth of Laurel and Gia. The continued abuse from Bianca and lack of affection from Lance. Seeing Nicolo in the mall, Rebecca's death and meeting Nicolo again at the beach last month.

Victoria didn't interrupt or ask questions. She didn't judge or infer. Her nods kept Heather calm enough to continue without apprehension. Heather trusted her and their connection immediately strengthened.

"He was so thin. You don't think he's dying and they rushed the wedding? Maybe she's pregnant too."

"Heather, relax."

"Sorry, I'm babbling." She wiped the mascara under her eyes, evidence of her shame. The heartbreak she hid all these years tore through her bones. No amount of drama in her life could ever make her forget what she did, what she lost. She never stopped loving him. Nicolo was always the one. Time only made it worse. Time she should be spending with him.

"Why didn't I mention where I worked?" Heather choked out. "He could have looked me up, found me."

"And done what?"

"If he's dying and I can't say goodbye...I should have stood up to Bianca back then. The one person that supported me, gave me courage and made me believe in myself, I wasn't strong enough to fight for."

"As we grow we learn. Whether or not it's too late is irrelevant. What's important is what you do with that knowledge now. Each time you had the opportunity to make a decision. You have that choice again now. "

"What am I supposed to do?"

Victoria studied the painting on the wall. "Maybe you weren't supposed to be together. Maybe he keeps entering your life to remind you of what he taught you."

Heather shifted in her cushion. No. That couldn't be the answer. She was being punished. Her fear of standing up to Bianca and telling Lance she didn't love him, and subsequently embarrassing her family, destroyed her happiness.

"What do you want Heather?"

"What I've always wanted, to be happy."

"And what makes you happy?"

"I was thinking about that yesterday when the girls opened their Easter baskets. They squealed with each little toy, with each tiny piece of candy. They were happy. I used to be that way. Before Lance."

"What do you mean?" Victoria ignored the noise from her beeper.

"My parents lived paycheck to paycheck. I had a hand-me-down bicycle, very few toys. I'd never been on a plane. Vacations, when we had them, consisted of drives to Pennsylvania Dutch Country or Busch Gardens. I had to beg my dad for change just to take the bus to the mall, and then once my friends and I got there, I had no money to buy anything or even eat."

"And you were miserable?"

"Not at all. The vacations meant so much to me. When they bought me a toy, I played with it forever. We had a ton of kids on our block and played SPUD in my backyard, made giant tents over my mother's clothesline, and we even ice-skated in the streets one winter when they froze over. I loved just *being* in the mall with my friends and we laughed non-stop.

"When I got my first baby-sitting job, I took the money and we all hopped on the train to the city, shopped in consignment shops, and went to punk-rock dance clubs at night in weird clothes. I dressed the way I wanted, listened to my music, and decorated my room with cool posters. They were the best years of my life. I was silly and crazy and did what I wanted. My parents only cared for my happiness."

"What changed?"

"I told my dad how Lance pestered me all summer. He said he seemed like a nice guy. My parents worried about me, they didn't want to see me struggle like them. They couldn't pay for college or buy me a car. They saw all the things my friends had. I thought if I dated Lance, they'd stop worrying, and maybe it was the secret to finding happiness."

"Your parents were miserable?" Victoria turned her beeper off and threw it on the couch.

"That's the thing. They were always hugging and kissing on the couch and goofing off while working on the yard. I wanted that. I always did. But I thought if I had the money too, it would make it even better."

"Were you ever happy with Lance?"

Heather leaned forward and rested her chin in her hand. "I kept making excuses. Senior year was busy and full of drama. Then college was grueling. We were both overworked and stressed. Having to clean and cook in our own apartment. Tests, projects, work. It was awful. I thought once we graduated it would finally get better."

"Did it?"

"That's the weird part. My first year of college, I was blown away by all the projects, plus working thirty hours a week. But despite the craziness, when I came into work and saw Nicolo, he made it all disappear. And then the year I did my internship, well, you know what a nightmare that is. Working seven days a week for ten months straight, projects coming out of my ass. I didn't think I could do it, but that was the year I had my affair with Nicolo, and you know what?"

Victoria's eyes widened.

"It was the best year of my life. He gave me something to look forward to every day. Supported me, cheered me on. All the years I made excuses about Lance and our relationship, it really did suck and he made the stress in my life worse."

Victoria heard them paging her overhead, but waved Heather on. "Then why didn't you break up with him?"

Heather rolled to her side and let her face hit the seat cushion. "That night at the engagement party, Lance made me feel like the most insensitive girlfriend in the world. There he was throwing me a surprise party, asking me to marry him, buying me this gorgeous ring, telling everyone why he fell in love with me and how I kept him going all those years, and there I was, off having sex with some guy, plotting to break up with him over dinner. How horrible is that? I was so guilt ridden."

"But if you didn't love him..."

"Brooke made me feel guiltier about the whole situation. Then my mother kept telling me how happy she was that I found someone like Lance. I guess I was out to prove that I wasn't a selfish whore and I *could* be a great wife. I've been trying to prove it for years. I also thought that with school behind us, the American dream in front of us, and with the money finally rolling in, that things would improve."

"But what about Nicolo?"

An image of Nicolo hugging her after she completed her internship entered her thoughts. His grip always squeezed out her pain. His smile, reassuring. His loving eyes spread joy to her core.

"Brooke told me he meant nothing. That he was just a distraction and our relationship would never amount to anything real. That I needed to grow up and stop playing games."

"Was that true?"

"At first I thought it was. I mean, it made sense. I was stressed out and depressed, and Nicolo made me forget everything. Plus, our relationship was based on having fun. We never dealt with any real couple problems."

"If it wasn't love, if he was only a distraction, then why didn't you just tell him it was over?"

Heather rolled over so that her back lay flat on the sofa. The ceiling had a brown stain from a leak. "I planned to tell him. I wanted to. I wrote down my speech on paper countless times. Each morning I re-read it and it sounded...there was just no right way to tell him. A week went by, then two. I went from feeling bad for him, to twisting it around and saying it was his fault. I became angry with him for asking for my number, for taking me out and buying me things and letting it get to this. He didn't push me away when I kissed him, he should have said it was wrong. I went as far to think that he should have known it could never work and it's his fault if he's upset."

"You threw your anger with yourself onto him."

"Yup." Heather sat up. Guilt ripped through her for the hundredth time. "But the day of the wedding, I knew. Whatever I tried to hide and squash that year came out. I knew I didn't love Lance, that it would never work and that I was always in love with Nicolo. I thought about the times we helped each other through many of life's problems and knew we would have been great together. It wasn't just fun and games, it was love. God, Victoria. I love him. I love him so much. I never stopped. It killed me to see him last month. See him without me in his arms."

Victoria nodded. "I don't know what to say."

The aroma of patient lunch trays seeped into the room. Heather glanced at the clock and stood. What was there to say? She lost the only man she ever loved. She couldn't deny it any further. Masking her feelings and drowning her life with distractions was no longer an option.

"So, what are you going to do now?"

"With the pregnancy?"

"With your life."

****

Heather returned from her Friday morning errands and dropped the container of fish food on the counter. Last weekend she cleaned her pond after the long winter and needed to buy new fish food.

She planned to tell Lance about her pregnancy, but still couldn't find the words. What was she afraid of, Lance yelling at her? It was all they did anymore anyway. Was it Bianca throwing it in her face for being so careless? Surely, it would ruin Lance's career. Or perhaps Bianca would say that she better have a son this time.

Maybe it was admitting that she was stuck with Lance forever, and telling him would make it real.

She thought briefly about having an abortion, not telling Lance about the pregnancy, then she could file for divorce and it would all be over. But Laurel and Gia made her laugh so hard the other night. She knew her children were the only things that brought happiness into her life.

What if it was a boy? Would Lance spend time with his child finally? Would Bianca spoil the boy and ignore the girls further?

Heather headed to the backyard, then crouched down and watched the fish swim in the clear water. Climbing in there last weekend barefoot, slime touching the underside of her feet, a bullfrog surprising her, scooping out piles of algae-covered leaves to find the fish that made it through the winter, was a tiring days' worth of work, but rewarding.

Four fish had made it. Three orange goldfish and one white one. Heather was glad the white one survived. The girls had named her Fantasia. Heather watched as it swam to the other side. The three others followed. She must be the leader. They continued to scoot along wherever she went.

She watched for another minute and then her thoughts shifted. They weren't following her. They were chasing her. Attacking and bullying her. Did fish do that?

Fantasia swam to the other side of the pond to escape, but the three refused to give up. She attempted to conceal herself under the unbloomed lily pad that sat upon the pump, but with nowhere to hide in the leaf-free, clear pond, she disappeared under the splashes and splatters from the waterfall. They were relentless.

What was their problem? Were they jealous of her white color? The more she observed, the angrier Heather became. She leaned in with her hand and smacked the water near the orange fish with powerful blows.

Heather opened the can of fish food and the overpowering odor entered her nose. She quickly sprinkled some food near Fantasia and then covered the container. It was too late. Her feet propelled her toward the back door, but unable to make it, she leaned over the bushes and threw up her egg sandwich behind the leafless barberry bush.

It was beginning. Heather never threw up with the girls. This would be a boy for sure and Bianca and Lance would win. They would get their name passed on and continue to spit in the female Milanesi's faces.

****

Three more days passed and Heather had yet to tell Lance. Granted, she had worked this weekend and as soon as she arrived home, he bolted. This morning, he left the house before she woke.

She had to tell him today. She calculated that she must be six weeks pregnant by now. Heather rehearsed her speech all day.

Lance I have to talk to you. I need to tell you something. Can you put your phone down for a second? Yes, this is important. No, it can't wait. Yes, now.

Heather leaned over the kitchen table and her head collapsed into her folded arms. *Fuck.* She made herself some coffee and then it happened again. Half way through the cup, she ran to the bathroom.

Toilet paper streamed across her lips as she crashed back onto the porcelain tiles. This was not supposed to happen. Her head knocked against the wall, her hand pounded the bathmat. She was supposed to ask Lance for a divorce, not tell him she was pregnant.

Gia turned five and would start kindergarten in the fall. The end of day care bills. No more baby stuff remained either. She gave everything away. Maternity clothes again? She wanted to run away with her children and avoid Lance and Bianca forever.

Heather crawled out of the bathroom and stumbled to the back door to get some air. May 2nd brought seventy-five degrees and no humidity. *Breathe.* The fresh cool air flowed through her nose. The trickling of the waterfall beckoned her and she made her way to the relaxing noise.

She bent over the side and found the three orange fish near the lily plant. She scowled at them as if they understood. Then she saw her. Fantasia. Floating on the top of the surface near the waterfall. Her body rolled and bobbled in the waves.

No! How long had she been dead? Heather squatted over the rocks and tilted in. The orange fish hid. She ran to the garage and grabbed a net. She scooped poor Fantasia out and laid her on the grass next to her. Limp. Depleted. Sorrowful eyes.

Heather took the net and smashed it into the water, aiming for the orange fish. She swatted and swiped, wishing them dead. They dove and hid behind the pump. Water splashed with each thump of the net and soaked Heather's hair. Water trickled down her forehead, onto her nose and into her mouth. She batted at the water and the fish until her arm gave out.

She collapsed onto the grass and beads of water from her bangs mixed with tears. How could they? Monsters.

Thought of Mr. Gentile and his kind words, came back. How he told her if he could do it all over again he wished he had the courage to express his feelings more, to live a life true to himself. *Now dead.*

She thought of Rebecca, encouraging her to stand up to anyone that made her feel less than the great person she was, to let them know she was special and perfect and capable of great things. *Now dead.*

She thought of Nicolo, telling her she was existing in someone else's life, giving up her dreams, not enjoying life to the fullest. *Now dying?*

Everyone that tried to help her, now gone. Why didn't she listen to any of them?

What happened to the person she used to be, the non-conformist, the crazy, silly girl from high school, the life of the party, the one always willing to open her mouth and stick up for herself? *Long dead.*

Why hadn't she listened to her own heart?

Heather tilted her head to the right and watched the sun beat off Fantasia's lifeless body. She scooped up the perfect white flesh and then with her nails, dug the soil next to the emerging hosta. Gouging and extracting the hard soil, rocks scraped her fingertips and chunks of soil imbedded under her nails.

Once down a good three inches, she laid Fantasia in the cold soil and with one last sob, covered her, knowing the erupting leaves from the hosta would soon shelter her. She kneeled before the grave and anger sprouted from the dirt beneath her nails, up her arms and into her chest. Vengeance. She glared at the three orange beasts and plunged her hands into their clear water, releasing the filth and stench from her fingers.

"Smell that? Taste that? It's death. Death you caused. What the hell did she ever do to you, you jealous fucks! Try finding food now. We'll see who wins. Maybe I should leave the gate open for the neighborhood cats to eat you, rip you to shreds and dig their teeth into your eyeballs!"

Heather took the net and threw it at them one more time. It plunged into the pond and sank to the bottom. She rose, sprinted inside and slammed the door behind her. She took a pillow from the couch and winged it at the far wall.

The shrieking of the kitchen phone pierced her ears. Who the fuck was it now? Heather headed to the aggravation and ripped it from its cradle. "What!" she shouted.

"There you are. I paged you at work five times." Brooke's obsession of calling until someone answered, caused fire bolts to rage through Heather's core.

"Obviously I'm not at work, and if I was, and I wasn't calling you back, clearly I'm busy *working*. That's what we normal people do. We *work*."

"No need to shout. I was just calling to invite you to my Home Interiors party. While I was waiting patiently for you to respond to my repeated calls, seventeen guests have already confirmed."

Heather held the phone away from her and strangled it wishing she had enough strength to snap it in half. Her other hand joined in and pretended it was Brooke's throat. After crushing several buttons multiple times, with Brooke's repeated *hellos* intertwined between the beeps, Heather returned it to her ear.

"Are you there, Heather?"

"What do you want?"

"Don't speak to me that way. It's not my fault you're all stressed out from your job."

"My job does not stress me out! I love working."

"You can't fool me. Your attitude says it all. Working full time, raising two kids with no help from anyone, and then having to do your own gardening and house cleaning. No wonder you're so crabby. Jaqueline Shultz told me that you were in the supermarket the other day in Old Navy sweats, your hair in a ponytail, and no make-up."

"Jacqueline Shultz needs to get laid by a big, fat, wide dick up her ass. That's what she needs."

"Heather, what the hell is wrong with you? Are you drunk?"

"No, I'm not drunk. I haven't had a drink in years. I have responsibilities, get it?"

"Then maybe you should start. You're clearly having anger management problems."

Why couldn't she have an old phone that she could smash back in its cradle? She took her finger and pressed the off button. Not as much satisfaction, but rid of Brooke, nonetheless.

The phone rang again. *Unbelievable*. She took a deep breath and held it until her face pulsed with pain. Her finger pressed the green button and she exhaled.

"What happened? The phone went dead."

Dead.

"It didn't go dead. I hung up on you."

"What? What's going on?"

"I'll tell you what's going on, I'm pregnant. How's that?"

"The two of you had sex?"

"Uh, yeah. We're married."

"But I thought..." Silence overtook the other end of the phone. Heather waited, wanting to hang up again. Then a huff spurted from Brooke's mouth. "Are you nuts? What on earth were you thinking?"

So much for support. Not that she expected it from her best friend anyway. Years of criticism. Abuse. Why the hell was she friends with this woman? Brooke loved to tell everyone that they had been best friends since middle school. Was Heather her trophy, or the only real friend that stuck by her for so long?

Maybe Heather was her only friend. That's why she kept her around, just to show off. Another tactic to make herself look important in everyone's eyes.

"Why are you friends with me Brooke?"

"What's that supposed to mean?"

"Exactly that. If I'm such an embarrassment to you then why continue the friendship?"

"We've been friends forever. Stop it."

"Answer the question."

Silence. Heather didn't want to know the answer, didn't care. The red button compressed under her finger again. The phone rang and the answering machine picked up four times. Heather grew more confident with each harrowing message. On Brooke's fifth plea, Heather picked up. "What is it!"

"Don't do that to me ever again."

"Don't tell me what to do. I'm done with you. You're a vile excuse for a friend and don't deserve me. I like who I am. I don't need to fit into your standards. You've tried to change me since twelfth grade. Fuck you! Go find someone else to harass. How about Jaqueline? You can discuss the cosmetic surgeries you've both had."

"Heather, please. I think this pregnancy's making you crazy."

"No, it's giving me strength. Finally."

"You're being unreasonable. I just wanted you to be happy, this is ridiculous."

"The only thing ridiculous is you. You didn't listen when I said I didn't love Lance and I begged you for help. You told me my relationship with Nicolo was a joke, and you've continued to insult me for over fifteen years. Why I put up with it is the most baffling part of the whole equation. Do...not...call me ever again. And you can tell all your fake friends, the next time you have one of your attention-seeking parties, that you lost your only real friend."

Heather clicked off the phone but then clicked it back on and left it under a cushion in the den. Her heart beat with such vigor that she raced to the bathroom and threw up, this time expelling all the animosity she ever stomached for Brooke.

****

Lance removed his suit, changed into his pale blue polo shirt and khaki shorts, and then fired up the barbeque.

Gia tumbled upside-down on the slide, landing on her head and laughter spewed from her mouth. Laurel tugged on the chains and propelled herself higher and higher on the swing. Lance ignored them both.

Still furious from this afternoon's blow out with Brooke, Heather watched from inside and waited for her moment. Lance cleaned the grates with the steel brush, closed the cover, gave the girls a weak smile and retreated into the den where Heather waited.

"I'm pregnant." She held her chin high, eyes remained stony, arms clutched tight around her chest.

Lance shook his head. "What? I don't have time for jokes."

"Oh, this is no joke. Trust me."

His nostrils flared. "Are you serious? This can't be happening."

"Um, you were there. You had no problems getting off."

"You forced me!"

"Forced?"

"Coerced me. I was asleep. That could constitute rape."

Heather snorted. He stood thirteen inches taller than her. "Are you insane? You didn't complain one bit and it only took your usual sixty-seconds to get off."

"Maybe that's because we haven't had sex in years."

"Why should we? It's always about you. No kissing, no foreplay. Pump me a few times then roll over. In fact, you've *never* lasted more than a few minutes." Heather bent forward and discharged one loud hoot.

"How dare you!" Lance's eyes flashed angrily. "You *will* get an abortion. I am not taking care of another child."

"Ha! When have you ever? Have you known the stench of a diarrhea-filled diaper? Held a bottle to their tiny lips as they fell asleep in your arms after only a few sips? Cleaned up puke at two a.m.? Taken them to the doctor, the dentist? When's the last time you've been to their school, a park or a—"

"Don't raise your voice to me."

"Don't tell me what to do." Heather gritted her teeth and took a step forward to stand face-to-face with him. "I'm having this baby and you won't interfere with any decisions in my life ever again. This is no longer about you."

Chapter 36

Nicolo

Nicolo stumbled out of the Fifty-Six Fighter Group restaurant with Dino and his two cousins Al and Carlo. The chicken cutlet Parmesan filled his stomach and he rubbed his belly. The belly that contained three, twenty-ounce glasses of Heineken tap beer, and drowned his poor chicken cutlet.

Dino drove them down the block to the Crazy Donkey and parked in the back of the already loaded parking lot. The line, at least twenty people long.

Dino cut the line, spoke to the bouncer, chuckled, shook his hand and then called the three of them over. "We have about nine more coming," Dino added.

"No problem." The brawny guy nodded. Nicolo used to be that built. He managed to gain back a lot of the weight, but struggled to regain all the mass he lost.

They shouldered their way into the mob and squeezed through until they reached the bar. Dino grabbed the first round and Nicolo gazed at the scene that swelled around him. He suddenly felt old. Was he really thirty-four?

He studied the women, early twenties, for sure. Micro minis, no underwear? Thongs. The shoes all spiked. Three, maybe four inches high and somehow, they danced in them as if barefoot. Their shirts, well, what was left of them, tight, strapless, or a thin string held them up but mainly belly shirts, quite a few on women that had a roll of fat waggling over their skirts. Most were hot and sexy, though. Grinding, drunk, lots of tongues were hanging out.

Dino handed him his fourth beer of the night. "Here's to Nicolo,"

Dino began. "His last week of being single. The fool that he is, taking the plunge into hell."

Nicolo laughed, knowing what an amazing life Dino and Carissa had. *Clink.* Their beer bottles met and then he raised his up to his mouth.

The cold, foamy liquid quenched his thirst and increased his buzz despite the large dinner. Along with giving up food and exercise for months, alcohol was another thing he barely stomached. Tonight, his appetite for all pleasures intensified. Food, beer and women.

Even with the cold beer sliding down his throat, warmth radiated throughout his body. A drumming persisted in his chest, unable to tell if it was from the music or not. Feeling rejuvenated, he slugged down the remainder of his beer and strutted onto the dance floor. The others guzzled their beers and joined him.

He danced alone at first. Not that anyone noticed in a crowded floor like this. Surrounded by gyrating bodies, he held his hands high and a grin ripped across his face. Life was indeed good. "Woo hoo!"

Nicolo wandered into the center of the dance floor and continued his solo dance. He turned at one point, noticed that his other group of friends showed up, some on the dance floor with Dino, some at the bar, but he continued to mingle in and out of sweaty, half-naked bodies that grazed his own.

His support team pointed at his brazenness. They howled and ridiculed him with distorted faces. He didn't care. His life, soon to be in sync with the rest of the clowns at the bar, took on a new outlook.

In one week, he would be a married man. Marrying his beautiful wife, expanding his family, three or four kids soon to follow. Kim's parents adored him, supportive and kind, they made him feel more than welcome. Her sisters kept Kim's head together and reassured her with all the phases of her life. His parents loved her too, and both sets of parents developed an awesome friendship.

Cold beer spilled down his arm and a scrawny kid apologized several times. Nicolo didn't care. He smacked him with a high five and continued his sultry moves, meandering through the wall of ecstasy.

Dino stopped trying to catch up with him. Winked at him instead. A good guy, great brother, and an amazing support system. He looked forward to Carissa and Kim hanging out more. The four of them, a solid team. Their kids playing together in their backyards.

Three girls surrounded Nicolo and raised their arms, adopting him as their new pet. He smirked, gave them his best dance moves and heard his name chanted by a dozen of his friends. A fourth girl returned, hands full of shots and she handed one to Nicolo. He downed it amongst their cheers and roars, and then a bunch of his crew, including Dino, finally caught up with him and joined him in his glory.

****

Dino half-carried, half-dragged Nicolo up his front walkway. Carissa held the door open with one hand and her robe closed with the other. They plopped him on the bed in the guest room and Carissa sneered at Dino for a minute, then a grin appeared on her face.

Dino made a quick call to Kim and explained that Nicolo would spend the night here. Unable to open his eyes without the double vision returning, Nicolo listened instead.

"No he's fine...He can't drive...It's too far...Don't you have to work early tomorrow?...How will he get his car then?...I'll drive him home in the afternoon...He's fine...He's here in the guest room...Kim, he had a good time...No...No...Kim, please..."

Carissa threw Nicolo's shoes in the corner and then tossed the blanket over him. She hurried to the kitchen and returned with a glass of water. A large glass. Nicolo twisted on the mattress and opened one eye. "Thanks," he slurred.

"Are you okay?" Carissa asked.

"Yeah, this'll hurt tomorrow."

"I left water on the nightstand. Try to drink it all."

He took a few sips and she helped him place it back on the counter. "I'm making a good decision, aren't I?"

"About sleeping here? Of course. Don't worry about Kim, she'll under—"

"No, I mean about marrying her."

Carissa tucked the comforter back over his shoulder and smiled. "She's a nice girl, Nicolo."

"I know, it's just..."

Carissa neared the door and gave him one last glance. "Just make sure when you're walking to the altar, it's Kim you're marrying."

****

Nicolo downed a shot of tequila. His third. On his fourth one, he asked for a lemon, the largest one the bartender could find.

"Lemon? What are ya, a pussy?" Nicolo's cousin blurted out. "Not even two hours into your wedding and Kim's got you whipped already." He laughed like a horse and then slapped Nicolo on the back repeatedly as he tried to drink the shot. The liquid dribbled down his chin.

Nicolo crammed the demolished lemon wedge into the shot glass and eyed the exit sign. He slipped past the guests while Kim danced with her sisters, twirling and kicking her toes out from beneath the gown. She was now Kim Trevisani.

He snuck downstairs to the cocktail-hour room. Darkness from the unlit chandeliers and the sun having set two hours earlier, made the once festive area look like a crime scene after the investigation.

He lifted the door handle that led to the narrow outside deck. Unlocked. After glancing over his shoulder, the door eased open, and he stepped out. Wind gusts greeted him and called him to the ocean. Gusts that always managed to comfort him, and shelter him from any disappointments in life. The welcoming briny smells coming off the cool breezes, the sea-weedy scent of low tide. He was home.

He crept to the far end and gazed at the black water. Lights from the catering hall reflected off the ocean like a painting destroyed by spilled liquid.

He twisted his neck and looked up at the well-lit reception room. The pounding music against the glass window let him know the stupid Cha-Cha Slide, as Kim requested, was underway. He covered his ears, but then decided, instead, to remove his tight leather shoes and socks, roll his pants up to his knees and step onto the sand. His feet immersed into the damp, cool grains, and particles flowed between his toes like brown sugar.

September twentieth, the last weekend of summer. Another summer had faded away. The waves that lapped over his feet were still warm with enthusiasm. He closed his eyes, thrust his hands into his pockets and let the salty air wander up his nose and into his throat.

The vision returned. After Heather and he had left the beach that final night, they snuck into his bedroom and planned their wedding. Hiding beneath his covers with a flashlight, they whispered their ideas to each other. Ones they both kept secretly, but now disclosed under his dark blue sheets.

Ceremony on the beach, under one of those frilly arches. Her in a white gown, short enough for her cute knees to show, but the back still long and flowing. He in a white linen suit, no tie. No shoes for either of them.

Only close friends and family. No dumb hand-shaking line to meet all the people you didn't know. No Uncle Joes and Aunt Marys that no one had heard from in twenty years. No bosses you felt obligated to invite, or nosey neighbors or people you needed to impress. No annoying cousins either.

They'd have the reception at a restaurant on the beach. Enjoy the summer warmth at an outside bar, tables with umbrellas, and a small dance floor. No Cha-Cha Slide.

They would say their vows with toes in the sand, take pictures as the sun set, dance a little, kiss a lot and then sneak off to their honeymoon on a tropical beach far away.

A vision, a plan, a conversation that happened a long time ago.

The waves continued to wash over his feet, eddying the sand away from underneath until they set two to three inches lower. He sank deeper into the hole. Restricted, locked in.

Chapter 37

Heather

A beautiful Christmas present. Nothing under the tree could top the birth of another child. She thought for sure she'd have a boy. Rori, the red king, she had chosen for him. With the birth of her third daughter, though, a beautiful bundle of sweetness with strawberry colored lips and the riotous cries she let out during delivery, she knew the name fit her perfectly.

Resentment during her pregnancy transformed into victory now.

The new year rocketed towards her and with that, a new stance. The endearing poofy-cheeked baby in her arms provided the outlook she needed. The menu changed, no longer serving up bland options. New choices brewed as she kissed Rori's tiny nose.

****

Heather adjusted Rori's bouncy seat so she could watch her while she exercised to an old VCR tape she found on the top shelf of her closet. Denise Austin's *Hips, Thighs & Buttocks* provided the needed motivation to get her body back in shape. Three kids, no regular exercise regimen, and finishing off Laurel and Gia's chicken nuggets and mac & cheese here and there, were taking their toll.

Lance entered the den with a rush of anticipation. "Who's here?"

Heather glanced up from her squat position and then looked away.

"Who's here to see me? There's a Jeep in the driveway."

"And that means they're here to see you?" Heather placed her hands on her hips and bent forward into a lunge.

"Who else would they be here to see, one of the kids?" He

chuckled loud and annoying.

"Maybe they're here to see me."

"You?" He scanned Heather's body as if looking at garbage pail full of rotten food. "Who's here to see you?"

"Nobody." Heather raised her hands above her head and peeked over at Rori. She could swear the adorable little girl just smiled at her.

"Is there something wrong with you? I asked you a question. Whose Jeep is that?"

"Mine."

Lance shook his head and gritted his teeth. "This isn't funny. What's with your attitude lately?"

Heather's eyebrows shot up and then she dropped her hand weights on the rug. They landed with a clunk. "You said I needed a bigger car so I bought a Jeep Grand Cherokee."

"We decided on a minivan." Lance said.

"No, *you* decided on a minivan. I told you I wouldn't be seen in one."

"Everyone drives a minivan."

"I'm not everyone. I refuse to sit in a giant dinosaur-egg. Like one of those 1950's silver RV's."

"Look, this is life. You get married, pop out a few kids, buy a minivan, go to PTA meetings, hob nob with the wives at the bus stop, make your husband dinner and then invite friends over for a barbecue. The American dream."

"Your dream," she mumbled. She rewound the tape and raised the volume.

****

Heather left work during her lunch hour and drove to FLEX, a small gym five minutes from the hospital. She had passed by it while pregnant with Rori and knew this was the one. A *man's* gym. No aerobics room, no daycare, no pink plastic three-pound weights. This was the real deal.

Heather headed to the front desk. The lobby already reeked of hot sweat, body odor and musty, humid air. Steel barbells, cast iron plates, power racks and a few benches covered the black and gray flooring.

"Can I help you?" A steroid infused mountain approached. His sheer, white tank top didn't cover his nipples.

"Yes, I'd like to join."

He leaned over the counter, examined Heather from her high heels to her unwavering glare and massaged the back of his neck. He snickered and gave her a suspicious half-smile.

"Problem?" she snarled.

A sneer touched the corner of his lips. "I think you're in the wrong place, sweetheart. Don't think you can handle this."

"I'm hoping your gym can handle me."

His look turned cool, he made a vague sound in his throat, then snapped up from the desk. "I'll show you what you're getting yourself into, babe."

She followed him to the pit. He purposely led her to the hub of the room where she became the focus. Thick non-ventilated air engulfed her.

"We don't got no yoga or Stairmasters. Strictly free-weights, bunch of machines."

Sweaty men, ranging from late twenties to early fifties eyed Heather. She placed her hands on her hips, squeezing the top of her red skirt. "That's all I need."

"No women in here," he growled.

"Good."

Chapter 38

Nicolo

Nicolo and Kim toasted to the incredible past year, on their first wedding anniversary, in the restaurant where their wedding took place. The year had flown by, and another summer with it.

They joked about the wedding antics and the hurricane that almost ruined their honeymoon. They chuckled about their new neighbor upstairs that clip-clopped in her heels all night long. They remembered the January snowstorm that kept them captive in their apartment for a day and a half. They spent the summer on the beach and at various wine-tasting tours.

Next month they planned a weekend in New Paltz, to see the colors transform along the countryside and enjoy everything the season had to offer.

"I booked a room for the third weekend in October," Nicolo said.

Kim removed her pocket calendar from her bag. "The twenty-third?"

"Yup. It's right near the Mohonk Preserve and the Shawangunks Mountains. They have rock climbing and hiking trails there, too. We should try that next time."

"Mountain climbing? Are you serious?"

"Why not? It looked cool."

"Can you see me climbing a rock?"

"Maybe we can check out the hiking trails at least."

"I thought we were going to farmers' markets and pumpkin picking. Buying some apple cider, Moon Pies."

"We are, it's just...there's so much to do up there. There's also the Split Rock Falls. Maybe we should bring bathing suits."

"Swimming in October?"

"If we hit a warm weekend, why not?"

"You know I'm not an outdoorsy person."

"You said that about the beach and now you love that."

The waiter brought his brownie sundae and Kim forked off a tiny corner. "You know you can order your own piece," he said.

"No way, too many calories."

He shook his head and polished off the rest.

After dessert, they returned to their apartment, and Kim surprised him with a new negligee. His eyes perked up. "Better than the brownie," he said.

"Your anniversary present."

He eased himself onto the bed and pulled her close to him. He lifted the red lace, kissed her belly and then slid his hands over her bare ass. Seeing her in these get-ups still excited him, but removing them was even more fun.

Later in the night, as they laid atop the sheets catching their breath, Nicolo removed the wet hair clinging to her damp face and grinned. Their sex life was still good after six years. He ran his hand diagonally across her belly, circled, and then gave it a pat. "You're gonna look so hot when you're pregnant."

Her smile plummeted. She turned away, averting his gaze.

"What? Did I say something wrong?"

"Nicolo, we've discussed this before. I told you, I don't know if I want children. Our life is perfect the way it is."

He withdrew his hand, ran his fingers through his hair and gaped at the ceiling. "And when exactly did we have this convo?"

"A few years ago."

"Years ago?" he shouted. "When?" He lurched up and faced her paralyzed expression.

"I don't know. I think we were at Wine & Corks."

"I've never been there! You go there with your sisters."

"I'm sure it was you. I remember sitting in the back near the wine racks. I told you the shrieking kids in the children's department were driving me crazy and that's why I asked to transfer to the lingerie department. I started crying, remember?"

"I was never in that place. I didn't even know about your transfer until after it happened. And from that, I'm supposed to get that you don't want kids?"

Kim yanked the covers until her head disappeared under them. "I specifically had this conversation with you." Her voice muffled. "I remember it all came out because I had too much to drink."

"Maybe that's why you thought I was there, because you were too goddamned drunk." He shot out of bed and yanked on his sweatpants. "Absolutely not. I want kids, lots of them. You know how much I adore Dante and Mariana."

"You can babysit them anytime you want."

He shuddered, then his face contorted. He lunged onto the bed and kneeled over her. "Are you serious? I want my own kids! And what in God's name do the kids in Macy's that are dragged around, exhausted, and bored to death have to do with us?"

The lump under the comforter was suddenly mute.

"I don't believe this. This is insane. We'll be great parents. I'll be an outstanding father. I'd even take on the majority of the responsibilities. Feeding, changing diapers, middle of the night fevers, puke—"

"I don't want our anniversary ruined any further."

"Ruin the anniversary? This can ruin our marriage!"

Kim sprang up. "Look. What can't you understand? I babysat my sisters all the time and then they up and left me."

"Left you? They're still with you. All the time."

"I had to share a room, my toys, my clothes—"

"You said you liked that. You had fun!"

"Yes, and then after sharing everything, they just deserted me."

"Did you want them to live with you forever? Kim, your sisters are here, all the time. What are you talking about?"

"You give and give and they just all end up leaving." Tears fell from her eyes,

Nicolo's eyes widened. He didn't understand where this was coming from. "Are you afraid if you have kids, they'll leave you?"

"They just want and want and it's never enough. The kids in Macy's, Dante and Mariana..."

"Hang on. Wait a second. They don't ask you for anything. Is this why you never wanted to babysit them? Is this why you refused to allow them in our wedding ceremony?"

Kim looked away.

"Why didn't you ever discuss this with me before?"

"I did."

"No. Never. Every time I bring up Dante and Mariana, you change the subject or walk away. I thought you just had a problem with them."

"Look, Nic. We're buying a house next month, how much more can we pile on?"

"I didn't say now, but for it not to be an option? Ever?" Nicolo crumpled onto the edge of the bed. "Please, say you don't mean it. Say you'll think about it."

She rolled back over and switched off the light. Leaving Nicolo in the dark.

Chapter 39

Heather

The end of the school year approached like a child on a brand new bicycle. Time played games with Heather. Her days at work dragged as if the batteries in the clocks napped. Her evenings flew by in a blur of homework and housework. At night, she wilted onto her bed and dissolved beneath the sheets until the sunlight warned that a new day was ready to harass her. The clock, finally catching up from its long afternoon snooze.

Heather unloaded Rori from her arms, watched her scuttle into the house with her sturdy walking legs and then dropped the diaper bag on the rug relieved it no longer contained jars of baby food or bottles.

She thanked the babysitter, boiled the water for the raviolis and reviewed Laurel and Gia's homework. The last of the homework before summer vacation.

She checked Gia's easier second grade assignments and then after checking Laurel's homework, placed it into her backpack. "What's this?" she asked. "You got your yearbook?" Heather couldn't believe Laurel was graduating from elementary school and starting fifth grade next year.

"Yeah," Laurel said. "Nancy Kalan and her sister's on every page."

"Nancy Kalan is only in third grade, and her sister's still in preschool. Why are they even in the yearbook?"

"Nancy Kalan's mom is in charge of the yearbook this year."

"So?" Heather flipped the pages. Faster and faster. At the fire department visit, Nancy and her sister Livia posed in front of the fire truck. For the Halloween party, the girls had a center shot hugging each other. At the Valentine's Day dance, both girls took over the dance floor with their red dresses, as other kids stood around and watched. Even at a stupid book fair, there was a large headshot of Nancy Kalan holding a freakin' pencil next to her face.

"Are there any pictures of you?" Heather reached the center of the book. A beautiful group shot of the fourth graders took over the centerfold. The children sat under a large flowering tree in the playground. Laurel was dead center. In the crack. A staple over her face.

Laurel bit down on her lip, but her chin still trembled violently. Heather tossed the book aside and hugged Laurel, whose sniffles turned into full-blown sobbing.

****

A week later, at the end-of-the-year celebration, Heather lugged in a huge box for Laurel's class party. She noticed Jessica Kalan in the main lobby.

Two women stood in front of Jessica, their eyes focused on her, pupils almost as large as their phony grins. They laughed ridiculously at her chatter. Praise and compliments sailed from their mouths, along with feigned enthusiasm.

"No, really. The yearbook came out wonderful." A woman around four-foot ten and two-hundred pounds, said.

"Yes, I loved all the backgrounds and embellishments." A petite mom wearing a turtleneck sweater in June, said.

"Thank you." Jessica closed her eyes and touched her heart as if she just won a noble peace prize. "It really was a difficult undertaking. Countless pictures had to be sorted."

"It couldn't have been that difficult." Heather interrupted. "Being that all the pictures were of your children."

The three women stared at her. Jessica's mouth dropped and her hand flew back to her chest. The two mothers glanced at Jessica for a reaction and then inspected the linoleum.

"They were not."

"They were on every page, in every activity."

"We are very active in our school's functions."

"Your daughter's not even graduating this year and Livia doesn't even go to this school yet."

"Listen, Heather, you're the only one that complained. Everyone else loved what I did. I'm sorry Laurel was unable to attend any of the functions because you work."

"She was at every function," Heather yelled. "With *me*."

"I don't recall seeing either of you."

"That's because your camera was shoved up your daughter's—"

"I noticed too."

Heather turned to find a woman wearing a black baseball cap backwards. She had on jean shorts, purple Converse High Tops and a T-shirt that read *Take No Prisoners*. Heather liked her immediately.

"Excuse me?" Jessica said.

The woman stepped closer. "My daughter was only in one picture. At the Hula Hoop Fundraiser, and it was the back of her head. The janitor was in more pictures than her."

"I can't be expected to get every fourth grader at just the right angle."

"But you were able to get two pictures of Nancy hula hooping, one of Livia looking dead on at you, and one of both of them dancing together on stage with their hula hoops?"

"I have to go," the woman in the turtleneck sweater, whispered. Humpty Dumpty waddled away with her.

"Look, I don't need this abuse. I did a fine job and I'm proud of myself."

"Is that what your therapist told you?" the woman continued.

Jessica huffed and then, before her temper exploded, stormed off.

"Nice!" Heather leaned over and high-fived her.

"I can't stand women like her. They take over the school and you're at their mercy. You have to kiss their ass otherwise they punish you."

"Is that why my daughter's not in any pictures?"

"Probably." She laughed. "My name's Roxanne Ferrari." She held out her hand, her fingernails were painted black. "But everyone calls me Roxie."

"You're Kylie's mom. Our daughters are in the same class. I'm Heather Milanesi."

"Laurel's mom, right? Kylie talks about her all the time. We should get them together over the summer."

"I'd like that."

Roxie eyed Heather's box. "Need help with that?"

"No, it's for the party. I'm in charge of arts and crafts."

"Oh, right. No more cupcakes. School ban. Isn't that ridiculous?"

"Especially since they have bake sales all the time and then send the kids out to sell chocolate bars and cookie dough for fundraisers."

"Gourmet cookie dough."

"Sorry. *Gourmet.*" Heather shut her eyes and flipped the hair away from her face, pretending to be Jessica.

Roxie giggled. "And the kids still bring in chips and doughnuts for snack every day. Kylie told me a girl brought in a chocolate sandwich the other day. A Hershey's chocolate bar in between two pieces of white bread."

"You're kidding me? They can't have cupcakes on their birthdays, but let them eat garbage every day."

"Exactly," Roxie said. "So, what craft did you bring in?"

"Decorate your own cupcakes."

"You didn't!"

"Totally. I don't follow rules anymore. Let them try to say something as the kids *ooh* and *ahh*. Plus, it's the last day of school. What are they gonna do to me?"

Chapter 40

Nicolo

Nicolo breathed in and out, nice and slow, even though his heart was slamming against his rib cage. Don't show too much emotion, the wrong emotion. It'll only upset Kim and any wrong vibe could put her over the edge.

He left their new home an hour later, convinced it was more than enough time without looking obvious. Also, because he couldn't restrain his feelings any longer.

After telling Kim he needed to pick up a bag of lawn fertilizer at Lowe's, he jumped into his truck and took off towards the elementary school a quarter mile down the road from their house. School had let out for the summer and he needed a deserted location.

His brakes screeched as he settled across four parking spots. He rocketed out, barely closing the door. Nicolo clutched his hair with both hands and paced. His sneakers pounded the sandy blacktop harder, quicker, as he thought about the morning and processed the information.

Relax.

He sprinted across the crabgrass, the weeds whacking him in the shins, and headed toward the playground. He grabbed hold of the first rung of the monkey bars and scaled to the other side.

Settle down.

Plopping down on the rubber seat of the swing, Nicolo soared into the clouds, pumping his legs and pulling on the chains with enthusiasm. He leaped off the swing and landed almost ten feet away, his construction boots driving the wood chips into a pile.

He scaled up the eight-foot slide, then ran across the wooden bridge to the corkscrew slide on the opposite end. He clutched the steel bar and thrust himself down the spiral. His shoulders and long legs wedged him within the chamber. He wriggled until he was able to finally slide upside down. His upper back landed with a plop onto the strewn wood chips. A man and a young boy stood above him, alarmed.

"I'm going to be a father!" Nicolo shouted.

The man's tensed glare shattered and then warped into a large grin with his eyebrows climbing just as high. "Congratulations!"

Nicolo took off again and jogged to the soccer field. Kim was pregnant. He saw the stick. A child, his child, would one day be in his arms.

Still unsure what convinced her, Nicolo shook his head and sat on a patch of grass. The neighbors for sure, and all their children. How many kids lived on their block? Eleven and counting. Kerrie was four months pregnant. She told everyone last month at her Memorial Day party.

Kim witnessed it for herself, though. Children ran all over Tom's front lawn, bicycles whizzed by, kids on scooters, boys with water guns and girls jumping rope and another handful played kickball. All of them laughing. Bubbles, giggles, playing tag and chasing the Mister Softee ice cream truck.

Their block sprouted into an amusement park this spring. They could have moved anywhere on Long Island, to a block with no kids, or one with older neighbors and children in college, and then his life would have continued down a childless path. But something saved them. The push Kim needed in the right direction.

Did she feel the love that other parents had for their kids? Had others hinted at her being next to have a baby? Did she realize what she'd be missing?

Little Chloe's first birthday party must have been the kicker. Piñata, farm animals. He was shocked to see Kim pick up a bottle to feed the animals. He watched her press the nipple to a baby lamb's mouth and his heart shriveled into the echoing void. A hopeless situation; the lamb mocked his longings for a child.

Something changed inside her, though. Extra quiet the following week, Kim wandered around their home planting flowers in the front and vegetables in the back. He didn't dare ask what was on her mind. He had in the past and she only snapped at him that she was fine.

She snuggled close to him one evening, and told him she stopped taking her pill. A month ago. For good. It was the most rewarding sex he ever had.

Chapter 41

Heather

Heather's beeper resounded in the cramped nurses' station. *Lance.* She sighed and fell back into her chair. Her plan of leaving the house early this morning and avoiding him all day, failed. What did he want now?

She dialed his office number, then turned her head away from the pulmonologist sitting next to her. Lance's voice cut through her ear, causing a massive hemorrhage. "Yes, Lance, what is it?"

"You ran out this morning."

"I needed to get to work early today," she lied.

"You didn't forget about tonight did you?"

Forget what? That her pathetic life would just repeat itself over and over again? No, she couldn't forget that. "Forget what?"

"The alumni reunion."

She drew a blank.

"Hofstra law school. My fifteenth reunion celebration."

"Tonight?"

"Yes," he shouted, then lowered his voice to a murmur. "We spoke about it last week."

"We? When?" Heather flipped through her *Josie & the Pussy Cats* pocket calendar she picked up at the dollar store. "I don't have any record of this." She attempted to act professional as the doctor stood and left.

"Are you kidding me? It's tonight at six o'clock at the Garden City hotel."

"There's no way. I have no one to watch the kids."

"Um, your mother," he said sarcastically.

"Um, how 'bout *your* mother," she returned the sarcasm.

His impatience exploded through the phone. "My mother is very busy. We've been through this countless times."

"Doing what? My mother's at work until five every day."

"Perfect, she can swing by and give the kids dinner."

"After working all day, all week? Are you insane? What's your mother done this past decade?"

A protracted sigh sifted through her earpiece and then silence.

"I have to stay late tonight anyway," Heather said. "My new boss wants me to help out for a catering event this evening."

"I don't care. You need to be there to support me. What would it look like if I showed up alone?"

"Like your hard-working wife was home watching our three children."

"Impossible."

"Lance, I work until four, then have to help her until at least five. There's no way I can go home, change, and be there by six."

"What are you wearing?"

"Excuse me?"

"Did you wear a presentable outfit today?"

"My outfits are always presentable."

"A suit perhaps? A dress?"

"I have my red suit on."

"Oh God, not that one. Must you stand out? Don't you have any black or grey suits?"

"For funerals, yes."

"Look Heather, call your mother, tell her to drive here right after work so I can at least get there on time. You leave work at precisely five, come directly to the hotel and I will meet you in the lobby."

Heather covered her eyes with her hand and inhaled. The smell of soap from the unit's bathroom invaded her nose. "Lance, even if this psychopath of a boss lets me leave exactly at five and I didn't spend a second freshening up and drove directly to you, there's no way I would make it by six. Not to mention, I don't know if my mother's even available."

"Is my dignity and self-respect not important to you? Must you always try to embarrass me?"

"Embarrass you?"

"Yes, my mother has pointed it out to me many times."

"I'm sure she has!" Heather did not care who heard now. The secretary popped her head out from behind the rack of charts. "If I'm such an embarrassment to you, why don't you just go alone?"

"No, no, I'll wait. Just sneak out, drive fast, do whatever it takes. If you're not there by six-ten, I guess I'll have to go in without you."

"Heaven forbid! A whole ten minutes. Thank you for your patience, and for suggesting I get fired and get a speeding ticket or leave our children motherless. So admirable of you."

He hung up the phone taking her reply as a 'yes'. *Asshole.*

Heather begged her mother to come, promising to take her out to lunch tomorrow with the girls. After all these years, her mother understood, but failed to suggest the unthinkable. Her mother would rather ruin her own social life than have her granddaughters go through a divorce.

Heather snuck downstairs fifteen minutes early, saw the wraps she had to prepare and glanced over at Maria, the salad room employee. "Mushroom, cream cheese and leek wraps?" Heather grimaced.

"She said it was healthy." Maria gagged in a teasing manner.

"For who?"

Heather dumped the ingredients into a large bowl, mashed it together and slapped it on the tortillas. All forty of them. Maria helped her with the last five and then they each took half, and cut them into small pinwheels.

Before the tyrant returned, Heather hurried back to her office. She brushed her teeth, threw lipstick on, and then flipped her hair up in a hair claw. She yanked on her sneakers, prepared for the hour-long ride to Garden City, and tossed her heels into a plastic Target bag.

She drove into the Garden City Hotel's parking lot at 6:20 p.m. After wiping the smudged eyeliner from beneath her eyes, she glanced down at her feet. The clock switched to 6:22 p.m and she grinned. She would do it.

Heather eased herself out of her car and strolled into the lobby. She meandered toward the large sign mounted on an easel: *Maurice A. Deane School of Law's Alumni Reunion.* The Cotillion Room.

She sauntered into the room like she was the guest of honor, snatched a glass of champagne from one of the waiters and then lingered by the buffet table, popping a golf-ball sized, stuffed, crimini mushroom into her mouth. Her back molars severed the ball in half releasing a torrent of boiling heat and vapors. The roof of her mouth seared, and she attempted to sip the carbonated champagne through her boiling, spinach-and-garlic-corked mouth.

"Why are you so late?" Lance screamed.

Heather rotated, trying to swallow the blistering globule. No words formed. She guzzled more champagne, chewing, swallowing. When the last bit went down, a coughing fit ensued. Instead of helping, Lance glanced around and hushed her.

Heather inhaled and wiped the tears from her face. The painful, charred flesh throbbed. She finished off the champagne, the effervescence stinging her again.

"What...the hell...are you wearing?"

She rubbed the roof of her mouth with her tongue and shook her head, tears still falling.

"Why are you wearing sneakers with skulls on them?"

Heather looked down at them, trying not to laugh. The pain helped. "I like skulls." Her garbled words inflamed the situation.

"Why are you wearing them in here?" he whispered.

"I ran out of work just like you said and forgot to grab my shoes."

Lance stepped back and his mouth dropped open. "You can't show up like this. And what happened to your jacket, why are you wearing a tank top?"

"Lance, its ninety degrees out there. I've been in my car for an hour."

"I don't care, this is a professional event."

"It's a reunion, Lance. Get over it." Heather looked over his shoulder, then waved.

"Heather! So good to see you!" Rex Bacon, Lance's old college buddy, the pirate she shared a bottle o' rum with, flew to her side and gave her a hug. "You're the only one dressed smart. Next time I'm coming in shorts and a Hawaiian T-shirt. What do ya think?"

"Only if you wear flip flops with it." She smiled.

"You're on!"

"Where's that great wife of yours?" Heather asked.

"Couldn't make it. Home with the kids."

Heather glared at Lance.

"More fun without her, though. I can catch up with my old friends and not have to worry about her being bored."

"I hear ya," Heather moaned.

"You look beautiful as always. How are the girls?"

"The three of them are absolutely amazing."

"Three? Did I miss one?'

This time Heather glowered at Lance. "I guess so. Rori. She's one and a half."

"Wow, I did miss it. I'm sure she's as wonderful as your other daughters."

"They're all remarkable."

"Gets it from their mom. So what have you been up to? Still working hard?"

Lance stepped behind Rex as he chatted, and motioned to Heather's teeth. He repeatedly poked at his own.

"Yup, switched hospitals, though. At Norlyn Plains Hospital now. Been there for about two and a half years. Horrible new boss though."

"Bosses always ruin the fun. You should think about starting your own private practice."

"It was always my dream but…"

Lance poked at his teeth again, then pointed to her. His face now red as the roasted peppers that passed behind him on a tray.

"What?" Heather looked over at Lance, interrupting Rex.

"Excuse us, Rex. Need to talk to the wifey for a second." Lance clamped down on Heather's arm and dragged her to the lobby. He let go of her and scowled.

"Now what?"

"You have a hunk of something green in your front teeth." Lance avoided looking at her, but instead, surveyed the deserted room for incoming.

This time, Heather could not hold back. She keeled forward and let out a roar.

"This isn't funny, this is a disgrace. And you smell of garlic."

"It's my new perfume. Garlic #5, for women." She bared her green teeth again for the full effect.

"That's it! My mother was right. You're intentionally trying to embarrass me! Go home, just leave. I'll make an excuse that you were sick."

"But, Rex. I enjoy talking to him. He's the only normal friend you have."

"Forget Rex. Just go."

"Fine. Tell him good-bye at least, will you?" Heather skipped through the lobby like a schoolgirl, but not before swiping a prosciutto-wrapped shrimp from a waiter.

Chapter 42

Nicolo

Nicolo took his son, Christopher to his friend Jeff's annual Fourth of July picnic in the park. Last year, Christopher spent most of the day in his stroller or in Nicolo's arms. Today, Nicolo needed his full strength to keep up after his sixteen-month-old son.

The two of them raced to the barbeque area, Christopher showing off his powerful legs, and Nicolo trying to haul the diaper bag, essential toys, a small cooler of food, and a case of Coronas. He unloaded the gear and his friend Jeff jogged over to him.

"Nic, great to see you." He shook his hand and then studied the almost three-foot tall twin beside him. "This is Christopher?" he said, squatting. "You got so tall."

Christopher paid no attention to Jeff and walked toward the open bag of pretzel rods.

"Uh, uh, uh. Not now, you just ate."

"Eh, give him one. He'll probably just suck the salt off it anyway. All my kids did that. A big soggy stick was all that was left." Christopher ignored them both and snagged a rod anyway. "Where's Kim?"

Nicolo scanned the woods to the left of the playground. "Uh, she went with her sisters to the vineyards today. Kind of a group thing with a bus picking them up."

"Sounds cool. Christopher's not much of a wine drinker?" He chuckled.

"Nah, he's just like his dad. To the T."

Jeff slapped Nicolo on the back. "Go get yourself something to eat. Foods already on the grill."

Nicolo hid Kim's breakdown from everyone.

After they told her she was having a girl, she gave birth to Christopher, in a difficult delivery that lasted thirteen hours and ended in a C-section. Crying in the maternity ward, she didn't want to breastfeed, as she had planned.

Her overwhelming exhaustion and difficulty bonding with Christopher after she came home, was labeled as postpartum depression. Crazy mood swings forced Nicolo to take over as the main caregiver.

He enjoyed every minute of it.

After months of refusing, Kim finally agreed to take medication. She leveled off, acting less unstable. Nicolo encouraged her to go out with her sisters to change up her atmosphere.

But Nicolo missed her, and wanted the old Kim back.

Christopher continued to suck on his now saturated pretzel, while Nicolo scarfed down a burger and a piece of watermelon. When mushy pretzel goo covered his hands and face, Nicolo wiped him down with a wet nap and then they hiked to the playground together.

Christopher's eyes widened like giant lollipops. "Daddy!" Christopher took off across the beige pebbles. Nicolo easily caught up after three or four steps. He helped him climb the ladder on the green slide, and the wind blew through Christopher's wavy black hair as he flew down, and into Nicolo's arms.

"Again, again!"

Eight plunges later, Nicolo dropped onto the pebbles, caught Christopher, rolled over and hugged him tight.

They say your life changes when you have kids. Lack of sleep, illnesses, piles of diapers and bottles. But no one talks about the effect on your heart. How a child can rip everything you believed in from you, and hand you a new view on it all. Now he understood why the Grinch's heart grew three sizes.

Nicolo laid on his back and lifted Christopher in the air with his feet. He balanced him on the soles of his sneakers and held his tiny hands. Soaring high, Christopher giggled and squealed.

His life was fun again. He was able to relive his own childhood, teach his son all the cool things he could do. Not to mention all the bad things too. "We won't tell mommy though, right?"

He put Christopher down and he tottered over to the swing. "Up, up." Nicolo lifted him into the infant swing and laughed. One day he'd be big like his dad and wouldn't be able to fit into such a tiny seat.

Once strapped in, Christopher kicked his feet numerous times wanting the ride to start. Instead, Nicolo squatted before him, held his tiny face in his large hands and kissed him on the forehead.

"Daddy, go."

Nicolo smiled, leaped up and ran behind him. The seat lifted a good four feet into the air, and then he let go.

Chapter 43

Heather

After four and a half years of working at the hospital, Grace, the fun and sassy dietitian, didn't return from her maternity leave. In came Catherine. Close in age to Heather, three children like Heather, but they had little else in common.

Victoria and Heather tried to control their giggling as they strode into the cafeteria. The tempting scent of almonds and grilled fish meandered throughout the room. Catherine had already settled herself into a booth with her perky yellow lunch bag that took up half the table. Heather prepared her routine salad with grilled chicken from the colorful salad bar. Victoria ordered the pepper steak over rice.

They sat across from Catherine and watched her unload her lunch, all in reusable containers. Out of a flat container came her turkey sandwich on whole wheat bread with lettuce, tomato and mustard. A small, blue container held a bunch of green grapes plucked off their vines. Heather was sure there were exactly seventeen, the correct portion size. A rectangular, clear container housed strips of red peppers. In a small piece of tin foil was her dessert. Six vanilla wafers. The same amount they gave their patients for dessert. She brought her own water bottle. Pink and transparent.

"What did you two do this weekend?" Victoria cut the long strips of steak in half.

"I took the girls to Sunken Meadow Beach. Holding on to the last few days of summer. I got some great shots of them climbing on the boulders."

"Nice. I can't wait to see them. What about you, Catherine?"

"Fall cleaning weekend. A little behind I'm sad to say. Bought a steam cleaner for the rugs and did all four bedrooms, even the living room and den."

"Wow, sounds like a ton of fun!" Heather smiled like a hyperactive clown at a five-year olds birthday party.

"It works really well. You have to see the difference."

"Can't wait. Maybe we can all come over on another beautiful seventy degree day and watch."

Victoria kicked Heather under the table. "It *was* really nice this weekend. Surely you went out and did something fun."

"Peter took the kids to play miniature golf on Saturday."

"You didn't go?"

"No. So much to do." Catherine picked up her container of grapes and after shifting a few around, speared the largest one with a fork. Heather's eyebrows raised.

"Do you have any hobbies, Catherine?" Victoria tried to look interested.

"Perhaps coin collecting? Knitting? Shopping in Coldwater Creek catalogs?" Heather's sarcasm earned her another kick.

"My kids are my hobbies. They occupy all my free time."

"But there must be something you enjoy. Something to relieve stress."

"I'm perfectly stress free. The kids do well in school, I'm married to a successful stockbroker, my house is clean and organized..."

"That's because you haven't worked in seven years." Heather pointed out.

"I wanted to wait until all my kids were in school full-time. Now that they are, work is my passion."

Heather bit into her chocolate chip cookie and looked over her shoulder for a diversion. She suddenly longed for Samantha and Cara's wild weekend stories of binging and vomiting, after having sex with various strangers behind smelly dumpsters.

****

Heather grabbed the new lab coat that she purchased online and slipped her arms through each sleeve. She admired herself in their office's full-length mirror. The short, fitted lab coat still allowed her funky, clothes to stand out.

She spent the past weekend shopping for new clothes. Short skirts, body-hugging shirts and loads of tank tops to show off her new body. The dedicated hours she put in at the gym over the past few years, gave her the body she could only imagine. She was more muscular now than with Nicolo. She made friends with the usuals at FLEX and devoured any advice they threw her way.

They shifted from sneering and gawking at her, to becoming her spotting partners. She asked countless questions and they were happy to guide her. They pushed her hard, but she never complained. Heather needed these workouts to release the anger that seemed to boil inside her every day. Planting pretty flowers was no longer an effective distraction. Her body fat dropped to fourteen percent and muscles protruded from every body part. Her new six-pack was something that Lance would never see.

Since Rori's birth, Lance's distance from her and the girls grew. Laurel and Gia preoccupied themselves with their friends and neighborhood kids, but Rori, almost four, clung to her familiar surroundings. Lance waved her aside like she was a thing, a mindless rodent that needed too much care.

Laurel sprouted into a beautiful twelve-year-old and Heather feared what seventh grade would bring this year. Would boys start asking her out? Still helpful, and always concerned, Laurel acted like the second mother in the house. Heather loved the one-on-one conversations they had privately. Something that had remained consistent since her curious toddler days. All Heather could hope was that she taught her enough about boys to make the right decisions when the time came.

Gia on the other hand, became a defiant and stubborn, soon to be ten-year-old. She wanted it her way. Always. Rebellious to the point that Heather refused to care anymore how she dressed. Skirts went into the basement with the hope that Rori would wear them one day. Gia replaced them with jeans that had tears and writing scribbled all over them. No more pretty, flowery tops. T-shirts with wacky sayings prevailed. She asked if she could paint a mural on her wall and within a day, the quote: *"In order to be someone, you must first be yourself"* appeared, surrounded by magazine photos of *Pink*. For her birthday, she chose a purple bike with black tires and skulls-and-crossbones on the frame.

Heather threw a piece of gum in her mouth and reached for her binder. The phone in the office rang and she snatched it. "Hello?" she groaned.

The caller hung up. *Good.* Probably another patient calling the wrong office and wanting another serving of French-fries. Heather grabbed her things and the chiming resounded again. This time Catherine answered it.

"Good morning. Registered dietitian's office, Catherine Bordeau speaking, how may I direct your call, please?"

Oh God. The person on the other end could be dead by the time she finished.

"No, Bentley. I'm very busy. Did you brush your teeth? Make your bed? Well, hurry up before you miss the bus." Catherine leaned in close to her desk and whispered. "Don't speak to me that way. Do you hear me?"

Victoria nudged Heather out the door and towards the cafeteria. "Leave, before you strangle her with the cord."

"Three months and it's not getting any better."

"She's just different, that's all. She hasn't worked in years and is trying hard."

"Trying to annoy me."

"Did you miss a session at the gym or something?"

"What?"

"You've been extra moody lately."

Heather tried to maintain her tough persona, but a grin crept onto her face instead. "No, I didn't miss a session. I'm just..." She ordered her eggs at the grill counter and walked towards the milk containers. "I'm just bored Victoria. Don't you feel that way? There has to be something more than this."

"Than what?"

"Marriage, kids, work. Is this it?"

"What do you want?" Victoria hid her face and grabbed some raisins for her oatmeal.

"You feel it too. Don't you?"

"No. Well, sometimes. But that's why I joined the Cancer Foundation."

"And that helps? I should join a group?"

"I'm not sure that'll help you, Heather." She plucked out a few napkins and sat at the back table.

"What's that supposed to mean?"

"I just meant that I joined because I felt like my brain was being drained of all its intelligence. I needed to resuscitate it."

"Oh." Heather sliced her omelet into a million pieces.

"What are you looking for?"

"I don't know Victoria, but I feel like a volcano ready to explode."

****

After Lance's reunion fiasco two and a half years ago, he insisted on buying Heather a cell phone. The last thing she wanted was for him to track her down and be at his disposal. She reluctantly took it, and frequently left it at home, the battery dead most of the time.

When she finally relied on it to keep track of her daughters' whereabouts, the harassment started. Lance ignored Heather when she asked him not to give Bianca her phone number. He took it as an insult and despite Heather's numerous reasons why, he gave it to his mother anyway. Then the texts began.

Never random, but always preplanned and calculated, Bianca seemed to know exactly where Heather was and what she was doing.

At the pool last summer: *Glad you have time to enjoy the nice weather while Lance slaves away at the office.*

Christmas shopping at the mall: *Hope you're spending your money on someone other than yourself.*

At lunch one Monday with Roxie: *Amazing how you can spend your day dining and drinking and not feel guilty about that messy house of yours.*

And at the park last evening with the girls: *No wonder Lance always complains about your cooking. You're too busy playing at the park instead of preparing a wholesome dinner for him.*

Bianca's texts were out of control. Heather woke the following morning in a rage. She watched Lance load papers into his briefcase. Coffee pulsed through her body, increasing her bitterness. She drifted within six inches of him and stared at his chin.

"Where's your scar?"

"What scar?" He stepped back two feet. "I don't have any scars."

"I know. Every guy has a scar on his chin."

"I don't."

"No broken bones?"

"What? What did you pour into your coffee this morning?"

"Did you get into any trouble at all when you were little? Break things, steal objects, hurt yourself?"

"I'm an honest lawyer and have been that way my whole life. What you see is what you get."

Ugh. She knew all too well. "Didn't you ever jump off your roof and try to make it into the pool? Run up a down escalator? Fall out of a tree, get into a brawl, do anything scary?"

"Heather, I don't have time for this. I had a normal childhood like everyone else."

"Normal?" She stepped closer. "I broke my arm climbing my cousin's tree when I was eight. I gashed my right shin riding my bike when I was ten. My friends and I got caught stealing lip-gloss from Super-X when I was thirteen. We stole rum from my dad's bar and I spent the night puking in my neighbor's bushes. I took an entire box of chocolate-covered cherries, emptied it into a gallon of Chunky Monkey ice cream, and ate the whole thing after doing bong hits all night at Ryan Bontigliano's senior party."

Lance leaned onto the kitchen counter and shook his head. "Are you having a nervous breakdown? Drugs? You're on drugs. What's that woman Roxie giving you?"

Heather collapsed in the kitchen chair. "Lance, name one crazy thing you did when you were little. Just one, and I'll leave you alone."

He appeared to be thinking. Searching perhaps, but then his mouth opened to a lot of nothing. "I was in the boy scouts. I played chess. I was on the debate team in high school. My parents took me on many vacations abroad. We just did family things." With that, he grabbed his briefcase and left.

Gia strolled into the kitchen and looked at her bowl. "Cheerios again? I refuse to eat!"

The simmering blood within Heather boiled. Heather glared at Gia. Gia stood her ground, hands jammed into her hips and head bent forward.

"Fine with me. One less dish to wash." Heather stomped into her bedroom and slammed the door. After years of Laurel's helpful, kindhearted nature, Heather was ill prepared for Gia's pre-teen hormone tantrums.

****

Heather slumped in the back of Victoria's car on the way to the new restaurant, Peaz and Chaoz. Her anger only grew as the months passed. Heather refused to let anyone talk down to her ever again. She became a fiery ball of resentment. Granted, she was PMS'ing, but Bianca's text at the park last night started her on this incensed rage. Lance's insufficient answer this morning, and Gia's rebelliousness, amplified her mood.

She attempted to calm down when she arrived to work this morning, but her boss' Monday meeting dragged her back into the piping turbulence. And now, sitting in the back seat, listening to Catherine ramble on about how a few cups of prune juice really helped one of her patients, made Heather dig her nails deep into Victoria's seat cushions. She wished torturous death for everyone in her path.

"It's just amazing what little prune juice can do to change a person's mood."

Was Catherine hinting at Heather? She had better not be. She eyed Catherine's neatly gelled ponytail wanting to rip a single hair from it. Victoria scowled at her from the rear view mirror. Was she that easy to read?

"So, then, the patient in the next bed said 'can I have prune juice, too' and the next thing I know, I'm calling the diet office giving them a long list of food preferences for both patients." Catherine tittered. "It really makes me feel good to help."

Heather pretended to barf into her shoes. "You realize that annoys the diet office, right?"

"Excuse me?" Catherine turned her head and met Heather's gaze.

"The diet office receives hundreds of phone calls all day long from patients bitching that they need seven containers of syrup, that they didn't like the soup, they want three pieces of pound cake sent up, or they suddenly decide in the middle of the lunch line that they'd like a grilled cheese on rye with tomato and a side salad for lunch. Then you call and give them a whole slew of food preferences when the patients can easily just fill out their own menus. You like something? Circle it. You don't like something? Don't circle it."

"I'm just trying to help." Catherine's meek voice faded into the classic rock music from the radio.

"We're not waitresses. I didn't go to school for seven years to help a perfectly capable patient fill out a menu. We're hired to prevent malnutrition and the progression of diseases."

"Okay," Victoria interrupted. "Maybe we should discuss what we're doing for National Nutrition Month, then."

"I'm not talking about work while I'm at lunch."

Silence overtook the car. They drove the final five minutes without a word. The friction only intensified in the past six months since Catherine started at the hospital. Victoria tried to keep peace between them, but it only soured her relationship with Heather.

Heather crumpled into a ball in the back seat and reclined until the seat belt touched her throat. Every time she inched toward happiness, something stormed in to ruin it. There was no end, no peace. What else was up the road for her? Divorce? Fired? Who cared anymore.

Victoria pulled into a parking lot with a purple-and-green striped building. Why'd she agree to go out to lunch? They should have gone without her. Leaving the building to escape their boss, only to listen to Catherine ramble on for an hour, was not an improvement.

They grabbed a booth at the back end of the restaurant and Heather ordered a beer. Such a long time since she drank, but she hoped the coolness of the beer would drop her anger a few degrees.

It didn't work. Nothing could rescue her from this misery.

Chapter 44

Nicolo

Nicolo dug inside his Ford F-150's glove compartment wondering why they still called it that. Did anyone keep gloves in there? He found a case of Christopher's baby wipes for the grime on his face.

His cousin Al jumped into the front seat next to him and Marc, a nineteen-year-old who was new to the construction crew, piled into the back with Nicolo's tools and Christopher's car seat. The three of them used up the case of wipes, scrubbing off as much of the dirt as they could.

Al had started them on a new line of houses in the Madison Hills area. Although shot at the end of the day, Nicolo welcomed the physical labor that construction provided after years of sitting on his ass in a patrol car. In the past six months, he managed to shave off ten pounds of body fat and put on more muscle than he had in years. He needed to be a role model for Christopher.

They drove into Peaz and Chaoz, a new restaurant down the road from the neighborhood they were working in. The hostess lead them to a table in the back of the restaurant.

"I'm getting the bacon cheeseburger with curly fries," the young trainee said. Nicolo remembered when he was that scrawny. Back in middle school. The kid needed to put some meat on his bones.

Al placed the menu down. "That sounds good." Al needed to lose a good twenty-five pounds. And lay off all the beers. "Hey, there's some action here today. Three chicks on the other side. I thought there was only two, but another one just showed up."

"Any my age?" Marc asked.

"What, thirteen?" Al snorted.

Nicolo took a sip of water to hide his laughter, then assessed the three women to his left. The older one Al could have. She looked like a CEO of a company and he needed someone to keep him in line. His wife let him get away with way too much as it was.

The second one looked pathetic, even Marc could do better than her. The woman tucked several pieces of stray hairs behind her ears, then smoothed her eyebrows down. "Maybe you'd like a nice cougar," Nicolo elbowed the boy.

The third woman, who appeared to be staring out the window, reached into her black jacket, pulled out a couple of bills, threw one on the table and then turned to the CEO. Nicolo snapped back. It was *her*.

It couldn't be. Why would she be all the way out east? He fidgeted in his seat, unsure what to do. The waitress approached Nicolo, but when he saw the pathetic woman pull out her wallet also, he knew he had to make a move. "Tell her I want the grilled chicken club," Nicolo blurted out.

"Where you going?" Al raised his palms.

He didn't answer. He walked toward her, legs shaky.

Nicolo towered over their table, no longer seeing the other two. He fixed his eyes on Heather waiting for her to look up. When she finally did, she squinted. An irritated expression filled her face. Was she mad at him? She did seem annoyed that day at the beach and obviously wanted nothing to do with him. His insides coiled into a hard mass.

He stood up straight, played cool, and smiled, lifting his chin in confidence. Then her face froze. Melted. She inhaled loudly, as if her lungs couldn't keep up with her heart, and then shoved the pathetic woman several times, almost causing her to fall out of the booth and onto her ass.

Heather stood before him in a tight, pink tank top. Many years had passed, but he was looking at a different woman than the motherly one he spoke to at the beach that day. Her brown hair was long again, the ends flipping up just over her breasts. New blonde highlights reflected the sunlight from the window. Her arms, her shoulders...*shit*. She was muscular, toned, firm and hot.

They practically raced to the bar on the opposite end of the restaurant and each hopped up on a stool. Whatever she was mad at before had disappeared. She sat in front of him and her cheekbones climbed up to her sparkling green eyes. She squeezed his knee and her fingers, like embers, radiated heat onto his thigh.

"How are you?" Her smile intoxicating as always.

"I'm great, you?"

"Terrific. Now at least. Having a bad morning."

He nodded toward the pathetic girl. "Anything to do with her?"

Heather let out a thunderous laugh. God, he missed that. He wanted to tickle her and record that laugh so he could take it home. Grab her, kiss her, never let go.

"She's part of it." Heather rubbed her temples.

"I knew it. I know you so well. She's probably annoying the crap out of you, right?"

"Totally. You still know me after all these years, eh?"

"How long has it been?"

"Not sure. Five years or so? Last time I saw you we were on the beach, you looked..."

"Gross?"

"No!" She laughed hard again. "I just didn't recognize you. I actually thought you were...dying," she whispered.

"Dying? What the hell?" Nicolo let out a rampant cough like he was choking. "Well, I was getting married so, technically..."

She slapped him on the knee. "You're terrible. That poor woman. You're probably torturing her."

"Her? She's torturing me. If it wasn't for my son—"

"You have a son?" Her eyes lit up.

"Yes. Christopher."

"I love that name. What's he like?"

"Just like me, only smaller. He turned two this month."

Heather shook her head. "You look amazing, Nicolo, even after returning from the dead."

"Look who's talking. Where'd you get these from?" He reached over and squeezed her bicep.

"Target. They had a sale, two for twenty dollars."

"Nice. I couldn't get these on sale." He raised his arm up and flexed. "Had to pay full price."

"Stop." She stuck her tongue out.

He wanted to bite it off remembering that he once saw this gorgeous creature totally naked. Heather leaned in further. Why was she being so flirtatious? Was she drunk? The day on the beach she looked like she couldn't wait to run from him.

"How 'bout you? Two girls, I remember?"

"Three."

"Three? Did I miss one?"

"No I...got pregnant right after I saw you, actually."

"That was a big year for both of us, I guess."

"I guess." She said no more. Her hands clutched the rim of her bar stool and her eyes pierced him, as if she was trying to tell him something. He wished he could read her mind. Was she thinking the same thing he was?

Heather looked over his shoulder and her face plunged. Her co-workers had walked behind him and out the door.

"You have to leave?"

"God forbid we're late. Not sure who's worse, my horrible boss or my rule-following friends."

"Come back to work with me," he joked. "I do construction part time now, Frame houses. I'm retiring from the force next year and then I'll do this full time."

"Really?"

"I'll have my twenty years in by then and I need to be there for my son. This way I can get him off the bus when he starts school, plus, I didn't need him worrying about me getting killed on the job."

"As if a large beam couldn't come crashing down into your head?"

"Thanks, now I'm worried again." He thumped her on the shoulder.

"Sorry, just kidding." She slapped his knee again and this time he grabbed her hand. He squeezed it, not wanting her to go. Could he drive her back to work? Have Al get his sandwich to go?

Heather grumbled. "Great, now she's spying on us through the door. What a dork. I should go."

Nicolo frowned. "Let me give you my number. Call me. Maybe we could…get together for coffee or something."

She looked over his shoulder again, distracted. "Yes, your number. Great."

Nicolo wrote his number on a paper napkin from the bar. He remembered the last time he gave his number to her. Would it happen again?

She gave him a powerful hug and then a peck on the cheek. The warmth from her body and lips overwhelmed him. He thought he would never feel her again. He held her tighter, refusing to let go, until she twisted away. Heather threw him one last smile and exited behind the purple and green balloons.

Chapter 45

Heather

Heather stood over the black garbage pail in front of her house. She stared at the napkin in her hand and the cute boyish handwriting it held. The garbage truck screeched at the end of her block. Only four more houses and it would be here.

Five more years had passed and Nicolo entered her life once more. It was no longer a coincidence. Victoria told her she was given a chance again, but Heather knew it was only to punish her. The first time, Heather was pregnant. The second, Nicolo was engaged. Now, he had a wife, a toddler, a new career path. None of which included her.

She crumpled the napkin in her fist before the phone number etched in her memory, tossed it in the pail and stepped back as the truck came to a sudden halt.

"Hey, Jimmy," Heather said.

"Morning." He nodded. Jimmy grabbed the pail and smashed it against the inside of the truck. His eyebrows narrowed at Heather's troubled gaze.

It was gone. For the best. What would happen anyway? Nicolo and Heather would sneak phone calls here and there? Meet for that innocent cup of coffee? Would it progress to a casual drink? They'd get buzzed and then what?

Nicolo had moved on, unlike her. Recently married, his son only two. He would retire and change jobs. They probably lived in a cute little house in a quaint neighborhood and his wife cooked crown leg of lamb and had charming Tupperware parties. Heather would not ruin his life for her own selfish reasons. She'd already done that once.

Heather wheeled the garbage pail back into the garage. Maybe next year, when Rori turned five, she could think of leaving Lance. But go where? He would never leave his home and the girls would be devastated to lose their friends. She needed to find another way to escape this hell, and destroying Nicolo's life would not be it.

****

Heather strolled into the ICU and dumped her books on the counter. A trio of nurses tried to squelch their laughs. "What's going on?" Heather tilted her head, looking for an answer.

"Playing with the new doctor," Hazel, the one with bottle-dyed black hair, said.

Heather searched the unit. "What do you mean?"

"He wanted the light turned on in the patients' room, but the light switches are out here, by the monitors."

"Right. You have to switch them on and off from the nurses station." Heather's baffled expression made them giggle more.

"So, this little, arrogant pipsqueak asked where the light switch was and we told him that Clappers were installed in all the rooms and he had to clap to turn the light on."

"You didn't!"

The nurses grabbed their stomachs and tears rolled down one of their faces. "Yup. So, he goes in and starts clapping and I turn the lights on. Then I turn it off and he's looking around trying to figure out what's wrong, so I scream, "you must have clapped one too many times." So, he claps again and the light goes on."

"You're crazy."

"Screw that. All the abuse we put up with from those jackasses. They think we're their servants."

The young doctor strolled out of the room and the laughter ceased.

"Oh, doctor. Don't forget to turn the light out."

"Sorry." He walked back in and began clapping. Hazel turned off the light.

"What're you going to do the next time he's in here and tries to clap to turn it on?" Heather whispered.

"That's the best part. He'll stand there clapping and clapping and everyone will think he's nuts, and he'll insist that it worked last time."

"You're evil, pure evil!"

The doctor walked toward them with a pretentious smile on his face and then sat across from Heather. She reached for a chart and flipped open the cover. Something caught her eye. Something gorgeous and sexy.

Dr. Silvatri headed toward the back of the ICU not noticing Heather seated behind the thick column. He greeted the patient, his back still to her and then turned to close the curtain for the patient's privacy. Then he noticed. He threw her a wink before the curtain closed him off.

Her heart pounded. Dr. Silvatri, a new gastroenterologist, approached her daily for weeks. Each encounter brought a new dream for her to build upon when she slept. The perfect escape to her wretched life.

Joking with him during the day, avoiding Lance in the evening and then dreaming lustful things about her doctor friend all night, worked. Although not a cure for her depression, flirting gave her something to look forward to each day. Heather even started fantasizing about some of the guys at FLEX.

Heather never forgot her last encounter with Nicolo, tied to his Jeep. What would he have done if that car hadn't scared her? Mind-blowing things, for sure. Probably more incredible than the images she dreamed of with Silvatri. Her ridiculous shyness that night at the beach, caused her to miss probably some of the best sex of her life. Over the years, she dreamed of having sex outdoors, in the open, people watching her.

She shook her head and went back to the chart. Dr. Silvatri's shoes moved under the curtain. Her thoughts were not on her colon-resection patient's needs.

Victoria noticed the change in Heather, but Heather refused to reveal her source of happiness. She told Victoria she'd been out of line this past year and was trying to control her anger toward everyone. Even her daily outbursts aimed at Catherine subsided. Poor Catherine was the 'Heather' that Samantha and Cara endured for many years. No wonder they hated her. She probably did bore them to death. Which, of course, meant Lance was right.

For now, Heather was happy and had something to look forward to every day. Innocent flirting made her feel that someone out there wanted her, and not just the hormone-crazed bodybuilders at the gym.

And Silvatri took her mind off Nicolo. Another distraction to keep her from falling apart.

****

Heather rested her head in her left hand while her pen barely scribbled across the pediatric patient's chart. Her yawn twisted into a loud gulp of air. She covered her mouth when the elderly nurse across from her frowned.

She signed her name at the bottom of her assessment, but before she could close the chart, a meaty forearm brushed up against her and made the hairs on her arm stand up. *Dr. Silvatri.*

He slipped a note under her elbow, then reached for a chart to hide the deed. She drifted it into her lap and glanced down. *Miss me?*

Miss him? She spoke to him daily and dreamed about him every night. Did he dream of her too? Would their dreams ever become reality? This was ridiculous. But then...

Silvatri's foot glided down her calf, locked onto her heel, and knocked her shoe off. It clunked under the counter, unnoticed. She bit down on her lip and pretended to flip through the chart. A slip of paper, held in just the right position, blocked the nurse from seeing Heather write him back.

Yes.

With the note hidden in her palm, she let her hand fall beside her, and extended it towards his thigh. She misjudged his distance and hit the bulge under the thin, loose scrub pants instead.

He grabbed her hand and squeezed, refusing to let go. Heather's body ignited from his powerful grip. Not wanting the nurse to notice, she reached into her lab coat with her other hand and pulled out her calculator. He separated her fingers and removed the tiny shred of paper.

She spied the empty bed in room 437 and inhaled. Her vision of Silvatri carrying her in there and tearing off her clothes emerged.

She peeled her hand from his and casually wiped her sweat-filled palm on her skirt.

Chapter 46

Nicolo

Nicolo drove his truck into the Peaz and Chaoz parking lot and parked under the purple awning.

"Not here again," Al grumbled. "Can't we pick a new place? Sick of eating the same crap."

"Stop eating crap then."

"I like eating crap, just not this crap."

"I think he comes here to find that girl." Marc slapped the back of Al's seat.

Nicolo shot his head up and located Marc in his rearview mirror, then fired off a glare.

"Yeah, what ever happened to that babe?" Al nodded to Nicolo.

"She's not a babe, just an...old friend."

They hopped out of his truck and waited for the waitress to seat them. Each time was the same. He acted casually in front of the guys, but searched every booth and table for her. Today would be the day. He sensed it. Today was the Friday before Memorial Day weekend and Heather would convince the others to go out for lunch to start the three-day weekend off right.

Nicolo scanned his menu, but flinched at the slightest movement. He remembered she left at one o'clock last time and convinced the others to eat at noon since then.

Forty-five minutes later, with a final piece of broccoli remaining, Nicolo dumped his napkin onto the plate. No sign of her, again. Why hadn't she called? He should have taken her phone number, too.

She seemed so excited to see him, but his phone remained lifeless. Each time it rang, heat radiated through his chest, but the droning of

2000

the voice on the other end left him empty.

The day after their meeting, he saw an unfamiliar phone number and knew it was Heather. The sound of a female's voice sent him flying out of the park bench and away from the playground. The shrieking children, gusts of wind tearing through the tree branches, and Christopher calling to him as he dashed away, obscured the voice further.

"Hi," he shouted. "How are you!" His enthusiasm exploded like a busted fire hydrant.

"I'm fine," Kim said. "Expecting someone else?"

Sadly, he was. And each time Kim called, he became more irritated. After two years of Kim's crying jags and nasty outbursts, he desperately wanted to hear an upbeat voice.

Was Heather's life with Lance that great? Nicolo could've offered her so much. Why didn't she give him a chance? She promised to spend the rest of her life with him. It didn't make any sense.

That day at the beach, she blew him off, stating she had to get her girls out of the water. The girls were fine. She could've kept an eye on them from the boardwalk.

Then she takes his phone number only to blow him off again? Did she have some hidden mental disorder he was unaware of?

What was with that woman? She couldn't fucking call him? Nicolo's body tensed. He threw a fake smile at the waitress when she took their money.

He heaved himself out of the booth. "Yeah, you're right, Al. This place sucks."

Nicolo shoved his wallet into his back pocket. He glared at the two bar stools Heather and he had sat on during their last meeting. He pictured her bright eyes, smiling face, and the loud, echoing laugh. Where was she now and was she really that happy?

Chapter 47

Heather

Heather swung on her hammock in the balmy summer night. With her family tucked in bed after a long day at the neighbor's Memorial Day barbeque, she knew no one would wake up and find her in this secluded part of their backyard. She unwrapped the security of the chenille blanket and let it fall onto both sides of the hammock.

She felt prudish in front of the crickets and fireflies. The stars ogled her naked flesh, sending down a teasing breeze to reject her shyness. Ridiculous, since she spent the afternoon having sex with Silvatri in her office.

Heather's fingers wandered in between her legs, evoking memories of her afternoon. She shook her head, ran her hand across her forehead and laughed. Did she really sit on top of Catherine's desk naked?

She watched him thrust into her, her legs spread wide. A surge of adrenaline erased the realism that someone could knock on the door. The open, well-lit room reminded her of the beach, his Jeep, feeling exposed. This time, however, she welcomed the reckless behavior, paralleling herself to a stripper on stage, in full view of an audience.

Did she feel guilty? Not at all. The deviant behavior empowered her. In fact, she didn't care if she got caught. What would be the worst that could happen? He'd divorce her? A victory, not a tragedy.

There would be no more fear.

Silvatri was in the process of divorce himself. Heather would enjoy the wild ride with him. Her numb, frozen state had melted.

The neighbor's bedroom light flicked on, high up on the second floor. Heather sat up on the hammock and a cool breeze reminded her she was naked. She leaped off, leaving the blanket behind, almost wishing the neighbor would see her. She skipped through the back yard, fresh cut grass sticking to the soles of her feet, trees swaying from the strong gusts.

She leaned back on her shed, chest heaving, and her hands glided across both breasts, sensing their hard nipples. She wanted Silvatri with her now, the urge to have sex insatiable. How long would she have to wait to feel him again, to feel his hands exploring her body?

Would there be a second time?

Panic ran through her. She refused to go back to her old life. She needed to feed her ravenous soul. This had to continue.

Chapter 48

Nicolo

Nicolo took over at one of the grills at his neighborhood block party and kept an eye on Christopher, who pushed his plastic lawn mower up and down the crowded street. Christopher stopped to watch three older girls show off their hula-hoop skills.

Pete, the newest neighbor on their block, having moved in just six weeks ago, strutted toward him. He wore a pair of shorts clearly left over from his high school days. So short, they showed off his white, chicken legs. Luckily, his knee-high, striped socks covered a good part of them.

"Hey, Nic, manning the grill?"

Nicolo gawked at him and held the tongs up to his face.

"Whatcha got on there? Any dogs?"

Nicolo stared into the grill. The grill that had twenty-four hot dogs spread across the grates. "I think so. You want one?"

Pete squinted down the block, but didn't answer. His yellow T-shirt, tucked into his elastic waistband shorts, had a picture of Tony Soprano on it. He hopped around trying to appear cool. Nicolo ignored him and continued to watch Christopher in the corner of his eye.

"You're wife, what's her name? Kate?"

"Kim."

"Yeah, Kim, nice lady. Where is she?"

"Why?" Nicolo snapped. He pointed the barbecue tongs near Pete's face. He was in no mood to entertain this loser.

"Haven't seen her all day, that's all."

Was he checking out his wife? This guy was way too slick and he didn't want anyone bothering Kim in her condition. "I saw her about a half hour ago. Went into Wendy's house for something. New drapes, I think."

"Wendy's? Okay, cool, yeah cool." Pete spit on his hand, patted his hair down and hiked away. Towards Wendy's house. *What the fuck?*

Nicolo pinched the two dozen hot dogs and dropped them into a foil tray. He left his post and spotted Christopher playing with little Chloe. She held his hand and they spun in circles singing, "Ring Around the Rosie." Bubbles floated toward them from Chloe's mom. They giggled when any popped on their noses.

"Can you watch Christopher for a minute?" he asked. "I just have to find Kim."

"Sure, go ahead. They're having a blast."

All Kim did around him was cry, and he didn't want anyone upsetting her. Hopefully this party would cheer her up.

Nicolo took off up the hill and headed three doors down. He cut across Wendy's lawn towards the front door. His finger hovered over the doorbell, but laughter escaped from the kitchen window. Kim's voice monopolized the conversation. Who else was in the room? Had Pete made it to the house or was she talking to Wendy?

"It was probably the most amazing night of my life. I'll never forget it." Kim giggled.

It had been ages since he heard her laugh. She was probably talking about their wedding night, or was it the first night in their new home when they lost power?

"Wow, some heck of a story," Pete's voice seeped out the window. Nicolo's body tensed. He *was* in there.

"Wasn't it? I'll never forget it. The people, the chaos, the craziness of it all."

"What were you thinking when it happened?"

"That I was the luckiest woman in the world."

"Really, with all that wacky bedlam?"

Bedlam? Who the hell says that? Nicolo's hand seized the door handle.

"But they wanted the best of everything for me and that's all that mattered. It meant the world to me. The chandelier crashing to the floor and one of the staff stealing my cake, just added to the memories."

"Wish I was there to see you, I mean, see your reaction. That's what I meant."

"Silly, why would you be at my bridal shower?"

"I always wanted to see what a bridal shower was like. And of course see you in all your glory."

What the fuck! What the hell was this guy's problem? Fucking moron. And where was Wendy? Nicolo tipped his head to the left and peered into the window. Kim sat in one of the kitchen chairs with a glass of wine in her hand. Another full glass rested on the far end of the table.

Pete edged closer to Kim and clutched the top of the chair next to her. His asinine red shorts blocked her face, but Nicolo had heard enough.

The door wrenched open and Nicolo charged down the hallway. His foot hit the kitchen tiles just as Wendy approached with a new bottle of wine.

Nicolo walked directly between Kim and Pete. "What the hell's going on!"

Wendy stepped back. Pete raised his hands in the air like he was arrested, and as if this wasn't the first time he'd run through this drill. Kim flinched and then scowled at Nicolo.

"What's your problem?" Kim slammed her glass down on the table.

"I was about to ask him the same thing." Nicolo bent in until he smelled the cigarette stench on Pete's breath.

"Woah, woah, woah, cowboy. Just making some friendly chatter with the ladies."

"The ladies on this block are all married. You picked the wrong block to move onto."

"Nic, we're just talking." Kim tried to push Nicolo aside.

"What happened to the hot dog you wanted?"

Pete touched a random magnet on the fridge. "Changed my mind, that's all."

"Look, dirt bag. I don't want to see you near my wife again, you hear?"

Kim's teeth clenched. "He was just being friendly."

Nicolo glared at Kim and then took a step closer to her. "He came right up to me and asked where you were, then took off to find you."

Kim hesitated as if alarmed. She glanced at Pete and then back at Nicolo searching his eyes for the truth.

"Kim, I'm sorry. I'm just trying to protect—"

"No." Kim sat back down. "You're just angry I'm not spending time with you. They're trying to have a conversation with me and you're jealous. Must I be around you all the time? Jesus, Nic. Give me some space, will you?"

Soft snickers came from behind him. Nicolo shook his head and dragged his fingers through his hair. "Fine." Nicolo turned to leave and ignored the grin under Pete's sickening mustache. "Sit inside all day and talk. Chatter up some more bedlam. I'll take care of Christopher myself. As usual."

He tramped down the hill, but then stumbled and launched into a jog. He ran past three homes, around the yellow police tape and back to the party. Christopher noticed and ran into his dad's arms.

"Daddy! Daddy!" Christopher hugged his dad tight. "I was all alone."

"No, you weren't. You were with Chloe's mom. You're all right, kid."

"No, I was scared."

Nicolo hugged him tighter. "Me too kid, but sometimes we worry for no reason."

Was he wrong? Did Kim need his protection? Had he been smothering her? He wasn't sure how to act in front of her anymore. The nicer he was, the more she seemed to cry or yell.

She said she wanted to be alone, though, and alone always seemed to mean away from him. She was never alone. Friends from work, her sisters, neighborhood Pampered Chef parties. When did she want to be alone with him? Patient and understanding through her depression, Nicolo did everything he could to make her happy.

He tried to remember the last time they had fun together.

On their first night in their new home, a nor'easter ripped through, and with unpacked boxes thrown all over the place, and dinner not yet cooked, the power blew out leaving them in darkness. They managed to find one apple-scented candle, an engagement party gift. Their dinner consisted of the chocolate-covered strawberries that Carissa made for them as a house-warming present.

They sprawled out on their mattress and stuffed strawberry after strawberry into their mouths. The candle gave them enough light to study each other's faces, their laughter echoed in the mostly vacant room. They talked all night, until she fell asleep in his arms and they woke to sunlight streaming into their curtainless bedroom.

Had her depression erased all their good memories?

Chapter 49

Heather

Heather left the indoor rock climbing facility under the cloudless sky. Silvatri sauntered off to his truck, Heather strolling to hers.

They drove in separate vehicles to an abandoned parking lot two buildings down. The industrial park, devoid of all its daytime employees, provided a perfect location for them to explore each other's bodies.

Their vehicles lined up side by side and then Silvatri climbed into her Jeep. Before the door slammed shut, his hand already clutched her breast and his mouth covered her lips. He removed her shirt and bra before she had time to shift herself away from the steering wheel, and then dropped her seat back, falling on top of her.

Heather stared at the light-gray, cloth headliner above her. He tugged hard on her breast lifting her off the seat slightly. This was what she wanted, right? To feel again. To have someone crave her and her body?

"You should dump the junk in your back cargo area so we can put the seats down and have all that space," he said.

She thought of all the beach chairs and toys jammed back there. Where would she put it all?

Silvatri turned the ignition key and opened the sunroof. "Come here."

He guided her up through the sunroof, jerking her climbing pants down around her sneakers. The hot and humid, thick air hit her as she surfaced. Silvatri tried to fit in the sunroof also, but his huge chest prevented it. He kneeled on the seat instead, spreading her legs, letting his tongue explore. Her breasts plunked onto the moist roof, mixing with the muck and grime while his mouth hammered between her legs causing her to sway. Her breasts left swirls on the roof like kindergarten finger paints.

Heather scanned the barren parking lot. A crushed water bottle scuttled across from a sudden breeze. She raised her hands in the air to feel the full effect of her pampering and let the tiny cloud that shimmied past the moon watch her. She had found her escape.

What a turn her life had made in just a few short months.

Silvatri pulled her back down. His mouth covered hers again and she could taste herself on his tongue. "Come on." He opened the passenger door and jumped out.

Heather looked at Silvatri, still fully clothed and standing before her holding the door open. She struggled to remove her sneakers and the pants from her around her ankles, then crawled out beside him.

The breeze engulfed her body instantly and the realization of her complete nakedness hit her. She glanced back at her clothes lying in a ball on the floor mats. Secure and safe, unlike her. Heather took two steps to her left and then the door slammed beside her. Why did she suddenly feel like a sex slave taken to a camp?

Silvatri propped her against the Jeep near her front tire and grinded his loose cargo pants against her pelvic bone. "I was hard all night, Heather."

Without removing any of his clothes, he guided her behind a row of four-foot high bushes and pushed her shoulders against the wall. The cold brick caressed her ass. Silvatri seized both her hands with one of his, lifted them high above her head and pressed them against the hard surface.

Heather surrendered to him. Tired of being in control and taking care of multiple obligations, it was her turn not to plan, not to think, not to reflect. Enjoy, and refuse to worry about the consequences.

The more time she spent with Silvatri, the less she cared about Lance. There was no guilt, as if she lived two different lives. She could turn it on when with Silvatri, and turn it off when she reentered her home.

Heather moaned into the night, unafraid of anyone hearing. There was something about having sex outside in the open like this. She dreamed of campgrounds, beaches, public parks, and playgrounds. The visual of having sex on a slide or on top of a picnic table, took over. A mattress would no longer do.

She wanted a car to come around the corner, pull in, and see her. Watch her reach orgasm.

Silvatri spun her around and leaned her against the wall face first. Heather spread her arms out to brace herself while he spread her legs. He lowered his pants enough to release himself and plunged inside.

As she reached her high point, she fought back the tears. What was it? What was she feeling? She wasn't sad, not at all. She hadn't felt this way since one of her daughters was born. Pure rapture.

****

Heather thought it was just some silly sex thing, but it had grown into so much more. She wouldn't dare tell Victoria or Catherine what she thought about when alone.

She pictured divorcing Lance. She wouldn't put up a fight, take whatever he gave her, if anything, and move out. Silvatri and she would marry and their wedding would be upstate or on the beach, but outdoors, for sure.

They'd sell both their houses and buy a bigger one for all of them to live in, close to the hospital. On their lunch-hour, they'd sneak off to their home and have sex in the outdoor hot tub, in the treehouse portion of the playground or even on the roof. Yes, they'd buy a house together far away from any neighbors and do it doggie style on the roof!

She let her mind wander to backyard barbecues, combining their families during the holidays, and inviting other doctors to their home. She'd be a doctor's wife now.

They'd teach their children to rock climb, have adventures upstate on long weekends, and watch the leaves change colors. He'd love her daughters as she would love his son. The children would each have a brother or sister, completing their family.

Would he want more children? She turned forty last year. Too old to have anymore? But hey, why not, if he wanted to. Honeymoon conception!

She needed to slow down, unsure if Silvatri felt this way about her. She would wait for the sign, for him to let her know that he was in love with her too.

Sex with Silvatri last night filled her mind. His animalistic behavior. How could he not love her? The way he absorbed every inch of her, tasting, squeezing, unable to control himself. Only a week passed between each encounter, but each time his desire for her grew.

Last night she was sure he would tell her he loved her. The look in his eyes, feral. Their time together, insufficient. What he wanted to do with her, never ending.

No one ever studied her body like he had. The way he ogled her as he ran his fingers over her skin. The way he explored and probed like an animal who caught its prey. Operating like his only job was to pleasure her endlessly.

When it was his turn, though, he let loose like a wild man who had suppressed his cravings for years. He thrust into her with such intensity, then howled like a wolf when he finished.

They planned to travel upstate and rock climb outdoors next month. An entire day away to talk and hold hands, to laugh and kiss, to run off and have sex in scandalous places. If it didn't happen before then, she knew that weekend would solidify her life with him. They would tell each other how madly in love they were with each other. Then she would tell her co-workers of her crazy plans that she dreamed up daily.

****

The weather in New Paltz, warm, sunny, and with no humidity made for some incredible climbing. They had stayed later than anticipated. Their romp behind some dense area of woods delayed their departure by an additional half hour. Driving home with the sunset following her in the passenger window, Heather struggled to keep her eyes open.

Silvatri reached for her hand and gave it a squeeze. The reassurance she needed. She had to tell him how she felt.

She hoped he would speak first, but his actions today did it for him. The soft lingering kisses, affectionate touches to her face, deep eye contact, caressing her skin with slow movements, it all showed that he had fallen in love with her, too.

They had snuggled side-by-side on a flat boulder eating the Mallomars she brought for a snack. She nudged his arm and he nudged back. Heather titled her head on his shoulder before their last climb and he gave her a cute pat on her head. If their guide wasn't with them, he definitely would have kissed her. On the long walk back to his truck, if they didn't have to carry all those heavy ropes, he would have held her hand.

When they entered I-87 and made their way home, she would tell him. When there was no confusion as to which road to take, no red lights, no cars pulling up next to them, no wrong turns or unfamiliar on-ramps. She would tell him how amazing the day was and that she was madly in love with him. He would smile and grab her hand again and tell her he felt the same.

The rest of the ride home, they would plan their future and laugh about all the things they would do differently the second time around. Everything from a small wedding to a bigger house, to backyard parties and holiday celebrations. Heather would tell him everything. Except that, she fell asleep.

****

Heather drove into the church parking lot near her home and threw her car into park before it came to a full stop. Unable to stop her trembling, she needed to find a way to calm down. Sleep would be impossible.

What just happened? What had she done? She looked at the clock in her Jeep. Ten-thirty. Was it too late to call Catherine?

Heather sent Catherine a text instead. *If you're awake, alone, and can talk, please call me.*

Five minutes passed and Heather gripped the car keys to restart her car. The phone rang. "Catherine?"

"Heather, what's wrong?"

"I don't know. I don't know what just happened, I'm fucked up."

"Where are you?"

"In a parking lot near my house."

"Did you have a fight with Lance? Wait, you were with Silvatri tonight. Are you drunk? Do you need a ride?"

"No, not that kind of fucked up." Heather closed her eyes and collapsed her head onto the steering wheel. "I slept with Tyrell."

"Tyrell? Wait, what? You were with Silvatri, rock climbing. Tyrell? But..."

Heather whimpered into the receiver. "I left the new rock climbing place with Silvatri. He invited me back to his house, his home. I thought for sure tonight was the night. He never invited me to his home before. I was going to tell him I loved him, but then..."

"What happened? You're scaring me. Did he hurt you?"

"In ways I never imagined."

"Heather, do you need medical attention?"

"No, no. He told me he loved his *wife,* not me. His wife. That he was doing everything possible to get back together with her. He was only using me for sex, he said that, said he had needs. I'm such an idiot!"

"Oh, Heather, I don't even know what to say. What a bastard. Arrogant jerk. He wants to get back together with his wife, but has no problem sleeping with you until then?"

Heather filled Catherine in on his previous affair, how his wife caught him, and how he missed his son and loved his wife more than anything in the world.

"Loves her so much he cheated on her twice? Damn, Heather, you've been sleeping together for six months. Was he going to let this go on for a year or two and then say, 'okay, done with you, getting back together with my wife now.' What a pig! "

"He was actually mad that I developed feelings for him. That I ruined his fun and I didn't want to continue with it anymore."

"Are you serious? If you ever speak to him again, Heather—"

"No, you don't have to worry about that. I'm done." Heather wiped her nose with a napkin from her glove compartment.

"But wait, Tyrell? I'm still confused."

"I ran out of Silvatri's house barely dressed, I think my shirt was on backwards. I drove fast, not knowing where to go. I couldn't go home and face Lance. I'm not sure what came over me. I pulled over, ripped out my cell phone, Tyrell's number flashed in front of my eyes, and I just called him. He was close and I was crying too hard to see the road. I just wanted to talk, that's all. I swear."

"What happened then?" Her words slow and careful.

"I asked for a beer, drank it fast, but Catherine it wasn't that. I was completely sober. I knew exactly what I was doing. He looked shocked I was there, unsure what to say to me. I blabbered on about my pathetic life for over an hour and then..." She wiped her eyes, then her nose again. "Then, he squeezed my hand and I wanted that feeling back. The one that kept me alive and going the past six months. I just want someone to love me, damn it! What's wrong with me?"

"Not a thing. You just chose another asshole, that's all. He'll be wishing he treated you better in the end. Both of them will."

"Tyrell must think I'm such a slut. I used him like Silvatri used me."

"I'm sure Tyrell didn't mind one bit. He's had his eye on you for years. Every time you walk into the kitchen, he drools. Besides, you guys are friends. He gets it, trust me."

"Catherine, what am I going to do now? This was my chance at happiness. I can't go back to my old life. This was the first time I've been completely happy in years."

Chapter 50

Nicolo

"**N**icolo!" Kim shoved the front door wide open, smashing it into the house. "Nicolo!"

He glanced up. Kim held Christopher's hand in hers and waved. He turned off the lawn mower and hiked over to them. "What is it?"

"He needs to use the potty."

"Okay, so...why can't you take him?"

"I have a hair appointment now. Plus we decided potty training would be your job." Kim dropped Christopher's hand and picked up her white leather handbag instead.

"But, I'm in the middle of mowing the lawn and I'm covered in sweat and grass." His held up his work boot, green and slimy.

"I can do it myself, Daddy."

"I know, Chris. Let me help you, though, just in case." Nicolo tore off his work boots leaving them outside. He steered Christopher to their main bathroom and propped up the two toilet seats.

"No Cheerios?" Christopher held up his tiny palms.

Nicolo snorted. "Hmm, let's see if you can aim without them this time."

"No, please. I like them."

Nicolo ran back to the kitchen and then let several Cheerios fall into his hand. He dumped the tiny life preservers into the toilet and waited while Christopher sprayed all over the seat, onto the floor and finally, the shower curtain, as he rocked and fell off the step stool.

"Sorry, Daddy."

He chuckled, again. "You did better this time, actually." Nicolo helped him wash his hands, then sopped up the mess around the toilet.

"I'm almost done with the lawn, then do you wanna go to the pool?"

"With mommy, too?"

Nicolo threw the soaked toilet paper into the garbage can. "No, mommy has to get her hair done."

"But she never comes with us."

"We like to do manly things, I guess."

"The pool and park are manly things? I see mommies there."

Nicolo lowered his head, slumped onto the closed toilet seat and drew Christopher into him. "Mommy likes to hang out with her friends."

"But not me?" Christopher's chin quivered, his eyes drowned in a puddle of tears.

Nicolo wiped the bead of stinging sweat from his forehead before another drop could penetrate his eye. He held his head high and bent in close to Christopher. "Listen, there's no one in this world that loves you more than your mom and me. You're an amazing son, no one could be prouder. You make us laugh, you're smart." He paused and wiped the tear that found its way onto Christopher's cheek. "I love taking you to the pool and park so that we can be best buddies and do man things like...grunt and scream, and climb and jump. Things that mommies sometimes don't do."

Christopher nodded.

"You have special times with mommy too."

"When?" Christopher sniffled.

"Well...what to you guys do in the morning when I'm at work? Before day care?"

He shook his head not answering.

"You must do something fun. Mommy doesn't have to be at work until ten."

"She talks on the phone or watches Kelly and Regents."

"You mean Regis?"

He shrugged his shoulders, not taking his eyes off his Hulk sneakers.

"She must read you books. I see them on the kitchen table when we get home."

"I read them to Barley bear. He likes when I read."

His heart clenched, jerking him forward. He held back his own tears now. "Listen, I'm almost done with the front lawn. Sit on the front porch with Barley bear and then I'll take you to the pool."

Christopher lowered his head.

"And maybe tomorrow we can go to Chuck E Cheese."

"Really?" Christopher jumped up and down and threw his hands in the air. "I love Chuck E. I'm not scared either, no." He shook his head with his serious grown-up face. "Mommy too? Lots of mommies go there. More than daddies."

"Not this time. Maybe we can get her to go next time."

"I'm sure she'd like it. The pizza too, she will. It's yummy. Mommies likes pizza."

"I'll ask her tonight. Go get Barley and watch me on the porch. You'll be mowing the lawn next summer so you better learn." Nicolo winked.

"I'm strong." Christopher made a muscle with his arm.

"Almost as big as mine. Impressive." Nicolo leaned forward and kissed him on his bicep, then messed up his hair.

The ache still lingered in his throat. Christopher deserved more.

****

Nicolo steadied himself on the narrow top plate of the exterior wall of the new house. His tool belt heavy from the hammer, tape measure, a level, speed square, chalk line and nails. He positioned his nail gun over his next mark. The shots rang out like a battlefield under attack, an army of woodpeckers pounding their target.

Nicolo lowered the nail gun to the ground with the incoming boom truck. The crew was installing the trusses today. He glanced at his watch. They were late and he needed to pick up Christopher from day care in two hours.

Nicolo relocated to the center of the room. The smell of lumber and sawdust filled his nose as the wind kicked up debris from the ground. He climbed up the scaffolding. Circular saws resounded behind him like the sharpening of a dozen knives.

"You take the far end," Al shouted to him.

"You sure?"

"Yeah, let Marc give it a go."

"Me?" Marc pointed to his chest, his eyes widened.

"Yeah you," Al barked. "Get up in the center and steady it as it comes in."

Marc hesitated for an additional minute, then hurried to the scaffolding and began his climb up the steel frame. The wind picked up. He steadied himself on the top wood base and then brushed the remnants of sawdust off the landing.

"What's a matter, too dirty? Want Nicolo to vacuum it for you?" Al's sarcasm blasted him.

Marc's face flushed while the assembly of workers chuckled behind him. He spread his legs wide, raised his arms into the air, and froze.

"There's nothing there yet." Al said. "You waiting to catch a bird falling out of its nest or something?"

Nicolo laughed now, but hid his face in his shoulder. The poor kid.

The crane operator lifted the truss above their heads and Al grabbed hold of the rope secured to one end. He teetered along the narrow beam paralleling the side of the house and pulled the truss with him. Marc reached out with both hands, but Al was still over thirty feet away. Al shook his head and continued his stride.

Al pulled on the rope guiding it into position. Marc trembled, making it appear as if the scaffolding was shaking. Al took his last few steps until he stood directly across from Marc and Nicolo, and tugged on the rope while the crane operator lowered the truss. Nicolo reached up, grabbing his end of the gable and helped Al steer it into place.

Marc leaned in and snatched the two center web beams that connected the top and the bottom chords and yanked them into him. Either the weight was too much or the wind pulled back, but Marc and the truss propelled forward. The sudden force knocked Nicolo off his feet.

Nicolo hung onto the truss with one hand and wobbled on his left foot. The wind swung the truss forward again and he whipped around. As his last finger slipped from the beam, his broad eyes found Al's. "Christopher," he screamed.

****

Nicolo opened his eyes. Fluorescent lights, ear piercing beeps. He turned his head to the right. Nausea and dizziness filled him and the bright lights deepened his headache. He closed his eyes again and waited. He took another deep breath through his nose and opened them once more.

Al stood up. "You awake for good now?"

"Was I asleep?" Nicolo glanced around. "Where am I?" He gazed at his white and blue nightgown and attempted to bolt up. "Oh," he wailed, clutching his head. The continuous beeping made his head throb. Lights flashed, like the time he worked in the heat with little food or hydration. Spacey and lightheaded, Nicolo covered his mouth and closed his eyes again.

"You can't possibly puke again. There ain't nothing left in ya."

He struggled to remember something, anything. Had he thrown

up before? The clock on the wall with its orange light, blurred, focused and then blurred again. He strained to read it. His heart jerked. Four thirty-one.

"Christopher!"

"He's okay. Carissa got him."

"Carissa? You mean Kim." He rubbed the back of his head.

"We couldn't get a hold of Kim. Marc tried."

"Marc? Does he even know how to use a cell phone?"

"Her phone went right to voice mail. He left messages, several. I called Dino and he got hold of Carissa."

"Why didn't he call Macy's? She's at work." Nicolo laid back down.

"He did." Al sat down himself, then eyed the nurse walking by.

"And?"

"She ain't there. They said she called in sick."

Nicolo closed his eyes, trying to think. Then drifted off again.

He awoke to a nurse touching his IV. She smiled at him, but her face blurred as well. She could have been a man for all he knew. "It's just a concussion Mr. Trevisani. You're okay. They did a head CT"

CT. His son's initials. "CT?"

"Yes, a CAT scan."

"Where's my son?"

The nurse glanced behind her. Al came around and tapped him on the shoulder. "He's okay. Kim's on her way here."

Kim. What had Al said before? He struggled to remember. Couldn't get a hold of her. Not at work. What day was it? Tuesday. She had work. Wednesday was her day off. Was it Tuesday? "Al, what day is it?"

Al glanced at the nurse, concerned.

"I'm fine, really, it's just...Kim has off on Wednesdays. It's Tuesday, right? She should be at work."

The nurse opened her mouth to talk.

"Al," Kim shouted. She pushed back the blue curtain that matched the color of the nurses' scrubs. "Nic, are you all right?" She looked worried, but anger grew inside him. The annoying orange clock read five-thirteen.

"Where were you?" he asked.

"I'm right here, Nic. Can you see me?"

"Yes, I can see you! I'm not blind. I have a fucking concussion."

"Al told me. I know."

"You know? How nice of you to know. And the *last* one to know it seems."

"You need your rest. They're keeping you here over night. I'll come back in the morning. Carissa will keep Christopher overnight." She threw her bag over her shoulder as if ready to bolt back out the door.

"Why's she keeping him? Why aren't you? Where the hell were you?"

Kim's glance shot back and forth from the nurse to Al like a tennis match. "Please, not now."

He didn't smell it right away. In fact, he didn't smell anything at all. But now, coconut made its way up his nose.

"Are you wearing suntan lotion?" She eased back a few inches as if to hide the scent. "Where…were…you…today? They said you called in sick to work. You didn't tell me anything this morning."

The nursed left and Al followed.

"I decided to play hooky. Go to the beach with my sisters."

"With your sisters. What a surprise. And when did you decide this? Right after I left the house? Or was it last night? Last week?"

Kim hesitated, unable to form the lies. Hadn't she had time to think up an excuse on her way here? Or had his anger surprised her? He had been overly nice to her for years, shielding her from anything that might worsen her depression. But how much more could he take on by himself?

"Well?"

"I went to the beach. I never get out."

"Excuse me? I ask you to go out all the time. With my friends, you and me alone, with Christopher."

"Sorry that I want to hang out with my sisters. Is that a crime?"

"You have a family."

"They are my family."

"And what am I? What is Christopher? They called you for hours. No answer, no one could reach you. Your son needed you. I needed you. You lied to me, snuck behind my back and you're not even sorry."

"I don't need this. I work hard. I need a break."

Nicolo covered his eyes with his hand. "You work in the lingerie department. How hard is it to fold underwear, Kim?"

"How dare you. I deserve to go out and have fun."

"We all do, but you have responsibilities. I take care of Christopher ninety percent of the time. He's your son too."

"You wanted him," she murmured.

Nicolo snapped back. The pounding in his head intensified. He tried to look past her eyes, past the vacancy he now saw. What was she saying? She didn't want Christopher? He thought she had moved past her fears of having a child. Hadn't she?

It must be the postpartum depression. He knew he shouldn't yell at her, it wasn't her fault. He had never yelled before, but now, years of pent up hostility released from the fall he had today. The thought of dying, and Christopher growing up with someone that didn't want him, cut through his heart.

Chapter 51

Heather

Heather left the lawyer's office Monday afternoon, discouraged. Lance and Bianca had found every tactic they could use. Heather was losing and would lose it all. She hoped Lance's father would stop their malicious actions, but he had no control over Bianca. No one did.

It turned into a case of survival. Surviving the divorce proceedings, but also sheltering her daughters. Money she put aside drained, as legal fees mushroomed. She took out a loan against her retirement fund, but that disappeared as well. The stock market crash had pocketed their money further, leaving Lance desperate to hold onto whatever he had left.

Her parents had no money to give, not that she would ask them. She could sell the Jeep, it was only six years old, or as they suggested, let Lance buy her out and fork the house over to him. Bianca pointed out it was her money that allowed them to put a down payment on the house in the first place.

They tried for full custody, but Heather knew he wouldn't last a day with the girls. His performance weakened the more she pitched this fact. It was her only victory, but was keeping your daughters really a victory? It was in this case.

She could find a small home or even an apartment that they could live in. Laurel and Gia bitched about having to leave their friends and their school. Rori blamed herself. Heather put her in therapy. All of them fought with Heather even though they breathed in the madness for years.

Her work at the hospital suffered. Victoria pointed out several items she documented wrong, important history left out of the charts, meetings she forgot to attend. She counseled less patients, unable to concentrate enough to carry on a professional conversation. But more because arguing with a patient that didn't get four sausage patties at breakfast, seemed asinine with all that was happening in the world around her.

Today the lawyer reviewed Lance's demands with her, his final considerate offer before he withdrew his generosity. She cried in the car. How could a father screw his daughters over like this? Was he that cold-hearted? Yes, he always was. She spent her whole life trying to convince him that she was worthy of him, but all along, he wasn't worthy of her.

Heather entered her home and kicked her flip-flops onto the rug. She'd take a nap before the girls arrived home from school, clear her head and relax. She had perfected her look of "everything is fine," which perhaps let the girls believe Lance suffered while she flourished. She would not stoop to his level, though. They would realize in the end. She wouldn't be one of those parents that put their children in between them.

It looked like another cereal-for-dinner night.

The front door cracked open like a slab of wood splintering from a tornado. "Heather, where are you?" It was Bianca. "Don't try to hide, I saw your truck. Or are you sleeping again?"

Heather bolted up, but not before Bianca spotted her jump off the couch. The blanket tangled around her legs, she tripped and fell forward, her hands scraped across the Berber rug.

Bianca stood over her like a vulture, hands on her waist. The red lipstick on her pursed lips displayed the only color on her pallid skin. Her face was sunken, and her neck exposed its veins, like underground tunnels to Satan's lair. Her merciless eyes peered from under a wide-brimmed straw hat. Her red nail polish, like blood dripping from clawing hands.

"Get up," she demanded.

Heather scrambled to her feet after loosening the blanket that restrained her. For the first time, she wished Lance were here to limit Bianca's assault. Could she simply walk away? Ask her to leave?

"I read Lance's recent proposal to you. So unlike him to ignore my charitable suggestions without a word about it to me, especially since I'm paying the lawyer fees. But luckily, I had the sense to call and inquire about the progress." She twisted the large gold earring on her sagging earlobe.

Heather shifted on her feet, aware of her trembling legs. She wrapped her arms around herself to prepare for the blow.

"There will be no alimony awarded to you. This house, paid for mostly by Lance and myself, will go to him. Your children and you will vacate it within thirty days of settlement. Since I donated the majority of the furniture, he will keep it. You can have the bedroom set. I never liked your choice of wood, anyway. I will allow you to take the gardening tools, although I fail to see why you'd need them when the four of you will be forced to move to a squalid apartment in an equally seedy neighborhood. You should be thankful. Less space means less cleaning which you never seemed to keep up with anyway."

Despair tore at Heather's heart and suffocated her. With no money left to fight, an entire law firm behind him, and a relentless witch conducting the persecution, there would only be more torture and intimidation to follow. Bianca continued, but Heather could hear no more. Her ears clogged and she drifted off like she did on the evening of her engagement party.

Her eyes glanced outside at all the perennials she planted, now bursting from their hidden graves. The annuals bloomed and grew almost daily it seemed. The pond, the lush green lawn, the perfectly trimmed hedges, would all be taken from her.

She scanned the inside of her home where she had painted a border across the den walls, hung pictures of her daughters, and vacuumed the rug daily. But her clearest sight was that of her and the girls playing twister on the carpet, the evenings they read books by the fireplace, and girls' nights where they slept on the pull-out sofa and watched movies. This was her home, her memories. How was this fair? How could this be happening to her and her innocent girls?

She could make new memories though, no matter where they forced them to live. They could make old-fashioned Jiffy-Pop popcorn, toast marshmallows over the stove, and watch movies in the king-sized bed Bianca hated so much. An apartment would be temporary and mostly for sleeping in anyway. They would make memories like always. Outside in the snow, on the beach and on hiking trips.

"Are you even listening to me, you little tramp? You're lucky you get anything after the way you embarrassed Lance at his reunion, the way you traipse around in your ridiculous clothes, your disrespectful attitude. All ploys to ruin his career. I may change my mind and just let Lance keep it all, everything."

Heather knew her legs could not hold her up any longer. She hoped Bianca would make her exit before she collapsed. Maybe she deserved all of this. Heather cheated on Lance not once, but twice.

"Your lawyer will be receiving a new drafted agreement which you *will* sign." Bianca, with her nose held high, cut through the kitchen and then left the house.

Heather wavered, but caught hold of the arm of the couch before sinking. She straightened and then staggered to the front door, knocked it closed and dead bolted it. She sank to the floor and wept.

She pounded the hardwood floors repeatedly with her fists, and new energy surged up her forearms. Heather lurched up, ran to their bedroom and glanced at the furniture. It was her favorite in the house. She would leave him the boring tan sheets and buy herself fuckin' Mickey Mouse ones.

She opened his dresser and searched through his revolting boxer shorts, glad she no longer did his laundry. She rifled under his shirts and jeans, his socks and shorts.

She swung open his closet doors and searched in his jackets and pants pockets, not sure what she was looking for, but hoped to find something they were hiding from her. Legal papers, documents, another plan to destroy her? The mattress provided no help either. She moved on to his end table feeling more discouraged. Anything important they would keep off premises in his office, but maybe he brought some papers home to look over and buried them under nonsense.

Lance's elementary school photo album lay on top of the heap of junk. She lifted it out, tossed it on the bed and hunted under an empty watch box, an extra pair of reading glasses, a flashlight, small box of tissues, and greeting cards the girls had made him for Father's day and his birthdays. The card on top, handmade by Rori, said, *Happy Birfday dady, you are my love.*

Heather chucked it aside and lifted up papers, mostly of receipts for home repairs, new carpeting, and the sprinkler system they installed years ago. Further down were proofs of purchase and work orders for the new roof, Andersen windows and the central air conditioning unit.

Nothing.

She let the heavy stack of papers fall and spread back out along the bottom of the drawer. She positioned all the other objects back inside, then spied a corner end of a photograph sticking out from the Andersen Window receipt. She pinched the corner and lifted it to her eyes.

In the picture was Lance in his new charcoal gray suit with a lavender shirt and plum tie. He had never worn such colorful combinations before. More unbelievable though, was who stood next to him. Brooke. She wore a tight purple dress that barely covered her chunky thighs. Low cut, of course, her boobs protruding as if intentionally taped together and shoved up.

She remembered that suit combination on Lance. It was a Friday night a few weeks ago. He didn't come home after work. Heather awoke at three a.m. from a commotion in the hallway and then the front door slamming shut. Lance knocked off his shoes or tripped over them, but a loud *thud* followed. Then silence. When she didn't hear any further noise, Heather slid out of bed, only to find him passed out on the couch. The scent of stale beer filled the room. He was wearing the purple Barney get up. She had never seen it before that night.

Somehow, Brooke was back in the picture, but who called who? Lance probably needed someone to accompany him on one of his conferences. God forbid he showed up alone. Heather was surprised he didn't bring his mother. How dare he call her former best friend after almost six years! He knew how angry she was about the way Brooke treated her.

But why hide it? Why hide the picture and the night? Why not throw it in her face? She already felt dejected. Stick it on the refrigerator with arrows pointing to it.

Heather slid the picture back under the pile. *Fine.* Let him use her as his escort on important get-togethers. They deserved each other. She shoved the drawer closed with her foot.

How could Brooke? Obviously, he told her about the divorce. Was she shocked? Was this Brooke's way of getting back at her? She always told Heather that Lance was a catch. Maybe she'll find out for herself that he'll just use her for his own selfish reasons. Once the event was over, he probably blew her off. Serves her right. *Asshole.*

Heather lowered herself onto the bed. *Crunch.* She had sat on his elementary school photo album. Why did Brooke accompany him anyway? She was still married. Heather would have heard about any divorce or separation through their gossipy friends, in an instant. Brooke would never allow such slanderous talk to materialize. She'd stay with her husband until he died, feigning her happiness until she was ninety.

She flung the album in the drawer. Another photograph fell out. Probably some stupid nerdy picture of him from first grade in a dorky suit and tie, playing chess. But no. It was another shot of him as an adult. This time shirtless, in yellow, Hawaiian-print bathing trunks.

Brooke was by his side again. They appeared to be in a hotel room, possibly the camera on a timer because Brooke stood next to him in a tiny yellow bikini bottom. She was topless. Lance had his arm around her, but instead of her waist, his hand completely encircled her right fake boob, squeezing it. Her large, dark nipple stared at Heather like a one-eyed monster, leering and mocking her. They laughed hysterically, mouths wide open.

Heather sat down on the edge of the bed and began to cry. She slumped forward and slid off the bed, her ass landed on the hardwood floor.

She recognized the bathing suit Lance wore.

He hated the beach and the pool, who knows why? Maybe he felt he was above the riff raff there. When they left for Jamaica, before Rebecca died, before her pregnancy with Rori, she ran to Marshall's to buy Lance a bathing suit since he didn't own one. He wore it once or twice on that trip, then never again.

Two years later, while putting his clean laundry away, she saw the bathing suit. The elastic waistband had dry rotted and stretched out enough to fit a three hundred pound man. She dumped it. He hadn't owned a bathing suit since.

Heather noticed Brooke's hair too. It was short in this picture like she had always worn it. Blonde, shoulder length and wavy. In the recent picture of her in the purple prostitute dress, her hair was much longer and with a bad attempt at flat ironing.

How long had this been going on? When was this? She remembered the weekend she saw Nicolo on the beach six years ago. Lance had left that weekend to go on a golf outing with his friends. Heather never questioned him because she was glad he'd be away for the two nights. She practically pushed him out the door.

There was no golf outing. He went away with Brooke and had mad sex with her!

Bile reached her throat. The night he came home from that vacation was the night she slept with him and conceived Rori. He fucked Brooke all weekend and then she stupidly gave him some more when he came home. What an idiot! Lance probably thought Heather missed him and craved his body. How gross.

She crammed the picture back in the photo album and slammed the drawer shut. No wonder Lance was so angry when she told him she was pregnant. No wonder Brooke was appalled when she confided in her. Were they planning to run off together? It all made sense now. Anger burned the shackles over her heart and now it beat hard and strong for revenge.

****

Heather and Victoria ordered their eggs and oatmeal, then hid in their favorite corner in the back of the cafeteria. Victoria's usual perkiness escaped her, while Heather's impatience leaped out of every pore.

"What's going on with you this morning?" Victoria asked.

"You're never going to believe this. I would've called, but you never know if they wire tapped my phones."

"That's illegal you know."

"Ha! Like that would stop them." Heather shoveled a forkful of eggs in her mouth and then told Victoria about the photographs she found.

Victoria stopped eating. Her spoon plunked down, smashing her oatmeal. "Wow, didn't see that coming. What a little shit."

"Which one?"

"We already knew about Lance, but Brooke?"

"The sad thing is, he sucks in bed. He'll just pump away for forty-nine seconds and then the snoring begins."

Victoria repressed a laugh and then grabbed a napkin. "You're sick."

"It's true. He gets a hard-on, rolls onto your thigh while you're asleep and then before you can fully wake up, he's freakin' done."

"I'm surprised you have three children." She scooped the last of her oatmeal and her expression turned pensive again. "What's Bianca's maiden name?"

"Vincenzo...why?"

"This weekend I was working on that article for the *Long Island Perspective Magazine*. The one on how farmland has changed on Long Island over the past century. There's a family owned farm in Woodbury, fifth generation, there since 1924."

"Okay."

"Meyer's Farm I think it's called. There was an article in a town newspaper about the construction of the farm's new greenhouse, dated November 12, 1965."

"I'm missing the punch line. Did Bianca pick corn there as a teenager or something?

Victoria pushed the bowl away and focused on her. She reached into her lab coat and white computer paper, folded in four, appeared. She opened it and handed it to Heather.

Two Women Arrested in Community Park for Possession of Drugs and Public Nudity

November 12, 1965 - Giavanna Vincenzo, 39, and Rosa Celano, 38, of Woodbury, were discovered by police at Syosset-Woodbury Park under the influence of what appeared to be the hallucinatory drug, LSD, which was found on the front seat of Vincenzo's car. A small amount of Marijuana was also recovered.

While thousands sat trapped in New York City, during Tuesdays thirteen hour Northeast Blackout that crippled five states, the two women spent their evening celebrating under the full moon.

Police found the barefoot women, dancing to loud music from their car's stereo. Giovanna and Rosa were topless despite the cold November temperatures. Both resisted arrest.

Giavanna is married to Frank Vincenzo, a prominent local lawyer, and has two children, Charles, a junior in college, and Bianca Milanesi, who recently married this past summer.

Both women have been charged with possession of a narcotic, disorderly conduct and public nudity. They are to appear in court December 5.

Heather gazed back at the top of the paper as if to read it again. Her eyes narrowed, then stared at Victoria.

Victoria's eyebrows lifted. "I think that would be Bianca's mother. Lance's grandmother, right?"

"I never met her. She died before we graduated high school. He never mentions her. No one does." She placed the article down on the table. "This explains why Bianca's so afraid of me embarrassing her family."

"Well, if she would've caught you hanging from that roll bar, naked at the beach..."

"Okay, okay, but I wasn't having a 'sixties-hippie, mothers-little-helper' moment."

"No, but you were having an, 'I don't give a shit, I'm going to cheat on my boyfriend at a public beach' moment." Victoria stuck her tongue out.

"Touché."

"Her mother humiliated her and she probably felt you would do the same. She was just protecting her and her son."

"Over protecting. But that's no reason to hate her grandchildren." Heather grabbed the newspaper article again, then laughed through her nose. "You know, Gia is named after his grandmother. I chose the name. I didn't tell anyone until she was born. Lance seemed to be happy with the idea." She folded the paper and placed it in her lab coat. "No wonder Bianca refused to visit Gia in the hospital. And Gia is *so* much like her great-grandmother."

"What are you going to do with the pictures you found of Lance? Are you going to use it against him in court?"

"No. I cheated on him, too. I was just upset that it was with Brooke. I'm angrier with her than him. Who knows how long this has been going on." Heather shuddered at the thought. How could Brooke do this to her? Heather swallowed her abuse for years, yet stood by her and provided support when Brooke needed it. How could one person be so jealous and conniving?

****

Heather's legs barely functioned when she left work and drove home on Saturday. Glad that her parents had offered to watch the girls over the weekend, she could relax in a quiet house, eat a big, fat brownie for dinner and read a book.

Lance came home later and later, sometimes not at all. She couldn't help wondering if he saw Brooke those nights. Where would they go? Some cheesy motel? Knowing him, he probably convinced her to meet behind some dumpster to give him a quick blowjob, then split the second she finished, citing some big court case he needed to work on.

She hoped it was true in a way. Hoped he used her for his own pleasure, then blew her off. Brooke would stand for it too, so eager to please, still desperately wanting men to desire her. Had she changed at all since high school? Lance and Brooke still held on to their high school days. The days they were the center of attention.

Tonight would be peaceful, though. She borrowed a book from the library and could drift off reading it. She chose a simple romance, hoping it would restore her optimism for the future.

Heather slipped on her B-52's T-shirt and a pair of gray sweat-shorts, then headed for the couch. She glanced outside the kitchen window and paused. She couldn't pass up the last few hours of such a gorgeous day.

She filled a tall glass with ice cubes and water, tucked her novel under her arm and then eased herself into the rocking chair on her front porch. The evening sun still blazed, heating her pale skin. Was she the only person without tan lines in the middle of July?

Heather leaned back, rocked in the warmth of the sun and started her book. Her mind was elsewhere, though. She glanced around at her neighbors. Would they care when she left? Would they keep in touch or take Lance's side? He had a way of schmoozing everyone, and the women on the block hovered around him at parties. It was high school all over again.

She didn't care anymore if she moved. She wanted out and away from Lance. After finding the pictures of Brooke and him two weeks ago, she started sleeping in Rori's bed.

The *screech* of the mailman's truck in front of her house shifted her attention away from her book again. Eddie emerged with his mailbag and hiked up her front walk.

"Gorgeous day," she said to him.

"Yes, but a hot one." Eddie handed her the mail and tipped his head.

"Keep cool."

"Almost done. One section to do after your block, then I'm finished."

"Enjoy."

Bills. Nothing she needed to care about anymore. Let Lance figure out how to budget the house. She placed the mail under her and leaned back in the chair.

The slow rhythmic rocking, the warmth of the sun, and lack of sleep, lulled Heather into a peaceful slumber. The book plopped to the floor. The book she would never finish. The chair slowed and she drifted further into her tranquil state.

She pictured her daughters and her under a large tree with a picnic basket; one of those old fashioned ones. They sat on a red-and-white checkered blanket. Rori held her doll, Gia did cartwheels and Laurel read her book.

A car door slammed. Then another, jolting Heather awake. She looked to her far right and saw them coming. Heather froze in her chair. If only she could melt through the holes of the wicker rocker.

The pair walked up the beige-and-coral walkway with determination in their eyes. They floated toward her at an unhurried pace, delaying the torture. Heather shuddered, unsure what to do. She sat back, but then, at the last second, fled inside the house.

Should she call the police? It was still her house, after all. What would she say?

The front door opened, but no footsteps followed. Instead, aggressive whispering, like the heat from outside, made its way into her air-conditioned home. Heather took another step back, eyed the phone on the wall, but before her hand could reach it, the front door slammed shut as if a boom of thunder had shaken the house.

With her heart beating desperately, she turned toward the den, but it was too late.

"Running away?" Bianca sneered. "Seems so perfect at a time like this. When time has run out."

Heather pictured Dorothy clutching the hourglass as the last grains of sand fell through the narrow, bulb neck. She looked down at her bare feet and noticed that the blue nail polish had chipped on her big toe.

"You have yet to respond to the new agreement, Heather. You've had more than enough time to answer."

"Just sign the papers," Lance chimed in. "You're postponing the inevitable. You can't win."

Bianca stepped forward until she stood only inches from Heather's face. The smell of her musk cologne, like a cluster of elderly women in a nursing home, penetrated her nose. Heather slowly inched back.

"Don't walk away from me." Bianca glanced back at Lance. "Do you believe this?"

"You were right all along, Mom."

If Heather weren't so tense, she would have collapsed onto the floor. This was so unfair to her daughters. This was their home. Bianca would never stop torturing her and she was allowing it.

Allowing it.

The vision of Bianca towering over her at the engagement party reappeared. She should've stood up to Bianca back then. Sure, she would have humiliated her family, and Brooke may have disowned her right then and there, but she would have had peace.

How could they be so cruel? Had they no heart? Heather heard Laurel crying on the phone the other night to one of her friends. Her words barely coherent. Gia had become more rebellious. Her once excellent grades plummeted. Was therapy really helping Rori?

This was it. She would agree to their terms. End this torture now before her daughters suffered further. There was nothing more she could do to protect them.

"You have off Monday." Bianca removed a small calendar. "I've secured an appointment with our lawyer and you'll meet us at his office at ten a.m. to sign these papers. You've procrastinated long enough."

"It's really doing you no good, Heather. It's over. Admit it. Just sign already." Lance folded his arm on his chest and sat upon the kitchen table. His ass was getting fat.

Heather bit her bottom lip, preventing herself from laughing. His stomach swelled since high school, too. The once-handsome, preppy guy, now had mushy flesh, a puffy face and man-boobs. She wondered what Brooke felt like getting an older, sloppier version of Lance.

Where was Brooke now? Was her marriage as perfect as she said? Were her sons happy with her tight hold around them, not allowing them to have fun? Hadn't she put on a lot of weight herself?

She looked at Bianca, the once adored and worshipped goddess, now sixty-two, looked frail and heavily made up. Her expensive clothes could not hide the aging process. Years of resentment had taken a toll on her.

Heather couldn't believe that she ever looked up to these three, even as a young girl. She tried desperately to get them to like her, make them see the good person she was, and convince them that she was special.

Heather folded her arms as Bianca continued.

"We want you out of here before Labor Day. The girls need to start school in their new neighborhood, wherever that may be." Her tone made it quite clear that Bianca's vision of the girls' future saw them as one of the deprived and destitute children running around this unforgiving planet.

Heather chuckled at how ludicrous Bianca was being. Softly at first, then fiercer, disrupting her mother-in-law's speech.

"How dare you. What on earth is so funny?" Bianca glanced at Lance. "Do you believe this insolence?" She bent forward so that her nose almost touched Heathers, her eyes glittering with rage, her voice bitter. "This ends, now!"

Bianca's threat hung in the air but Heather didn't respond. Instead, she remembered the plastic Target bag she'd left on the kitchen table when she arrived home from work. Inside was her *Oxygen Magazine*, a camp newsletter and...

Ignoring her husband and mother-in-law's dark threats, Heather went to the counter, opened the bag and rifled through the contents. She turned to them, her hand clutching three papers as if they were rare autographed documents.

She never intended on using them, but enough was enough. There's only so much one woman can put up with in a lifetime. Fuck 'em.

"Heather this is not a time for you to gap out."

"I'm not listening to you anymore, Bianca. Or you, Lance. There will be no more manipulation, threats, or mistreatment to me or my children."

Heather took once last deep breath and smiled like she had done when she stood on top of the mountain in New Paltz.

"Lance, you have made me feel worthless for many years and I took it. I spent my life trying to prove to you that I was worthy. That I could be the perfect wife everyone thought you deserved. But I've realized that you don't deserve *me*. You never have. You've done nothing but try to change me, mold me into some Stepford wife and tried to squash all that energy and vibrancy you supposedly fell in love with."

"Fell in love? If you're trying to make up with me now, it's too late." Lance snorted and shook his head at his mother.

"Of all things," Bianca said. "Unbelievable."

"After the way you humiliated me at the firm with your divorce proceedings, I no longer love you. I've moved on, Heather."

"When did you move on Lance? When?" Heather crossed her arms behind her.

"It was difficult when you asked for the divorce, but my mother gave me strength. Just this past month I've started to feel like maybe there's someone better out there for me."

"Oh, please." Heather groaned. "I think it was a lot sooner." She held out a sheet of paper with the photo of Brooke and him at the awards ceremony. She had blown it up to fit the page.

Lance snatched the paper away. "Where'd you get this? Did Brooke send it to you? I thought the two of you weren't speaking—"

"What is it, dear?" Bianca tried to peek over his arm at the picture.

"Nothing. I had an awards banquet to attend and Brooke was nice enough to take time away from her family to accompany me. It would have been disgraceful to attend alone."

"Indeed," Bianca said.

Heather's grin widened. "Then it must have been even more difficult for her to accompany you on your weekend golf trip six years ago." Heather shoved a second photo in his face. She managed to enlarge this one when she printed it out. Brooke's big, fat boob stood out nicely. The photocopy darkened her nipple, making it obvious.

Lance's face blanched. "Where did you get this? What is this, a joke?"

"What now?" Bianca grumbled.

Before Bianca secured a firm look, Lance seized the paper from Heather's hand and crumpled it.

"What on earth was that?"

Lance scowled at Heather and then crushed the paper further. Did the picture embarrass Lance or did he not want Bianca to know about his relationship with Brooke?

"Rip it up all you want," Heather said. "I have plenty more copies and the original pictures are hidden in a very secure spot."

"Who the hell do you think you are?" Lance stuttered.

"What's going on?" Bianca slammed her hand on the counter top, irritated she was left out of the festivities.

"It appears Lance and Brooke have been having an affair. For at least six years now."

Bianca looked at him, her face expressionless. No emotion showed in her once vindictive eyes. Had she known?

"Seems like Lance isn't so perfect after all," Heather said.

Bianca recovered, then pursed her lips. "It appears that Lance had no choice after putting up with you all these years. Disrespectful and uncouth, he obviously turned to Brooke for support. Probably felt abandoned and he simply lost it one night. The stress too great, the pressure of being perfect. It wears away at you until you finally snap."

Heather narrowed her eyes at the woman who had tormented her all these years, and then a grin slowly crept on her face. "I guess the acorn doesn't fall far from the tree then, does it, Bianca, you miserable bitch."

The old woman glared furiously at her. "How dare you! What are you talking about?"

"You mean Lance never heard about the night your mother went to jail?"

Bianca's eyes flew open in horror. She strained to keep her

composure. Her fists clenched and body shook with fury.

"What are you babbling about?" Lance barked at his wife, stepping into the ring.

Heather revealed the last of her papers, dangling it a few inches in front of Bianca's face. Bianca knew. Heather could see it in her frightened expression.

"What is that?" Lance demanded.

Bianca grasped the paper with both hands ripping one of the corners that Heather held onto. She swung it behind her back away from Lance's view. Her face inflamed, finally giving some color to the usual pasty complexion.

"Let me see," Lance held out his hand to his mother.

"Lance, no!"

He stood unyielding. She finally gave in, her composure shattered, a shell of the imposing figure she usually presented.

Heather watched them, waiting for his reaction. She only realized now how fast her heart was hammering in her chest.

Lance scanned the newspaper article and then looked at his mother, confusion etched on his features. "You knew about this? Why'd you hide it from me? Why didn't you ever—"

"It was for your safety, your protection. You didn't need to know."

"You never let me see her. You never explained why."

"She wouldn't have given you the attention you needed. Only left you feeling unloved."

"My own grandmother? What are you talking about?"

Bianca's chin quivered, her hands curled inward. Then she remembered Heather's presence. "We'll discuss this matter later." She composed herself, her overconfidence returned. "Heather, your little detective work proves nothing and has no bearing on this divorce."

"No, but you know, the Internet is a funny thing. It has a way of spreading information to scores of people, quickly."

"You wouldn't!" Bianca's face drained of all its color as she grabbed hold of Lance's arm to prevent herself from collapsing.

"Oh, I will. And Lance, I *will* be using these pictures as evidence. I'm sure your law firm will be concerned about any negative publicity. You're not getting this house, you're not kicking my daughters out and I will drag this on as long as it takes." She pointed to the front door. "Now get the hell out of my house!"

In a state of shock, Lance and Bianca wandered out the front door in a daze.

Heather's legs quivered, her body temperature seemed to double.

Once their car pulled away, she ran out of her house. Adrenaline pulsed through her like no workout had ever done. Her flip-flops slapped along the sidewalk. She rounded the corner and headed south to the neighborhood near the elementary school.

She didn't intend to use that against Lance, but she knew he'd stop at nothing to destroy her. Yes, Heather had cheated on him. Twice. Something else she would have to live with for the rest of her life. But there was no reason for her daughters to suffer for the rest of their lives. They were innocent.

Heather reached the next block and went into a full sprint. She stood up to them. She did it! And it felt amazing. She needed to stay strong and get through this new phase. She would take out a loan, sell her personal items, anything. The girls deserved better, she didn't care about herself.

Heather crossed the street and veered left down the next block not noticing the mail truck barreling down the road. She flew back and then leaped out of its way. Once on the sidewalk, she caught her breath.

"So sorry!" Eddie jumped out of his mail truck.

"No, it's my fault. I should be watching where I run."

"Actually, I was coming back to you. This fell under my seat." He handed her a long, white envelope. "It must've dropped."

"Thanks. And thanks for coming back."

The mail truck took off again and Heather continued on her journey at a much slower pace. She wandered toward the next block and glanced at the envelope, her name was hand written on the front, no name on the return address. Heather sliced open the top and withdrew the folded paper. It was typed. What now?

Dear Heather,

Hope you are well. I know this is a stressful time for you and only wish you the strength you need to get through it. I must add though, that I overheard Lance talking to one of his colleagues and I was dismayed at the unfair and malicious tactics involving your divorce, as well as the heartless proposals. As you may have heard, Lance and I severed our ties several months ago.

I am writing to offer you any assistance I can. If you need legal advice, I would be happy to help you. You and your beautiful daughters are in my thoughts and I'd like to protect your best interests. I wish you only the best.

Rex Bacon

Chapter 52

Nicolo

Nicolo helped Christopher climb up Dino and Carissa's front steps toward the shrieking kids in costumes. Christopher's Batman get-up dragged over his black shoes, and the sleeves that Nicolo tried to roll up slunk down over his hands again. "Let me fix your sleeves before you get hurt."

"No! I want to see Dante and Mariana's costumes." He charged into the house amidst a blur of children cloaked in disguises. "Which ones are they?" Christopher held up his palms, his hands still hidden under the fabric, then took off down the hall.

Nicolo entered the kitchen with an eighteen-inch, twelve-pound fruit platter. "Hey," he said.

Carissa spun around in her Mini-Mouse outfit with a tray of cheese and crackers. The yellow and white slabs were shaped like tiny ghosts. "You're here! We were wondering what happened to you."

"A little problem with the costumes." Nicolo held his arms out, demonstrating his homemade Batman costume.

"Looks good to me," Carissa said. "Dino is setting up the eyeball scavenger-hunt."

"Sounds creepy." He tossed his mask on the kitchen table.

"Where's the new kindergartener?"

"Looking for his cousins."

"And Kim?"

"She had to work."

Carissa frowned. "She couldn't ask for the day off? I mailed the invitations a month ago."

"I guess others wanted off."

"I've been in that Macy's. Everyone that works there is ninety-years-old. Why do they need the weekend before Halloween off?"

"Ninety? Stop. Do you need any help?"

"I'm sorry, Nicolo, but it's rude. This is the third time I invited you guys over and she didn't show."

"She's in retail, what do you want?"

"She can take off any day she wants, don't give me that shit. She gets off when it comes to spending the weekend at the wineries or that trip with her sisters to Atlantic City for one of their birthdays. Had no problem taking off then."

Nicolo collapsed into the kitchen chair and rubbed his eyes. "Carissa, I don't want to fight. Kim's just very unstable. I don't want to upset her. If this is what she needs to become her old self again, then—"

"Old self? Is that what you're waiting for? It's been over five years! She's playing you. There's nothing wrong with her."

"That's not true. Her doctor said she was depressed. I was there."

"*Was*, Nicolo. *Was*. She found a way to extend this act and leave you with all the responsibilities, while she's off living the single life. You fall for her performance over and over again."

Nicolo bent forward, his elbows resting on his knees. Was Carissa right? No. She didn't understand that Kim came home from work too tired to cook dinner, or help Christopher with his baths. She'd fall onto their bed exhausted, begging to eat in the bedroom. They didn't see Kim crying on the weekends because there was an entire house full of cleaning to do. He understood that Kim didn't want Christopher seeing her like that, so when she asked him to take Christopher away, he did.

"No, she's still depressed. You just don't see it."

"No one does, Nicolo. Only you. She turns it on when she has to be a responsible parent, and then turns it off when she's around others. Magic! Go figure." Carissa tossed a large bowl into the sink and then swiped her arm along the counter, dumping several utensils on top of it.

The sound jerked him back. "No, it just takes time."

"Time? How much more time are you going to lose before you realize? It's an act. Everyone notices, but you. You're blind. I'm sorry to be the one to tell you, but I can't see you guys like this anymore. It's not fair to you or Christopher."

His eyes remained locked on the floor mat. "Look, I'm here, and Christopher is too. Can we just have fun? I had a long week and needed this party."

She tossed the dishtowel into the drain board and then grabbed a seat next to him. "I'm sorry. I've wanted to say that to you for a long time, but I held it in. I didn't mean for it to come out today. I'm thrilled that you and Christopher are here and we're gonna have a blast." She squeezed his hand. "You want a beer?"

He tried to act like her words didn't cut, but they did. "Nah. I'm more in the mood for Frankenfooters, creepy chili, and worms in blood casserole."

"Your imagination is better than mine."

"Yeah, right. I know you."

She wiggled her fingers near her ears. "Go find Dino. I'm sure he's losing it by now."

Nicolo made his way towards the living room where fifteen kids screamed at full volume every time they uncovered another hidden eyeball. Christopher snuck up behind him and grabbed his cape. "Hey kid, having fun?"

"I got three eyeballs and now they're having a pin-the-spider-on-the-web game."

"Cool. You want something to eat?"

"I'm not hungry." Christopher took off before Nicolo could change his mind.

After eating a few mozzarella sticks, Nicolo stepped onto the back porch. Leaves blew up and around like a mini tornado, sending a bone-chilling gust up his thin costume. He shivered in the icy temperatures, hoping that on Halloween this Wednesday, it would be warmer for Christopher to go trick-or-treating.

He thought about what Carissa had said. Kim *had* drifted further out of their lives.

You wanted him.

He couldn't get her remark out of his head. It wasn't fair. Christopher was a good kid. No, a great kid. What happened to that mother-and-son bond? Was it depression, or a way to dodge her responsibilities?

Christopher noticed. Not even six-years-old and he felt her pulling away. Or was she ever really there?

****

The frigid winter, mutated into an unusually cold spring, and now June provided nothing but rain. Christopher wanted out. Nicolo wanted out. Kim never seemed to be home.

Christopher stared out the kitchen window at the pouring rain. Relentless, it tortured the boy. He leaned on his elbows and a lingering yawn escaped his mouth.

Nicolo carried him into the den. He had grown almost four inches this year. Much taller than most six-year-olds, Christopher towered over the kids in kindergarten. He threw a blanket on top of him, turned the TV on, and after fifteen minutes, he easily fell asleep. It was that kind of a day.

After washing the lunch dishes, Nicolo wandered toward his bedroom. The hallway closet remained ajar after Kim grabbed her raincoat this morning. He tried to shut it, but a telephone book prevented it from closing. She couldn't take two minutes to pick it up and put it back on the shelf?

He lifted it off its dusty surroundings and flipped the pages until it closed. He sighed. Then an idea flashed. Yes, he could try.

Nicolo grabbed a pen, then closed the bedroom door behind him. He strummed through the phone book and checked the area hospitals, circling the ones closest to Peaz and Chaoz.

With only three in a fifteen-mile radius, he clicked the phone on.

"Good afternoon, Norlyn Plains Hospital, Samantha speaking, how may I direct your call?"

"Um, yes, I was looking for a dietitian, her name is Heather Di...I mean..." Damn, what was Lance's last name?

"Hello?"

"Sorry, I was looking for a dietitian—"

"One moment please." Classical music replaced her voice before he could finish. The phone rang five times and then an answering machine clicked on.

"You have reached the nutrition department. If you're calling for a missing patient tray, please check your census to make sure the correct diet was ordered..."

Nicolo hung up and dialed the operator again asking for the direct line. He called back every five minutes. On the third try, he reached a human.

"Diet office, Anna speaking, may I help you?"

Nicolo sprang from his reclined position. "Yes, I was looking for a dietitian. I was there..."

"Oh, you have the wrong office. One second, I'll connect you."

All this time wasted on the wrong phone number. More classical music played until the phone rang some more.

"Dietitian's office, Catherine speaking."

Nicolo's body jolted. "Um, yes, I..." He picked up the pen and flicked it back and forth between his fingers. "I was a patient there and

I saw a dietitian and—"

"Your name please?"

"My name? It's...David. I spoke to—"

"Last name?"

Last name? What was this, a government agency? He flipped the pages in the phone book. Damn. It was the yellow pages. He looked on the top right. Sumps. "Sump, uh, Sumper."

"Sumper? Can you spell that?"

"S-u-m-p-e-r."

"I don't see that name."

Was she scanning through a list? "Well, it was a while ago."

"The computer doesn't show anyone with that name."

Computer? Oh, man. He was screwed. "I mean a long time ago, like a few months ago."

"The computer holds every admission that's ever come through here. Is there something I could help you with?"

It *was* a government agency. FBI. Fort Knox. "I just had a question on a diet, that's all." Good save. Act natural.

"You have a question about a diet you were given *months* ago?"

The radio in the background muted and then muffling overtook the receiver. Whispering and mumbling followed. What was she saying about him? Nicolo lurched up from his bed and raced toward the den. His heart smashed against his chest and a blaze ignited throughout his body with each stride.

"Um, I..." He opened the sliding glass door to get air. The rain continued to pour, smashing on top of his patio table and barbecue. Warm air streamed through the screen door and whisked across his face.

Then he hung up the phone.

How hard was it to find out if she worked there? Yes or no? Wait. Had he asked for her specifically? Did he ever say her name? He thought he did. No, he hadn't. He started to with the operator. He couldn't call back now. How stupid.

What was he doing? He slid the screen door open and stepped onto the back step underneath the overhang. It could have been the rain or the dreary, miserable day, but he couldn't help but feel hollow inside. Lost and in pain.

Nothing relieved it. Contacting Heather wouldn't have fixed it either. She wanted no part of him.

His marriage was a fucking joke. What had he done wrong? They had purchased a gorgeous home and he busted his ass to fix it up for her. He bought her so many gifts in the past. Flowers, cards, romantic dinners. He listened to her vent and gave supportive advice. They attended neighborhood parties and he accompanied her on all her stupid outings.

He had no shame telling his friends that he changed diapers, gave Christopher nighttime bottles and wiped up puke. Let them laugh. Every moment spent with Christopher was a blessing. What more did Kim want from him?

He picked up a broken tree branch and winged it across the backyard. It smashed into a tree and cracked in half.

Nicolo examined the empty patio table with its eight chairs. Chairs they rarely used. He always pictured hearty morning breakfasts served at that table. His family sitting around waiting for him to bring out his special Eggs-in-a-Basket on a large tray. Kim, Christopher and their other children would pound their forks until he arrived, laughing when he finally served the food onto their plates. Strawberries and blueberries in a bowl, large glasses of chocolate milk.

The table seemed dull now. Never had they eaten breakfast there. There'd be no more children. His dream of a large family faded. Divorce sounded horrible though, he couldn't do that to her. Never. His parents had celebrated their forty-fifth anniversary last month. That was his dream.

One night, a long time ago, he had told Heather that he planned to make every day of her life fun and memorable. Where were *his* fun times? Maybe Heather was right. She said you grow up and mature and move on. Maybe he was delusional.

The rain intensified, as if blurring his summer breakfast dream. It fell sideways and drenched his bare calves. The hair on his arms caught the blowing rain, and mist soaked his face.

Nicolo stepped back into the den and slammed the screen shut. He wiped the droplets off his arms and legs, then rubbed it over the back of his shorts. A smirk crept up his face. A final memory. He thought he recollected them all, but one final one remained.

Heather and he sat on his parent's large wooden swing in their backyard under the weeping willow. The air was warm, but clouds had moved in relieving them from the humid, sultry day. Heather brought bubbles and blew them in his face whenever he tried to kiss her. Nicolo pulled on the chain and kicked his feet to push the swing higher and knock her off balance. He rocked back and forth to jolt her body and shake her bubble-wielding arm. She persisted despite his efforts.

He jumped from the swing and ran to the side of the house. She chased after him, cornering him by the gate. Rain left the clouds and sprinkled on them, but they didn't seem to notice. She continued to blow bubbles despite the raindrops popping them before they touched him.

Nicolo unlatched the gate when the downpours no longer let the bubbles shape on the stick, and he ran down the driveway. Puddles had already formed in the street and Heather darted after him running through the flowing streams. Soaked hair clung to Heather's neck and muddy water splashed their bare legs as she charged after him. Before they reached his neighbor's house, he stopped and threw his arms around her, linked his wet shirt with hers, and kissed her.

His neighbor drove by and eyed his disapproval at the two drenched kids dancing and kissing in the rain. Heather waved at the man as if she was drunk, then Nicolo pulled her onto the sodden grass. He never wanted to let go.

Christopher awoke, kicked the blanket onto the floor and rubbed his right eye. "Still raining, daddy?"

Nicolo ruffled the waves in his son's hair and squatted down next to him. "Yup, but I think I know a way we can still have fun."

"How?"

Nicolo scooped him up and carried him to the garage. The garage door groaned as it opened, revealing the opportunity.

"Where we going?"

"Nowhere." Nicolo handed him his shark umbrella, clutched his hand and ran onto the driveway.

Christopher blinked at the wind and rain blowing around him, unsure what his dad was up to. When they reached the street puddles, he paused. He watched his dad shove his hands deep into his jean pockets, spring up and land in the puddle, barefooted. The gush of water spurted in all directions. Christopher's eyes lit up.

Christopher inched toward the puddle and touched it with his toe. He leaped in. The smile grew on his face, his eyes and mouth enlarged, and with each jump, Christopher vaulted higher. Soon he tossed the umbrella aside and ran down the street, shadowing his dad and kicking the rain with his feet.

The two of them laughed, whooping loudly and Christopher's eyes widened and glowed as the beam on his face continued to grow.

After ten minutes of hopping in the puddles, the rain diminished and Nicolo lifted him into his arms and crashed onto the grass beneath a tree. He tickled Christopher until his laughter muted from lack of air. Nicolo stopped and hugged him instead. Rain from the leaves dripped on their heads. This felt good. Almost as good as it did when he was with *her*.

****

"And now, let's welcome this year's kindergarten graduates." The principal at Christopher's school secured the microphone under her armpit and her hands smacked together in thunderous bursts. Applause and cheers erupted throughout the gymnasium. Tiny children in red caps and gowns marched single file into the expansive room with their heads held low. An occasional child glanced up when a parent called their name, but most examined their shoes.

Nicolo examined the room. For Kim. He snapped several pictures of Christopher, waved and then sat back in his seat. Nicolo arrived early to secure two chairs in the front row, but now that the principal's ten-minute speech about how proud she was of the graduates and how she herself used to be an English teacher ended, the celebration was well under way, and Kim was more than a little late.

Christopher stood in the back row due to his height. Nicolo had slicked Christopher's black hair with gel and dressed him in a dark blue polo shirt and a pair of shorts. He appeared naked under the gown.

With his fingers in his mouth, Nicolo's high-pitched whistle echoed in the gymnasium as the applause faded. Christopher held his thumb up and gave his dad an exaggerated wink. Nicolo chuckled, but when the principal returned to yet another speech, he searched the room again for Kim. The hand on his watch ticked as if in a rush and now her lateness could be nothing more than another intentional blow off.

He had no idea what she did on her days off. She never answered her phone when he called, always voice mail. She claimed to work late, but her paycheck didn't reflect this. The weekends Nicolo worked, he came home to laundry still unfolded, toys left in their same places, and dishes in the sink.

When emergencies broke out or he had to make important decisions, her phone went unanswered. Nicolo called Macy's but she never returned his calls stating she didn't receive them. The more Kim pulled away, the more freedom he gave her, and the more responsibilities he took on. He finally saw the light. She wasn't depressed. She was taking advantage of him.

"And now the talented kindergarteners, with the help of Ms. Hooley, will entertain you with three songs that they worked very,

very hard on this year."

He spent his afternoons with Christopher, getting him off the bus, helping with his homework, cooking dinner for the two of them and playing with him in the bath. The nights Kim came home for dinner, she ate in silence, and read the mail or newspaper.

Nicolo signed Christopher up for T-ball, and made trips to the park and library. He read him stories in bed and tucked him in. Nicolo became a whiz at school arts and crafts projects and Christopher appeared as content as any six-year-old could be.

He found a local gym that had a daycare center and brought Christopher with him when he worked out. Christopher made friends there quickly with his wacky sense of humor. The babysitters loved how he willingly shared and had compassion for the other kids.

"Now it's time for the graduates to come up and receive their diplomas. Get your cameras ready, parents."

Parents. That was a joke. He felt like a single parent. Luckily, he wasn't close with anyone, otherwise they'd start asking questions. Does Christopher have a mommy? Are you divorced? Where's your wife?

Six years he had tried with Kim. Six years he ignored her insults and her callousness to their son, but this was the end. Missing Christopher's graduation, there was no excuse.

"Christopher Trevisani!" they called. Nicolo leaped up and snapped away at the camera. Christopher smiled and waved the diploma in his hand, then placed it by his chin for his dad to take several more shots.

"Way to go, champ!" Nicolo held up his hand for him to high five it.

Christopher smiled and then looked behind his dad. "Where's mommy?"

Nicolo pulled his truck into the driveway and Christopher hopped out and ran to the swing set his dad had installed. Kim's car wasn't in the garage. "I'll start your lunch," he hollered. But Christopher's long legs shot him into the backyard before Nicolo's voice reached his ears.

He removed a can of tuna from the cabinet and whole wheat bread from the fridge. After cutting it into two triangles, he sliced up a red pepper for a side dish, then poured some milk into Christopher's plastic Avengers cup.

The knob on the door leading in from the garage, jiggled, then rolled towards him in a calculated pace. The door creaked open a few inches, paused, then continued its skulk until wide-open and unmasked. A tan pocketbook plopped onto the rug.

Christopher's Avengers plate shook under his intense grip. The innocent sandwich twitched and threatened to topple over. Pounding thundered inside his ears.

He set the plate down before the sandwich fell to the floor, and glared at her, waiting for the moment of recognition to hit. Kim kicked off her sandals and placed her hands on her hips. Her head remained forward and eyes fixed on the door leading to the backyard. She bent back as if stiff and worn-out, then raised her hands in the air and stretched. A grin spread across her face like a crack in a windshield.

Nicolo, with the knife still clenched in his fist, his arm pulsing with rage, lifted the hefty blade and tossed it, producing a loud *clang* in the stainless steel basin behind him.

Kim flinched, then twisted her head toward the noise. Her grin faded. She stared him down and he gladly returned the favor. Both without words, both with animosity building inside every cell.

Nicolo shook his head, expecting Kim to apologize like always. Bark out some ridiculous excuse, then flutter off as if he was being unreasonable. But not this time. Her nostrils flared as if hiding a laugh.

"Where were you?" he asked.

"Excuse me?" Her sarcastic tone hissed through his bones.

"Let me guess, you *forgot* your son was graduating today? Is that it?"

"No, not at all. I knew."

"You knew? And you deliberately missed it? What...what the hell?" Nicolo's skin ignited.

"He's not my son. He's yours."

"What did you say?" He stepped closer.

"You wanted him. I never did."

"Yes, you did. It was your decision. You stopped taking the pill."

"You forced me."

"I did not. Once we moved in, I never mentioned it again. I threw myself into repairing the house."

"To butter me up so I would change my mind." She folded her arms.

"What! You couldn't wait to buy this house. You made a list of things that needed repairs and only cared how the damn house looked to everyone instead of enjoying it. Every tax return went to fixing this place up instead of the three of us taking vacations together."

"Vacation? With a kid? How's that fun?"

"That's what parents do. Christopher's been dying to go on a plane. But no, we need a new dining room set and a new front door and let's not forget the carpeting."

"I knew the day he came out I made a mistake. Your mistake. Now I have to pay for the rest of my life?" She pointed to her chest.

"Are you drunk again?"

"Perfectly sober."

"He's the most amazing son you could have. Well-mannered, smart as a whip, good-looking, compassionate, funny. What the hell is wrong with you?"

"I was not cut out to be a mother. I have more fun with my sisters than with the two of you."

"I'm so sick of hearing about your fucking sisters. Maybe they're still single for a reason. The four of you deserve to grow old and alone in some nursing home, wiping each other's asses."

"Fuck you!"

"No. Fuck you, Kim! You just wait. One day, someone, not sure who, but someone will sweep one, if not all of your sisters off their feet and they'll drop you in a second."

"No, they won't."

"And you'll be left alone. You won't even know your own son and you'll wish you had us back."

"No, I won't. I made a decision. I was at a lawyer's office today. My second visit actually. I filed for divorce."

Nicolo exhaled as if releasing six years of tension. "On your son's graduation, you made an appointment with a lawyer?"

"Don't worry. I don't want this energy-draining house. Or him. I want out. In fact, I rented a cute little apartment starting July first—"

"You can't even say his name! How can you abandon your son?"

"I can't live this life anymore, surrounded by all these fake, cheesy families."

"You think our neighbors are fake? They love their children, more than anything. *That's* normal. I've done everything for you to make you happy. I've changed for you, let you have your space, but it's never enough. I don't even know you, Kim. Not sure I ever did. What the hell did I see in you?"

Christopher came in through the back door and paused. "Mommy!" He ran and threw his arms around her waist. Kim stiffened, her arms dangled beside her. "You missed my graduation, mommy. I sang three songs."

Kim kept her eyes focused on the back door, unhooked his arms from around her, and stepped aside. Christopher's eyes widened. His bottom lip quivered. She snatched her bag from the floor and stomped past him towards her bedroom.

Christopher fled out the back door in a silent hysteria.

Nicolo rushed to console him, but before he could leave the kitchen, Kim's nails dug into his forearm.

"I can't stand the sight of you anymore either." She released his arm, the ache remained, then she sauntered off to the bedroom as if she won an academy award.

His shoulders collapsed, bowing his spine. His facial features sagged as if melting. Wet, dull eyes searched their kitchen for something to say, but he had no words for her. It was over. This was it. All he tried to do was make her happy, make everyone happy and—

Just then, a tiny pixie-looking thing skipped past his kitchen window in a half-run, half-prancing motion. *"You try to make everyone happy, but end up miserable yourself."* He could still hear her saying those words to him.

The bedroom door clobbered the sheetrock with such force, the framed picture of Christopher fell off the wall and shattered.

Kim's head bolted up. She tumbled backward and tripped over her bag at the sight of Nicolo entering the room.

Nicolo parked himself in front of their bedroom door. Kim's clear victory was no longer at her fingertips. Her power over him was about to be crushed. "Wipe that smart-ass grin off your face," he snarled.

Kim struggled to stand, searched the room as if looking for a weapon, but only a pink, lace pillow laughed at her.

Nicolo didn't move any closer. He didn't have to. With his feet rooted securely in place, his body shook. The heat from the first hot day of summer filled his forehead with beads of sweat. The whites of his eyes became more prominent.

He jerked open the closet, the tiny, crème-colored floral doorknob yanked off in his fist. He chucked it across the room, smashing it into the wall just as the flowing curtain sailed open from a howling wind.

Nicolo gripped the two suitcases from the floor and flung them across the room. One crashed into another, and then they both hit the baseboard near her dresser.

"Get...out." Nicolo whispered in a tone so eerie, she recoiled.

Kim pushed the invisible hair away from her face and stared back at Nicolo, hiding her parched breath.

"You don't deserve us. And to think I thought you were so fucking sweet. You fooled everyone, but you're just pure bitch. Greedy, hateful bitch. You're a miserable person that'll never be happy. Looking at you now, really looking at you, you sicken me. I thought you'd make me happy, but you've kept me from going after what I always wanted."

The mask of spitefulness that shielded Kim for so long, dissipated and the shy vulnerable girl reappeared. She shrunk before him, unable to speak.

"You faked your depression long enough. I was a fool to believe you. I wanted to, but..." He sneered at her and then snickered, reaching for her top dresser drawer. "You know what? Just go. Take your crap and get the hell out of here, now."

Mounds of clothes heaved themselves into the luggage beneath him. Unfamiliar pink and lavender thong underwear, red bras, and with ones with black polka dots, all made their way into the get-the-fuck-out-of-here suitcases. He stomped on the clothes with his black leather shoe and reached for the next drawer.

"Stop it!"

Nicolo attacked the final drawer. The heaps of clothes overflowed her two vehicles of freedom, now her route to hell. He kicked them out of his room and down the hall until they careened into the front door. The doorknob twisted in his intense grip. "Say hello to the new Nicolo Trevisani."

Chapter 53

Heather

Heather's algae filled pond groaned like a neglected child. She needed to find time to scrub it in the next few weeks. She caught a flutter here and there and hoped all the fish made it through the winter. Hard to tell for sure with the black leaves that occupied the majority of the mucky bottom. The four, beautiful, white fish were fighters, though.

She strolled inside hopeful it would warm up for today's spring festival in town. Last year, it only reached fifty-two degrees, and hats and coats were the collective fashion for the day. They promised sixty-three today, but the early morning chill tricked the emerging perennials into thinking winter still lingered. And what a busy winter it was.

Binghamton University accepted Laurel in next fall's admission. Between the senior ski trip, the upcoming prom and turning over her old Jeep to the newly licensed teenager, Heather felt herself reliving her own senior year. Luckily, Laurel was doing exactly what she wanted.

Heather and Laurel continued their long talks. Talks that began when Laurel was barely two. Laurel shared stories that most teenagers would never tell their moms. Rumors and gossip that sailed around the school, made it to Heather's ears. Laurel loved hearing her mom's advice and asked many questions. Answers were always honest and direct.

Heather guided her as best she could when each new boy entered Laurel's life. Her choice of boyfriends far exceeded her expectations. In fact, they trumped Heather's pathetic, lifeless dates.

Gia managed to make it through her first year of high school despite a rough start. By the end of September, she begged to be home-schooled when her friends turned into snobby, boy crazy, drama queens. They forced her to dress a certain way, told her she could only talk to certain boys, and that she couldn't listen to her alternative music anymore. They turned against Gia, shunning her when she refused. She was friendless, one month into her first year of high school.

Luckily, she found a great group of kids that came from one of the merged middle schools, and black became her new clothing color. She cut her hair short, joined the school yearbook and once she bought contact lenses, eyeliner found its way around her green eyes. When Gia raced out of the house one morning wearing Heather's Depeche Mode T-shirt, she knew she'd be all right.

Rori started third grade and outgrew her shyness. Tales of what she and her crazy family did over the weekend, always grabbed her classmate's attention. Super Bowl parties at the house, trips into the city, playing ice hockey on frozen ponds and rock climbing on the weekends, filled her with enough stories each week to break out of her shell.

Interaction with Heather's new friends and the constant get-togethers at their home, taught Rori how to socialize. She made many friends and they practically begged to come over to play. The neighborhood kids found their way onto Rori's front lawn every afternoon, and Heather couldn't be happier.

Laurel and Gia both refused to see their father anymore. Occasional and random visits proved awkward and kept them away from their friends. Rori soon followed, wondering why she had to go if her sisters didn't have to. Holidays were still a challenge, but they kept their visits short. Fortunately, the three of them had each other to talk to while Lance did his usual schmoozing and bragging to his fans.

As much as Heather cherished weekends by herself in the beginning, her sporadic dates were dull, and she decided she'd rather spend time with her daughters. Now that Laurel and Gia were in high school, though, it appeared Rori was the only one available on the weekends.

Heather wrote *pond* on her spring to do list and then turned on her computer. She deleted the three SPAM emails on her account and then switched over to Facebook. Nine notifications and one message.

She skimmed over the *likes* then looked at the one comment from Roxie about the picture she posted from last week's girls night at her house. Heather had posted a photograph of Roxie and her lying on the couch in hysterics. She briefly remembered the joke Roxie told and chuckled again. Roxie had commented *Bunch of nutjobs!* underneath it.

One private message remained. She clicked on it. It was from Brooke.

Heather stared at the name for a minute. It wasn't registering. Brooke? How long had it been? But it was her. She glanced at the tiny profile picture that only contained a head shot, mostly hair. Her message was less clear.

Heather please, I know its been forever and years and I know your mad but please I need to talk to someone youre the only one that understands me no one will listenThe neighbors have blown me off they wont talk to me and its not my fault I don't even know how they found out plus Clifford is leavign me and I cant be divorced I cant. it's a mess everything Jacobs doing drugs and Daniel got kicked out of another school and Heather please you're the only real friend I ever had and I did do it I did. I did eat the gummy bear off the floor. it was green. I remember it was the same color as your feather earrings. I'm sorry, so sorry please please write back

Heather leaned back in her chair and gaped. The time on the message read 2:36 a.m. Was she drunk? She clicked Brooke's profile picture to enlarge it. It had been ten years since she saw her, not counting the picture of her with Lance at the banquet. It looked like she attempted to chemically straighten her curly hair and dye the blonde to brown, but instead, it appeared scorched and over processed. Heavy makeup coated her face.

Her cover photo displayed a professional picture of Brooke, Clifford, Jacob and Daniel. They all wore lavender T-shirts and blue jeans. Clifford lost all his hair, and wore thick glasses. Did he think expensive designer eyewear looked better on his bare head?

The photograph was old, though. Jacob, who should be graduating high school with Laurel this year, looked like he was thirteen. Daniel looked barely ten. Had they no recent photos of the four of them?

The rest of her wall was private, but it didn't matter. Heather deleted the message. She thought twice about blocking her from future contacts, but reveled in the possibility of more rants.

Did she need the drama, though? Did she care? No. She had purged her life of anyone that drained it. She never imagined life could be this peaceful. She went into *settings* and blocked Brooke after all.

Heather jumped into the shower and then made the girls French toast while her hair air-dried. Her daughters fought over the powdered sugar until a covering of snow fell across the kitchen table.

"Mom, I found a prom dress I like." Laurel swallowed a gulp of milk. "It's sexy, but not slutty."

"Well, that's a good thing."

"Ack." Gia stuck her fingers in her mouth. "Proms are for girls to show off that they have a boyfriend and boobs."

"Boobs is a bad word," Rori said.

"No, it's not," Gia hollered.

"Hey." Heather held up the spatula. "Be nice, otherwise I'll use this thing on you."

"As if." Gia rolled her eyes. "What are you gonna do? Slap a blueberry at us?"

"I'm getting pretty good at racquet ball, so, I'd be scared if I was you. Now, hurry up. I want to get to the festival while there's still good parking."

After the French toast party ended, Rori and Gia climbed into Heather's car. Laurel took the Jeep, her new toy, and picked up her best friend Debbi on the way.

Rori and Heather skipped into the community park while Gia, Laurel and Debbi pretended they didn't know them. Sausage and peppers whizzed past their noses as soon as they reached the ticket booth. Once inside, Laurel and Debbi took off, but were to meet by the Philly Cheesesteak stand for lunch at one o'clock.

The sun warmed their pale skin. A gentle breeze fluttered through the long strands of Rori's hair and she skipped along, not noticing a golden retriever coming toward her. Gia stayed three feet in front, in case any boys from her school approached.

Heather paid for Rori to get her face painted like a tiger. Bright orange and black paint coated her unblemished skin. Gold glitter accented her eyes. Gia settled for a small black skull and crossbones on her right hand.

They drank pink lemonade and listened to the band play classic rock songs on stage until Gia spotted her friend Jada. That was the last she saw of her until lunch. Heather spent the next hour with Rori on the kiddie rides, the house of mirrors, and playing a few carnival games.

After stuffing their faces with hamburgers and hot dogs, they shared a dozen zeppoles between them. Powdered sugar laced the strands of hair around Rori's face, but Gia intentionally smeared the moist sugar around her lips. The mustache-look did her proud.

Several hours later, the group made their way back to the parking lot. Gia hopped into the Jeep with Laurel and Debbi. Hopefully, they'd be home for dinner.

Once they neared their home, Rori jumped out of the car and ran to the neighbors, leaving Heather alone.

She made her way back to her computer wishing that she didn't block Brooke after all. Maybe there would've been another message from her by now. One of realization that she wrote to Heather late at night, possibly while drunk. Heather considered unblocking her just for the fun of it.

Brooke had never let on that her life was flawed. Heather had heard stories here and there from old friends, but every time they spoke, Brooke only graced her with the epic moments in her life. Heather never brought up the rumors that she'd heard. Didn't Brooke realize she would support her no matter what? That she could confide in her and share her secrets?

Looking back, Brooke had always talked down to her. Heather told her all of her darkest secrets and failures in life. Her affair with Nicolo, the problems with Bianca and Lance, her former horrible co-workers, Rebecca's death and her unplanned pregnancy with Rori. Brooke must have thought Heather was a complete loser.

In Heather's eyes, Brooke had always been the queen of good fortune. Perfect loving husband that provided for her so that she never had to work. A nanny to do the chores they all hated. Accolades from the moms and neighbors that looked up to her. Had she mentioned the neighbors stopped talking to her?

Her drunken rant blurred into one giant incoherent sentence. Her two cute boys, who excelled in school, looked like nerdy mama's boys in that old photo. What did they look like now? What had she said about them kicking out Daniel from yet another school? And innocent Jacob with a drug problem?

Maybe her life wasn't so perfect. Maybe it was always a sham. Heather had no regrets. She loved two men passionately, even if only for a short time. She raised three gorgeous, intelligent daughters that would one day rule the world. She had amazing friends and co-workers supporting her, too. Heather refused to let drama enter her life anymore.

The photographs of Lance and Brooke entered her mind. Maybe Brooke envied Heather in some way. Had she seen past Heather's tales of doom and recognized that she had everything going for her? That Heather had the ability to find happiness? Maybe Brooke noticed before Heather did.

Her computer booted and showed no new emails. She flipped back to Facebook. Three comments on the picture she took with Roxie last weekend. All hysterical. But there was a friend request and another message. Had Brooke somehow broken through her block? Had Heather done it incorrectly?

She clicked on the new friend request. *Nicolo Trevisani.*

Heather flinched. The letters on the screen intensified. She swallowed hard and read his message.

Hey Heather. Hope you are good. I just joined Facebook and I'm not even sure if I'm doing this right. I only have three friends so far. Ha Ha. My brother forced me to join. I got divorced six months ago and he told me to get on here to find some old friends. The only old friend I want to talk to is you. You look beautiful in your picture. And your girls are the spitting image of you. Four beautiful girls. Hope you get this message. Love you to the moon.

Heather's body immersed with goose bumps. She read the message again, positive she read it wrong. It was his name and definitely his silly nature.

She fidgeted in her chair for a while, not sure what to write, while twenty years of emotions crowded her heart. Ones she held in for too long. Heathers' fingers hovered above the keys, but she hesitated longer. Her fears had always destroyed her path to happiness. She refused to let it happen again. There would be no more fear.

Her fingers flew across the keyboard with little effort, no barriers to her thoughts. No more holding back.

Hello. So glad to hear from you and so happy you thought to seek me out.

Nicolo, I have wanted to tell you so many things over the past two decades. But each encounter, with its unexpected situations and time limits, had prevented me from doing so.

First, let me say how truly sorry I am for having left you the way I did that wonderful summer of '93. It was not only wrong, but immature and cruel. I was selfish. Scared. And too embarrassed to face you.

You did nothing wrong and I meant everything I said to you that last night on the beach, and every other time. Lance sprang a surprise engagement party on me that Sunday I was supposed to break up with him. Circumstances that I thought were beyond my control at the time, threw me down a different road, a road I never should have traveled.

I'm embarrassed to tell you that I saw you in the mall five years later. Although you were clear across the other side of the concourse, I recognized you immediately. I was nine months pregnant and looked hideous, so I ducked and hid. But that wasn't the real reason I hid from you. I think you can figure out why.

I felt your breeze as you passed, and smelled your familiar cologne. I regretted that decision as well. I watched you walk into Macy's and stared until you were no longer visible.

That day at the beach with your fiancée, you caught me by surprise. I didn't know what to say to you and for the first time in my life, jealousy surfaced upon seeing you with someone else. I was humiliated and ran away. I dreamed of you though, it was so real. I wanted it to be at least.

When I saw you in Peaz in Chaoz, I was indeed miserable. My entire life was falling apart around me. Seeing you melted all my anger. You always knew how to make me smile. I had every intention of calling you, but for what? My own selfish needs again? You were newly married and had a toddler. I couldn't ruin the happiness you found. You had moved on after someone you planned to spend the rest of your life with deserted you. Yes, I was miserable, and have been since I left you, but that was my own doing and I could not let you feel the pain of ME again.

I would've loved having you back in my life, but the profound love I felt for you never disappeared and I knew I couldn't control myself. That would've been unfair to you. You found happiness and love and someone that could give you everything you deserved. Unlike me. I hurt you and I'm sure you forgot all about the girl that treated you like crap.

I'm sorry to hear that you're divorced. I only wished the best for you and that someone wonderful would give you what I could not. Christopher must be seven by now. I'm sure he's tall and as handsome as you are. (By the way, get a profile picture. That blue silhouette's gottta go. Not fair that I can't see what you look like. ;p)

Nicolo, I must tell you that I too am divorced. Almost four years now. I never should have married Lance, not that you want to hear that now, but I was persuaded to believe that this was the true path to happiness. I instead found another fifteen years of misery and regret. If it wasn't for my girls, I'm not sure how I would have coped. The methods I tried all failed. The men I dated, all fiascos.

Would I like to be friends with you? I'm shocked you want to, but I'd like nothing more than to have you back in my life. A five-minute conversation with you was not enough to learn all the things you've experienced in your life. Things I missed, things I should have been a part of.

If you can find it in you to forgive me and we can possibly be friends, I would love that. I wish I gave you half the happiness you gave me.

***

Heather slouched inside the booth at *T.G.I. Friday's* across from her Saturday night date. And yawned. Laurel and her boyfriend were at the movies, and Gia was at her best friend Squiggy's house.

A straw wrapper skyrocketed toward Heather's head, poking her in the eye.

"Ooh, sorry, Mommy." Rori plunged the straw into her red kid's cup and took a sip of the raspberry lemonade. "Mmm, so yummy."

Heather blinked a few times relieving the sting, then opened her straw and shot the paper across the table back at Rori. It missed and hit an old man behind her in the back of the head. "Sorry." Heather waved her hand. The man gave her a fierce look. Was everyone so unhappy?

She needed to drop Rori off at her parent's tomorrow morning and felt guilty that she was dumping her there. At nine years old, Rori still needed supervision. Laurel and Gia had plans with their friends and couldn't watch her all day, anyway. Who knew how long she would be gone. Better safe than sorry.

An exciting dinner out with just the two of them would make Rori feel special. The waitress took their orders and then Rori sat back, opened her *Diary of Wimpy Kid* book, and buried her nose inside. So much for stimulating conversation.

Heather glanced at the couples at the surrounding tables, able to tell which ones were new loves and which were old. A gray-haired woman sat with her arms folded and surveyed the patrons behind her. Her companion, a bald man with age spots on his head, looked out the window. On the other side of the room, a boy around twenty, held a girl's hand and they leaned in close and giggled.

At forty-five, she couldn't believe all the years that passed without feeling intimacy like that. For someone to stroke her face with gentle caresses and look into her eyes when they spoke. Someone to say, 'I love you' while clutching the back of her head. Someone to laugh with.

A guy strutted by that looked like her old boss, Barry, from Northford Insurance Company. He winked at her. Obviously, these were the only men she attracted lately. Her dates over the past three years were like lethargic patients given too much medication. She wondered if she really loved Nicolo and Silvatri or was it just the thrill of sneaking around, the spontaneous sex and the precarious locations.

Rori giggled at the page opened in front of her. She turned it toward Heather and after reading it to her mom in her cute little voice, they both chuckled out loud. The old man behind Rori gave Heather another foul glare.

She was thankful for the laughter she shared with her girls at least, despite what the uptight people in the world thought. "Just having fun with my daughter on a Saturday night, is that a problem?"

The old man huffed and went back to his loaded potato skins.

****

Heather glanced out the window again. Dense black clouds emerged over the northern part of the island. *Damn.* The weather report said a chance of a late evening thunderstorm. It was only noon.

Jacket? She stepped onto her front porch to investigate. The overcast sky threatened with showers, but the warm May afternoon wrapped Heather in comfort. A breeze kicked up. Gusts flipped the soft waves of her hair and caressed her face. A cool and refreshing break from the humid air. Rainclouds charged in, controlled by strong winds.

She reentered the kitchen, tossed her sweatshirt on the chair and watched the clock on her stove change to 12:03 p.m. A distant rumble filled the silence. The wind whipped through the neighborhood trees, savagely bending their branches and kicking her rocking chairs against the house. The rumbling increased, closing in on her home, the grumble and growl that led her to close the kitchen windows.

Heather latched the final window fearing the impending rain, but a sudden jolt threw her back. Although she anticipated his arrival, seeing him ride up on a motorcycle, knocked her off her feet. Black biker boots and faded blue jeans stood out from the all-aluminum frame. A tight black T-shirt spread across his broad back. He removed his helmet and black spikes of hair jiggled when he shook his head. The rapid beating of her heart pounded in her ears. She couldn't do this.

Nicolo dismounted and laid his helmet on the seat. He paused for a minute, surveyed her home and beamed. She grabbed her sweatshirt and exited, slamming the door behind her. Although propelled by adrenaline, Heather's timid feet hindered her progress. This was not real.

Nicolo swallowed hard. Heather's eyes locked on his as she glided towards him. Time made her more striking. No longer cautious or afraid, she looked at him for the first time with confidence and purpose. The Heather he'd once known, flourished into the beautiful, confident woman, no longer hidden behind hurdles and barriers. Instead of weathered, she'd improved with age, like an antique car.

He stepped forward. Neither of them spoke. What *do* you say after all these years? He pushed the strands of hair back behind her ear and let his hand touch the glow upon her cheek. Her cool skin felt identical to the first time he touched her in the gym.

Heather closed her eyes and let the warmth of his touch dissolve the years of sadness, of yearning, of need. She stood before him, trembling. Her hand covered his and her eyes filled with moisture. Each time their paths had crossed, she couldn't express how she felt. Now alone, she found herself mute.

Her mouth parted, but a surge of tears threatened to fall. Nicolo placed a finger over her lips, hushing her. Heather collapsed into his chest. She needed to be held. Now. By him. Know that her punishment had finally ended.

Nicolo wrapped his arms around her and kissed the top of her silky hair. He embraced her, and the feel of her chest against his, brought him back to the night in Northford's parking lot when they hugged for the first time.

Their warmth merged, and bonded them together, evermore. Memories he treasured, the moments he never forgot, saturated his thoughts. It had been an eternity since he felt her heartbeat next to his, but when he closed his eyes, they were back on the beach again. The vision replaced all his years of doubt.

Nicolo pulled away and looked into her misty eyes. He reached up to touch the silky skin of her neck, to draw her into him. Would she still taste the same?

Heather tried hard to smile while fighting back the tears that held decades of emotions. Her final attempt to speak was silenced by Nicolo's soft lips. He tasted exactly the same. She was finally home.

Nicolo gazed at Heather's beautiful smile, then held her hand, guiding her to his bike. His muscular leg swung over the seat and he gave Heather a wink. She shadowed him, her warm thighs surrounding his rugged jeans. They didn't need to speak.

Heather's arms encircled his waist, her fingers caressed the cylinders of muscle underneath. She rested her head on his back and knew she would never let go again. The black clouds lifted. It would not rain on them today.

****

"This is unbelievable." Gia threw her arms in the air and stomped away from the back door.

"Wow, this does stink." Laurel plopped onto the couch.

"Are we still going, Mommy?" Rori asked.

"I'm not sure, honey. We'll figure something out."

The rain continued to drain from the clouds, ruining their plans to go to Superstorm Adventure Park. How many times could it possibly rain in one summer? The streets pooled with water from overflowing sewers, kicking off Labor Day weekend with a dreary start.

At noon, the doorbell rang promising some hope. "I'll get it." Rori scampered to the front door, unlocking the deadbolt. "Yay! They're here."

Heather tied the pink laces on her black converse high tops and then made it into the kitchen before they entered. They turned the corner from the foyer and sprang into the kitchen as if the rain was only an illusion. Their faces lit up the house from pure joy. Her eyes sparkled as they always did when she saw him.

"Hello," Nicolo said, in his melodious tone. He arched forward and let his lips gently land on Heather's mouth. Soft, wet and yummy.

"Oooh," Christopher cooed. "You gonna get married?"

Heather chuckled and Nicolo stepped over to Christopher and yanked his baseball cap over his eyes. "Go play with Rori in her room. Show her your new toy."

Christopher skipped off with Rori and headed for her room with his Transformers Bot Shots.

With the kids out of range, Nicolo clutched Heather in his arms, nestled her in his muscular chest, and squished her on purpose. She gasped for air as he squeezed her ribs, but she loved every second of it. Feeling Nicolo's warm body and heartbeat gave her comfort and security. She had a partner now to enjoy life with. Someone to support her, push her to be the best person she could be. Someone that loved having fun with their kids, and brought the kid out of her as well.

"You had something to do with the weather didn't you?" Nicolo asked.

"Me?" Heather pointed to her chest and smirked. "What makes you say that?"

"Anything to get out of going on the roller coaster."

"I had every intention of going."

"We can still go to the arcade there. Maybe the weather will turn around."

"Hurray!" Cheers erupted from down the hall. Their four children ran into the kitchen jumping up and down as if on a giant trampoline. Christopher and Rori hugged their parents, and Laurel and Gia layered around them creating a huddle. A tight knot needed by all of them.

The six of them climbed out of Nicolo's truck and raced toward the indoor arcade at Superstorm Adventure Park. Nicolo carried Heather on his back, galloping into the building like a bunch of ten year olds. He purchased an equal amount of tokens for each of their four children and then Laurel and Gia dove onto the Pump It Up Dance Machine as soon as the tokens hit their palms. Rori and Christopher lingered a moment, not sure which direction to take off in.

Rori caught sight of the skee ball machines and dragged Christopher by the arm. Although three years younger, Christopher stood at the same height as Rori. They reminded Heather of Hansel and Gretel skipping off into the woods.

Heather stepped forward to follow them, but Nicolo grasped her hand before they entered the maelstrom of hyperactive children juiced up on soda and candy, and hypnotized by deafening explosions. He dragged her behind a row of racecar simulators. Finally alone, he clutched her cheeks in his hands and his eyes absorbed all her attention. Nicolo tilted his head, studied each detail of her lips and then kissed her.

Each moment with him erased her heartache and replaced it with hope. Was this still one of her dreams? Could this ever truly be reality? Would she capture complete happiness and have everything she ever wanted? His lips told her "yes." Everything would be perfect.

Nicolo would protect her and her daughters. His son would gain three sisters and a caring mother. Her daughters would learn what real love and companionship was. They'd all experience a lifetime of adventures and laughter. Six kids on water slides, rock climbing, and late nights watching the sun set on the beaches of Long Island. Go-cart racing and ferry rides to Fire Island. Movie nights by the fireplace and breakfast on the back patio. Six pairs of Converse high tops would hike up trails and watch the fireworks over Northport Harbor.

He gently removed his moist, hungry lips, never taking his eyes off her. The color of her cheeks deepened from the transfer of love to her. She ran her finger over his eyelid and onto his lips.

An overexcited middle school boy tackled the racecar next to them and inserted his token. With their concentration slashed, Heather looked away and searched for Rori and Christopher.

Nicolo stepped in front of her. "I'll go. You make sure Laurel and Gia aren't getting picked up by some—"

"Some hot guys that will sweep them off their feet and promise them the world?"

"No. Hell no. I was thinking more on the lines of some uninspiring, lethargic momma's boy that expects them to cater to him."

"Oh, not my girls. I've taught them well."

He tapped her on the nose, bent in for one last kiss and hurried off to find them.

She spotted the girls still on the dance machine, giggling, as they attempted to copy the screen. She waved to Laurel and Gia, and then zigzagged through the maze of arcade games in pursuit of the other three.

Heather made her way to the skee ball machines, but saw none of them. She glanced to the left, then traveled to her right and turned down an aisle and there it was. Heather floated to it. Stared. Then a grin grew on her face. She reached into her pocket, removed a token, and inserted it.

With three middle fingers positioned on the trackball, she began her battle. She made her way back and forth across the screen, spiraling down, further, faster. The spider appeared and sprang at her and she twirled the ball to avoid it. She swooped up to the left and then back down, firing laser shots through a field of mushrooms.

No time had passed. Her skill remained as if tucked away but not extinguished. Heather avoided the spider and destroyed each segment of the centipede. She would not be defeated. Tougher, stronger, she would defend her right. Succeed and conquer. Find her happiness. Win.

EPILOGUE

Heather's toes sank into the cool sand. Tingling, like that from festive sparklers, weaved along the soles of her feet and piloted her closer to the shimmering waves. The soft grains crunched between her toes as she stepped. Brilliant greens and blues of the ocean joined the white foam waves that slapped with calming lulls.

Puffs of clouds, like bursting white roses, watched over them. A melody, romantic yet sensual, accompanied Heather on her journey to her future-forever.

Nicolo lifted his head an inch, peeked at Heather from the slivers of his eyes, and his familiar grin swelled as she stepped closer to him. His posture straightened, and with his head now held high, the golden sunlight glistened off his glossy eyes. A single teardrop slid down his cheek.

Heather's sexy white dress revealed her toned legs while the long white train cascaded over the bronze sand. She joined Laurel and Gia under the gazebo but her gaze remained on Nicolo as his eyes dampened further. Dino and Carissa stood beside them and Rori and Christopher held their wedding bands. Her delicate finger wiped the tear from his cheek just as one dropped onto hers.

The reverend began his welcoming blessing. Nicolo's white linen shirt fluttered in the ocean breeze. He glanced down at Heather's rainbow colored toenails, chuckled and then slipped his toes over hers. Heather bowed her head to hide her giggling, but when she peeked, gorgeous black eyes absorbed her.

Heather rose up on her toes and stole a kiss from Nicolo. She didn't want to wait a minute longer. How many years did they waste already?

"We usually wait until the end for that." The reverend shook his head.

Nicolo arched towards Heather and whispered, "Rule breaker."

Nicolo squished her toes under his, then wiggled his finger in jest. She flicked sand at his calf and then a small stephanotis flower winged at them, courtesy of Gia.

The reverend paused again. "This is highly unusual."

"*We're* highly unusual." Gia made a silly face.

"We've just waited so long for this moment," Heather beamed.

"Too long." Nicolo leaned in and kissed her again.

"Why don't we just skip to your vows?" The reverend closed his notebook.

Heather removed a slip of paper from her bouquet, breathed in the salty air and then began.

"I knew the day you stood on top of that desk at Northfords, to throw that giant rubber band ball, I loved you. And I knew you were someone that would make me happy for the rest of my life. Make me laugh, make me enjoy every second of every day, and have as much fun as any human being could have.

"Although many years were lost, I promise from this day forward, to buy only Jeeps. To cook wieners and roast marshmallows on a charcoal grill while the sun sets on a sparkling beach. To dance in the summer rainstorms, blow bubbles at you while you try to have a serious conversation with me, and eat Eggs-in-the-Basket on our back patio table. I promise to raise my hands in the air on giant waterslides and always open my eyes on roller coasters. Especially in Disney next week when the five of you torture me. Repeatedly. There will be nothing but laughter from this day forward.

"I look forward to engaging conversations by the fireplace, and your never-ending support and understanding. I intend to make you as happy as you made me, for the rest of our lives, and thereafter. I love you, Nicolo. I always have."

Heather grinned while Nicolo composed himself enough to speak. He wiped another tear away and shook his head in disbelief. With one last deep breath, he began his vows. No scrap of paper needed.

"Heather." He paused again, fighting back tears. His hands shook. "Heather, no one has ever made me feel the way you do. You've always believed in me. Your laugh melts my fears and you make me feel courageous and powerful. Smart and invincible. Things you taught me years ago, never left me. Instead, they kept me going, pushed me to discover the potential you said I held.

"To think of all the times our paths crossed, and how we never stopped thinking about one another, just blows my mind." Nicolo laughed and shook his head. "I cannot believe I'm standing here, now, about to marry you. I'm the luckiest man in the world. I love you more than you will ever know. Love to the moon."

The reverend smiled. Finally. He stepped closer and asked for the wedding bands. Heather and Nicolo stood only inches apart, a breeze from the heavens blew wildly, whipping their clothes and hair about. The sunlight shimmered on their smiling faces. They held hands, gazed deeply into each other's eyes and saw their future.

Most people want to recapture their younger days, but Heather and Nicolo, well, they looked forward to the second half. The rest of their lives. The half they waited so long for and intended to enjoy with every beat of their hearts.

"Congratulations!" The reverend sang out. "I now present to you, Nicolo and Heather Trevisani!"

The End

Author's Notes

Dear Reader,

Thank you for reading *Every Five Years.* I hope you enjoyed it. If you did, I would love it if you would write a review at your favorite book review site. Reviews are the best way for readers to discover great new books. I look forward to seeing your review on Amazon or Goodreads.

I also invite you to visit my Website at:
Christine-Ardigo-Author.com/,
or on FaceBook at:
Christine.Ardigo.Author, to stay in touch with me and follow my next book project.

You can also follow me on Goodreads.

Thank you for spending a few hours with my story and its characters. I hope you had fun living in their world as much as I did. Heather and Nicolo's love story will always hold a special place in my heart. How about you?

Christine

About the Author

I'm a registered dietitian/personal trainer who writes contemporary romance novels in my spare time. When weight lifting, rock climbing, white water rafting and jumping out of airplanes wasn't enough, I decided to fulfill a dream I had as a child: to write a book.

I've lived in New York my entire life and can't imagine living anywhere else. I have the beaches, the bay and the city, all a half hour away. I've built memories here with my husband, two silly daughters and a bunch of crazy friends, all whom I love very much.

14106263R00177

Printed in Great Britain
by Amazon.co.uk, Ltd.,
Marston Gate.